AIR & ESSENCE

AN ELEMENTS OF ITERIA NOVEL

FATE OF THE ACNA BOOK TWO

MIKAYLA D. HORNEDO

CONTENTS

AUTHOR'S NOTE

Please visit my website mikayladhornedo.com/air-and-essence for an up to date list of content warnings.

Thank you so much for wanting to continue with Daya's story! This journey has been such a labor of love, and I really hope everyone can see a little bit of themselves in these pages. A reminder that this is the second book in the Fate of the Acna series, as well as the over-arching Elements of Iteria series. You'll get a hint as to what the future books in the Elements of Iteria will involve at the end! If you've made it this far, then that means you love a morally gray, feisty, violent, bi bruja, and I think that means you're my kind of person lol Enjoy!!

Listen to playlist on Spotify –

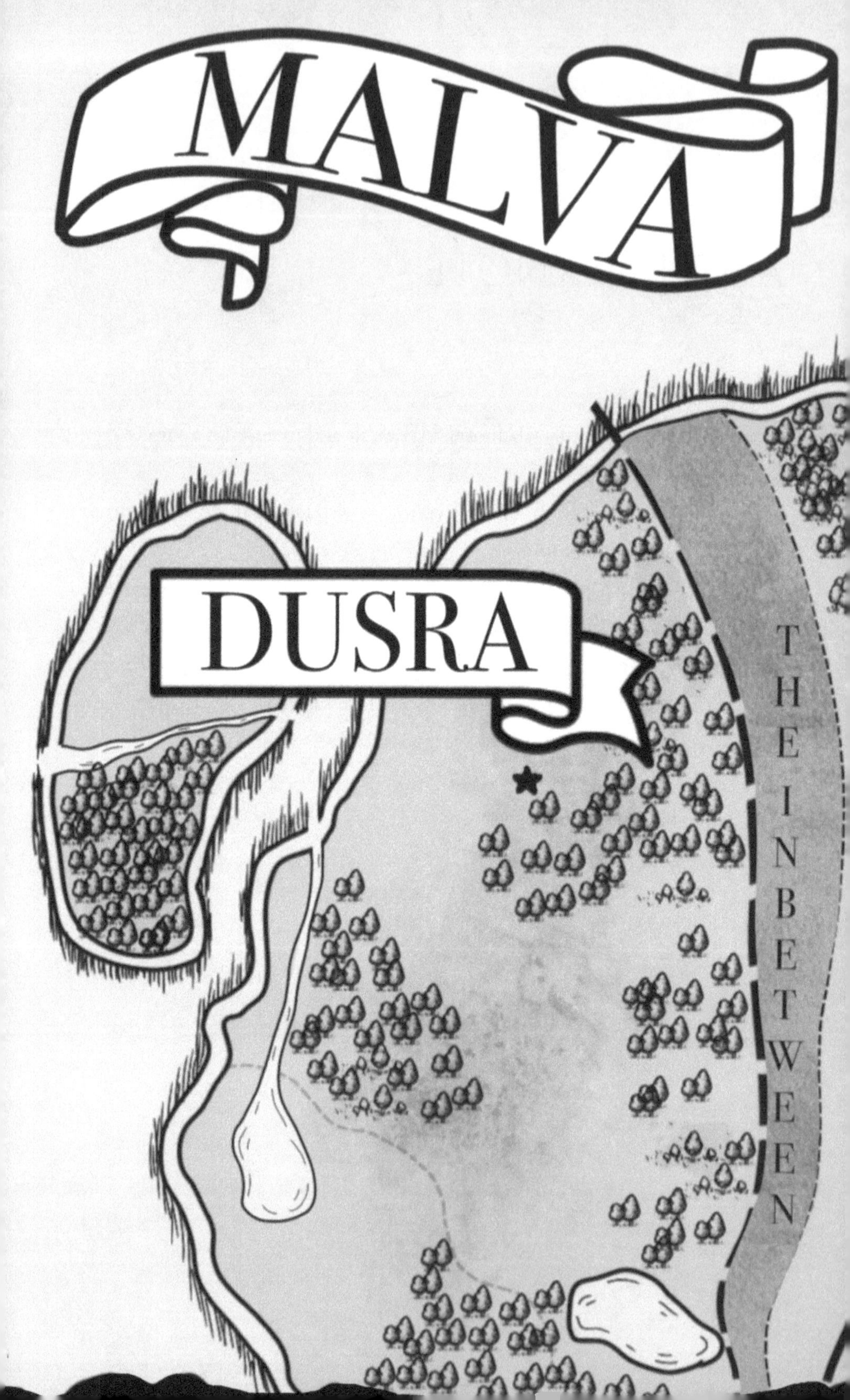

MALVA
DUSRA
THE INBETWEEN

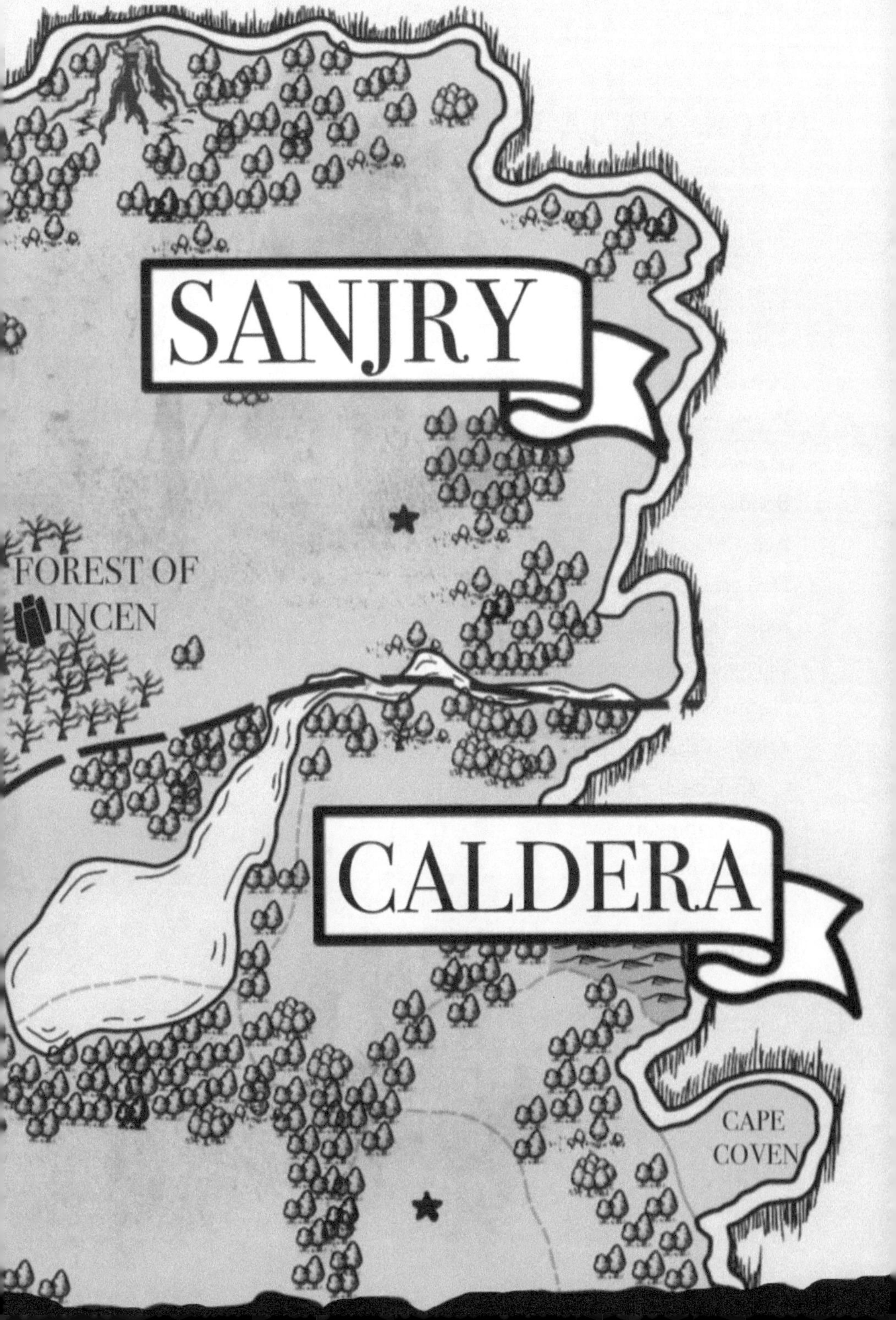

SANJRY
CALDERA
FOREST OF INCEN
CAPE COVEN

PROUNCIATION GUIDE

Sanjry- Sahn-jree

   Caldera- Kahl-dehr-a

   Iteria- Eh-tear-e-uh

   Dusra- Doo-srah

   Malva- Mahl-va

   Bonda- Bohn-duh

   Acna- Ahk-nuh

   Dayanara- Dai-uh-naa-ruh

   Kaizer- Kai-zur

   Sanguijuela- Sahn-gee-hweh-la

   Naom- Nay-ohm

   Zalvoh- Zahl-voh

   Coleb- Co-leb

   Cama- Cahm-ah

   Chuah- Ch-ew-ah

Full Map of Iteria-

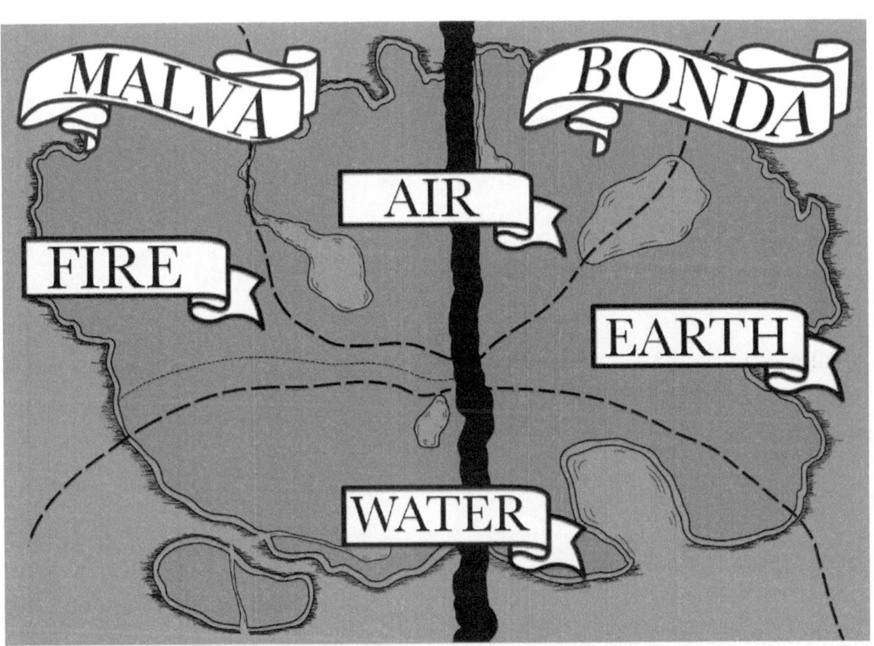
MALVA
BONDA
AIR
FIRE
EARTH
WATER

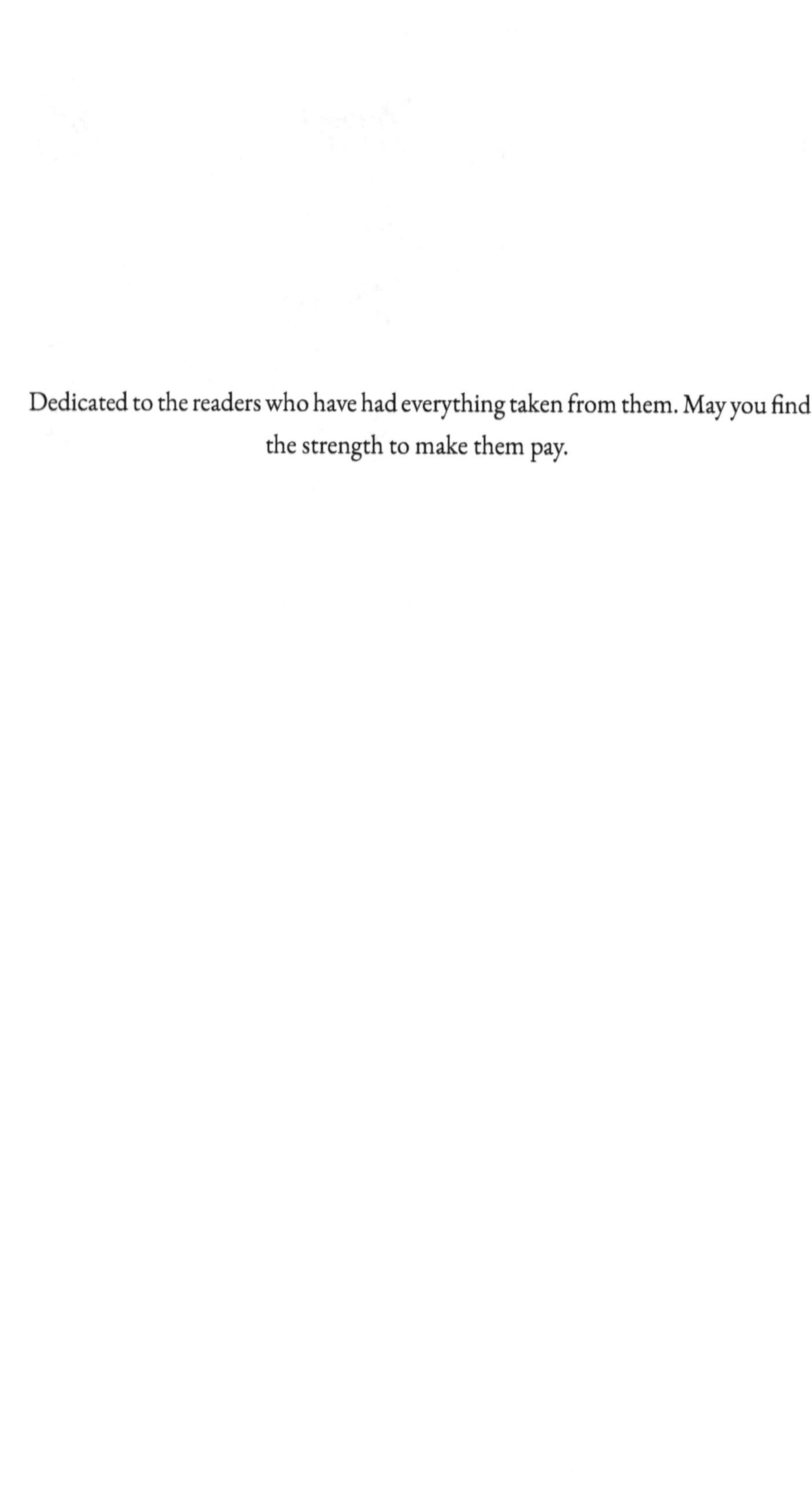

Dedicated to the readers who have had everything taken from them. May you find the strength to make them pay.

What Happened in the Last Book?

The mortals have said we are resting—myself and the other goddesses. They were right, but we saw more than they thought. Not everything, and we couldn't do anything to stop the terrible things coming, but we watched. Especially me, the Goddess of Air and Essence. I had a direct connection to my brujas through Dayanara.

My poor child. When we created this world, we did not design it to be one of heartbreak, but it still found the mortals. I had hoped that Dayanara's mother, Lupe Amapola, would have made better decisions. Using her daughter the way she did, abusing her with the desire for power. That vision Lupe saw had tipped all of Malva into the wrong direction—the one where she killed Dayanara, and I came down from the sky to help the brujas. It wasn't me she saw with wings and essence flowing in her skin. It *was* her daughter. I never wanted her to sacrifice Dayanara. I certainly didn't want her to align with Kaizer Curran, the king of Sanjry.

I wished I could have told Dayanara not to trust him. Kaizer was only looking out for himself, and some of what he'd done was even kept from our vision. But he only wanted Dayanara as a weapon. He was no better than her mother. When he'd stolen Caldera, the land I'd given to my brujas, I wanted to rage. But I knew Dayanara would eventually see him for what he was, and she shattered the binds of that magical agreement and escaped. I hope she makes him pay.

Thankfully, Dayanara found Zuri and Axel—the hearts that beat with hers. She also found out that Zuri was Dusran, and Zuri was stolen by Sanjry before they could rectify it. I have faith that nothing will stop Dayanara from getting her back, though. Axel will help her, and now she has the whole Dusran army behind her.

The other goddesses and I had done what we could all those centuries ago, but now the mortals will have to fight. Chaos is coming for them all.

—The Goddess of *Air & Essence*
Naom

PART ONE

"Hold fast to dreams, for if dreams die, life is a broken-winged bird that cannot fly."

—Langston Hughes

Chapter One

Zuri

My favorite version of myself, of my life, was one that wasn't real. A rendition of my existence where I'd met Daya on different terms and never lied to her about who I was. One where we could have lived happily. Where the weight of all of those who came before us wasn't pulling us down to the ocean floor and flooding our lungs with water. I clung to that fantasy, thinking of how I would have brought her flowers every day on my way home from the market. Where we could have lived out in a forest, where Daya could have been connected to the world the way she preferred. Our home would have had open walls like there were in Dusra, and she'd never feel confined or stuck again. I'd scour the land for the perfect location. One where the moon would shine wide between the trees and bathe her in those silver rays that made her resemble a goddess.

It had been easy to envision it when I had initially gotten captured. But now the image was hazy. I grasped at the invisible strings of what we could have been, watching them turn to cobwebs in my hands. Blood dribbled into the dirt around me as my body slowly healed from the torture I'd been through yesterday.

A sure reminder that as much as I fantasized about it, that wasn't my life. I lived in the real world. Where I'd broken trust with Dayanara and would regret it for the rest of my life. The reality where Daya hated me, even if she said she didn't. I knew her well enough to know that wasn't completely true. She was pissed and just seemed to tolerate my presence. It would take some time before I got into her good graces. Now, I couldn't even try.

I didn't even sense the brujas who took me. They grabbed me so fast I barely registered it before they doused me in magic suppressant and threw me in the dungeon. I didn't stay there; they moved me around multiple times a day, but that didn't put a stop to the beatings I was receiving. Dark purples and blues covered my once rich brown skin, only small windows of it left across my body.

They had me in some forest near Sanjry's volcano. The strong, acrid smell of burning magma in its base saturated the dense air. The earth here gave way to beautiful plants and flowers, which was one bright side of my current outdoor prison. I'd already counted each individual flower in my vicinity. Fifty-three purple, forty-two yellow, and thirty-three red. I counted the purple twice. Pulling at the chains bolted to the tree, I tried to get more comfortable, but there was no use. I was here to be made *uncomfortable*, to succumb to my conditions and give them what they wanted. There weren't even walls at this location, leaving me exposed to the harsh elements. The forest surrounding the volcano was dense, far enough from civilization that no one would come searching for me. With rocky mountains and intense drop-offs around the corner, it was the perfect place to hide a prisoner.

I'd overheard the guards talking about the fact Dayanara hadn't been found yet. They also had no idea how powerful she was or the magic she now had access to. I only hoped that she would be safe with Axel for now. The fucking bastard.

We'd never really gotten along in all the years we'd known each other. We had love for one another, but we were too much alike not to butt heads. Things defaulted to heated arguments between us, regardless of the scenario. There honestly wasn't a worse person to have caught Dayanara's eye while we were fighting. He was arrogant, and I had heard far too many stories about just how *sufficient* of a lover he was. It couldn't come close to what I had with Daya, that I was sure.

Purple smoke bloomed to life a few yards away between the trees, and my heart skipped a beat as I struggled to my feet. It was too pale, though. A light lavender to my girl's violet. It wasn't Dayanara. A bruja stepped through the smoke with Kaizer on her heels and Otto behind him.

"Ah, Zuri," Kaizer tsked. "You don't look so well."

I offered no response as Otto dropped their torture devices onto the ground with a clank that promised pain. He was having far too much fun with this. Otto was a wild card. I'd heard throughout the castle that he was evil many times, but I'd never seen it until now. Much like the other high-ranking assholes in Sanjry, he kept up a facade. Appearing as the devout adviser, but behind closed doors, he was a heathen. There was no way their *deity* ignored the things he'd done to me.

"You know the drill." Otto picked up a blade with a curved edge. "Tell us where Dayanara is."

Lifting my chin, I glared at him directly in the eye and snarled. I'd take a lifetime of bleeding, give up my very life for that woman. They could cut me down to nothing, piece by piece, and I'd never speak.

"I've been thinking about your resilience," Kaizer said as he, too, picked up a weapon. "I'm wondering what would make someone hold up to a week of torture and not mutter a word."

Otto chuckled. "There could really only be a few reasons."

The breath caught in my chest as their smiles grew, but I kept my face stone cold. I'd give them nothing.

"What could you want from her? Protection? Friendship?" Kaizer asked with a smirk. "Love?"

I stayed silent.

"It had to hurt for that love not to be reciprocated. Is that why you're doing this? You hope you'll earn that love?"

Well, he's not completely off.

Otto flipped the knife in his hand and sank it into my thigh. I groaned through my teeth, but I refused to scream for these assholes. Even if the pain spread like burning lightning straight down to my bone, pulsating with every beat of my heart. They didn't know how gifted of a healer I was. The magic I had couldn't be suppressed. Similar to most of the magic in Malva outside of our elements, I did need blood to be able to heal myself, something they were giving me just barely enough of. I kept all the bruising and blood on the surface, but I quickly healed any internal wounds. My healing did nothing for the pain when inflicted, and with a combination of old and new wounds, it was getting more difficult not to react.

"Tell us where she is, and this all can stop," Kaizer said before crouching down in my eyeline.

I spit in his face, and he chuckled. "Move her closer to the mouth of the volcano. She can sweat out her loyalty."

I should have warned Daya about Kaizer. I couldn't have said much, even I didn't know what he was up to. I *still* didn't fully know. But she had concerns, and I could have done more to help. Kaizer wasn't going to stop until he found her. That much was evident. The real question was, what was it about *her* that he needed? He said he loved her, which was possible. I fell in love with her in the same amount of time that he did. There seemed to be more with Otto in on it. It had to be some sort of war tactic as well. They wanted her as a weapon.

The fact they thought that they could control Dayanara fucking Amapola now was comical. My woman would slice them to pieces before they even had a chance to command her. She wasn't weak; she never had been, but now she was unfathomably strong. Emotionally, physically, magically. She'd been controlled for far too long to be held under some weak excuse of a vampire.

I prayed Dayanara would let me go. I'd do anything I could to return to Dusra, but I didn't want her to come after me. Her risking her life to save me—the woman who lied to her since the moment we'd met. . . I wasn't worth it. But I'd do everything I could to protect her from where I was. Starting with not giving these assholes a shred of information.

One of the guards slid a key into the lock that was holding me to the tree trunk. The heavy chains pulled my wrists down to the ground with a thud. I needed them to get the knife out of my thigh so I could begin healing the tear in my muscles.

"Stand up," the guard growled.

I looked up at him, my matted curls falling in front of my brow and then at the knife in my thigh. The guard rolled his eyes and yanked it out, causing a groan from my throat that I tried my best to stifle. Kaizer turned around, and his gaze immediately fell on the blood flowing down my leg as his nostrils flared.

"Get her patched up. Can't have her dying on us before we get our use. Let's stretch her blood supply too, see how she likes bloodlust," he said with a smile that promised more pain.

The other guard kneeled down and aggressively wrapped a bandage around me with absolutely no regard for the pain he was causing. The moment he sat up, I stitched the muscles together before partially faking a groan and standing.

"You know, there are more. . . inventive ways, barbaric ways to get you to talk," Otto said with his back turned. He moved to face me and ran his finger down my jaw in a way that had me wanting to rip his throat out with my teeth. "Think about that before the next time we return."

Kaizer cast one more glance over me, face unreadable, before he snapped his fingers at the witch to open a portal. A gust of hot wind burst through the portal with the mouth of the volcano so close. The guards pulled me by my chains, and sweat gathered on all of my exposed skin the moment my feet stepped through the opening.

I love you, Dayanara.

Chapter Two

Dayanara

My lips pulled into a grin at the screams beneath me. The villagers panicked in terror, eyes wide and skin slick with terror. I inhaled deeply, feeling my rage gather and pool in my chest. Magic expelled from every crevice of my body, finding a living soul beneath me and ending them. If Zuri wasn't here, nobody needed to be.

I knew pain—emotional, physical. But this pain cut me to my bones, wherever inside me my essence lay. I paced around the garden, trying to think of what I had missed. It had been three weeks. Three weeks since my heart was ripped out of my chest, three weeks since I'd slept, and three weeks since Zuri was taken.

We'd gotten absolutely nowhere in finding her. Every location I'd suggested we search came up fruitless. I had a suspicion they were moving her often with portal magic to keep us from finding her. Our contact in Sanjry hadn't seen her in the palace yet, but that didn't mean she wasn't there. I'd seen the secret passageways and was sure there were even more places to hide her.

I was losing my mind, and every person I'd come in contact with had known it. The only thing I made sure I did for myself was get my blood intake. I didn't want there to be any chance of getting to her and my reserves being too low.

"Who's blood is that?" Ishani's voice cut through my thoughts.

I looked down, finding my entire body covered in the substance. It hadn't dawned on me until this moment just how much of it there was. Caked in my hair, under my nails, the creases between my fingers.

"Nobody that matters," I quipped, continuing my pacing.

The Dusrans couldn't cross the border without possible repercussions. Axel had pushed the limits of the agreement before when we went to Caldera. They could technically go if he didn't know about it, but Axel had been more cautious. He said he felt how close the magic was, as if it was watching and waiting for him to take it a step further. Magical agreements were fickle that way; mortals could set their own parameters, but the magic took a life of its own. Whatever ethereal creature in charge of it enjoyed watching us suffer.

Ishani watched cautiously from the low brick wall separating the beds of flowers. Her dark curly hair swayed in the breeze, rustling the surrounding plants, but her gaze stayed locked on me. I focused on the grass below my feet or where the grass was before this became the spot where I worked through my thoughts. I'd made a clear, worn down trail over the last hour. Bruja magic was seeping out of me and only adding to the disaster. My emotions were all over the place. I *hated* what Zuri did, hated the fact she lied to me, but I'd never felt for any man or woman what I felt for her. I was *so* mad at her, but I'd forgiven her, and a small piece of me hoped that one day we could revisit whatever it was we were working toward before her betrayal. That possibility being ripped away from me by my own clan, people who were supposed to be loyal to me. . .

"Woah there," Ishani gasped.

My body was glowing, and my hair floated around my head again. Everything within a few feet of me was shriveling to its death, and I worked hard to reel it back in. My anger had made that part of my gifts so hard to manage. The wings came with ease, but tapping into that well of power—or more so, controlling it—was difficult. Ishani sent a blanket of water over the plants as my magic dissipated. The vegetation bloomed back to life, and I peered back up at her.

"How'd you do that? That feels like earth magic," I asked, curiosity getting the better of me.

"The elements all go hand in hand. You can steal the oxygen from a flame, but you can also add to it and grow it larger. Earth magic and water are similar. I can pull the water from the plants," she said as she balled her hand into a fist, and the plants she just brought back to life withered again. "Or I can push the water into it."

Ishani opened her hand, and the flowers bloomed to life once more. I ran my hand through my hair, not entirely interested in the 'we're all one' speech at the moment. She bit the inside of her cheek as she surveyed me, her green eyes full of worry, as they had been since we told her what happened to Zuri.

"We'll get her back," she whispered.

"Everyone keeps saying that, but we're no closer than we were three weeks ago," I snapped.

They'd been working hard from this side of the border, but there was only so much they could do. I knew that's why Kaizer took Zuri. He wanted me to make a rash decision and show up alone. I was getting closer and closer to taking that risk, and all of them grew more worried about it daily. I'd kept to the outskirts of Sanjry thus far, not too close to the capital or any of the big cities. Close enough to see if I could get enough information. But this last time, coming up short *again*. . . I'd seen red. Once I realized they had no information, I cut through them all with my blade or magic.

There were moments where I swore I could feel Zuri's pain, when my breathing would catch, and I'd sense a sting beneath my skin I couldn't explain. Part of me thought it was anxiety, but another part knew it was something else. I just didn't know what.

"It's almost time for dinner. I'm sure you skipped breakfast and lunch, but you need to eat," Ishani said.

"How did you do it?" I asked as I stepped closer to her. "How did you stay sane when Axel was captured? How did you rescue him?"

Nobody knew what she did, or if they did, they never spoke of it. The only person close enough to her to know was Xavier, and he didn't particularly enjoy my presence. Ishani's body went tight, and she looked out into the garden, away from me.

"What I did was." She shook her head. "It wouldn't work this time. I got my brother back, but that price was heavy, Dayanara. It's not something I'd want anyone to endure."

"Well, what—"

Ishani raised her hand. "Let's get some dinner."

Her eyes glazed over, and her fingers were flexing on what appeared like their own accord. I reluctantly agreed. I couldn't remember the last time I had actual food. Blood could sustain me for long enough, but I was pushing it with the lack of real sustenance.

With one last glance into the endless green beyond the garden, I followed her into the castle. I missed being one with nature. Dusra was full of it. Hills and forests gave way to beaches and seas. I was a lot more at home here than in Sanjry. Even so, there were moments when I felt outside of my body, like I wasn't in control. It was almost as if I was watching myself live, rather than living. I knew that it had nothing to do with my location, and everything to do with my circumstances. But I longed for Calderan soil, the endless trees and wildflowers.

I realized then that it had happened again. I didn't remember half of the halls we'd passed to get here. My heart skipped a beat when I saw Axel heading in our direction. Zuri getting captured had triggered him for different reasons than me. It was hard to look at him, knowing he might have some idea of what was happening to her. It wasn't the same captor, but the same kingdom. I missed him, though. I really did.

That guilt was nearly debilitating, wrapping around my heart like thorny vines. How could I entertain anything with him when Zuri was most likely being tortured? Axel had understood without me having to spell it out. But fuck, did I want to fall into his arms and let him do anything to make me feel better—again.

"Hey," he said as his gaze ran up and down my body the same way Ishani's had. His sister looked between us and ducked into the dining hall without saying anything to either of us.

"Hi," I gulped.

The man was magnetic. I moved closer to him without even realizing it, the two of us sharing breaths as we held each other's gaze. Axel towered over me, and his presence brought me comfort. That feeling of safety I always searched for rushed up and down my spine. He reached out his hand and put his palm to my cheek, and the touch of his skin against mine made those breaths come in easier. That spark, that tingle I got every time he touched me. . . I wanted to melt into it. But I couldn't.

I stepped back, breaking our contact and staring back to the ground. That moment was selfish. I shouldn't have let him think I was ready for anything yet, and I hated the fact I could hear his heart start beating faster.

"I want to be here for you, Daya," he muttered.

"I know, I just," I sighed. "I need her back, Ax."

"I'm doing everything I can, I promise."

The pain and desperation in his tone had those thorny vines squeezing tighter around my heart. He was doing everything. Short of risking the possible magical repercussions of adventuring into Sanjry uninvited, he'd been nearly as restless as I was. I wanted to soothe that hurt in his voice, even tried to reach back for his fingers, but my hand stayed glued to my side. My heart, it hurt too much.

"I know you are, but it's my fault. I shouldn't have let her come with us. I should have sent her back with Akari."

Axel grabbed my chin and brought my gaze back to his. "She wanted to come. This is not your fault."

Lust was what I was comfortable with. It was easy—surface level. But it wasn't just lust I saw in those hazel eyes of his anymore, and that was dangerous. Eyes had looked at me that way before, and they were now shut forever. The other ones. . .

"Caring for me always comes with a cost. You should remember that," I said before trying to pull myself from his grasp. His grip tightened as his water magic lapped over my body. The blood and gore that was stuck to me lifted from my clothes, skin, and hair. His gaze still locked on mine as he expelled it.

"I'm the last person to tell you how to work through this, but. . . maybe try to take someone with you next time. Don't tell me who or why," he said as he released me and walked through the doorway.

The moment my feet crossed the threshold, everyone stopped talking. I'd sucked the joy out of every room I'd been in the last three weeks. Like a whirlpool with no care for who was pulled into my current.

Akari and Ishani were at one end of the table, sharing a bottle of wine. Xavier and Paxx were already eating while they studied some papers between them. Axel stepped around me and went to sit beside them, and my hands balled into fists again. They were happy, enjoying themselves, and I could barely find it in me to fucking eat.

I sat a distance from everyone. Axel looked at one of the palace staff members with the blank facial expression he usually used when he was mind-speaking. The staff nodded and left the room quickly. I poured myself a glass of wine on the table, and by the time I took my first sip, the staff members came back in with their arms full of plates. They sat them down, full of my favorite foods I'd grown to love here and double if not triple the average portion. I could see Axel trying his best not to make eye contact with me, but my stomach was growling so loud I decided not to let that bother me.

The first scoop of the potato and cauliflowers doused in orange sauce had an audible moan escaping me. I ripped a piece of the flattened bread, similar to tortillas from my region but slightly thicker, and stuffed it down my throat. Before I knew it, every last crumb of food was gone, and I quickly realized everyone was watching me.

"What?" I bit out.

They all pretended to be doing something else, and I sighed as I grabbed the jug of blood and poured myself a glass. The tingle of my reserves filling bloomed in my chest, and for the first time in the last couple of weeks, I felt fully satisfied—physically, that was. The rest of me, my frantic mind and the pain that had made itself home in my chest, remained.

Axel pointed to something on the papers between Xavier and Paxx, and I lifted my chin to see what they were doing.

"What's that a map of?" I asked as I scooched out of my chair and went to stand behind Axel.

"It's Sanjry. These are all the places we've checked, but as you know, it's very possible that she's being moved around. We're continuing to monitor, but thus far, there still hasn't been any word," Paxx exclaimed.

I picked up a piece of charcoal and marked an 'x' through the area of Sanjry I'd just come from. "She's not here either."

Ishani looked between me and the mark. "That's closer to the capital than you've gone before."

"She's not on the outskirts. I have to move further. I'm a half a second from storming the fucking palace."

What was I supposed to do? Continue waiting around for someone else to solve the problem? I was so, *so* tired of my fate and happiness resting in someone else's hands. If that meant destroying village by village, leaving a wake of blood behind until I made it to Kaizer's doorstep, so be it.

"That's what he wants, Daya," Axel sighed.

I didn't care.

"He doesn't know you're here. He's still searching, and we know she's alive at the very least," Paxx added.

"How do we know that?" I asked.

Akari stood and moved to our end of the table. "When a lobo dies, the pack can feel it. I'm her only remaining blood relative, and I haven't felt her death."

An intuition between lobos wasn't something I could see or feel, so I couldn't trust that yet. Most of the major cities were checked off, a few spots near the Inbetween, and some places along the coast, but one place had no marks.

"What's here?" I inquired.

Axel's jaw ticked. "It's the only place taking significantly longer than the rest due to the terrain and their patrols. It's mostly farmlands, but there's a volcano and mountains in the general area too. Deadly drop-offs, unstable rock, it's not easy to get through."

"So she could be there," I said as I bit my lip. I felt Axel's gaze on the side of my face, his presence filling my mind but no words spoken.

"She could be anywhere. We're checking Caldera, too, but my gut tells me that Kaizer will keep her on his own land," Xavier replied.

"In other news, we did find quite a few brujas who are loyal to you being hunted by Kaizer's people. We can. . . potentially go and get them tomorrow and bring them out to the coast with the others. Hypothetically," Paxx said, trying to work around the agreement since Ax was in the room.

I nodded. "Okay."

Finally, something I can do.

"All right, we'll reconvene in the morning. Everyone, get some rest," Axel commanded.

"Stay," he spoke into my mind before I could leave.

I looked back to fight him on it, but the desperation on his face had my feet planted in place. Ishani squeezed my arm as she left and closed the door softly behind her.

"You can't go after her alone," he said.

I folded my arms across my chest. "I don't think any of you could stop me."

In a fucked up twisted way, I wanted someone to try. I wanted to fight, to explode my life even further. Self-sabotage wasn't the way, I knew that, but I just wanted to feel. . . something else outside of hurt.

"I have some friends that might be able to help. I was saving it for a last resort, but if you're thinking about going into the capital now, we can visit them."

"Friends?" I asked, unable to hide the intrigue in my tone.

Axel nodded once. I wasn't sure what friends could help in this situation, but I'd take anything I could.

"Paxx has his people on constant surveillance. There's no stone in Sanjry they're going to leave unturned. Zuri is strong. She'll be holding out, if not for you alone," Axel reassured.

He placed his fingers in mine, and I let my hand stay limp, not wrapping them around his. He scooted his chair back and stood to exit the room, but I grabbed his wrist before he made it past me. "Ax, it's not you. You know that, right?"

"I know, Daya. I'm here for you, no matter what you can give me right now."

Chapter Three

Dayanara

Fuck, I missed this.

I sliced through the vampire, charging me, in one swift move, his top half falling to the ground while his bottom half stayed upright for a few more seconds. My bruja magic sparked in my hand, and I shot a stream of it into the chest of a witch who would not be shown mercy despite being from my clan. Any bruja siding with Kaizer was no bruja at all.

The witch pulsated as my magic shocked her, and she fell to the ground with a hand on her chest. I brought my blade down on the back of her neck, and her blood splattered across my body. I was already covered in it. I couldn't tell what was hers or the other handful of vampires and witches I'd taken down. We were in the marshes, the sanction on the other side of Sabia, near the silver lake we'd gone to when looking for Rosa. The landscape didn't make it easy for battle, but I didn't let it stop me. My boots and legs were covered in thick mud, and the bits and pieces of soldiers around me were already starting to sink into the shallow water.

Ishani and Paxx had cleared a good bit of the water out, but the moment we made it into the land, we were met with soldiers, so there wasn't enough time to clear out the whole marsh. My brujas were battered. If we had been any later, there might not have been anyone to save. It was too much between the witches siding with Kaizer and the vampires they sent to retrieve them. There were about seventy-five brujas, which didn't seem like a lot, but I had to admit it felt good to save *somebody*.

The surrounding water vibrated and lifted into the air, sliding over my leathers and skin and pulling the mud and blood from my body. I turned around to find Ishani with her hand outstretched, her body clean as well.

"Everyone's down. We need to get out of here before more show up," she said.

I nodded and scanned the area for Cat. "Let's take them to the coast!" I yelled once I found her. Cat snapped at two of the witches we'd saved from the desert, and they both held hands as they opened a portal back to the coast.

Too lost to my anger, I didn't keep anyone else alive, but there had to be someone around who hadn't crossed over quite yet. The severed body parts in my area proved that theory wrong, but a few hundred yards out, I saw a large man crawling toward a witch who was twitching slightly. I quickly portaled over to them and sliced through the witch in Sanjry colors to make sure she didn't try to get back to the kingdom.

"Going somewhere?" I grabbed the soldier and tossed him through a portal to Axel's office in Dusra.

Axel stood from his desk without a single question, grabbing the soldier by his neck and lifting him in the air for me. I licked my lips as I moved before the bastard, his Sanjryan general ring reflecting the light in my eyes. He might have some information.

"What does Kaizer want? Where's Zuri?" I asked.

He held his chin up and squeezed his mouth shut. I lifted my blade, but Ax was faster. The vampire groaned as his back arched and his eyes went wide. I didn't realize what Ax had done until I moved to the side. He had stuck his hand right through the man's back and gripped the soldier's heart.

"Speak, or I crush it," Ax snarled.

The man gasped like a fish out of water, trying to will his mouth to form words, and I stepped closer, lifting my blade.

"Nobody knows where she is. They move her. I don't know, I swear it," he barely got out. "He said you're integral in some bigger plan, but only Otto and Abel know."

He clutched his chest in expectation of us letting him go, but Ax ripped his heart out through his back. It disintegrated into dust with Axel's magic before the soldier even made it to the ground.

I was in the training wing, where I'd spent almost all of my time in the last few weeks. Nobody bothered me, which was nice. Whether they were scared of me or respecting my personal space, I wasn't sure, but I didn't care. There was a comfort that came with moving my body in a way I was confident in. These drills I'd done thousands of times—they were second nature. I hated many things about my mother, but this wasn't one of them. Giving me these tools to be self-assured, even if her goal was self-serving, had benefited me. Focusing on my muscles stretching and contracting, I took quick breaths with each movement. I'd gone through enough training dummies that I'd resorted to bringing in large trunks of trees to hack up as I pleased.

I felt a presence behind me and took one more hit against the wood with a training sword before turning around to see who it was. Paxx was walking toward me with a tray of food. I'd lost track of time again. It was well past lunch.

"Hey," he said as he sat the tray down.

I nodded at him before twirling back around and kicking the tree trunk hard enough for the pain to reverberate in my shin. Paxx didn't say anything, just sat at the table on the outskirts of the room and watched me.

"Did you need to update me on something?" I asked, not facing him.

He grunted, and I heard his boots brushing through the grass closer to me. I still hadn't talked much with Paxx and couldn't find the energy to foster any new relationships.

"No updates. Just. . . wanted to bring you food."

I wiped the sweat leaking from my hairline and flicked my gaze over to him. "I didn't think you even liked me."

He shrugged as he rolled up his sleeves, exposing his forearms. "Never said that. I don't like uncertainty. The way you're fighting for Zuri has made me a little less uncertain about you."

The matte black ink scrawled across his rich mahogany skin caught my attention. I hadn't seen them before. Xavier and Axel had similar styles, but Paxx's seemed as if they were from a different world entirely. I'd come back to that.

"You've worked with her for a while, haven't you?"

Paxx slid on the padded gloves and wrapped the bandages around them so they'd stay in place. He brought his hands up in request for me to punch them, and I lifted my eyebrows. He continued staring at me, his face conveying that he knew there was a risk of me hurting him, but he didn't mind.

I threw the first punch, then an elbow, and he shifted his feet to get a better stance. "She's been with me for a long time. I trained her and helped her see she had a purpose after her parents died. It took a long time, but we helped each other through some things. I care about her."

I tried to study his face. He was hard to read, but whatever emotion he was trying to bury around Zuri being gone wasn't easily hidden. I never asked her about any of her past relationships. She never really wanted to talk about anything like that, which I now knew why.

"You love her?" I asked.

His jaw ticked. "I have love for her. I haven't felt *that* kind of love for her in a while. Regardless, I want her back."

I punched his left hand twice as hard and twirled around. Paxx groaned as I drove my knee into the pad with enough force to make him stumble.

"Trust me, there's no competition here. It's been decades since we were anything," he said as he set himself back in a defensive position.

I believed him. Zuri was great at her job, a fantastic actress, but some things you couldn't fake—not on that level. At least I hoped not. Paxx had never crossed any boundaries with her from what I'd seen; he was always very respectable when she was around.

"I believe you. Just know I'll gut you if you ever try anything with her again," I said.

Paxx laughed, a warm laugh I didn't think I'd heard come from him yet. Axel had spoken highly of Paxx, who didn't engage much with the others as freely. He seemed content just being around everyone. The fact that he'd tear the world apart for everyone he cared about was evident even in that stoic silence.

"I don't doubt that. You're a bit complicated, aren't you? I have a feeling you'd react similarly if I'd been talking about Ax." He pulled the padded gloves off.

"You sure you want to discuss the intricacies of my romantic life?" I asked, hand on my hip.

He grimaced. "I really, really don't. I'm saying I care about them both."

"Is that a threat, Paxx?"

"I feel like you only have one type of reaction, and it's violence." Paxx laughed.

I wiggled my fingers to determine whether I'd broken anything this time. Everything seemed to still be whole. "You're not exactly wrong. I don't know much else."

As he did often, Paxx didn't respond immediately. He watched me, or the air around me, I couldn't tell.

"I don't think it's a bad thing. It does make you a little predictable, though," he finally responded.

I humphed. "Ax is taking me to see friends in a few days. You have any idea who they are? He said they might be able to help."

Paxx's smile faded, and he tilted his head, which was one of the most evident changes of demeanor I'd seen on him. "That's not a good idea."

"What isn't?"

He shook his head and walked over to the table. "He can explain. Eat the food. It's getting cold."

Paxx swiftly left the room, leaving me still questioning who the 'friends' were and why it was such a bad idea.

Chapter Four

Dayanara

I was freezing.

Like I'd never known warmth, as if ice flowed through my veins. My entire body shivered as I brought my knees to my chest, and it was then I realized I was completely naked. Wind blew, sending my hair into a tizzy around my head. I couldn't see through the downpour of rain, but it pelted my body like thousands of tiny arrows. The elements continued bearing down on me until darkness enveloped me completely. A single flickering light in the distance grew and then vanished completely.

"Dayanara," a voice I'd never be able to forget drawled somewhere in the darkness.

My chest heaved as I realized I had to be dreaming, but the last time I was this deep into a dream, my mother was able to hurt me. *Wake up. Wake up. Wake up.* As much as I didn't want to panic, my body remembered. That instinct to protect myself and get as far away from danger as possible blared, but nothing happened. I had no control during these nightmares, so I had to wait for whatever forces controlled these hellscapes to grant me the courtesy of visibility.

The gusts of wind grew deafening, my eardrums on the brink of bursting. With a single snap of fingers, the wind completely stopped, and the space I was in silenced. Another snap and clouds of smoke bound for me like an incoming storm, green witch magic sparking inside. The darkness waned into a dim light, and my mother appeared sitting on a rock, dressed in heavy black robes that pooled at her feet. I now wore some sort of torn rags, and we were in the middle of a dark forest. My mother smirked, her skin glowing and her emerald eyes narrowing on me.

"You have fought hard not to let me take control. I'm almost impressed," she said with her hands in her lap.

I had. It was mainly because I hadn't actually slept in weeks, and when I did, it was such light sleep I barely dreamed. I felt her trying to get her claws into me when I ventured too close to deep sleep, and I accidentally let myself drift here now. For years I'd trained myself to stay calm in her presence, to control my heart rate and not give her anything to use. It was difficult, but I let that calmness ground me. As soon as I relaxed, my fear morphed into anger.

"Why are you this persistent in trying to get into my head," I snapped. You would have thought the fact she was fucking dead—by my hands—would be enough of a deterrent.

"I have unfinished business." Her eyes glowed as she stood from the rock, and the surrounding scenery changed. We were in the dungeon, and I was strung up in chains like I had been many times before. I pulled at my binds but didn't make it anywhere. My mother flipped her hands so her palms were facing up, and knives manifested. I closed my eyes, trying to wake myself up, but they opened on their own accord every time I closed them.

"What the fuck do you want?" I screamed.

She tsked. "You haven't figured it out by now? I want the brujas on top where they belong. We shouldn't bow to anyone, let alone lowly vampires."

"And torturing me helps that plan by?" I squinted my eyes in confusion.

"You can do it. You can do what I meant to, but your heart isn't in it. I only wish to..." She paused, twisting the knife in her hand. "Convince you to follow in my footsteps."

"I'm not going to take over all of Malva, Mother. That is a waste of my energy, and I have no interest in running *three* kingdoms."

She smiled cruelly, like that was the answer she was hoping for. I blinked, and she was before me, dragging the knife down my side. Pain here was tenfold. I knew she only stabbed me with one knife, but I felt the slice through my flesh everywhere. The blade carved through my side and down to my hip as if it were sliding through butter. My agonized screams waned into pure fury, and my body lit brightly. She gasped for air, and her entire being flickered as the color was pulled from her hair, the emerald green turning forest green. My mother reached for her throat as I pulled out of my chains, screaming so loud my throat threatened to close. Driven by some sort of instinct, I clenched my hands into fists, and she fell to the ground, staring back up at me with colorless eyes.

Someone was trying to wake me, but I wanted to end this now. I focused all of my power on her, she twitched and convulsed as her body drained of color. Just as I thought it would be enough to kill her, she disappeared, and I blinked awake. A practically naked Ax jumped back from the slash of my nails, throwing his hands up to show he meant no harm, and my chest heaved as I caught my breath. Something was off. There was a breeze when no windows or doors were open in the room, but a clear night sky sparkled above me..

"What the fuck," I mumbled as I looked back over at Ax.

"You blew the fucking ceiling off your room." He cautiously took a step closer to me. "Your mother?"

I nodded, realizing that he was towering over me more than usual because my bed frame had cracked. The middle sank into the floor, and the mattress was split, with a gaping hole beneath me.

Axel pulled me out of my shock and jutted his hand for me to grab. "You can stay with me, come on."

I let him help me up, glancing back at the absolute disaster in my room. I couldn't lose control like that again. I wasn't even completely sure what I did or if it was just a figment of the nightmare. Axel pushed his door open and held it for me, going into his bathroom and returning with a wet cloth. He swept my hair to one side and wiped my face, and only then did I realize I had rubble and debris on me from the ceiling.

"Thanks," I grumbled, making sure the rest of me was clean before getting in his bed. Axel flipped open the covers to let me know he didn't seem to mind, and I laid down on the side closest to the bathroom. He got into the bed on the other side and stayed a few feet away. We sat in silence for what felt like hours until he rolled to face me and cleared his throat.

"Do you want to talk about it?" he asked before he blew out the last candle in the room, sending us into pitch-black darkness.

"Not really," I mumbled.

"Do you want to not *talk about it?"* Axel spoke into my mind instead.

"How does that work?" I said, rolling closer to him. "Can I talk back to you in my head?"

"Once I establish a connection, yes. I essentially give you access to communicate with me. It won't work from too far away, but if you wanted to talk to me, you'd merely have to wish it, and I would answer."

I bit the inside of my cheek and turned away from him. I really didn't want to talk, but pretending I was having a conversation with myself wasn't too hard.

"She wants me to take over everything for the brujas. I don't have any interest in that. But I have no control in those nightmares. She cut me again, and the pain was debilitating. I screamed, and I swore I was pulling the very essence from her body. A few minutes longer, and I might have killed her, a death I don't think would grant her access into the spirit world."

"That has to be hard. Going from not having any control, regaining it by killing her, to losing control again."

"I'm not convinced I've ever had, or will ever have, control of anything. You don't know what I am. You say I am goddess-blessed, but I am *cursed,* everything around me crumbles. I am a disease, everyone who cares about me..."* I trailed off, not even wanting to speak that into my mind.

Axel had his arms around me in a heartbeat, pulling me close to his chest in one swift move. I wanted to tell him that I didn't want to be touched, that if he thought right now was the moment for sex, he had definitely read the moment wrong. But he simply embraced me, held me like if he let go, I might have drifted away from him into the night.

"I know *who* you are. You are perfect, Dayanara. A victim of circumstance, of very shitty circumstances. You have not broken yet, and you won't. You deserve for people to care about you and want to be there for you. Your mother doesn't get to take that from you, no matter what."

I didn't know what to say, so I let him hold me, taking solace in the warmth of his body and his steady heartbeat against my back. I let it ground me the same way Zuri had, not wanting to think too much about that situation when I still felt out of control. Ax's fingers trailed through my hair, rubbing softly over my temples until I fell into a dark, dreamless sleep.

Soft light filtered in through the tall scalloped windows as I blinked awake. My head was lying on Ax's bare chest as it raised and lowered evenly. Tilting my chin up, I let myself look at him, *really* look at him. I hadn't let myself take any joy in him in weeks, and I'd almost forgotten just how beautiful he was. His dark olive skin was covered in stubble, an almost full beard now. His lips twitched into a small smile, and I chuckled internally as I wondered what he was dreaming about.

"You," he said into my mind.

"Hey!" I sat up. "No reading my mind, it's rude."

He laughed and opened his eyes, his hazel irises pinning me down, making me forgive him without a word. "The line of communication was still open, not really my fault."

"Well, how do I close it? My mind is not a safe space for anyone who wants to wander in," I said as I stretched my arms above my head.

"Close your eyes and focus on me," he commanded.

My suspicion was surely written in my face, but I closed my eyes and did as he asked. The mattress dipped as he shifted to sit up and placed his hand on my forearm. "Focus on me, our connection. Do you see anything?"

I squeezed my eyes tight as if that would help me focus, but something sparkled behind my lids. A dark ball of what looked like witch magic floated, small silver sparks extending from it every few seconds.

"I see the essence of your magic."

"If you can see that, the connection is still open. Should you want to communicate with me when we're apart, that is what you wish back into your mind. You can push it out just the same, lock it up in another 'room' essentially."

"Just push?"

"Mhm."

I tried to get it to move, but it only stared back at me. It almost felt like it was growing in size. I focused all of my energy, but it still didn't move. Opening one eye, I peeked at him, and his brows pulled together right as I put my arm on his shoulder and pushed him off the bed. I closed my eyes again as I heard the thud of his massive body hitting the floor, and his magic was gone.

"Not exactly what I meant, but that works too." He laughed from the floor. "I'll get someone to start fixing your room. I know you need your space right now."

I was glad he understood. I was worried that the connection we'd established would disappear due to the stress I was under, but it didn't. He still continued to understand me, somehow. Walking over to his bathroom, I checked out the rest of his room. It was usually neat and put together, but it had been weeks since I'd been here, and it was much messier than before.

His ceiling was as high as mine with thick stone pillars supporting it. Each one was full of complex designs, painted in reds and dark browns. I ran my fingers over the closest pillar, wondering how long ago these were decorated. Piles of paper were stacked everywhere and a huge map of Sanjry was stretched across his desk—markings all over it. I ran my finger over the writings, all places he suspected Zuri could be, places he remembered being taken when captured. Some had different names under the writing from where he'd gotten the intel from.

"Zuri actually stole this map for us a few years ago," Axel said.

There were two very clear handwriting patterns, and I could tell which one was whose without having to ask. "I barely got to talk to her about any of this."

Ax put his hand on my shoulder. "She's helping in her own rescue. It's very. . . her."

I smiled, but my face pulled down with a dark thought I'd been ignoring. "What if she's already. . . What if we're too late."

"Akari will know," he whispered.

For some reason, that fact still hadn't made me feel better, but I turned to face Ax and nodded. "I'm going to shower, go ahead and check in on everyone."

Ax smirked. "I love that you know I need to do that."

I shrugged and moved into the bathroom. I'd gotten pretty used to the shower. It was nice not having to wait for a bath to fill up, even though I enjoyed the relaxation the tub brought. I turned the knob and waited for the steam to pour out of the contraption before stepping out of my clothes. The door was cracked, and I looked into Ax's room to find his gaze already on me.

"*Need help?*" he asked, his voice dark and husky.

I bit my lip, wanting so badly to agree, but I just. . . couldn't. Even after last night and him telling me I deserved people to care about me, I still felt like I shouldn't. He nodded. I wasn't sure if I accidentally left the communication line open or if he read it on my face, but he turned around and picked up a stack of papers beside his bed with a soft smile.

The steam covered the mirrors in the bathroom, and I stepped into the shower to let the scorching hot water pour over my body. Small bits of stone rushed down the drain. Pieces from the ceiling Ax must have missed. I grabbed the soap, and it smelled *exactly* like him. I practically moaned as I took a sniff and covered my entire body with it. Running my fingers through my hair, I did one more rinse off and turned the knob on the wall. The towel was as soft as a blanket, and I was tempted to stay wrapped in it in the steamy bathroom until I heard the door to Ax's bedroom open and close.

I tucked the corner of the towel into the spot, pulled it across my chest, and walked out into his bedroom. Axel had one of my witch leather suits in his arms, along with my boots.

"Builders are working on your room now, but we need to go out to the coast. Xavier said we're needed regarding a witch we rescued from the marshes."

I took the suit from him, dropped my towel, and blasted my body with hot air. "He say what about?"

Axel's eyes were on my naked body, but I quickly pulled on my suit. "Ax, what is it about? Do they know something?"

He cleared his throat. "He only said to meet him there as soon as possible."

I hadn't spent much time at the coast, but I'd been there enough to be able to open a portal. Axel handed me over my weapons, and I strapped them to my body before snapping open a portal to our destination.

Chapter Five

Dayanara

We were met with a warm, salty breeze and the sound of waves crashing somewhere in the distance. I moved toward the site where the witches would be, but didn't sense Ax following me. I looked over my shoulder to find him still with his eyes closed, his face toward the water. I wondered if he felt the way I did when the breeze blew by the Piedra or when I'd been inside for a long time and came out to the fresh air. Our connection to the elements we wielded was strong, something that brought us a certain calm. I tried to sense what he did, to understand the water.

There were rivers and lakes in Caldera, but I never really got to marvel at a body of water this vast. The waves rose and fell in a tempo that resembled a song—one ancient and natural. Water stretched so far and wide that my mind had difficulty comprehending the pure size. The space between the orange sky and the blue water wasn't stark—they melded together as if they were one. Ripples of white foam floated between the massive rocks at the coast, being interrupted every few seconds by the rhythm of the waves. It all felt. . . above me. As if I was too mortal and imperfect to experience the spectacle. When I finally glanced back at Axel, he was already watching me. We didn't speak, but the smile pulling across his full lips said enough.

Shouting behind us was a quick reminder that we needed to get moving. Xavier and Ishani spent a lot of time on the coast and had on-site offices in the main building. Thousands of rooms were set up for the army and all the witches we had brought with us. Like the palace, everything was open, the same scalloped doorways and designs found here. I followed the open-air hallways to Xavier's office. I knocked twice before entering, not bothering for a response because I needed to know whatever information he had. The door swung open, and Ishani sat across from Xavier, appearing to be deep in conversation, but he shook his head when he noticed us.

"You guys came fast," Xavier said.

"*Not exactly true,*" Axel spoke into my mind, reminding me of our time in the pub. That felt so long ago—a lifetime ago—but the memory of our first time having sex still made the corner of my mouth tick up slightly.

"What is it?" I asked.

Xavier waved his hand for us to sit, and I plopped down, leaning forward in anticipation.

"There's a witch here. We were running our usual screens on anyone we're bringing in. She claims she was on Kaizer's side before but is now on yours. I thought you might want to be there for the rest of her questioning."

My lip twitched as I thought about the once-traitor. I didn't know if anything she said could be trusted. She could still have been playing both sides. But I'd rather hear what she had to say and decide later if she could be believed.

"Very well. Where is she?"

"She's being held in one of the training rooms. I want to mention she offered this information willingly and has been cooperative thus far," Ishani answered with an eyebrow raised.

"So don't kill her right away, got it," I teased.

Ax chuckled beside me, and Ishani rolled her eyes with a small smile before leading us out of the office and toward the training room.

"Any problems with the others thus far?" I asked.

Xavier shook his head. "No, they have all passed the screenings except this one. They're all more than eager to join the army."

"A few of them mentioned that Kaizer's people weren't even giving them an option on what side to pick, anyone left behind in Caldera has been assumed the enemy," Ishani added.

"I wouldn't give any witches I found in Sanjry a second to explain either," I growled.

We reached the room, and I found a bruja with honey skin and shoulder-length black hair. Carmen, a high-ranking witch from Adriana's sanction, awaited us. I should have guessed Adriana's sanction would have been with them. She wasn't among the ones we saved from the desert. Every other sanction lead was there except her. Plenty of high-ranking brujas were missing, but the leaders had all sided with me.

"Carmen," I said as I walked around her and sat in the chair across from her.

"Acna." Carmen dipped her chin before lowering her brown eyes. Xavier and Axel sat beside me, Ishani on the other side of Xavier.

I folded my hands and sat forward, my face relaxing into a deadpan. "You sided with Kaizer originally?" I asked.

"Adriana," she growled. "Adriana sided with them immediately. With our border against Sanjry, she was worried we'd be the first to die when it came to war. She didn't tell any of us; they just showed up the day after the Ritual, and we either followed them or they killed us. I always stood with you. I had to get away without being killed."

"Where's Adriana now?" I asked.

"When I got out, she was in Sanjry. Because of her ranking in Caldera, Kaizer offered her a position in his council. She's the only sanction head there. I haven't seen any of them in Sanjry."

"The rest of them are already here," Axel answered.

Carmen nodded. "Good. Adriana kept me close. I know parts of the plan. A lot of it was left between Kaizer and Otto, but there are bits and pieces I know."

"I assume you wouldn't mind if I did a truth spell?" I asked.

She shook her head. She didn't really have a choice. I was going to do it either way, but her thinking I was being nice might help. I slipped off my bracelet and picked off the chrysocolla stone. This spell required me to destroy it, so I'd have to get another one to replace it. Placing it in the palm of my hand, I sent a spark of my witch magic into it and disintegrated it into powder. I stood up and walked around the table, blowing the substance into her face and whispering the spell. Carmen's eyes dilated, and she blinked a few times, which was an indication that the spell had worked.

I brushed my hands against my leathers and sat back down. "Do you know where Zuri is?"

She shook her head. "They don't keep her in one location. The last place they mentioned was near Caldera's border, but that was a week ago, and she could be anywhere now."

I bit the inside of my cheek. "What's Kaizer's plan?"

"He needs you for something. I don't understand what it is. Neither do Otto nor Abel. I've seen them argue about it multiple times. I do know that he thinks he'll be able to wield all four elements after he finds some sort of old relic. He believes it is here in Dusra. He has a group of witches trying to figure out a way through the barrier. They're having to be very specific about how they go about it to avoid the agreement taking a price."

"None of that is new information," I muttered.

"There's a woman with red hair that's always with Kaizer—Athena, I think her name is. I overheard her saying they were going to Joriv to meet with some of the nobles and lords about their place in his plan. I'm not supposed to know, but I listen when people don't think I am. I promise I've only ever been on your side."

I watched, waiting for one of the blood vessels in her eye to blow should that have been a lie, but she was telling the truth.

"Can you take—"

Ax cut me off. "I should leave. The details of the agreement state that I can't knowingly send someone to Sanjry's lands. You should be fine if you do it without me knowing."

I nodded, and he got up quickly and left the room. I watched as he glanced back one more time before closing the door, worry pulled across his features. He didn't want me to go without him—he didn't want me to go at all, but he also knew who I was.

Looking back at Carmen, I flicked my wrist, urging her to continue.

"Do you have a map?" Carmen asked.

"This could be a trap," Ishani whispered into my ear.

"It's not," Carmen offered. "It is not a trap."

She widened her eyes, showing that the truth spell didn't indicate it was a lie, and I turned to Xavier. "You have the map?"

Xavier sighed but retrieved it as Ishani sat back as if she was already plotting what to do next.

Carmen trailed her finger across the map, tapping twice on a spot I hadn't searched yet but had been to before. "They're meeting here. Joriv."

"I'm familiar," I said as I traced a path from Dusra's border to the other side of Sanjry. "Tracked a thieving vampire there once. When's the meeting?"

"Two days."

"If all of them are in one place, we could get information, weaken Kaizer's side, maybe even bring one back for questioning," I said.

"Just remember you can't question a dead vampire," Ishani added, ever the one to try to keep me on track.

"Do you have any more information on the relic?" Xavier asked.

"No, not what it is specifically. Only that he's searching," Carmen answered. "Am I good to go back with my sanction?"

Xavier looked to me, and I answered, "Yes, should we need you, we'll come and find you."

Carmen left, and I watched as one of the guards standing in the hallway directed her down the hall. Axel must have been waiting near the door because he came back into the room as soon as Carmen left. He sat where she was sitting across from me and put his hands behind his head.

"She said they're trying to make it through the barrier. Would they be able to do that? What is it made of?" I questioned.

I'd always been curious. To keep every single other Malvan out of Dusra, and to constantly maintain it, the source would have to be vast.

"It's our mother's magic, we have no idea how she did it. The only reason we know it's hers was because we recognized the signature. Went up not too long after she passed," Axel responded.

"It hasn't wavered since?"

"Not in the slightest," Axel said. "I don't completely understand it. Her existence alone was an anomaly, being both lobo and witch. Or more so, that she had the ability to tap into both sides and the witch blood didn't snuff out the lobo. Regardless, I don't imagine they'd be able to get through it easily."

Ishani was biting the inside of her cheek and tapping her fingers against her leg. I couldn't quite tell what the problem was, but when she noticed I saw it, she stopped.

"You're going to the jungle on the island tomorrow, right?" Ishani asked.

"That was the plan, yes," Ax answered his sister.

"You're going to see the Triori?" Xavier practically gasped.

"Well, I hadn't made that quite clear yet," he said, looking over at me. "But, yes."

"The Triori are still alive?" I said as I sat forward.

The Triori were part of the ethereal creatures that left with the goddesses, or at least we thought. Nobody had seen them since. The past, the present, and the future represented across the three of them—The Fates. They were said to be where the seer gift originated, as they could peer into your future at their own will and tell you about your past and your present if they wished. Most seers couldn't control it. They got their visions whenever the magic granted them access, but the Triori were in full control. People had lost their lives fooling with the Triori. It always came at a price—whatever you went to them for.

"They are. They've been hidden in the jungle for a few millennia. My mother discovered them a while back, and Ishani and I continued keeping their secret," Axel replied.

"And you are going to ask them for what exactly? Help to find Zuri? How to stop Kaizer? What would the price for something like that be?" Xavier asked Axel.

"I don't know. We'll find out when we get there. If it's too heavy, we can return to square one."

"Maybe that should wait until other things unfold. I feel that should be a very last resort," Xavier added.

Ax looked at me, letting me make the decision. I bit my lip as I weighed my options. We still needed to figure out what Kaizer was up to. I didn't think there was anyone who would be able to give us any direction outside of asking Kaizer himself.

"We still need to know what we're up against. Has Paxx made any more headway on that?" I asked.

Axel shook his head. "They're being very deliberate about not sharing that information with anyone they don't trust. Outside of kidnapping one of them, we may be on our own."

All three of us went quiet.

"Great," Axel groaned. "Don't tell me anything else."

"I think we. . . follow up on some leads first and then go to them. There's a chance some other things might come to light."

Trying to make sure Axel wasn't implicated in our plan was going to be difficult, so if it were up to me, we'd be going as soon as possible.

"All right, that's fine. Make sure you tell Paxx your plan. He may have some helpful intel."

Chapter Six

Dayanara

Snapping open a portal in the hallway, I stepped through and into the training wing, where Akari should be at this hour. We hadn't talked much since Zuri was taken. Part of me figured she blamed me. I blamed myself. Regardless, she was Zuri's family, so she should be involved in getting her back. I scanned the area and saw her blonde braids shifting as she dodged someone's blade. She rolled and popped up behind the man, swiping his feet and angling her blade for his neck. The man tossed his sword to the side, and she chuckled before helping him up. When she noticed me, her smile immediately faded.

Nice to see you too.

She said something to the man that had him looking over his shoulder at me and walking in the opposite direction. All the rooms surrounding the wide courtyard were empty, and the blades that were usually strewn about were missing and in the weaponry closet.

"Hey," I said awkwardly.

She didn't make eye contact, just cleaned her sword and regarded me with all the warmth reserved for a bug. "What do you need?"

"We've got a lead. We don't know where Zuri is, but we're hoping to find out," I said, and her off-putting demeanor shifted.

"When are we going?"

"First thing tomorrow if you'd like to join us."

Akari nodded rapidly. "Yes, do you need more soldiers?"

"No, I think we need to move light. The witch who brought us the intel is going to take us to them; we don't need much more. Her, me, Ishani, you, and Cat. They have detection spells set up for my magic signature. I won't be able to portal us in."

"First light?" She tapped her hand against her weapon. She was still here with me, but I could see the thoughts swirling in her mind.

"I'd like to get there before everyone wakes. We can meet in the courtyard."

"I'll let Nia know, but I'll be there."

I walked out of the training wing, breathing a little easier than I had this morning. We had a plan, somewhat of a plan. It was more than we had to go off, and that thought reminded me that I needed to go update Paxx.

His office was on the other side of the palace, as most of the offices were away from the training arena. I let myself marvel at the beauty of this palace. I was still in awe at the design that made me feel like I was running through the garden outside. Caldera's architecture let air flow in and had many open halls and windows, but the high ceilings and glass roofs here gave the actual illusion of being outside. Along with the breeze that was always there, it was somewhere I could stay forever. There were murals sporadically placed throughout the palace, all of varying designs. Some depicted battles fought, others portrayed love stories.

Plants, art, sculptures, all working together to create an incredibly welcoming place. I knocked on Paxx's door and waited for him to answer, something I didn't exactly offer Xavier and Ishani earlier. I wanted to ask her why they were so intense when I came in, but didn't get the chance yet. They were close, and I wondered if they were closer than I had originally thought. Ishani meddled in my business. I didn't see why I couldn't meddle in hers.

"Come in," Paxx boomed.

I turned the handle and stepped into his office. He sat behind his desk in the same position he always was when I came in here. It was still a little weird knowing that he'd been with Zuri, that he'd loved her, but I didn't see him as a threat. Paxx seemed damaged, as did most people in Malva, but I wondered if he was quiet and closed off for a reason. We weren't close, but I could take a guess that he had some sort of tragic backstory like Axel.

"I've got news." I sat in the chair across from him. "There's a witch who was in Sanjry that we brought in from the marshes. She gave us a tip about a meeting that's happening with the leaders of Sanjry. We're going to see if we can kidnap one of them."

"Is there a plan, or is *that* the whole plan?" Paxx inquired.

Ishani, Xavier and I had talked through what we thought would be the best course of action, but with such little information, there wasn't a lot to report.

"I'll take one of my brujas and Ishani, Akari, maybe one more. We'll go and survey the area and look for an opportunity to get information."

"I don't love that the whole plan fits in two sentences, but I understand. Do you need anything from me?"

"Nope, just wanted to let you know what was happening," I said with a bang of my knuckles on his desk.

Paxx sat back and crossed his arms across his chest. "Ax can't know because of the agreement, right?"

I nodded.

"Well, I appreciate you keeping me up to date. Actually," he said as he looked out the window beside his desk. "Can you help me with something?"

Nobody had asked anything of me in weeks. I wasn't sure if it was because they knew how focused I was on finding Zuri or if they were afraid to ask. Paxx hadn't treated me any differently though. He got a bit nicer, yes, but he was one of the few that didn't walk on eggshells. I wondered if it had even occurred to him that I might have said no.

"What do you need?" I asked.

"I usually have some of the witches here help me with the spell to communicate with the spies. I can handle the ones nearby, but these are too far. I was going to go get one of the brujas, but since you're here?"

I was actually eager to perform any sort of brujeria.

"What's the spell?"

Paxx stuck his hand into the drawer and pulled out a substantial chunk of aquamarine stone. I was curious as to how he communicated with Zuri and the spies he had in Caldera. Now that I saw the stone, I racked my brain on whether I'd ever seen Zuri with a piece of this in her room.

"Stone connection, I don't know why I didn't think about that," I muttered.

"Well, you typically can portal to whoever you want to talk to," Paxx chuckled.

"True. Yeah, I can help," I said as I rubbed my hands. "How many connections are there?"

"Only need to check in on the ones in Sanjry, so four connections. You know the spell?"

"I do," I said before picking up the stone and whispering the spell into the stone until it glowed from within. I passed it back to him and he spoke into it, checking with each of his spies, but none of them had any updates on Zuri.

"Looks like this is the only plan, then," Paxx sighed.

"It appears that way. I'll have someone update you when we leave. Remember not to tell Ax about the plan. It could come back to bite us."

"Got it," Paxx responded quickly.

I got up from my seat and moved toward the door, placing my hand on the handle, but paused. "Thanks for your help. I've never had this many people genuinely want to help me. . . Just. . . thanks."

I didn't wait to see if he responded as I slammed the door behind me and walked back toward the courtyard. The words had slipped out before I could stop them. They felt odd and foreign, but with an actual plan, there was a sort of. . . optimism growing in my heart. Optimism might not have been the right word. It surely wasn't hope, but it was a change.

I needed to get into my normal mission mode, but it was really fucking hard to treat this like any other mission I'd been on. There were far too many unknown factors, and I wasn't really sure how to prepare for them. Thinking about the repercussions of failing was not going to help. But if we got caught, Kaizer would likely have me drugged and behind so many guards I might not ever see the light of fucking day again. That wasn't an option, and it wouldn't deter me from trying either.

I sat on the bench in the courtyard, which had become the place where I did most of my thinking. Someone had watered the grass, most likely Ishani, because the path I'd worn into the ground was gone. I'd spent enough time here that the fields beyond the garden felt like a painting. Nothing changed, the same terrain, dips and hills. Trees and flowers bent in the breeze, but when it stopped, everything was still and constant. It was nice, knowing what to expect when I sat in this exact spot.

Especially because I had no idea what to expect from this mission. The only part I could plan out was entering Sanjry. We could go in through the border of Caldera to avoid the Inbetween altogether. One of the other witches would have to make the portal. Who knew where they had the magic detection set up? We knew for sure at the capital, at least, doing it for all of both kingdoms would be quite the feat. Going by portal to the border further north, outside of Adriana's sanction, was worth the risk. Otherwise, it would take far too long to travel by foot.

The advantage of being trapped in Sanjry before was I knew where their weak spots were around the walls. Or where the weak spots were before, but Kaizer wasn't the kind to change too much of his defenses. Vampires were all offense. We'd have to figure out that part as we went. I could do a spell to hide my identity, but that magical signature would radiate through me while hidden. Had it just been vampires around, I wouldn't have been worried, but brujas knew how to read those signatures with ease. It would have to be the non-magical route, which was something I'd trained myself for battle, but not for this kind of work.

"Daya!" Cat's voice came from behind me.

I couldn't help the smile pulling across my face. I really didn't deserve Cat. She had helped so much in the last few weeks. Especially with the witches on the coast, and before, making sure those who followed me didn't die because of it. I'd barely been able to check in on them, but Cat had checked in on me almost daily.

"Ishani said you might need me?" she said as she plopped down at my side and dug her heels into the dirt.

The gesture had a breath of contentment rising in me. We'd always done that as kids. No matter where we were, if we were outside, we wanted to be as connected with nature as possible. Sometimes we'd even dig our fingers into it as well to see if we could feel the magic in the soil.

"We have a lead. It's not the best plan, but it's the only one we have," I said as I followed suit and pressed my heels into the dirt beside her.

I filled her in, and she nodded, making suggestions for entrance since it was in her homeland. Thankfully, the desert didn't cover all of her sanction, only part of it, and few lived near the border. Thankfully, that part wouldn't add to the difficulty.

"You really want to go with that few of us?" Cat asked, shifting her long sheet of black hair from one shoulder to the other.

"If there's too many, the chances of us being successful are slim. The truth spell worked on Carmen, but I'm not sure what we'll be facing. I trust you more than anyone, so I'd like you with me."

Cat bit her cheek, staring off into the distance and calculating. "All right, well, let me get back to the coast and put someone else in charge for tomorrow. How long you think we'll be gone?"

"I'd say two, three days tops."

"Okay, I'll be here first thing tomorrow," Cat said before snapping open a portal and disappearing within a matter of seconds. I followed behind her, opening a portal to my bedroom and pulling off my leathers to get more comfortable. Thankfully, whoever Axel had fixing my room did it quickly; it looked like there was probably some more work to do but at least it wasn't a danger zone anymore.

"Are you done discussing things I can't know about?" Axel spoke in my mind, startling me, but somehow, in a way, I didn't mind too much.

I closed my eyes, saw his magic bouncing around, and I invited it to stay so I could respond. *"Yes, where are you?"*

"Listening to Xavier tell me how idiotic I am for wanting to take you to the Triori. He's been going for quite some time. I'm not sure I even need to be here for the monologue."

I laughed, wondering if he could hear my amusement. *"Any valid points?"*

His dark chuckling filled my head. I supposed he could most likely hear mine before. *"Oh, tons. We're out of good options. It's just the best of the worst."*

"Are you worried about my recent best of the worst plan?" I didn't say what it was specifically, trying to skirt the lines of the magic.

He remained in my mind, but no words were spoken for a few moments. *"I feel lucky to be someone you'd fight for."*

I didn't know what to say, and instead of embracing that very heartfelt moment, I joked, *"Hey, that doesn't mean you should go and get yourself captured or anything."*

"Shit, Xavier knows I'm not listening. I'll come check on you when I get back."

His magic retreated suddenly, and it left me feeling empty. Like the moments after mediocre sex, where you go from being filled and they retreat, leaving you wanting more. But goddess, sex with him was anything but mediocre.

Fuck, did I want to experience that again, and as soon as I got Zuri back, I'd let myself enjoy all that he was. I plopped down on my bed and rolled over onto my back to stare at the ceiling. That thought alone was complicated. What the fuck was I going to do when they were both here? I needed them both for different reasons; they fulfilled different parts of my life, and I didn't want to give either of them up. Axel was half-witch, but he was still a bit of an alpha male, and Zuri was a literal alpha female. The chances of them easily agreeing to me being with both of them were pretty much zero.

A flash of what all of us together might be like rolled through my head, and I almost moaned at how real the fantasy felt. Zuri sitting on my face while Axel pumped into me. She'd turn back to kiss him as she came on my tongue, his hands roaming up my body and flipping the both of us on our backs.

My knees fell open as my fingers grazed down my naked body. Just because I didn't want to have sex with Axel quite yet didn't mean I couldn't please myself. I grazed my lips, the slightest touch already sensitive. I trailed lower, finding myself very much aroused by the thought of having them both.

I closed my eyes and thought about what would happen next. Axel would line himself up with me as he reached over to Zuri and plunged his fingers into her the same moment he moved inside me. She'd gasp and fall apart as Axel switched over to fuck her. I pretended my hand was his, pumping his fingers in and out of me. I wouldn't be jealous to see Axel with Zuri; the two most attractive people I knew together felt like some sort of perfection to witness. Zuri would reach over and caress my breasts, pinching my nipples as we made eye contact, and she'd come so hard her legs would shake. I moaned as my very real orgasm built, and I hooked my fingers inside, thinking about Axel flipping me onto all fours and fucking me hard and wild—the way I liked it. Zuri would move closer to rub my clit. . . I muffled my scream as I came, both in the fantasy and in real life. I heaved a breath, right as I heard Axel's door shut across the hall.

Fuck, if only it could be real.

Chapter Seven

Dayanara

As promised, Axel came to see me last night, just an hour after my little self-love session. I wasn't sure if he knew what happened when he was coming down the hall, but he looked over at the bed a few times while we were talking. He left me with a necklace he'd recently found in his mother's collection, one of pure rose quartz, meant to help conceal my magical signature. It had been enchanted long ago to do so. There were a few relics that held this much power. We had one in Caldera—a moonstone vase. But this one felt even more potent. I wondered how it had come to be in her possession, but however it made its way into Dusra, I was thankful to have it. I had a feeling once he found out I was venturing so far into Sanjry, allegedly, he made it a priority to locate it.

We kept it brief, me not giving him any details of what was happening, but he still wished me luck and safety before kissing my forehead and letting me get to bed early. I was thankful for it, as it was about that hour when you couldn't decipher whether it was morning or night, the moon still fully out, and just the faintest glow of orange on the horizon.

It was chilly, a hazy cloud blowing from my mouth with each deep breath I took to try to relax. Cat, Ishani, Akari, and Carmen would be meeting me here outside the palace soon, but I wanted a moment alone before the crazy picked up. I tucked a piece of hair that escaped my braid behind my ear, the black color of it catching me off guard for the slightest second. I dyed it last night, as I couldn't use my own magic to hide my identity without facing possible repercussions. The black dye was the best I could do to hide the purple of my hair, which would identify me immediately.

There were a plethora of different scenarios that could play out and so many factors that had to go right for us to succeed. The first was the spot we planned on entering Sanjry from Caldera not being guarded to the teeth. The familiar tingle of Axel's magic filled my mind: *"Kill anyone who so much as looks at you wrong. Come back to me."*

He retreated before I could offer a response, and Cat came through the gates with Ishani on her heels. "Can't remember the last time I was up this early," Cat said with a stretch of her arms.

"Can't say I've ever volunteered to be up at this time," I laughed. "Well, unless I hadn't gone to sleep yet."

"This is my favorite time of the day," Ishani said with a wide smile.

"Of course it is, you little beam of fucking starlight." I lifted the pendant on the necklace Ax left me. "Can you feel my signature?"

Ishani closed her eyes and placed her hand on my shoulder. "No, not even when I touch you."

"Perfect." I clapped my hands.

Carmen smiled, but I could tell she was nervous—I could hear her heart beating at a fast pace.

Cat quirked an eyebrow. "Nervous?"

"Not excited to go back. I barely got out the last time," Carmen responded.

"Well, I can promise you'll die if this goes wrong, if that helps?" I offered.

Cat side-eyed me, and I shrugged as Akari approached the palace doors with more than enough weapons strapped to her. I rubbed my hands together and rolled my shoulders as I prepared to portal us into Caldera. It was a big jump and would take quite a bit of magic. I directed us all to get our fill of blood before meeting out here. As great as my Acna powers were, they didn't necessarily help with portaling, and I surely couldn't fly all of us anywhere, so we needed to stay strong. We had some blood with us, but we also needed to use that as a last resort.

"All right. We're portaling to your sanction, Cat. We'll cross the border and then portal to right outside of the city. From there, we just have to take whatever is thrown at us."

They all nodded, and I snapped open a portal to the border of Cat's sanction. The forest offered us coverage as we cleared the purple smoke and quickly surveyed our surroundings. I could hear the rushing water of the river that straddled our borders, and we moved toward the sound as quietly as possible. Nothing was out of place yet, but we stayed low as we reached the tree line.

"You think it's safe to portal across the river?" Akari asked.

I homed in on my witch hearing, listening for any heartbeats nearby, and heard none. "Smell anything?"

Akari shook her head. "The water could be affecting it, but no, I don't sense anyone anywhere nearby."

"Cat, you've got this one. Don't want to risk my magic from this point forward."

Cat opened a portal, and I watched as it sparked to life across the water near some bushes. She directed Carmen in first, and then we all followed behind them quickly. I still didn't hear anyone, but I pulled out one of my daggers from my thigh just in case. We pushed forward, still trying to be as quiet as possible. Before cresting a hill, both I and Akari lifted our hands to stop the procession simultaneously. Someone was nearby, but for the life of me, I couldn't figure out where. The sound was muffled, and Akari's nose twitched like she was having a hard time pinning down the scent, too. We slid onto our bellies and crawled to the top of the hill, finding a whole battalion of vampires wrapped in an air shield. I looked around for the witches who had to be here maintaining the shield, and found them on the front line of the group.

"What are they doing?" Cat asked from beside me.

They seemed to be digging for something, but it wasn't clear what they were looking for. They definitely hadn't been successful yet, and with the thick air shield, I assumed it was a secret. Three witches were maintaining it together, their hands linked, and the two on the outside stretched high.

"They're trying to find something. Let's not stick around," I said.

A grunt sounded behind me as Akari yanked her sword from a vampire's chest, and another one came behind him. I stretched my hand to use my magic, but growled as I remembered I needed to avoid it. I tossed the dagger in my other hand forward, landing it in his neck and dropping him to the floor. Pulling my sword from my back, I twirled around to make sure nobody else was coming. Cat was straddled across another man, her dagger dragging across his neck as she smiled down at him devilishly.

Carmen, to my surprise, was also splattered with blood. She wasn't a warrior; fighting was in a bruja's genes, but she'd never fought in any wars, and I didn't know if she'd homed in on the skill at all. Cat had been drinking from one of the glass containers of blood when we stopped. She must have dropped it when she heard the first soldier because it was shattered across the tree roots.

"Can you save that?" I asked Akari.

"Blood isn't the same as water, and it's forbidden to even try," she said.

"Fuck. Turn them to ash to get rid of the evidence, and let's get the fuck out of here," I said.

Carmen and Cat listened, the dead vampires' bodies floating into the wind as Akari and I kept our heads on a swivel. Nobody else came, and Carmen snapped open another portal to the next location we agreed on outside of Joriv. We stepped through and were immediately met with guards, of course. I slashed through the first one with the sword Zuri gifted me, letting it glimmer in the light of Cat and Carmen's magic. A non-witch growl sounded as Akari, quite literally, ripped out a vampire's throat with her teeth and spat the flesh onto the floor. We were all covered in blood by the time the last guard fell, and we moved closer to the wall quickly.

"So much for an easy entrance," Cat joked as she wiped the gore from her face.

"We're low on blood. Let's try to reserve magic once we get into the city."

"We'll be fine. I can drink from Akari if I need to get us back," Ishani reassured.

"Still, let's be careful." I looked down at my body. "Akari, can you help us out here?"

Akari lifted her hand, pulling water from the atmosphere and letting it coat our bodies to remove the dirt and blood that were sure to mark us as intruders immediately. I pulled my hood back up. Even though my hair was dyed, I didn't want to take any chances. The guards we killed were just the first line of defense, but this side was still not nearly as bad as the alternate routes. Cat pulled a dagger from her ankle and tossed it behind me, the sound of pierced flesh and a grunt reaching me as I turned to find a dead witch.

"Thanks," I whispered.

We crept over to the closest guard tower, a much smaller stone wall around this city than the capital, but a wall the same. We found four guards across it, one of them far enough not to hear us coming. Akari flicked her wrists, a blob of water rising to the top of the wall and encasing one of the guard's heads. Ishani mimicked the movement, the other guard now covered in water as well. They convulsed as they forced the water down their throats and drowned them within a minute. Cat yanked the last guard from the wall with a rope of air, softening their landing with another blanket of air to avoid the loud thud. I twisted, bringing my sword down on their neck before they even realized what happened. The last guard was moving away from us. I pointed two fingers toward where the guards once were, signaling them to push forward. Carmen and Cat moved as one as they lifted us in a gust to the other side of the wall.

"No more magic," I reminded them as I adjusted my hood to ensure it was covering my face. This city was a near replica of the capital on a much smaller scale. They all seemed to follow the same model: rings of homes surrounding the main stronghold, the poorer ones furthest away. Everything was covered in a thick layer of dust, no green around, no grass, no plants or trees, only dirt. The homes were dilapidated, some of them missing their entire roof, just thick cloths draped over the spots missing.

"What the fuck is this?" Cat asked, her nose scrunched in disgust.

Nobody lived like this in Caldera. Everyone was taken care of, had equal opportunity to make their living, and had the resources to do as needed. I'd never seen anything remotely similar to this outside of Sanjry. Kaizer charged such high taxes that these people barely had any money left over. They gave it up for shelter, even if it was as shitty as some of these houses. Some of these people came to court with the illusion that Kaizer was there to help, but he didn't do anything for them. They were so far beneath the people in the palace that nobody appeared to care about them. I felt a tug on my cloak and I whipped around to find a little girl pulling on the hem. She looked up at me with the biggest brown eyes I'd ever seen, her loose curls falling wildly around her round face. I stopped, turning to face her fully. "What?"

"My mama hasn't come home. I don't know what to do," she whimpered as tears filled her eyes.

Nobody paid her any mind; nobody came to help her or make sure she was safe around the strangers walking down their street. I never considered myself a great person, but fuck, even I felt like I should do something for her.

"When's the last time you saw her?" Cat asked.

"Two sleeps." She raised three fingers. "She went outside with a scary man, and she didn't come back."

"What are we supposed to do?" I whispered.

They all shrugged, and I cursed Kaizer for failing his people and picked her up to rest her on my hip. She poked at one of the daggers on the other hip and I yanked her back. "Don't touch that," I snapped, and her lip quivered.

I was not cut out for this shit. Cat laughed as we took the child with us, still not really sure what to do with her. We made it to the next ring, an area clearly better off than the last, but still not the best. Akari pointed toward a building and I followed to where her fingers were stretched.

"There's a church," she muttered.

"You ever been to church?" I asked the little girl.

She shook her head, the curls shifting with the movement. "Me either," I chuckled. "Let's see what they're about. What do you say?"

"Okay," she whispered with her gaze weary on the building.

Cat followed me as Carmen and Akari stayed on the street with their heads on a swivel. I pushed the large wooden door and found someone in orange robes, but the crazy demeanor in the eyes of the acolytes in the palace was missing from this woman.

"Hi, I'm not exactly sure how this works. Her mom's missing." I mouthed the words 'probably dead.' "Is that something you help with?"

The acolyte sighed, her hand moving to her chest as she moved toward us, and I had to stop myself from grabbing my knife. "We do. May the Flame bless her mother. Come here, child." She stretched her arms out.

The girl clutched onto my clothes and tightened her legs around my body. The woman dropped her hands for a second and watched the little girl.

"Hey," I muttered into the girl's hair. "This lady is going to help you, okay?"

She shook her head, keeping her face buried in my armpit. I looked over at Cat, wanting some advice on what exactly I was supposed to do, but she just shrugged. Neither of us had any kind of experience with children. I bent down and sat the girl on my knee, tucking the hair behind her ear.

"Are you scared?" I asked.

She nodded, wiping some of the tears from her cheeks.

"Not gonna lie, kid, I don't blame you. You want to know what to do when you're scared?"

"Yes."

"You close your eyes, look inside of you, and find the warrior that lives there."

"There's no warrior in me," she said. "My mama said I'd grow up and be like her. I don't think her job was a warrior."

My jaw ticked. "Fuck her."

"Ma'am!" the acolyte gasped.

Cat laughed and took a step back, but I brought my gaze back to the little girl. "You decide where your life goes. You have a warrior in you, I can feel it. Anytime you're scared, you remember that. You fight, and you fight hard. Do you understand?"

The girl hopped off my lap, her posture tall and her shoulders pulled back. "I'm a warrior."

"Yes, you are," I said as I stood up. "Take care of her," I demanded of the acolyte, with my hand on my dagger. "Or there will be repercussions."

The woman took my words for what they were, quickly grabbed the little girl's hand, and bent her neck as she muttered a prayer.

"She deserved better than that," I snapped to Cat.

"She did," Cat said with her gaze on me.

Finding a helpless little girl was not part of the plan, but I hoped she grew up in a world better than the one she was born into. It was never my plan to take all of Sanjry, but I could do a fuck ton better than Kaizer seemed to.

Chapter Eight

Dayanara

We'd made it to a safe place to stay for the night, far enough from the lord's estate but close enough to surveil what was going on. The inn we'd found was at the base of the hill the mansion sat atop, and we'd snagged a room facing that direction. It wasn't the nicest, but it would do the job. After questioning a nearby shop owner, we found out that there'd be festivities tonight to welcome Kaizer and the leaders of Sanjry. Apparently, this city didn't get many visitors, and their lord was going all out for them. The streets of the inner ring were clean, with banners and decorations around. All adorned in the burning tree sigil of this kingdom. It made me want to barf.

We'd purchased some Sanjryan attire to try to fit in. Hiding in plain sight would be our best option tomorrow. From the sound of it, there were going to be enough people filling the streets and the estate that blending in wouldn't be too hard. I hated being back in these colors, but if I was closer to stopping Kaizer and getting Zuri, I could suck it up.

Carmen and Cat went to find us food, and Akari was wandering around to see if she could see something from the other side. Which left Ishani and me sitting in the courtyard watching the estate. I toyed with one of my daggers, balancing it on my finger and tossing it from hand to hand.

"You always get this restless on missions?" Ishani asked.

"I haven't rested in weeks," I responded.

"We've noticed. You know we're all trying, right? Taking a day or two to rest and make sure you're in the best shape isn't a bad thing."

I dropped the dagger into my palm and squeezed the hilt. "I can't. No matter how hard I try, awake or asleep, I can't find peace."

"You blame yourself?"

"How could I not? I was there. If I had been faster, not lost in anger over my clan, I might have seen it coming."

It was easy to forget that she and Axel were twins. With Ishani's long hair and green eyes, and the permanent smile on her face. But their movements and mannerisms mirrored each other. The tilt of her head and her eyelids low as she watched me cautiously reminded me so much of her brother.

"Zuri knew the risks of going with you."

"She didn't know the risks of caring about me."

At least, that's what I told myself. But it wasn't true. She did know. She knew what happened to Ximena, and it didn't deter her. Zuri knew exactly what could happen. . . that she could be used against me. And she *still* stayed.

"The same way Ax cares about you." Not a question, a statement—an observation.

"He shouldn't. Not if he doesn't want to get hurt."

Her face remained serious, that hint of a smile always dancing on her lips gone. "You wouldn't hurt him."

"I wouldn't, but fate tends to think everyone who cares about me deserves pain."

"Hm," Ishani sounded, her gaze rising back to the top of the hill. "You know, when I first met you, when I saw you with Ax in Sanjry, I could sense your connection. Like it was in the air, tying the two of you together. You two seemed to feel it as some sort of magnetization, but I saw it for what it was. When Zuri told me about the two of you, I figured that it was just a fling. I didn't see how you could have *that* with Axel and someone else. But then I saw it between you and Zuri. Even in all that anger you had with her, it was there."

I tried not to let that do anything to the ice in my chest. It was one thing for me to feel connected to them both, but for it to be evident to Ishani? Someone who was close to the both of them, who had seen them at the worst and best. I wasn't looking for any sort of validation. I honestly wanted a reason to keep them at bay—to keep them safe from me. But each word beat against the wall I'd built, fracturing and splintering to the point it trembled.

"You say this as if I meant for it to happen," I replied.

"That's not what I'm saying, Daya. I'm saying that none of you are in control here. The connections you have can't be denied. You say the fates punish them, but I think they gave you all to each other. Regardless of our current circumstances. Would anyone else fight this hard to get Zuri back?"

I deflected. "You all care about her too."

"We do. But not the same way as you. I don't think there's a force in this world that could come between you all."

"Well, Zuri seems to hate Ax. So I'm not exactly sure what's in store for us."

"Zuri wasn't around when Axel was at his lowest. She doesn't see how far he's come. How long it took him to really get to where he is."

"When he was captured?"

Ishani nodded. "It made me physically ill. I felt his pain like it was my own, a twin thing, I suppose."

"What did you do? To save him?"

I'd been curious since Axel told me, and nobody knew. The ability to do damage like that was something we'd probably need by the end of it all. Ishani's eyes turned sad, her fingers falling to the hem of her shirt and pulling like a nervous tick.

"If it's too much, you don't have to tell me," I offered.

"No." She shook her head. "You should know. Especially because you might be in the same situation soon."

"What do you mean?"

"The other day when you saw me and Xavier arguing? It was about this. . . mostly. He's the only one I told about what happened. When Axel was captured, I went to the Triori. I asked them to help me get him back. They gave me an. . . ability. But in order for me to use it, they took a price. They told me within the year, the people I hated the most would die. At the time, I didn't think too much about it. I only wanted to save my brother. The people I hated the most ended up being my parents.”

My eyebrows rose. “They died because of the Triori?”

“They died because I couldn’t stop for a second and think about what the Triori were saying. They tried to talk to me, tried to give me some sort of riddle to explain, but I didn’t listen. When you go to the Triori, listen to *every* word, Daya. Everything they say has meaning and power. Few people are able to even get to them, so they play their games with the few who know of their existence. Be careful.”

“You didn’t say what the ability was.”

Ishani looked out into the crowd, biting her cheek. “I have blood magic.”

“Blood magic?”

“I can manipulate blood just as I can water.”

My mouth fell open. “Akari said it’s forbidden.”

A small part of me… no, a large part of me was curious about what that looked like.

“It’s forbidden if you aren’t gifted it. I was. The only one in a thousand years.” She tossed her head back like it was a joke. “It’s not easy, though. The toll it takes on me, on my body. I was sick for weeks after I saved Axel. I don’t use it anymore, and Xavier makes sure of it. He saw me. He gave me blood when I was so sick that I could barely walk. I didn’t let the rest of them see it. They were too focused on getting Axel healthy.”

“So the Triori took their price, and then they kept taking it,” I responded.

Ishani nodded. “I’m not sure if they made it that I get sick or not, but I do know that they will take a price for any help they give you.”

“Does Axel know? About the blood magic?”

“No. I understand that I shouldn’t ask you not to say anything to him, but he’ll blame himself. If you can avoid it, I’d ask that you don’t say anything. He’s gone this long without knowing.”

“Thanks for that,” I joked. “I’ll take this as a bonding moment between us.”

Her mouth pulled into a playful smirk. “I do like you, Daya. You know that?”

"You are one of the few ones who have made that pretty clear." I laughed. "Paxx and I have made it to somewhat of an understanding. Akari and Xavier, I'm not sure about."

"Xavier has good intentions. He's been around us the longest, he knows about all our ups and downs. You brought a lot of. . . drama with you."

"That's one way to put it," I mumbled. "I'm about tired of my drama myself. Have you and Xavier ever. . . ?"

"Oh, we have, and we've done it well." She chuckled. "Xavier is too serious. He doesn't understand why I am the way I am. I'm free-spirited. I move where the world takes me. He wants a structure I'm not sure I'll ever be able to give him. We are drawn to each other, though. No matter where we go, who we go with. It's been decades since we've been anything serious."

"Will you outlive him?"

"I try not to think about that. The fact I have to see so many of my friends die while I am still moving on in life. Much like you, I suppose."

"Witches seem to live forever when not killed by something. That is true. Have you ever heard of soul-tying?"

Ishani shook her head.

"There's a ritual where you can tie your soul to someone. It was something that they did in Caldera. When you met the one you wanted to spend your life with, we didn't have wedding ceremonies. We tied souls. Making it that one would never have to live without the other, whoever had the strongest soul was the one who carried them both. It's in the grimoire. My mother had to perform it."

"Interesting," Ishani said as she sipped her water. "What about Zuri? You were pissed before."

"I am, I'm still pissed." I threw my dagger into a nearby tree. "I'd never let myself open up to someone like that. Not since. . . my mother killed the only other person I cared about that way. I haven't even let myself fully go there with Ax yet. I want to so badly, but I find it. . . difficult. It wasn't difficult with Zuri."

I was fairly sure that Ishani wouldn't judge me over Ximena, but that possibility had me keeping it to myself.

"Why do you think that is?" she asked.

I didn't realize when I stayed back with Ishani that we'd be getting this deeply into things. But much like Zuri, it wasn't difficult to talk to her. It could have been because I felt so much of Axel in her, or it could have been the kind of person she was.

"Part of me wants to believe that it was a tactic she used, something Paxx taught her. Another part tells me she's just a dirty fucking liar."

Ishani leaned forward in expectation. "But?"

"But, I know it's not true. Even if we never were able to get back to that place we were in, she doesn't deserve what's happening to her. They targeted her because they wanted to get to me. And that pisses me off even more."

"Does the fact Zuri lied about where she was from change the connection you two had?"

"It doesn't fucking help," I said as I got up and yanked my dagger from the tree before sitting back down. "Determining what's real and fake is what changes the connection. All the little lies told to maintain that big lie. I get why she did it, more than most, really. That's the hard part. The guilt, though, that's eating at me."

"You certainly have some things to talk through," Ishani said.

"You two see anything?" Akari said as she approached us.

I kicked the dirt beneath my feet. "Nothing yet. A few people have gone up, but nothing to note."

Akari scratched her jaw and left a streak of blood on her sienna skin. "I figured out where the meeting is."

"I assume the source of this information is dead?" I asked.

"To put it simply." Akari shrugged. "They won't be telling anyone, that's for sure."

Cat and Carmen turned the corner, their arms full of food, and Ishani made space for them at the table. Akari grabbed an apple and bit into it before saying, "Kaizer and his people should be arriving tonight. The other lords are already here, and everyone is staying in the east wing. Party begins tonight at dusk, and the meeting is tomorrow morning."

Cat eyed Akari. "How'd you find that all out?"

"Someone who worked the estate. Information is sound," Akari replied.

"All right. Well if everyone will be here today, maybe we can complete the mission tonight. Get back before the meeting even starts."

"You don't want to try to infiltrate the meeting itself?" Carmen asked.

"I don't imagine we'd be able to if only his trusted allies were in this secluded area. Unless anyone has an idea?" No one spoke, so I continued. "We see what we can figure out tonight, and take someone with us for questioning if needed."

Ishani pointed toward the estate. "There they are."

Kaizer stepped out of a carriage, reaching back and holding Athena's hand to help her down. Abel followed behind them, Otto not seeming to be traveling with them. A man greeted them at the entrance of the estate, and they walked inside without sparing a glance toward the city. My magic pressed beneath my skin, and I fought to keep it down as my blood boiled with the knowledge Kaizer was this close. I could kill him here and now.

"Whatever you're thinking," Cat said with a hand on my arm. "Stop before you lose control."

"I'm trying," I said through tight teeth.

By pure will, I calmed the rage inside me and took a deep breath. Akari picked up a stick from the ground and drew the layout of what she'd seen, pointing us toward where they'd be staying for the evening and where the meeting was to be. The party would be going all night, with the estate courtyard open for drinks and dancing.

"They were giving out these masks." Carmen set five full-face masks on the table. "Apparently, it's some Sanjryan holiday," Cat added.

"Ah, that's right. Flame Founding, it's said to be the day that the forest gifted a vampire the ability to wield fire. That's why they're here. The capital usually has a big festival, but I'd guess they're trying to win over the city leaders by letting them host it," I said.

"So there could be some possible dissent that we could take advantage of," Ishani suggested.

A boom going off at the top of the hill had us all on our feet with weapons raised. We lowered them once we saw the sparkling firecrackers shooting into the sky.

I grabbed the mask and fastened it to my face. "Possibly. Let's find out."

Chapter Nine

Kaizer

Lord Byrne had been a thorn in my side ever since I'd brought him into my plans. I was close to having him killed and replaced, but he offered to house our council meeting. So, there was hope that he might finally get on board. Flame Founding was a great opportunity to win him over as well. Letting him throw the festival here rather than in the capital had been one of Athena's ideas. We needed his land and his people. I could demand it as the king, but Otto and Abel had advised against it. Being unified was more important than ever.

They'd gone all out, the firecrackers lighting up the sky evident enough. Byrne's estate was one of the biggest ones in Sanjry, and being connected to Caldera's border, it was a vital location. I felt closer to Daya just being in proximity to the land she came from—our land. We'd gotten no further in finding her. We'd sent out a battalion to figure out what happened to the last witch retrieval, and it was evident she'd been there. Nobody cleared a battlefield like her.

"Baby, can you help me," Athena drawled from behind the changing screen.

She'd made herself useful in the last month. But we both knew the moment I found Daya, Athena was gone. Well, I knew. I had a feeling she was working hard on changing that future. Athena had a way with the lords and nobles of Sanjry that couldn't be denied. She stepped around the changing screen, a red dress hugging her slight curves and pooling at her feet. It wasn't a typical dress she wore, the neckline deeper and the shoulders out.

"This is different," I said as I tightened the strings at her back.

With an uncharacteristic hint of shyness, she said, "Thought I'd try a different style."

We looked at each other, a beat of silence passing between us. It was something Daya would wear. I couldn't be sure if that was why she wore it, but it certainly wasn't out of the question.

"We really should have traveled with a handmaiden or two," she said, breaking the silence.

"I'll be sure to remember that the next time," I responded. Sometimes, it was easier to tell her what she wanted to hear right away than to listen to her complain continuously.

Athena reached for my bare chest, but I brushed her off and pulled on my tunic. "We don't have time."

"There's always time," she responded with a step toward me.

A knock at the door proved my point, a voice coming through the wood saying, "They're ready for you."

I grabbed my porcelain mask, mine only covering half of my face instead of the full thing like most people. Athena complained that it would ruin her makeup, so she didn't want to wear hers. They weren't required, but the people enjoyed their symbolic nature. The fact that the Flame saw us all the same, that it could wipe us all clean no matter who or what we were.

The sentiment was nice, but I wasn't too sure how true it was. Regardless, I'd follow whatever voice it was that had been guiding me to our victory. We walked out of the room, Athena's hand finding the crook of my arm per usual. All the lords were waiting downstairs for me to officially start the festival. I usually gave a generic speech about how strong Sanjry was and what the Flame had in store for us for the next year. Joseph and Abel typically wrote it, but this one I wrote myself—short and impactful.

We descended the spiral stairs, both of us the picture of power and grace. The lords lined the hall out to the veranda, forming a tunnel of respect. A plethora of city dwellers filled the courtyard, some spilling out and down the hill. Athena went to stand beside Otto as I stepped out onto the balcony. The excited energy of the crowd was palpable. I raised my hand, and everyone screamed and shouted. That never got old.

"My people," I belted, and the crowd silenced. "We have had many wins this year, our land has doubled, and our stronghold within Malva has grown. There have been losses." I paused, my hands balling at my side. "But we shall continue prospering with the help of the Flame! I call to you, my kingdom, to have faith and continue our path to righteousness!"

More firecrackers erupted as the sea of people clapped, and I let them show their excitement for a few more minutes before yelling out, "Let the festival begin!"

Music played immediately, some people on the hill shifting toward the streets where the pub and louder instruments sounded. Lord Byrne's estate-men ushered people off the dance floor and set up some tables of refreshments on the perimeter. I turned to find Athena waiting for me, switching her long braid from one shoulder to the other. The lords all watched her, her choice of fashion surely causing their eyes to wander. She was typically watched this way; how she walked demanded attention. Not an inkling of jealousy rose in me. She could take her turn with all of them for all I cared. She absorbed every look of desire like it was feeding her soul, and I walked beside her until we reached the courtyard.

Lord Byrne had a throne ready for me at the back of the space, a raised platform with a table and tray of food waiting atop it. He and his wife, the Lady Byrne, stood with some of their guards, their smiles soft as I met them.

"King Kaizer, it's a pleasure having you here," Lord Byrne said. His black hair had started to go gray the last time I saw him, but now the spots of silver overtook him from crown to nape. He wore a light gray tunic—close to the shade of his hair—that caused a reflection from the moon to highlight his dark skin.

"Thank you for hosting," I said, turning to his wife. "I'm sure this was all more you than him."

She smiled, delicate lines forming around her mouth. "Believe it or not, he had quite a hand in this."

"Does your passion for the festival mean you're finally ready to join the cause?" I asked.

His wife bowed her head and left the two of us to speak. I climbed the stairs of the dais and sat atop the throne, waiting for his response as I took a sip from the wine.

"Your Majesty, I meant no offense with my concerns. What you're saying is. . . difficult to comprehend."

"Do you not believe in the Flame?" I questioned.

"Those were not my words, sire. The Flame represents many things but has not spoken to anyone directly in a very long time."

"It sounds like we're due, then."

"Maybe. But I've been around for a long time, and I've seen a lot of things. I can only put up so much of a fight. I know as well as anyone else that you can take these lands that have been in my family for centuries. Take my men and my soldiers. I just hope that when it comes down to it, you aren't wrong."

"I won't be. This is the future of our kingdom, the future of this world."

"If you say so, Your Majesty." Lord Byrne bent at the waist and waited for me to dismiss him.

"Thank you," I said with a wave of my hand.

As Lord Byrne left, Athena floated over to the dais and made a show of bowing dramatically. Her breasts spilled from the deep neckline, and she placed one of her hands atop her chest. She slowly climbed the stairs seductively, but she wouldn't make any moves out in the open like this. Many of the lords partook in plenty of heinous activities but never where our subjects could see. The people of our kingdom saw us not only as leaders but as religious figures. When the civilians went home and the estate doors closed, I was sure Lord Byrne had something up his sleeve.

"Abel sent me to see if you needed anything," Athena drawled, her tongue tracing her lip.

"Where is Abel?"

Athena pointed across the yard to where he sat with Lord Pyke and Lord Nyr. "They're already talking about the meeting tomorrow."

"I'm fine, thank you," I said.

She bit her lip as she stood there for another moment. I doubted Abel sent her. She stood with anticipation, looking to want something but too afraid to ask.

"I want to dance," she blurted.

"Then dance." I stared back out into the crowd in dismissal, but she placed herself directly in my eyeline.

"With you," she followed up.

"I don't dance at these events."

"A fact, but doesn't have to be," she said, stepping closer and reaching for me.

A few people in the crowd turned toward the dais, and I smiled tightly before taking her hand and helping her down the stairs. There were times I quite enjoyed the showmanship of being king, but times like this, I did not. I couldn't react how I wanted to, not in front of all these people, so I had to pretend that I wanted to dance. Thankfully, the song changed into something slower, and I placed my hands where I'd been taught to. I wasn't raised among these people. I wasn't schooled on the intricacies of fine living. I grew up under a lord, but just a spare son. My city had since been obliterated—one of my first acts as king. To vanish any ties of my life before I sat on the throne.

Abel and Otto were the ones who caught me up on many things. They had served my cousin, the previous king, the one I slew. I had no real fondness for the man; we shared a last name and blood. He treated my father poorly, and even though I didn't necessarily have a fondness for him either, it always rubbed me the wrong way. My cousin especially didn't like me; he'd said once that I didn't look Curran enough. I had the white hair, but my skin, and, well, everything else came from my mother. Flame rest her soul.

Being king had been something that fell into my lap, not something I set out venturing for. I'd done what was needed to obtain and maintain my position, but it wasn't something I expected. I thought about what Daya said, about how exhausting it was to keep up the facade and make everyone happy. Maybe she was onto something.

I fell into the next steps of the dance, letting my muscle memory guide me as I smiled at Athena. I was getting lonelier and lonelier. Athena was a good distraction, and she did have sound advice at times, but I longed for more. More anything. More power, more of a connection, like the one I'd felt with Daya. Not one *like* it—I wanted *her*.

She was integral to my plan. I needed her to defeat Dusra and finally bring Malva to what it always could have been. A great united kingdom. I wanted this to be the last war my people saw, securing our future and the future of all Malvans. Dusra wouldn't go down easy, but the journal seemed to think we were on the right path. It hadn't guided me in the wrong direction yet, and it agreed that Dayanara was needed to be successful. She was the only one powerful enough to wield the scepter. Even I couldn't deny that she surpassed me in power. The hairs on the back of my neck stood, and I turned Athena—thankfully to the tempo of the music—to see what my body was alerting me of. I saw nothing, merely tons of masked vampires dancing, drinking, eating, and celebrating.

"What's wrong?" Athena asked as the song ended.

"Nothing." I made to move back to the dais, but she held onto my hand.

With wide eyes and a slight pout, she urged, "One more?"

We'd have to talk about this. She hadn't been this outright about her desires until today. I wasn't sure what her angle was, but I was sure there had to be one. She hadn't brought up anything about making her queen like she had before, but it didn't mean it was out of the question.

I squeezed her hand tighter. "This is the last one."

Chapter Ten

Dayanara

The sea of masks was unnerving. Brujas never needed to hide their identity with such a thing when we had magic. But since I wasn't able to use mine without possibly alerting someone, I was thankful for the ugly things. The rose quartz pendant was cold against my chest beneath my clothes, but I didn't want anything further to mark me as a witch. There were quite a few around the estate, none I recognized yet.

We elbowed our way through the crowd in the courtyard, the music loud enough for people not to hear us trying to get around them. The stone floor looked like it was made of one huge slab of granite, silver gleaming in the veins running the length. They really brought out all of their finery for their king, so many sculptures and lanterns throughout to be maneuvered around. I kept the hood of my cloak up, hiding my eyes in the shadow it cast. We decided to split up. I was with Ishani, Carmen and Cat were together, and Akari ventured off by herself. She still wasn't too keen on me, so I was happy not to be partnered with her.

Ishani wrapped her hand around mine to guide us through the room, and we went over to the table with refreshments. I spotted Abel at the other end and took my time choosing some snacks and a drink. He'd taken off his mask as he appeared to be discussing something of great importance.

"You all must do your part," he said. "Byrne's lands are necessary to our advancement. He's the last one with any reservations."

One of the men he spoke to grunted. "Why do we care about his reservations? The king should take what's already his."

"We need unity," Abel responded. "Byrne has one of the largest lands here and treats his people well. They're loyal to him. Dividing people at a time like this would not bode well. That is a last resort. You'll all be happy when the king does as promised."

He clearly hadn't been to the outer circle of this city. I'd been choosing between two different types of cheese for too long, I had to move. I turned to go back to where Ishani was nibbling on her food, clearly listening for anything. As I lifted my glass to my mouth, I surveyed the area. I noticed a throne at the back of the yard, but Kaizer wasn't sitting in it.

"Two lords are over with Abel," I uttered.

"The man in silver is the owner of the state, Lord Byrne," Ishani whispered.

I spotted Cat and Carmen entering the estate and turned back to watch the Lord Byrne. There had to be a reason he didn't trust Kaizer, and one of us needed to figure it out.

"See if you can get anything out of him," I said as I left her side and entered the dancing.

A familiar redhead, not wearing a mask, brushed past me, and I turned to find Kaizer only a few feet away from me. Before I could think any better of it, I threw my voice an octave higher and said, "Care to dance?"

Kaizer's gaze ran up and down my body, nothing pointing toward my identity. I could see his jaw tick in the small space beneath his mask, but he nodded and raised his hands. There was a dagger beneath my cloak strapped to my chest and one at my thigh. It would be so easy to slide one of them out and watch his blood run all over this dance floor.

"I'm going to be honest with you," Kaizer started. "I'm not very good. You seem to know what you're doing."

"Hm," I sounded.

"Lord Byrne has thrown quite the party. He treats you all well, does he not?"

"He does," I said as I contemplated how quickly I could reach one of my weapons. The position of our hands made it difficult to get to the one on my chest. Maybe the one on my thigh would work.

"I find him. . . different from the others." He paused. "I'm sorry. I'm not sure why I'm telling you all this."

"It's okay," I responded.

"I'd like for him to join with me. I know what we can do as a kingdom would be incredible should we all be united. Maybe you could put in a good word with your people? Our secret?" he said, the teasing in his tone had me thankful that the mask was covering the confused curl of my lip.

He seemed content to move in silence. He spun me out, and I moved gracefully. There was no way he couldn't feel the absolute disdain radiating from me, but he didn't miss a beat. A couple of the others on the dance floor stopped and pointed, delighted that their king was dancing with someone from their city. I was surprised to find him here and not sitting on this throne.

We continued until the song ended, and I bowed with my hand on my belly. This was my shot. I slowly moved my fingers higher, the tip of my pointer grazing over the hilt of my dagger before Abel came to Kaizer's side. *Fuck.*

"You're needed," Abel said to Kaizer.

"It was a pleasure dancing with you," Kaizer said to me, and I kept my eyes low.

They turned and left. I wasn't above stabbing him in the back, not after what he'd done to me. I wrapped my hand fully around my weapon, dodging bodies to try to keep up with him. Someone tugged on my arm, which had me truly ready to use the blade.

"That was reckless," Ishani hissed.

"I was so close," I pleaded as I tried to see where he'd gone. "I could have ended it all."

"We would not all have made it out alive," she responded.

"We don't know that for sure."

After being so far from any sort of success, and then being this close, I wanted to scream and send my magic into all the surrounding bodies. I had to focus. What

I was about to do might not have helped Zuri. Otto wasn't here, and he would have followed through on any of Kaizer's plans. Ishani was right. Even if I hated it.

We shifted back toward the perimeter of the space, but the lords were congregating toward the building. There were a few guards by the doors who looked like they were going to close them off soon, and me and Ishani slipped into the crowd to get inside. The doors slammed shut behind us, a lock clicking as music bloomed to life in one of the rooms. We followed the group of people into a small ballroom, the men and most of the women seeming to split off into different spaces. Ishani and I were reasonably tall, and with our hair covered, the cloaks, and masks over our faces, no one should have suspected we didn't belong in either room.

Athena's voice caught my attention, "Oh, she's pathetic really. Kaizer is completely over her. He just needs her for her power now."

"That's not what I heard," another female voice responded, someone I partially recognized, but not enough to remember a name. "I heard he stays up all night muttering her name, searching for her all hours of the day."

"As the one who is with him at night, I can assure you her name isn't uttered from his lips," Athena responded. "They are having quite some fun with her handmaiden, though."

Ishani stepped in front of me the moment my foot shuffled in their direction. "Just wait."

"Oh, do tell," another female voice said.

"They think they're close to breaking her. I joined in on the last interrogation. It was…" She paused, seeming to savor the next word. "Gruesome. One last piece of the puzzle, and Kaizer will have everything he needs."

"And you still expect him to make you queen?"

"I'm the only logical choice," Athena preened, her gaze snagging on something across the room. "Oh, you ladies will have to excuse me for a moment."

She rose and left the room swiftly, and we waited a moment before following her. I could barely hear my own thoughts, everything inside me *needing* to kill her. The way she spoke about Zuri was enough to end her. Maybe she knew where she was. Carmen and Cat spotted us, and Cat's hand immediately found my arm. Even completely covered and with my magic blocked she could sense what I was feeling.

"Akari is outside. She said she was waiting for instructions on what you wanted to do next. What's going on?" Cat asked.

"I want Athena," I growled.

"Wouldn't one of the lords make more sense?" Carmen asked.

"No, she has more information than all of them combined from the looks of it. The only one better would be Abel, but I doubt he'll leave Kaizer's side for the rest of the evening."

"All right," Ishani said as she led us out of the room. "Cat and Carmen, you two should go let Akari know we're coming. Meet back at the room, if we aren't there by morning, portal home."

Cat glanced at me for confirmation, and I nodded. "Go ahead, we'll be fine."

She held my gaze for a moment longer, but turned and left with Carmen. Cat hated when I went rogue, and I went rogue a lot. Ishani seemed to also pick up on that. I listened for Athena, hearing her voice coming from upstairs. We slowly turned the corner, ascending the stairs cautiously.

"As much as you think you belong in that room, you don't," Abel snapped.

"You really think he doesn't tell me everything, anyway?" Athena responded. "What's the difference?"

"The difference is you may have the title of lady, but you and I both know you aren't one. Plus, I don't think you could handle what's currently happening in there."

"What does that mean?" Athena's voice turned from vicious to concerned.

"Your king currently has two women in his lap, one of them he's drinking from and the other he's fuc—"

The loud crack of a slap sounded, and I had to hold down my laugh. Go Athena.

"Why don't we just take them both?" I said to Ishani, listening for if anyone was nearby. "They're the only ones in the hall right now."

Ishani shrugged and climbed the stairs, but the slam of a door had both of us pausing. Footsteps stormed toward us, and Athena reached the top of the stairs where we stood. She went to move around us, but I put my arm out to stop her, unfastening my mask with my other hand.

"Where do you think you're going?" I purred.

Athena opened her mouth to scream, but Ishani created a bubble of water and gagged her with it. Grabbing her by her arms, I dragged her back up the stairs as she unsuccessfully tried to get away. Her back slammed into the wall as I forced her up by her throat. I looked over at Ishani, and she lifted the water away from Athena's mouth, letting it hover an inch in front of her.

"What is wrong with you!" She gasped, the sound not quite a scream with my hand on her throat.

"I think we're due for a little chat, wouldn't you say?" I bared my canines.

"What do you want to know? I'll tell you!"

I chuckled, shaking my head. "Oh no, I'd rather have you at my disposal for more than a question or two."

"Pleas—" Athena was cut off as Ishani shortened her plea with the blob of water.

"Open a portal to the inn," I said as I took both of Athena's hands and held them behind her back.

Ishani's magic sparked, Akari perked up on the portal's other side and grabbed her weapon. I pushed Athena through, and Akari pulled her by the neck the rest of the way. Athena would be useful. If I found out she had anything to do with Zuri, I'd—

A door handle rattled, startling me, and I turned to find Kaizer with blood dripping from the corners of his mouth, his shirt untucked and disheveled. His mouth opened with shock, his gaze flicking to where Athena was screaming and trying to pull out of Akari's hold. He took a step, a flame sparking and vanishing at his fingertips.

"You came back to me," he said as if an active kidnapping wasn't happening right in front of him.

"You think I came back for *you*?" I asked in the voice I used while dancing.

"That's why I felt comfortable talking to you." He took a step forward, and I lifted one of my throwing knives to stop him from coming any closer.

"Where is Zuri?" I asked.

Ishani put her hand on my wrist, trying to pull me into the portal.

"Agree to be with me, and I'll tell you," Kaizer said, careful with his words and movements.

If I was here by myself, I might have agreed. I might have gone with him and hoped for the best. But Kaizer knew who I was, knew the decisions I'd make. There was no way he'd give me Zuri. He'd take me away in hopes of using me for whatever power he sought. Everything inside me fought against my words, but I jumped into the portal, turning back and looking at him over my shoulder.

"I'll come for you next."

Ishani closed the portal into the inn quickly, and we watched as the estate lit with fire through the window. Guards ran around, forcing everyone out of the yard. I saw Kaizer on the hill, flames shooting from his hands and into the sky just as the firecrackers had. The people still at the party ran from him, shrieking in fear of his lack of control. Abel and Lord Byrne ushered them away and contained him as he yelled.

Athena was gagged and bound, her body still flailing like a fish. We all ignored her as Ishani opened a portal straight to Dusra, which was smaller than her usual portal. Probably because she needed blood and the fact the jump across the kingdom was vast.

I picked Athena up and tossed her through the portal, everyone following behind me quickly. Ishani had us at the front of the palace where we'd left from, and Dusran guards came running to make sure we didn't need any help. Ishani turned to the first one, sinking her fangs into them and drinking deeply. You could practically see her magic replenishing, her breathing coming easier, and her color brighter by the time she was finished.

"Thanks," she said as she wiped her mouth.

The guard bowed, a small smile pulling at his lips as his eyes sparkled.

"You do that often?" I asked as I pulled Athena to her feet.

"Often enough that they don't seem to mind," Akari mumbled.

"Oh, hush. I asked them if it was okay." Ishani pushed Akari to her side.

Athena's mumbled pleas for help had us all turning to her and sighing. I took the gag out, and she screamed again, so I pulled her close to my face quick enough to shock her.

"Shut *the fuck* up," I demanded. "No one here cares about your screams. You're in Dusra now, Lady Payne."

Chapter Eleven

Zuri

They weren't kidding when they said they were going to stretch my blood supply. I hadn't had blood in almost a week, and while I wasn't a vampire and wouldn't go into bloodlust, it didn't mean I wouldn't be in pain. Everything hurt, even places I had no bruises or cuts seemed to burn. I didn't need to see myself to know I looked terrible. I wished I could have shifted into my lobo form and ripped their fucking throats out. But that would be a dead giveaway as to who I was and where I was from. With such a low blood supply, I couldn't make the shift at this point, anyway.

They'd moved me almost to the mouth of the volcano for now. Every so often, lava would shoot in the distance, and I was starting to welcome the thought of jumping in and ending it. They'd most likely move me away later today. I only had to endure the heat for a few more hours. They never kept me in one place for too long. It was hard to keep track between the volcano, the dungeons, and random houses in the farmlands.

The chains on my wrists I'd once been able to move around in were heavy. I couldn't even adjust my position. The wind blew from the volcano, sending hot gusts of air over my body and shifting my tattered clothes. I was doing all of this for Daya. The longer she went undetected, both her location and her gifts, the better. We couldn't give them time to prepare.

I blinked a few times, trying to get the blurred world around me to clear, but I was delirious. I needed blood, I needed water, and I needed food. All of which I hadn't had nearly enough of in the last weeks. I just hoped wherever Daya was, she was okay, she was safe, and she was happy. I'd endure this for decades if it meant those three things were true. But they wouldn't give me decades—my days were numbered.

I smelled people before I saw them, a group of three bodies coming up the hill. The scent of fresh water hit me, and I peeled my tongue from the roof of my mouth as they got closer.

"Give her the water," Otto commanded.

A younger woman came over, her eyes scanning me over with concern. She held the water canteen up, but the chains were too heavy for me to lift my hands and grab it. Once she realized this, she brought the water to my lips and held it as I drank. An uncharacteristic metallic tang coated my tongue, and my brow bunched.

"You'll be sick if you go too fast," she whispered. "There's a healing tonic in it."

I couldn't stop myself, though. The dryness in my mouth and the lightness in my head were too much. I regretted it as my stomach ached, and the taste of bile filled my mouth, but I forced it down. Losing water wasn't an option. It had to be a witch tonic because I felt the magic of it coursing through me and healing any minor wounds. My own magic was still too far without blood, but I had more strength than I'd had since I got here.

"That's enough," Otto stated.

The young girl smiled weakly and backed up. I wished I could thank her and ask her who sent it, but that was too much of a risk. The other two people with them were Otto and a witch who must have been the one who brought them here.

"Open the portal," Otto demanded of the witch.

He came over, unlocking my cuffs and pulling them off my wrists before pulling me up by my arm. Lifting my chin took effort, but I did it. I still hadn't spoken a word to them, and I didn't plan on it. He kept his grip tight on me as if I was viable to actually run away. We stepped through the portal, but the witch and the girl didn't follow us through.

This location was new. Dark, unwashed stone walls and the smell of deep earth filled my nostrils. Dust and debris shuffled as they pushed me toward a wall, more chains and cuffs waiting for me. They didn't lock me in this time, and I didn't know if that was a good sign.

Kaizer came down a set of dark steps, his hair disheveled and a look in his eye I couldn't quite place. He was covered in dirt, and I didn't think I'd ever seen him so unkempt. Even when he'd come to question and torture, he was put together, sure, and confident. A chair went flying across the room, shattering into a hundred pieces from the force with which he kicked it. With my attention on the chair, I didn't see him cross the room until he lifted me by my shoulders.

"I saw her," he whispered. "I saw Daya."

My eyes widened, fear for her encompassing my very being. The rage in his eyes turned to something softer, and he set me back down. Otto was at his back, a smile crueler than anything I'd seen thus far stretched across his face.

"I've had enough of your silence. You're going to talk today. You're going to tell me where she is. We only have so much magic suppressant left. Either your life will run out, or I'll have no more use for you," Kaizer said as he took a deep breath.

Otto pulled out his favorite blades, ones I'd come to know pretty well in my weeks here. We were practically friends. Kaizer bent down and picked something up off the floor. He turned it in his hand, a small knob. All the furniture down here was in splinters, but he held it as if it were a small injured animal. He ran his finger over it with his gaze on the ground and his facial muscles twitching.

"I haven't been back here in years," Kaizer mumbled. "This place was where I was raised."

I didn't respond, but I hoped he continued. The man tended to monologue, but this one might actually hold some value.

"I was never supposed to be king. I'm sure you know this." He turned toward me. "Didn't even want to be king. But fate had other plans for me, and denying fate is something I had even less interest in than being king."

Otto watched him, not with the same manner of reverence he typically had, but with concern. I thought Kaizer snapped when Daya ran away with me, but the fear that it was just the tip of the blade coursed through me.

"I'll be honest. I don't know if I believe in the Flame. But I believe in. . . something. Something bigger and greater than us, and whatever that is, be it the Flame or another being entirely, they put me on this path. They want to see the entirety of Iteria in *my* hands. Well, mine and Daya's."

The knob he was holding went up in flames, smoke and embers cracking between us and hiding him from me. His face pushed through the smoke, hovering an inch from mine. "Don't you understand? That is the inevitable outcome. Whatever you think you're doing to protect her is futile. She will be mine again."

She was never yours, you fucking asshole. Now that I was more healed, every inch of the blade was evident as he plunged it into my side. There was no delirious numbness protecting me, but that also meant I was able to hold his gaze with my chin high. I didn't expect him to pull it out that quickly, and certainly didn't expect him to tear through the bare threads of my clothing.

"You will speak today," Otto said before pushing me to the ground.

My hip hit the ground first, and I tried to catch myself with my hands, but Otto was faster. A sudden heat, sweltering and torrid, radiated from my other hip. His hand pressed hard into my skin, glowing orange and blue with flame. The smell of my own burning flesh had more bile rising by the second. I'd thought the blades were the worst they could do, but I had never been more wrong. The scream that escaped me shocked even myself, and that had them both smirking. The most reaction I'd given them in some time.

Kaizer was next, his hand bigger than Otto's and charring more skin. I held in the scream that time, but that didn't stop them from continuing all the way from my hip to my armpit. Every time I thought the pain peaked, the next burn proved that wrong. My vision blurred, and the last one I felt grazed beneath my breast before my head hit the hard stone and I passed out.

* * *

I gasped as cold water encased me, and I jolted up out of complete darkness. The water dripped down my body, the open wounds on my side singing with agony. I couldn't get another gulp of air down, and my body convulsed until the pain subsided, and Kaizer came to stand beside me with a bucket. Trying to take count of the pain, I felt the burns in only a few more places since I passed out, now traveling further onto my back.

"Speak, or we give you matching ones on the other side," Otto drawled.

I could let them kill me. Let it all be over. Maybe it would be nice. I was sure they called it the long nap for a reason—it could be like drifting off to sleep. Being reunited with my family in the spirit world would be nice. I was sure they'd sensed me teetering on the line in the last month. They were probably waiting at the entrance for me to finally cross. My father's face appeared next to Kaizer's, his long gray locs dangling down to nearly his hips. He smiled as he bent down next to me, and the debris in the room shifted, as if moved with air magic. Kaizer and Otto stepped back, surveying the space with confusion.

"What is that?" Kaizer asked

Otto couldn't find an answer and ran up the stairs as Kaizer peered back at me once before following.

"You're not doing too well, pup," my father said with a smile, his voice echoing in my mind like Axel's magic. He brushed the side of my face and wiped the tear that fell from my eye. "It's not your time. You will do great things, I've been told."

"Told?" I whispered.

"I can not elaborate. Know you are strong; you have the strength of thousands of lobos running through you. Every single one that came before you, every single one that has been slaughtered, they're all lending you their strength."

"I'm tired, papa," I responded. "I want to be with you and my mothers. My brother. I will never tell them where she is."

"You don't need to tell them where she is, my daughter. You can tell them where she is not, and they will be none the wiser."

I swore I could smell his scent and leaned as close as my body allowed. "When they know I'm lying, they might kill me."

"They will not have the chance," he said, his brow raised in the same way he used to do when I wasn't supposed to ask any more questions. "You need to choose to fight, do you understand? Just a little longer, pup."

I closed my eyes and took a deep breath, and when I opened them again, my father was gone, and Kaizer and Otto were descending the stairs. Tell them where she is not. Where would she never go? Where would it take some time for them to search?

Otto rolled me over, the pressure on my burns forcing my eyes to roll back in my head. He lifted his hand to burn again, and I spoke for the first time, choosing my words carefully.

The sound of my voice felt odd and foreign as I croaked, "She's in the desert."

Chapter Twelve

Dayanara

"So, why her?" Axel questioned.

He reached for the glass pitcher of blood, and I passed it over to him. "When I was in Sanjry, Athena gave me information that ended up being true. Apparently, Kaizer is a pillow talker."

Axel chuckled as he sipped, running his tongue over his bottom lip. I stared, not able to hide my reaction. Oh, that man was so damn delicious.

Paxx cleared his throat. "You said they were digging for something when you crossed?"

"Yeah," Ishani answered for me. "Right on the other side of the river at the border. The site was huge, and they had brujas wielding a massive air shield. I don't think they wanted anyone to know why they were there."

"You remember anything being located there from your time in Sanjry?" Ax asked.

"No, I have no idea what they're looking for. Everyone keeps saying that a relic is here. Maybe it's a piece of it?" I responded.

"We need to go to the library," Axel mumbled, biting the inside of his cheek. I could see the wheels turning in his head as he tried to figure out where to go from here. There wasn't a lot Ax hadn't seen, definitely few things he wasn't educated on.

"I already told Uma to pull anything she thought was relevant. I've gone once thus far but haven't found anything of use. They're in one of the backrooms," Paxx added.

"Perfect. We'll go this evening." Axel sat up.

Documentation was so important as we moved through history. Ensuring that those left after us didn't make the same mistakes as we did. The library here was said to be the biggest and held more knowledge than any of the others in Malva. The Vohras, even before Axel's parents, had always been known for their investment in preservation. It was known across the nation, and it was probably part of the reason Kaizer was trying to get through. I had my own source of information that I was ready to crack.

"Where's Athena?" I asked Paxx.

"On the coast," he responded.

"I think I'll go pay her a visit." I smirked and stretched with the joy of bringing her pain. I hadn't gotten the chance to let out all of this pent-up energy with us going to Sanjry.

Paxx stood. "I'll go with you. I needed to go out there."

I watched him, wondering if there was some sort of angle he was working. Maybe he thought I couldn't be left alone with the prisoners.

"I'm sure you're entirely capable of handling it. I'd just like to see you work," he followed up.

"Oh," I started, looking over to Axel, who smirked at me. "Very well."

I asked Paxx to move her into one of the 'interrogation rooms' as they referred to them here. Gone was the beautifully crafted Dusran architecture. Only gray stone walls were left here. Finding Athena chained up in the room was comical, as if she was any physical threat. We'd been staring at each other for a few minutes now, her face twitching with anger and mine with amusement.

"So," I broke the silence. "I need information. You proved that Kaizer spoke about his plans to you before. I assume finding you on his arm would prove that to still be correct?"

She didn't say anything, and I flipped the knife in my hand and planted it in her thigh. She screamed, the red silk of her dress split, and the blood spread like spilled ink. It was actually a cute dress. What a shame.

"You can make this easy on yourself, or you can make it difficult. I'm in quite the violent mood, so I'm okay with either way."

She ground her jaw. "What is it you want to know?"

I laughed. "That easy, huh? So much for loyalty. Where's Zuri?"

"Otto handles that, and I'm the last person he shares information with."

"You seemed to know about her at the party." I yanked the knife from her leg and sliced into her arm before quickly moving it up to her neck. "Let's try again."

Her throat bobbed, but her nose scrunched in defiance. "Otto hates me. He thinks I'm a whore." I pressed the blade in slightly, and she quickly yelled, "They've seen what you've left behind thus far. They don't want to leave her anywhere for you to find!"

"What I've done is a fraction of what I'll do if I don't find her soon," I growled. "What is Kaizer trying to accomplish?"

"Other than being stupidly obsessed with finding you?" she snapped.

"Yes, precisely," I said as I wiped the bloodied knife on the sleeve of her shirt.

Athena rolled her eyes. "He wants everything. I want to be clear: my only loyalties are with myself. I thought I could convince him to forget about you. If you want information, I'll need to know you won't kill me."

"Hm," I said as I looked over at Paxx, silently leaning against the door frame. "What do you think? Let her sit in the dungeons for a few more weeks?"

"Don't see why not. I think the one she's in now is a little too comfortable. Could move her to the wet cells. You know, the ones the ocean fills with water at high tide?"

"What's a little water, right, Athena?" I quipped.

Doing this with Paxx is kind of fun.

"Flame, you're all insane," she groaned.

"Choice is yours." I shrugged.

"I give you something, and if you find it to be true, you move me to better accommodations. Then I'll give you more."

I sighed. "Still playing politics? Paxx, move her to the wet cells."

Paxx drifted out of the doorway without question, and I winked at Athena as I left as well.

"They're looking for seraphinite!" Athena yelled.

I turned. "There is none left. My mother already got rid of it all."

Athena shook her head. "It was part of her and Kaizer's deal. Your mother left some already activated, not enough to use in a battle, but enough for them to use it on. . . certain individuals for some time. She knew the river split a deposit, so she let them know where it was. It was a contingency."

"Seraphinite?" Paxx asked, his tone laced with confusion.

"Brujas refer to it as seraphinite. Everyone else knows it as the suppressant stone."

"That is less than ideal," he responded.

There was no way my mother gave them the spell for it. She cared more about that spell than she did about me. But I also knew not to doubt the level of my mother's stupidity.

I moved back into the room. "I've seen them digging for it. All she said was it's split by the river and not the exact location?"

Athena raised a single eyebrow, appearing to be waiting for her terms to be met. Sanjry getting the stone could be potentially disastrous. Weighing the risk of it against the threat to Athena, I bit my cheek.

"Fine. No wet cell. Speak."

"She said it was somewhere along the sanction on the north side of the border. Didn't give specific coordinates."

I didn't offer her a response and slammed the door behind me. Paxx's rushed steps matched my own as I opened a portal and brought us back to the palace.

I walked over the sandy hills with Axel, filling him in on what we'd found out from Athena on our way to the library.

"Apparently, there's a deposit of seraphinite, the suppressant stone, in Sanjry. They're looking for it. She doesn't know Zuri's location."

"Fuck." Axel dragged his hand across his face. "This treaty is really starting to become a burden. I can't do anything to help, and I feel like I can't even be there for you without the risk of breaking it."

I felt it too. It put distance between us, and I hated it. Especially because it had been even more difficult in the recent weeks. It was like we were both adrift in that beautiful ocean we'd admired, our fingers grazing with every pulse of a wave, but never able to reach each other. I had to focus on what we *could* do.

"Let Paxx deal with that. What can we do? Do you still want to go to the Triori?" I asked.

He nodded once. "Yes. As Xavier said, it's a last resort, but if we don't figure out what power Kaizer is seeking within the next week, then it's one we must turn to."

"Between the magic suppressant and the intel that he wants to control all the elements, I agree."

Last resorts were all we had. Ax brought us to the coast, but not the part that I'd seen thus far. It was further south, and we stood on a cliff with water much deeper than on the beach. The deep blues and greens seemed to go on even further, but where the water rippled softly against the coast, this one raged against the rocky base. People underestimated water just as they did air. We couldn't burn a hole through you or drop a ton of rocks atop your head. But there was power in water, even more than air, if I was honest. It was hard for me to understand how anyone thought differently, especially when looking out over a sea like this. The water had a mind of its own, moving with grace and strength.

Ax winked at me with two of his fingers in his mouth and pulled me out of my thoughts. He whistled a sound so high pitched I almost couldn't hear it and then crossed his arms to watch me smugly.

"Why are you looking at me like that?" I questioned.

"Just want to see your face when you see *that*." He tilted his chin out to the water.

Two waves seemed to populate out of nowhere, speeding toward us far quicker than the others. The water separated and scaled spines poked through the surface, sending the water trickling down the backs of two massive water dragons. They blended in with the ocean to the point you could barely see them outside of the parts that were exposed to the air. Axel grabbed me before he hurdled us off the ledge, and I couldn't help but laugh at the thrill, a feeling I hadn't really experienced in weeks. He floated me over to one of the dragons on a wave of water, and he landed on the other.

I straddled the spine and ran my hands over the wet scales, feeling the strong heartbeat thud beneath its skin. It was bigger than any animal I'd ever seen, with strong webbed wings pulled in tight to its sleek body and dark blue scales trailing up to the thick, long neck. The dragon tilted its head back to look at me, and I froze. That gaze was ancient—the realization that this magnificent beast may have been around far before me, maybe even before our world was split by the Piedra. It watched me with so much intensity that I almost took a dive off the spot where I was sitting.

"Don't worry, they're excellent judges of character," Ax offered over the sound of the waves.

"Not sure if that's reassuring."

"*Hold on tight. Create an air bubble around your head,*" Ax spoke into my mind.

I barely had a chance to follow his instructions before my dragon dove deep into the water, and I had to wrap a tendril of air around its neck to stay in position. Ax glanced over at me, a hollow blob of water around his mouth and nose, similar to my air bubble. He smiled, and I couldn't help the one I gave in return. This deep into the ocean was a wholly unique marvel I didn't think many people got to experience outside of Dusra. The sand shifted around us as we made it to the bottom and the dragon slowed near colorful coral going on for miles in every direction.

Small fish swam in and out of it, their reflective scales gleaming like precious stones. It almost seemed like they were playing, chasing each other through the tunnels within. I touched the very tip of my finger to the coral closest to me. I thought it would have been rough like rock, but it was. . . squishy. I jolted back when two eyeballs appeared, the rough purple texture fading into a smooth bright red. Ten tentacles lifted off the coral as the red creature swam out into the open water.

I looked up, tracking its path, to find endless ocean. It could have felt claustrophobic if it wasn't somehow still so open. The dragon sped up, my hair pulling behind me in the movement as bubbles surrounded us and a stream of white water was left behind. Axel's dragon crossed over in front of the one I was riding, and mine sped up to cut off the path of Axel's, starting a game between the beasts that felt more like a dance. I wondered if this was how the sirens always felt, living within the freedom and beauty found at the bottom of the ocean.

Suddenly, the other dragon peeled off, leaving a wake of bubbles behind it. I wondered what was happening as mine stayed still until I saw Ax wave to me from within the bubbles. Light blasted from him, more bubbles forming as something massive replaced where he once was. Axel had told me he was able to guide essence in a way similar to the lobos, but had the ability to replicate other animals. I hadn't had the chance to see it, even thought he was joking. As the bubbles cleared, I quickly realized he was serious. As big as the dragons we rode and, just as menacing, he slid through the water with grace. Black scales shined like the fish we'd seen, webbed wings stretching to a stop.

My dragon bucked me off, sending me flying over to Axel. He caught me on his back, and even if I'd never seen him shift, I'd known it was him. His magical signature radiated within the water, my power recognizing his immediately. I ran my fingers up his spines and down his scales, feeling all the muscle beneath them.

"Impressed?" Axel spoke in my mind.

"Don't think that's a big enough word," I replied.

I felt his contentment within my mind, and before I could say another word, he took off. The other dragons must have been holding back, because I could barely hold on to Ax. It seemed like he knew that, and his laughter filled my mind. He pulled his head up as we shot to the surface, the water breaking as he roared a mighty sound into the open air. Axel's wings spread open and stopped us abruptly on the coast of what I assumed was the island.

Axel shifted back in a flash, lifting us out of the water on a mighty wave that dispersed as we hit the sandy ground of the coast. My chest was still heaving, but for the first time in quite awhile, it wasn't from fear or anger. I placed my hand on his chest and blasted us both with hot air to dry us off. Didn't think the librarian would appreciate us entering her building sopping wet.

"Wow," I breathed as a smile pulled tight across my face. "I don't even have words. That was amazing."

"I don't do it very often, but figured it was time you saw that." He smiled.

Axel looked down at me, lifting a finger to trace the curve of my top lip and rubbing his thumb across the bottom. He held it there, pressing in slightly, which made me exhale and drop my lip more.

"I missed this," he said.

Those thorny vines of guilt left my heart and wrapped around my throat instead, locking up my words.

He took my hands and placed them on my chest. "I'm here, Daya. I'm real, and I'm here. I'll give you as much space as you need, but I'm *right here*. You're not alone anymore. Things will still move forward if you allow yourself a minute to breathe."

You're not alone anymore. It wasn't that I was unaware that the Dusrans were helping me, but after this long of being the only person to save myself, it was hard to let go. It was hard to give myself the permission to take a breath. They'd proven that they were helping. I'd even told Paxx that I appreciated it. . . I was just. . . unlearning some behaviors.

I let his words sink in and took a deep breath, feeling the constraints on my throat wane. "I'm. . . I'm sorry. Pushing you away wasn't my intention. I've just been so *angry*. Mostly at myself. But you're right. I feel more myself with you than anywhere else. There's space in my heart to worry about her and to be here with you."

"I would never get in your way of getting her back," he whispered on my brow.

"I know that," I said as I stared up into his eyes. "I don't deserve you."

"Incorrect." He smirked and pulled me into his side as he guided us away from the water.

We crested a huge dune, and the island folded out before us. A vast jungle sat to our left, untouched and as beautiful as the ocean. A small city sat to the right, people moving up and down the stone streets. Vampires and witches alike, maybe lobos as well, but they weren't easily detected outside of their wolf form. People smiled at us as we moved into the busy streets, all of them looking at Axel with reverence. He returned all of their smiles, nodding his head and even hugging a few of the children who ran up to him.

"The people of Sanjry would shit themselves if they saw who you truly are," I laughed.

"I earned my reputation at one point." Axel looked out into the distance, his eyes glazing over and tone shifting.

I stilled, feeling how serious he was. "What do you mean?"

"They targeted me that day for more than one reason. I was a way to get to my parents, but I'd dealt my fair share of pain to them personally. I'd gone into their lands and slayed hundreds, drowned them, brought down buildings, whatever to get an edge."

"That's war." I shrugged.

"It wasn't just soldiers who fell in my path." Ax pinned me down with his stare. "I know you look at me, and you see the easy-going king who has lived in peace for a while now. The one that makes you smile and laugh, but that is not who I am at my core, Daya. You don't understand the blood and the violence it took to get to this peaceful version of me. I am who they fear, who they tell their children to fear—the monster they see in their shadows. I haven't been that person for a long time, but by the time this war is over, you'll see. I'll become that monster again, for my kingdom, for you."

I took a beat to digest what he said. We were more alike than he knew, and I feared that maybe he saw me differently than who I was at *my* core. "You forget they fear me too. If you're lurking in the shadows, I'm there with you."

We were no sweet fairy tale, no pretty princess and handsome prince. He was right. We were monsters, bloodthirsty, and dangerous to anyone who opposed us. I'd never been anything else. My kingdom hadn't known peace as recently as Axel's had. I had to hope he heard the truth in that statement. He'd seen more of that monster inside me than I had him, but war brought out the worst in all of us. Or the best, depending on how you saw it.

Axel's eyes darkened like he did see that truth, and he wasn't deterred. He closed the space between us. "I look forward to it."

The wind blew his dark curls in front of his hazel eyes, and I reached up to move them back. Even dry, his olive brown skin was dewy, and I placed my hand on the hard edge of his jaw. Rubbing my thumb through his beard, I lifted my chin in expectation. He moved his hand to my lower back and pressed his body into mine, his head lowered to claim the kiss he'd been after for the last few weeks, and I let him.

The door behind him yanked open, and a small woman yelped, "My King! You scared me!"

Axel's jaw ticked, but he softened his features as he turned to the woman. I peered above her, realizing we had already made it to the library, a large stone building lined with tall windows and sconces. As many levels as the one in Sanjry, but this was an entire building.

"I apologize. I did send word that we were coming," Axel offered.

She nodded. "Yes, I was running out to grab a bite before you got here. Come in."

We stepped through the threshold and into a foyer with intricate paintings trailing up the walls, blues, purples, greens, all mixing to create something so much like the ocean bottom we had come from.

"I pulled out what Paxx requested. It's in your room," she said as she looked toward the end of the hall and back over at me. "Are you the witch queen?"

"Something like that. My name is Dayanara," I offered.

"I am Uma. It is a pleasure to meet you." She bowed deeply. "I run the library. Everyone is out right now, so it's only us for today."

"Feel free to go get your food. I have a feeling we'll be here for quite a while," Axel told Uma.

"Oh, that would be great. I'll check in on you when I'm done," Uma said, before rushing out of the foyer.

"Trying to get me alone, Ax?" I asked as I ran my fingers down the walls of the hall.

"If I ever pass up that opportunity, check me for sickness, because my death is surely near," he replied from behind me.

I laughed as I pushed open the door and the true size of the library appeared before me. Rows and rows of books unfurled, twisting around each other in a maze, like the pattern on coral. The distinct smell of the tomes filled my nose and brought me back to the years of my schooling. The times Ximena and I would be together in a place like this for hours learning. Ax took the lead, and I followed behind him, in awe of the amount of books we passed.

"Did Zuri ever tell you about Ximena?" I asked.

He shook his head. "No. Who is that?"

"Story for another day. Was just wondering."

Ax looked over his shoulder at me, realization it probably wasn't a fun story to tell running over his features. "Okay."

I'd tell him, but today I wanted to exist with him. I could let myself not be on high alert for a while with Axel while Paxx handled the most recent threat.

Chapter Thirteen

Dayanara

The room Ax brought me to was cozier than I expected from the massive size of the rest of the library. Our reflection startled me in the mirrors beside us, but the only things in the room were a table with two chairs, a couch, and bookshelves lining the other three walls. Some as old as the beginning of time, some were freshly bound, but they all peppered the room with color. The table was pushed up against the mirrored wall, and Ax and I sat on opposite ends of the small table.

Uma had pulled out quite a few books for us to read, and Ax stopped on our way back here to pull a few of his own. I'd never really thought about how centuries of living could make someone so smart if they took every small encounter, every big thing they'd been through and applied it to their future. Axel had done that; he was calculated and wise in a way Kaizer wasn't. Given the manipulation and loads of lies that I'd experienced in my century and a half, I could probably take some notes from him.

"The real question," Axel said as he sat back in his chair. "How accurate is any of our history? I mean across kingdoms. My family took pride in preserving knowledge, but to balance all four elements, that feels like something that would have been documented at the beginning of our time. Who really knows who is the keeper of that information."

I nodded. "We've been separated for thousands of years, between elements, kingdoms, and across the Piedra."

"Exactly. For neither of our kingdoms to have heard of this possibility, and for his somehow to find this, I wonder if we're here in vain."

"It just sounds outlandish. The ground we live on, the kingdom we're born in is what gives us our elemental magic. He'd have to somehow steal it from someone already with the other powers? I don't even know how that would work."

Axel bit his lip. "As much as I hate to admit it, neither do I."

"What's the oldest place here?"

"Actually..." He rubbed his chin. "The place the Triori are, that forest, it's been untouched since its creation, mostly."

"Might be able to find something there," I offered.

Ax smirked and leaned forward on his elbows. "I would think so as well."

My eyes fell to his shirt, where I knew the scars from the previous Sanjryan king were. I'd been avoiding asking him more about it, both for his sake and mine, but I couldn't anymore.

"Can I. . . ask you something?"

"Anything."

"I saw the scars, but how bad was it?"

I didn't need to explain what I meant. Axel closed the book and looked past my head for a moment before bringing his gaze back to mine.

"It was bad, I'm not going to lie to you. What I remember is horrible, but I told you about the blackouts? Sometimes I have dreams that seem like flashes of memory from those times, they seem even worse than what I remember."

"But you held on, what did you hold on for?"

"My sister, mostly. My kingdom, my friends. I didn't want to give Sanjry the satisfaction of me dying."

"That's how I felt with my mother. I don't think she would have let me die, but there were moments I felt close. I didn't have anything to hold on to then other than spite. I had a lot of it."

"If it helps, you would be what I held onto now. If it were to happen again."

He stared me down, his gaze darkening by the second. There hadn't been a moment since the last time I'd been this alone with Axel that I didn't want it to happen again. I realized I was punishing myself. Not giving myself any space to experience anything other than anger. But I didn't want to do that anymore.

"I think we have some unfinished business from earlier, no?" I asked as I popped the top button of my leathers open. Ax went still, so still I wasn't sure if I was somehow stuck in time. My chest rose and fell, the only indication that time was still moving. I blinked, and Ax shoved the desk into the couch and fell to his knees before me.

"I've been waiting, but fuck if I wait a moment longer," he growled before ripping open the rest of my buttons. He'd been waiting, he was right, patiently even from the looks of it, but now he was unleashed. He picked me up and spun us around to sit me in his lap, he somehow got my clothes off before I even straddled him. His fingers lightly grazed over every inch of my exposed skin as he sat back and watched it pebble under his touch. His thumb trailed up from my stomach to the base of my neck and he wrapped his fingers around it with more force than he'd shown until now. He pulled me forward, my body jerking from the quickness of the movement and pressed his lips against mine.

I'd forgotten how perfect he tasted, how soft his lips were in the weeks since my body had been entangled with his. He released his hold on my throat, and I wrapped my arms around his neck to push myself closer to him. The curls that hung from his nape tickled over my arms as he pulled my bottom lip into his mouth and ran his fang across it. My blood trickled out slowly and he sucked it out before running his tongue over the cut and pulling back to stare at me again.

"I want you in about nine different ways right now." He leaned forward and took my nipple between his teeth, flicking with his tongue. "But you tell me, forceful. How do you want it?"

He sucked my other nipple into his mouth as his fingers rubbed over my clit, robbing me of the ability to speak. He chuckled and turned me to face away from him, still on his lap, but toward the mirror. "Do you want to watch me fuck you? Watch yourself fall apart on my dick?"

I felt the full length of him twitch inside his pants beneath me, and I nodded as I leaned my head back on him.

"Haven't we talked about you using your words?"

"I want to watch you fuck me, Ax." I turned and bit his earlobe. "Now. How's that for words?"

He slipped out of his pants, his dick springing out and hitting me in the movement. I reached my hand down and wrapped my fingers around it, my touch making him groan. I dragged it through my wetness slowly before lining him up with my pussy. Axel wrapped his hand around my body, gripping me by my chin and raising my face to watch us in the mirror. He didn't go in gently, that wasn't our style; he drove straight into me with his hand still holding my face straight to the mirror. My eyes rolled back as I moaned and he pulled me to the side so he could watch too. I shifted my weight, keeping him inside as I rolled my hips. His gaze was at the point we were joined, and I watched as he slowly lifted it to my face. The hunger in his gaze had me wanting to feed him, to show him that I really did miss him, that I was sorry for how distant I'd been.

I placed my hands on his legs and lifted my hips to his tip before sinking back down on him. I did it again and again until I found a rhythm, a relentless pace that had him biting his lip and gripping onto the arms of the chair. His curls fell to his forehead as he watched me, and I watched him, watching me take him. He savored every bit of it, I wasn't sure if he was even blinking. He brought his fingers to my clit and rubbed circles over the nerves at the same unrelenting rate I was moving. Ax kissed up my neck before bringing his lips to my ear and whispering, "Come for me, Daya."

He thrust up as I pushed down, and I held the position as he continued rubbing circles, and just as he asked, I came. I screamed, hoping Uma was still out, but also not really caring if she heard.

"That's my girl," he muttered.

I leaned back on him fully as the orgasm burst through every inch of me and he didn't let up. My toes curled as it continued, tingling spreading into my arms and legs and Ax watched it all in our reflection. Finally, he removed his fingers and gripped me by my hips to hold me up, he must have known my legs wouldn't be working for at least a few more seconds. He brought me up and down a few times before pushing me forward and standing up behind me. Ax bent me over and put my hands on the mirror before pulling my head to the side by my hair and holding it there for me to watch.

He gripped my hips, and I watched as the muscles in his arms and chest strained. The tip of his cock ran up my pussy as he dragged it through all the evidence of the orgasm he'd just given me. Ax pushed in and I had to press my forearms to the mirror to keep myself up. The sound of our bodies slamming together bounced around the small space, mixing with the moans coming from the both of us. I fucking loved when he moaned. When he let me know how much I affected him. He slapped me on the ass and pulled me back up by my neck to be flush with his body. He had to bend his knees slightly to match my height, but it didn't stop him as he kept moving inside me, restricting my air and pinching my nipple with his other hand. I didn't know where to focus, on which part of him was bringing me the most pleasure. He was everywhere, and I didn't want it to end.

My breasts moved with every thrust from him and I reached my hand back to grip him by his hair as I screamed with another orgasm. His muscles, hard and rigid, pressed against me as I kept my grip on him. The man clearly wanted to torture me, because he moved his hand back down to rub around my clit and milk every bit of it he could.

The movement stopped abruptly as he pressed his hand against my pelvis and he groaned in my ear with his own release. We fell back into the chair still joined and I let my head fall onto his shoulder as I gasped for air. My core trembled, contracting around him every few seconds with the aftershocks of orgasms. He turned his head sluggishly and kissed me, moving his tongue in slowly as mine tangled with it.

"I've been thinking about this for about a month," he breathed.

"Me too," I rasped.

"Not just the sex," he said with a nip at my ear. "Just feeling you, being this close. The intimacy."

I stood, letting his dick slide out of me. "For the record, you'd be what I held onto now too."

A look flashed across his features, a tightness, like maybe he didn't believe me. I didn't know how to put into words what I felt for him and what I felt for Zuri. There was not a simple explanation. I didn't even know how it was possible. I'd moved through life for so long not caring about anyone in this way. Now I cared this strongly for more than one person. But I didn't want him to think he wasn't enough, or that there was something missing I had to get from someone else.

Ax twisted me around to face him and tucked a strand of hair behind my ear. "Hey, I believe you. You are my ending, of that I have absolutely no doubts."

"What's that mean?"

He pressed his lips to my forehead. "Story for another day," he said, mocking me with my own words.

Chapter Fourteen

Dayanara

"I have. . . information," Paxx broke the silence we'd been sitting in.

Uma wasn't entirely excited about it, but I had taken a few of the books from the library and brought them to Paxx's office while Axel was in a meeting.

"I wasn't sure if I should tell you yet, but I don't want to keep anything from you either," he followed up.

"Woah, Paxx. Are we friends now?" I smiled, but his rock-hard gaze had me settling back and waiting for him to tell me what it was.

"One of my spies contacted me. They said there's been some unusual activity northwest of the Sanjryan capital."

"Unusual how?"

"They thought it was just the army running drills at first, but most of them left, all but a few who have been seen going in and out of these ruins." Paxx pulled a map from goddess knew where.

"What's there? There isn't anything on the map," I said.

"It was a village, but it's not anymore. If my intel is correct, it's where Kaizer lived before becoming king."

"Interesting. Anything else for me to go off?"

Paxx stared, not blinking. "I'm coming with you."

"Going to be honest, Paxx. If we're just starting to get on good terms, I don't think that's the best idea. Also, I don't need a babysitter."

"Ax can't be there for you on this one, so I will," he replied, standing and grabbing his weapon. "I'd like to connect with my spies in person as well. It's been a while."

I rubbed my temples, checked that all my weapons were in their rightful place, and followed him out of the office. My sword was in the dining hall from breakfast after training, and I popped in to grab it. Ishani and Xavier were eating, sitting on the same side of the table next to each other.

"Hey..." I said before I grabbed my sword. "I'm going... out. Can you let Axel know I'll be back when I can? And that I'm taking Paxx."

Ishani leaned a fraction away from Xavier and smiled tightly. "Be safe."

I eyed her, the question of if she was okay in my eyes, but she nodded her head toward the door. Making the mental note to check on her when I got back, I listened and found Paxx standing in the hall with more armor on now. He finished fastening one of the ties on his shoulder plate as he glanced up at me, determination in his gaze.

There was a possibility Ax told him to keep an eye on me when he wasn't able to, but it also seemed like he just wanted to help. I knew he cared for Zuri, but for some reason, it also felt like he was starting to care about me. *Not entirely sure how I feel about that.*

Squeezing the hilt of the sword Zuri had made for me, I willed myself to sense that connection to her. There'd been times in the last few weeks I stared at it, wondering what directions she'd given the blacksmith to make it. If there were tweaks she'd made for me specifically. It was the most well-balanced weapon I had. It damn near melded to my hand.

"All right, where are we going?" I asked Paxx.

He pulled out the map we'd referenced earlier, circling his finger around the nearby cities. "You know any of these?"

"I do," I said as I scanned the parchment. "Here."

"That's not too far. Let's portal there," he suggested.

"Do you know what we're going up against?"

Paxx bit the inside of his cheek. "I know there's fewer than twenty people left at the ruins, according to my spies. No heavy artillery from what they've seen. They haven't seen Zuri, but it would be a good place to keep her so off the grid and away from people."

I clapped my hands. "Let's do this."

Thinking back to my time in Mijra, I tried to remember a good place to portal. There was a wooded area, but people lived there. I had to remember what side.

"There's a chance we step right into danger, so be prepared," I said as I opened the portal.

Paxx grunted a response as he stepped through. I cleared the smoke quickly with a burst of air, and thankfully, nobody was nearby. I waited to be attacked should they have set up a detection spell, but none came. I had the necklace Ax gave me from his mother's collection, but that only worked if I didn't actually use any magic.

Paxx pulled out one of the communication stones, whispering into it as it glowed. "Here," he said quickly.

The response came even quicker, "Inside."

"Okay, he's in the ruins. We'll meet him there." Paxx tucked the stone away.

"City is on the other side of the lake." I pointed through the trees to the body of water. "I suggest we fly in. Less of a chance we'll run right into someone."

Paxx's brow pinched with concern. "And you'll. . . what? Carry me?"

"Don't underestimate me now, Paxx," I replied with a slap to my biceps.

He looked like he regretted coming with me as he hung his head and dragged his feet in my direction. I smirked, unlatching the snap of my leathers and letting my wings unfurl from my back, focusing on not letting my skin glow. Deciding to make this as hilariously uncomfortable as possible, I quickly scooped Paxx up like a child, one arm at the back of his knees and the other around his back, before I shot into the sky. Paxx's body went tight, and I had to hold back the laughter bubbling up my throat as we parted through the clouds.

The ruins came into view far below, and I nudged Paxx to have a look as I circled within the clouds. There was one guard at either end, no movement happening between the main structure. I brought my wings in tight, shooting between the two on the other side, far away enough to make a landing without notifying them. Paxx quickly got to his feet the moment I set us on the ground, and I watched as he tried to right himself from the plunge.

I vanished my wings. "You saw the two guards?"

"Yup, let's take them out."

I hadn't seen Paxx in any kind of warrior mode, just training, studying, facilitating. But something fell over him, a new energy radiating from him as he pulled out his sword. He didn't move ahead of me like I thought he would, but he fell into pace behind me and let me lead the way to the first soldier. Listening for their location, I realized they were still where I'd last seen them. I slid the smallest knife from the holster on my hip and sent it flying through the air and into the soldier's neck. He fell to his knee with a thud and a grunt, the sound alerting the other one on the other side. The one I'd hit was still alive, and Paxx ran around him to fight the other.

A part of me needed to fight with my blades and fists to feel the impact of every hit. He came at me with his sword, and I smiled as it whizzed through the air. I elbowed him in his side as he missed me, baiting him and pissing him off.

"Come on, make this fun," I said as I gripped my dagger in my hand.

He let out a frustrated grumble and yanked the blade from his neck. Blood poured from the wound, but he charged me, not missing a step. With both hands on his sword, he plunged it toward my stomach, but I twisted and dragged my dagger across the side of his neck. He stumbled, the little color left in his face draining by the second.

"Ugh, you're boring." I jumped, flying through the air as I pulled my sword from my back. Holding it horizontally, I barely felt the impact of his head disconnecting from his body.

"That was unnecessary," Paxx said from behind me. "You could have killed him before I got to the other soldier."

I shrugged. "It's the little moments in life, ya know?"

A sound from inside the building had both of us turning and rushing over to the wall. A soldier stepped through the door, his eyes falling on the dead soldiers, his mouth opening to warn. I sent a stream of witch magic to zap him, then a blanket of air to pad his fall. A quick jab to his head, and he was gone. Paxx turned to me with a pointed look, displaying that I really could have killed the other soldier quicker, but I just rolled my eyes. We crept along the wall, and I listened to see if anyone was close.

"I don't hear anyone else nearby," I whispered.

Another man stepped through the entryway, somehow undetected by me, and Paxx put his hand on my arm before I killed him too. "He's one of mine."

The spy stood taller, respect in his eyes, as he said, "This part is clear. More people left earlier today, and the others are on the other side of the ruins. There are a few down the stairs, but it should be light work."

Paxx nodded, and we stepped through the entrance, finding the inside even worse than the outside. The walls themselves seemed to be crumbling, no furniture unbroken. The windows were all shattered, the outside breeze flowing in and shifting the dust and rubble. This wasn't the work of a natural disaster or a war, and as we walked down the hall, Paxx's suspicions were correct.

A family portrait was the only thing hanging on the wall. The canvas was curling at the edges, some tears and holes, but the image of Kaizer and his family stared back at me. He was much younger, not quite a child, but not quite a full adult either. His father's face was harsher, even more sharp edges than his, but those blue eyes were identical. Kaizer had never talked about his mother, not that I really asked, but I wasn't expecting her to be this beautiful. I'd once said that he was a pretty man, and that was because he looked so much like her. Her soft, light brown skin was precisely as smooth, the fullness of her lips the same, and the delicate slope of her nose. Kaizer was essentially the male version of her, a little lighter, but hair favoring his father. Another boy stood beside him, a brother I could assume, although he was the opposite of Kaizer, his father's face with his mother's dark hair. Even in the painting I could see the tension between the siblings. The bottom half of his brother's body was missing, rolled, and tattered.

His mother was left unmarked, no slashes in her like the ones in the depiction of everyone else—including him. There was a certain kindness in her dark eyes, one that didn't transfer to her son.

"He looks. . . normal," Paxx whispered.

"Well, he's a basket case now, so." I ushered us to keep moving forward.

The stairs at the end of the hall were dark, retreating deep underground. I heard heartbeats and used the Dusran signal Paxx taught me as we descended the stairs to let him know. The closer we got I realized it wasn't very many, just as Paxx's spy said, and I readied my blade before we turned the corner.

"Zuri's been here," Paxx stated.

He ran his finger over a divot in the wall, something that must have been a tell they used. That was all I needed. My Acna powers came to the forefront without me asking, my body glowing as I stepped around the corner, with streams of it shooting from my fingers and into the four people in the room. Paxx sliced through the one closest to us as their bodies quivered. I pulled back, focusing all of my energy on the soldier to my left until there was no body remaining. Just ash glittering in the air. The last two fell to their knees, and Paxx and I reached them simultaneously. I rolled my shoulders and took a deep breath, searching for other clues as my body returned to normal. I was happy to use those powers, but it seemed to be activated by knowing Zuri was nearby and not by my own will.

Paxx ran to the back of the space, chains hanging from the stone walls. "I can still sense her. She was here not too long ago."

That meant she was alive—or she was alive within the last couple of days—real proof. The relief I felt was profound, but it only meant we were closer to finding her. Not that we did.

"Do you see anything of hers that I could use to track?" I asked as I fell to my knees and searched. I heard something in the distance and pulled Paxx back into the shadows.

"Someone's coming."

I already had a weapon ready, but Paxx placed his hand on my wrist and shook his head. "Save this one for questioning."

A retort bubbled up in my throat, but he spoke again.

"Trust me."

His eyes bore into me, but a sense of trust did as well. "Okay."

Paxx moved quickly, quicker than I thought him capable, moving akin to a crashing wave in the sea. Like he and his water magic were one. He brought up a swell of water before the soldier, encasing him in it and freezing it over. The soldier's hands burned with fire, but not nearly enough to break the hold. Water sloshed within the ice as I opened a portal, and Paxx slid him in.

We stepped into the dungeons, a cell already ready and open for the soldier. Paxx melted the ice around his ankles, clipping a cuff and chain on them before doing the same thing with his wrists. Paxx dispersed the water and coated the walls with it before freezing it over and bringing the temperatures down so cold it was difficult to breathe. The soldier tried to blast us with fire, but it turned to smoke and ash before it reached us.

"Give me a couple of days. I'll bring you down if I need you," Paxx assured.

A chill ran over my body, and I nodded. "Fine. I'll interrogate the other prisoner."

Chapter Fifteen

Dayanara

"Where are you?" I asked Axel in our mind connection.

It was getting easier and easier to contact him this way. I didn't have to concentrate like before.

"My office."

"Want some company?"

"Ishani is here, but I'd love for you to come, anyway."

Slightly less exciting, but I had nothing better to do. I snapped open a portal, thankful I knew enough of the palace now to portal pretty much everywhere. Clearing the surrounding smoke, I pushed into his office with a smile.

"Good morning," I said to both of them.

"Hey, where are you coming from?" Ishani asked.

"Uh. . . Training," I sighed as I plopped down in the chair beside her. "What are you guys doing?"

"Ishani was updating me on the shore site. Even though I was there yesterday," Axel said with a pointed stare.

"Fine, I was just checking on you. Why do you have to make that so difficult?" she rolled her eyes.

"Checking on me regarding. . . ?" He leaned forward in expectation.

Ishani peered over at me and back to her brother. It felt like a 'get lost' look, which wasn't something I'd gotten from her before.

"I can leave if you need me to," I offered.

"Not necessary," Axel responded.

Ishani sat back. "Just wanted to make sure you were okay with. . . the possible future."

"I'm fine," Axel replied.

"And?" Ishani pressed.

"You're being incredibly invasive, Ish."

"You act like that's new," Ishani laughed.

I leaned onto the armrest. "We talking about Zuri? You seemed on board the last time we talked."

"Yes, I believe in the connection, but he has to be okay with it too." Ishani surveyed me, her gaze a little more prickly than usual. She'd been incredibly warm and inviting since I met her, but she was significantly more serious with her brother's happiness hanging in the air.

"What's the deal with you and Xavier? You guys looked to be in the middle of something when I came by," I asked Ishani.

Axel studied his sister with his brows high and his arms crossed. "Did you now?"

"Point made, Daya," Ishani laughed.

I shrugged, and the door to Axel's office swung open. Leaving it to only a few options as to who was coming through without a knock. Akari stormed in, covered in dirt and blood.

All three of us stood immediately. "What is it?" Ax asked.

"They put up a fight," Akari huffed as she dropped down into one of the chairs in the office. "We didn't get all the seraphinite, but we got a good amount."

"Deaths?" Ishani asked.

"Ten. Another few injured and in the infirmary now. We had the advantage of surprise. We took down a lot more of theirs."

"So Athena was telling the truth." I paused. "Interesting."

I was almost. . . impressed with her. Almost.

"Someone there has to have the spell," Ishani said.

"They'd have to have our spell book, the Amapola grimoire. That's not a spell my mother has told anyone else in centuries, especially after she took all the seraphinite from Caldera."

"Where's the grimoire located?" Ax asked.

"It's not at the palace. It's hidden in Caldera. We're the only ones who know the way. I've never even seen it, but I was told how to get to it should I ever need to."

"Do you think she would have given it to someone else?"

I shook my head. "It's protected by blood magic. Nobody else could read it but us. So Kaizer must still be betting on the fact I'm coming back."

"How are you feeling, Akari?" Ishani asked.

"Like shit. I need blood, and I need to rest. We can reconvene tomorrow," she said as she stood to exit the room. I snapped open a portal to her bedchamber hall, and she looked over at me with brows high.

"Just take the portal," I sighed.

Akari's eyes narrowed, but she stepped through. When she was all the way in, I closed it and turned back to Axel. "Care to torture a prisoner with me?"

Axel smiled. "I'd love to."

Me and Axel walked through the prison halls toward Athena's cell, on the other side of the dungeon I left Paxx in. I bumped into his side, pulling out my knife and spinning it in my hand. "Have you met Athena?"

"Haven't had the pleasure."

"Not much of a pleasure," I laughed. "I'll give it to her, she's surprised me. Let's see if she has any more surprises today."

I whistled the same tune I did when I'd come to visit her cell in Sanjry. Wrapping my hand around the bars of her cell, I leaned in. "Hello, Athena."

Athena sat prim and proper on the bench in her cell with her legs crossed. It looked like she might have gotten someone to wash her clothes, or she washed them herself in the trough of water. Her hair wasn't the mess that it was the last time I'd seen her, her face clear of dirt and grime.

"I take it my information panned out?" she asked as she stood and brushed her hands down her skirt.

"For now." I waved my hand to the guard on duty to open her cell. "Let's go."

I grabbed her by the back of the neck and dragged her with me to one of the interrogation rooms. Axel stood behind me with his arms across his chest, a smirk on his lips as I strapped Athena to the chair.

"We should play here later," he spoke into my mind, and I clamped my lips as I finished the last strap.

"I don't usually keep prisoners," I started, taking a seat across from her. "Axel, does Dusra usually keep prisoners?"

"Depends on how bored we are."

I chuckled. "You can make yourself useful, or you can die. Any other information you care to share to keep yourself alive?"

Her eyes narrowed on Axel, calculating before returning to me. "I'd like to tell you a story."

"Not exactly what I asked for, Lady Payne."

"All the same, I think it would help." She flicked her head to get a strand of hair out of her face. "Once upon a time, there was a little girl. A girl born into poverty on the outskirts of Sanjry. Her mother was a whore, her father a scam artist. They barely got by, and when she came of an acceptable age, she was forced to join her mother. They stayed in their dilapidated home for years, making enough to pay taxes and feed themselves, but no more. One day, her father ran a scam, a gambling ring that was set up to make him the most money he'd ever received. The scam went as planned, but one of the men didn't have all the money they were supposed to pay him. They gave him a journal, saying that their ancestors had passed it down, and that it was worth more money than what he owed. He thought he was lying but took it anyway. One of the other men was a lord and had to give up his title to her father. It was their way out." Athena adjusted her position in the seat and sighed.

"Get to the point," I snapped.

"They built their lives from the ground up. They demanded respect, even if they were covered in dirt and had empty bellies a few months prior. The girl saw it, saw a future where she didn't have to sell her body for a few coins. Her father promised she wouldn't have to do it much longer, but he allowed the mother to stop. She believed him, moreso out of hope for that outcome than actual belief in his words. She was given to other lords and other noblemen. Nobody would have guessed she was a whore. She looked just like the little daughter of a lord. It went on for years until all the relationships with the other nobles were solidified, and they were given respect. The girl thought it was finally over, but she was wrong. That damned journal," she growled and glared up at the ceiling. "That damned journal ruined her fucking life."

"How?" Axel pressed as he moved from his spot against the wall and sat beside me.

"It spoke to him. Through some sort of magic, the journal spoke to him. The girl's father used it one day simply to write down something of note. He'd forgotten that the family said it was special as he didn't believe him. When he wrote in it, an answer appeared on the other page. An answer from the Flame."

I laughed. "From the Flame, really?"

"I swear it. Or someone pretending to be the Flame, I don't know. Her father used it. He became a *holy man*. His biggest scam of all." She barked a laugh. "It sent him in the direction of Kaizer when he was still just a lord's second son, merely a cousin to a royal. Kaizer never wanted to be the king, but his white hair gave him away. He could never escape from the knowledge that he was of the Curran lineage. Even with his mother's tanned skin as opposed to the royals' icy pale. The girl's father said that this was the last time she'd have to whore. After this, every Sanjryan would bow to her. She'd never want for a thing. She put in her best work, fucked him in every way imaginable, got him to bend to her will, and pointed him in the direction of her father. While she laid this foundation, her father made himself a priest. Spewing out whatever the journal told him to, getting thousands to follow his word. The girl never told Kaizer that it was her father; she only said that there was a man rising to power with whom he should connect. He swayed Kaizer, him and the journal. They convinced him to overthrow the royals. It wasn't difficult. The royals were idiots; the King was far too affected by the loss to Dusra. Kaizer went in there. He killed them all. It's why they call it the red room, every bit of surface was covered in blood of the former king and queen. I didn't see what he did, but I heard it was absolutely astonishing."

"I always wondered why it was called that," I mumbled.

"Anyway. Kaizer sat himself on the throne and brought the girl with him. She thought it was done, finally. She thought that she would be queen, as she was the entire reason he got to where he was. Once again, she was wrong. He continued fucking her but fucked plenty of others too. At first, it didn't bother her. If she was to become queen, it would all be worth it. There were still men falling at her feet to be with her. That wasn't the issue. The issue came about when he told her he wouldn't be taking a queen any time soon. Not even her. He said they asked the journal, he and the girl's father, and the Flame said that he shouldn't take a queen yet. That there would eventually be a better option than anyone in Sanjry. They didn't know what it meant. Until you," Athena snapped.

"I can assure you I never wanted to be there." I rolled my eyes.

"All the same, Kaizer became obsessed with you. To the point that not even the girl's father could keep him in check. He sent her back and told her to get in however she could—to regain control. He sat at the head of the church, but they needed power coming from both angles."

"Okay, enough of the third-person shit. It's you, obviously. And your father." My mouth opened. "Fuck, your father is Joseph?"

Athena nodded only once. "We are the only reasons he has the power he does. He doesn't know that I'm Joseph's daughter, even to this day. We'd kept the scam up."

"And your mother?"

"She died. I always suspected he killed her but never had proof. I hold no fondness for either of them. They were shit parents, but I kept close enough to my father in hopes that I'd eventually be queen."

"So all of this to say there's some journal that he's conversing with?" Axel asked.

"He believes it to be the Flame. I'm not sure if it really is or if the Flame even exists. My father seems convinced enough, even if he doesn't follow any of the rules and laws he preaches to the Embers. The journal told them there was a relic here on your island," she said with her gaze directed at Axel. "It said that there's a scepter here created by an ethereal being that could house all four stones, that with it, anyone it's linked to could use all four elements. Some sort of fancy magic. They have to take the essence from someone of each element and place it into the scepter along with the stones. The scepter believes it's someone who holds the ability to wield the stone." She flicked her hands as far as she could while strapped to the chair. "All four elements."

"Well, fuck," I grumbled.

"Don't you see, Dayanara? We are the same, you and I. We have been used from the moment we came of age. Our parents, our families, they decided what our lives would be before we even had the chance. Kaizer told me about your mother, about what really happened, the agreement between them. I got myself out of the dungeons shortly after you left. He's kept me in his bedroom ever since. I know he figured he could throw me back in if you ever came back. I couldn't tell anyone what he was saying, so he told me many things."

"Look at you, finding yourself useful indeed." I stood up. "Keep it up. You might be able to leave your cell."

Axel followed behind me as I slammed the door shut and walked down the hall. "I've got to be honest. I was not expecting any of that."

"Me either. You know about a scepter?" I asked.

Axel shook his head. "This is not good. He has to be planning on taking down the Piedra to get a fae who wields earth, as well as the earth stone."

I stopped in my tracks, looking down at my feet. "That's why they need me," I mumbled.

Axel lifted my chin with his finger. "Why do they need you?"

"When I had that nightmare the other day, the one where I blew the ceiling off my room." I grimaced. "I was fighting with my mother. I don't know how to explain it, but I pulled the essence out of her body. The color in her faded, and her heart sputtered. How would someone know that I can do that? I'm not saying it's actually the Flame because that's ridiculous, but it has to be someone with crazy power."

"A seer, most likely. I'll send a notification that we're requesting to visit the Triori tomorrow morning."

"You have to ask?"

"It's a courtesy I offer them. I don't have to, but I'd like to make them as likely to help us as possible."

"Fair enough," I said as we started moving again. "Until then?"

"We do what we can to prepare."

Chapter Sixteen

Axel

How do you tell a woman like Dayanara that you've loved her for hundreds of years? Before she was born, before she was a thought in her mother's mind, I loved her. We were dangerously close to that information being revealed, and I didn't know how to go about it. I certainly didn't know how she'd react to it. But we'd be going to meet the Triori tomorrow, and I wouldn't be able to keep it from her any longer.

The fact I didn't know that Zuri would be part of my future, even after the Triori showed me, was odd. The Triori liked to play games, offering enough that you wanted to return and give them more of yourself. Ishani had pestered me over the last two days to tell Daya, but I just couldn't bring myself to do it.

"Axel!" Daya yelled as she came running over to me.

Fuck, I could listen to her say my name for hours. "Yes, forceful?"

The woman lived up to her name, that was for sure. I'd never met a force as strong as Dayanara fucking Amapola, and I never would. It hurt me to leave her in Sanjry, knowing she didn't belong there. Every touch from Kaizer or his use of the word 'my' in reference to her burned me to my core. I never would have guessed what would happen to her. The things she would have to endure before she showed up at my doorstep.

"You're supposed to be training," she said flatly. "Why have you been so out of it?"

"Have a lot on my mind." I wiped some sweat from her brow.

"It's not about. . . us, is it?"

The uncharacteristic nerves in her tone had me answering quickly. "No. Everything is fine."

Daya tilted her head but rolled her eyes instead of pushing me on it. "Come on, give me what you've got."

She tapped her sword on the one dangling in my hand, and I tightened my grip on it, knowing that was the only warning she'd give me before she swung. She twisted, bringing her blade across her body, and aimed for my side. I blocked it with my own, stumbling a step as I shook my head at the power in this creature. Daya smirked as she lifted her sword, pressing it into mine as she tested that strength of hers. There weren't many people who could match her in strength, but Ishani and I were the only ones to really give her a challenge.

If only brute strength could win wars, we had more than enough of it on our side. I retreated quickly, moving around her to her backside. My favorite side. That was a lie. I really couldn't pick a favorite side. She tried to turn, but I grabbed her waist and brought her flush with me. I tried to whisper in her ear, but before I could get any words out to distract her, she elbowed me and turned with her blade on my shoulder.

"Yield."

I chuckled. "I yield."

Daya shrugged smugly before sheathing her blade. "I'm about to go help Ishani on the coast. I'll see you at dinner?"

"Sounds great," I said as I wrapped my fingers around the back of her neck and pulled her toward me. I placed a kiss on her forehead, and she winked before running to find my twin sister. My eyes stayed on her until she exited the room, and I felt a presence coming up behind me.

"You're out of time."

I found Paxx at my back, his arms across his chest as he stared me down with those dark eyes that put everyone else on edge. Paxx was quieter than most, but he never had a problem telling me when I was wrong. Dusra had been living in peace mostly since the war with Sanjry, but that didn't mean there weren't times over the last half century we had problems. The devastation that was the death of Zuri's parents was one of them. The other was how Paxx came to be in my service.

"I know. I don't know how she's going to react. At this point, I've waited too long for it not to feel like I was withholding information purposely," I said as I set my sword back with the others.

"Well, it's either you or the Triori, and you know they won't make it easy."

I blew air between my lips. "Thanks for the reminder."

"Dayanara is a straight shooter. Tell her the truth. There is no need to make it into a spectacle."

I glared at him, and he shrugged. "Just trying to help."

"I'm just stressed. If I lose her, I'm not sure I'll be able to come back from that. She's what got me here. . . I don't. . . " I trailed off.

She was what kept me going all of these years, the reason I was even still here in the first place. If I lost that, my anchor to this world. . .

"It's okay. It'll all be fine. Come on, I need to show you something." Paxx turned, and I followed him out of the training arena. The sound of metal clanging faded as we made it over to Paxx's office. He pushed through the door, and piles of seraphinite littered his office.

"Why did you bring this all here?" I asked.

"There are too many witches out on the coast. I know Dayanara said nobody else has the spell to use it, but I wanted to keep an eye on it myself."

"Always so distrustful." I laughed and sat in the chair across from his desk. "Is that what you needed to show me?"

"One of the things, yes." He moved behind his desk and rolled out a scroll. "I pulled the battle strategies from the last war with Sanjry. Obviously, you're one of the few who fought in that war. I'm taking this over to Ishani and Xavier, but I wanted to know if you wanted to add anything."

Flashes of that war appeared in my mind, the sheer amount of death, the person I was back then. Young vampire men tended to be a bit violent and more arrogant than necessary, but I was far worse. The amount of power I received due to my odd lineage and the privileges I had from being royalty all created a man with far too much confidence and not enough care. I told myself it was war, and obliterating villages for the sake of battle was warranted. But it didn't bother me. I barely thought about it twice. Being captured—the torture—*that* I thought about far too often. There were still sleepless nights, even to this day, hundreds of years later. I'd go months without thinking about it, and the sight of a scar, the smell of the underground, would have me plummeting back to that place.

I cleared my throat. "I had these updated once I recovered. Everything here should be accurate."

Paxx didn't respond, only stared at me. He didn't have the gift of mind-speaking like I did, but he did have something else. The ability to sense emotions. He explained it as a person's vibrations, different colors radiating from their aura. It's why he always watched everyone the way he did. He could see things, sense things that weren't as obvious to other people. While someone could train themselves not to let someone like me into their head, hiding your emotions was far more difficult.

"You haven't had a reaction like that in a while," he muttered.

"It's the scenario that led me to the Triori, the reason I need to have that conversation with Dayanara. It just feels. . . fresh right now."

He nodded. "That makes sense. Do you want to come with me to the coast?"

"Sure." I shrugged. The distraction was welcome.

We made our way over to the portal door. Since only Ishani got the portal magic, I couldn't get us over there with a snap of my fingers. The fresh smell of the sea hit me as soon as we walked through, one of my favorite scents. Daya's laughter had me snapping my neck in the direction, wondering who could elicit that sound. I found her and Cat across the courtyard. They looked to be directing some sort of drill, but whatever Cat was doing had Daya in near tears. I left her there to follow Paxx into Xavier's office, where Ishani was sure to be. They were rarely too far from each other if they were both on the coast.

Their relationship had been off and on for centuries. Xavier loved my sister with his every fiber, but he didn't understand how she moved through the world so carefree. His urge to protect her, to get her to relax and settle down, it was too much for her. She loved him as well, but she loved herself more. Something I couldn't fault her for. Not to mention the thing none of us spoke about: she'd outlive him, and probably sooner rather than later. He was in great health but didn't have any witch blood in him. Vampires didn't live as long as the witches and lobos.

As I suspected, she was sitting on a couch in Xavier's office, her head turned toward the door as soon as we walked through.

"Thought I felt you," she muttered as she sat up. "Are we all here to talk about the fact Daya's going to cut you into pieces tomorrow?"

I rolled my eyes, ignoring her in favor of greeting Xavier.

"She's not wrong," Xavier said before I could even say hi.

"Already told him, he knows," Paxx responded for me.

With this group, I wasn't the king. While sometimes I greatly appreciated it, right now was not one of those times.

"I'll do it before we get there. Everyone can leave me the fuck alone about it now," I huffed.

They all laughed at my expense, and I looked over at Paxx for him to discuss whatever it was we were here for. Paxx pulled out the scroll and put it on Xavier's desk as Ishani joined. It was a map of the Sanjryan land we fought on the last time. Battle tactics and instructions were scribed on the sides, and crosses marked each place where a battle took place.

"These were the last battle plans. While obviously, many things have most likely changed since then, the land should be mostly the same. We'll have to move through the Inbetween, but I think we all agree it's better to bring the battle to them. If it comes to that," he cleared his throat, gaze on me. Everything had to be a hypothetical when it came to me being part of these conversations.

"I agree," Ishani added. "I would rather destroy their land than ours."

"Any new estimations on when the war might start, Paxx?"

"They're still very busy with whatever they're seeking. There have been no big moves with their armies. Nobody's been found trying to get into Dusra. It's quiet, no real guess."

I sat forward. "I don't like quiet."

"None of us do," Ishani agreed before swiping her hand across the scroll.

Her hand lingered on the area of the forest I was captured, her other hand balling tight into a fist. We all had trauma from that day. While I went through the actual torture, Ishani went through a torture of her own. She, too, went to see the Triori, and whatever they told her, whatever they gave her, it was what saved me, but it didn't come without cost.

While I didn't know what that was, she thought I was too far gone to notice. While I recovered, I saw it. Something plagued her. We were connected in ways that went beyond our comprehension. Twins, possibly the rarest twins to ever exist, and I knew her better than I knew myself. She wouldn't let me push the topic, and I stopped to give her peace, to let her cope. Xavier helped a lot with that. He never told me specifically what she went through, but he made sure I knew that she was getting better.

Xavier humphed. "What time do you leave tomorrow?"

"First light."

"I suppose we'll know more after then," Xavier responded.

"We'll know a lot more of something, that's for sure," Ishani mumbled.

"You all act like I have to tell her I killed her closest friend," I snapped.

"The girl has been lied to by too many people, Ax. You might as well be," Ishani responded before she plopped back down onto the couch, and the other two in the room averted their eyes.

Well, fuck.

Chapter Seventeen

Dayanara

Axel said we'd be leaving at first light, and he wasn't kidding. He didn't bother knocking. He knew I wouldn't be up at this time. I was awakened by him sitting beside me on my bed, gently running his hands through my hair. One of the best ways. I finished dressing and grabbed the boots I had left by the fireplace the previous night.

"Ready?" he asked.

I nodded. "Just need my weapons."

Sitting down on the chair, I pulled on my boots. By the time I was finished, he'd come over with my weapons and my leather back holster. I stood, and he slipped it over my head, holding out the straps for me to stick my arms through and tighten. Ax held his hands on the buckles at my side for a moment, his bottom lip between his teeth.

"You okay?" I questioned when he didn't move for an unnatural amount of time.

He quickly withdrew his hands and nodded. "You remember the island enough to portal us there?"

Not very convincing. "Yeah. You sure you're fine?"

"Nervous. I have to tell you a story when we get there."

I side-eyed him but snapped open the portal to the island. We stepped through, the light barely gracing the sky. The orange glow was subtle on the horizon, casting a beautiful warmth on the ocean. The moon was fading but still showing while the stars faintly sparkled around it. Axel's chin was turned up toward it, a calm sensation falling over him that was definitely not there prior to him seeing the water.

"Lead the way, big guy," I teased.

Axel turned us in the opposite direction, toward the thick forest behind us. We walked in silence until we reached the edge of the trees. Something washed over me. It wasn't magical in the way I knew magic; it was something older, something ancient.

"It's the Goddess Zalvoh's magic. She enchanted this forest herself. At least, that's what we're told. Either way, the magic is very old," Axel explained.

I wasn't sure how he knew the way, but he walked with purpose around trees, over small creeks, and up and down unstable terrain.

"So, that story?"

Axel cleared his throat. "I told you the story of when I was captured. I left out some. . . details."

Don't love that. "Okay?"

He peered over at me once and then back at the ground. "I said that I consulted some friends. Those friends were the Triori."

The deeper we made it into the forest, the darker it became. An eerie feeling that we didn't belong encompassed me, a gut reaction that I should turn around and go back to where I came from. Axel kept moving forward, though, so I kept following.

"When I arrived in Dusra, I was a shell of a being. I didn't see the point of moving on when everything felt so heavy. What was the point of existing if my existence was pure pain and sadness?" He lifted a single shoulder. "Every day I opened my eyes was a day too many. I was in a constant state of panic, thinking that I was back there. The flashbacks weren't just flashbacks; it was as if I was experiencing it all over again. The torture, the pieces of what I might have done during the blackouts, it was too much."

My brows pinched together, but I didn't know what to offer him. I nodded, encouraging him to continue.

"So I went to the Triori. I wanted to know if there was a future worth living for. They gave me a reason to keep living. Something to look forward to, something to hold on to." He cleared his throat. "They sat me down in this room, and they didn't just tell me what to expect, it was like I was there in these memories. They showed me as a young boy with Ishani, the joy we felt swimming in the sea with the dragons. They showed our wild smiles as we grew up together, nights with my mother, proof that I once knew happiness. They had me relive my recent present, showed me at my lowest, showed me the pain that stained my soul. The scars that stole that joy from me.

"My future. . . they showed me my happiness. They showed me a witch filled with rage and pain, so much like my own. A woman who felt the same darkness as I did. They showed me hand in hand with her. They showed us decimating battlefields together, covered in blood, but neither of us minded because we were together. They showed me well into my life, with that same witch, someone's lifespan who matched my own. I saw the shadows behind her eyes from her trauma fade as we moved together. I heard her laughter, I saw her smile, I heard her cries in battle, and I watched years upon years of my future. I saw the security we both experienced by simply being in each other's presence. Something unlike any love I'd ever seen. The price for them showing me this was that I wouldn't remember who she was. I wouldn't remember her face. I could know that my happiness was a possibility, that there was a future of joy, but I wasn't allowed to know her identity."

I swallowed, my hands shaking. He couldn't mean. . .

"Then I met you." He peered over at me with a small smile. "I knew right then and there who you were. When I heard your growl as you took down that drunk piece of shit in the pub, all the pieces clicked back together. That woman, that woman who had known true pain and loss. That woman who held so much power that she outshined even me. That woman who I saw overcome everything this life served her was. . . you. You climbed out of the depths of despair, and *you* looked at me like I meant something. Like I was worthy of this life. It was you,

Daya. You were the force that held my life together. *You* are the reason that I'm still here. It's always been you."

"That was. . . Hundreds of years ago?" was the only question I could form.

He nodded. "I've loved you for longer than I haven't. I don't say that in expectation of anything, but it is the truth. I fell in love with the possibility of you, and from the very first words you spoke to me, I fell in love with *you*."

"My first words were, 'Don't call me a bitch, and we have a deal.'" I laughed.

"The sweetest words I had ever heard."

Axel stopped at the edge of a deadly drop-off, stepped off the ledge, and disappeared.

"What the fuck," I whispered.

His hand reappeared and grabbed mine, pulling me off the ledge and into whatever magical illusion was ahead.

"We're here," Axel muttered.

Darkness, unlike our world, framed the land with no stars or moon shining. Orbs of lights levitated a few feet from the ground, all leading up a hill where a large black cottage sat at the top. Fog covered everything, the thickness reminding me of Cape Coven. The same feeling of being watched accompanied it, and my body geared into high alert. Even after what Axel had told me, all of my senses focused on the danger.

"I'm sorry I lied," Axel whispered. "Or withheld the truth. Whatever the wrong thing I did was, I am sorry. Part of me worried that our future would change if I told you. Then I realized I was more worried about how you'd react. If it'd be too much for you and you'd leave me. You didn't sign up for this, and with your kingdom and Zuri gone, I just kept waiting."

I shook my head. "It's a lot to digest. I'm not. . . mad. Or I don't think I am. I honestly don't know how to feel."

He loved me, and that was dangerous. He loved me before I was even born, before he met me or touched my skin. I didn't give any thought to the other thing poking at my mind. This seemed bigger than the average love. It felt like Verdaji—like he was fated to me. That kind of love couldn't be real, wasn't a love

I had ever witnessed, and yet here he was. The people who loved me tended to find themselves in danger if not dead.

He also kept it from me. Could I blame him for it, though? I might have run for the hills the moment he tried to tell me. Not that I'd been in a state to hear such a thing. I expected some sort of anger toward him for lying, but it wasn't there. Was it because, deep down, I wanted to be loved? Or was it because I was so fucked up by so many disastrous events that this didn't seem like the worst thing to happen to me? *Who knows.*

Axel watched me as we stood on the lit path. His body was rigid, and his hands at his sides.

I reached out to grab one, and his muscles instantly relaxed. "Let's worry about dealing with the Triori for now, but thank you for telling me, Ax."

He swallowed hard and nodded, staring up at the spooky cottage atop the hill. "Remember what we told you about the Triori. They will play their games. Don't give them more than you need to. Also, keep in mind that they pretty much know everything. Lying is pointless."

A soft humming came from the cottage, and the weight of the dark magic was overwhelming. I felt it everywhere, like phantom tendrils of shadow wrapping around my body. The voices were entrancing, definitely feminine, but there was a wholly unique range between them. Axel grabbed my hand and gave me a side glance that had me snapping myself out of the song's trance.

We reached the door of the cottage, and Axel knocked twice. The humming came closer and closer as unhurried footsteps stopped on the other side of the door. My breathing was suddenly uneven as the black door knob slowly turned and the door was pulled open. A woman stood before me, a woman so beautiful the urge to look away overcame me. Her warm brown skin glistened as if she were a freshly painted work of art. Every wave in her hair was set perfectly at her bare back, an ocean stuck in time. The dress she wore felt like something not of this age, silver fabric draped across her body, only held by a sparkling rope. Her dark eyes seemed to see straight through me as she stood with a stillness that had me wondering if she was even real.

"Dayanara, Axel. Welcome," she spoke with a voice that had me ready to do anything she asked me.

"Lachala." Axel bowed his head. "Still the most beautiful being in our existence."

Lachala pursed her lips and looked at me. "You once spoke that and meant it. Now I'm not sure. Come in."

I stumbled in with Axel, and the Fate closed the door behind us. I felt her hand on my arm, moving up to my cheek, and forgot how to breathe completely. It wasn't the touch of a mortal. Not just soft warmth, but an electrifying sensation that rippled through my entire body.

"You are divine. I'd love to sample what you have to offer." She ran her gaze up and down my body and then over to Ax. "The both of you. . . now that would be truly divine."

Axel cleared his throat. "Are your sisters ready?"

Lachala removed her hand from me, and I wasn't sure if the fluttering in my gut was fear or arousal. "Don't spoil my fun. They are in the sitting room."

Axel gripped my wrist and pulled me with him, leaving Lachala in the foyer. She chuckled from behind me, and I sensed Axel trying to enter my mind.

"Don't play into her advances. She has killed nearly every person she's laid with."

"Seems worth the risk," I mumbled as I peered at her over my shoulder. One touch on my arm was euphoric. I couldn't imagine more than that.

The inside of the cottage was as eerie as the outside. The floor creaked beneath our feet as we walked, and it felt as if the walls themselves were watching me. An awareness that I couldn't quite pin down. The paint peeled from the walls in the light of the sporadic candles, and I swore the house took a breath as we moved. Axel turned into a room more lit than the rest, and two more women sat in chairs facing away from us.

Axel stopped at the doorway and pointed his hand to the woman on the left. "Sartho, Makali. Thank you for your hospitality."

They both turned their heads, and while I thought Lachala was the most beautiful thing I'd seen, they both were just as beautiful. Sartho's skin was slightly lighter than Lachala's, and her curly hair was a few inches shorter. The same dark irises as Lachala, but her eyes were slightly upturned. The last sister's hair was much shorter, her curls not hanging from her head but resting atop it, with a few hanging over her forehead. Golden jewelry sparkled on her smooth, deep mahogany skin. So many piercings I couldn't keep track. The one on her nose was my favorite. Makali felt like the oldest of the three, although it was certainly hard to determine as they all looked to be in their prime years. Lachala handed Sartho a glass of dark red wine, and she took it without removing her gaze from me.

"Oh. We have been waiting for this," Sartho said with a devilish grin.

"What do you seek?" Makali asked bluntly.

We moved to sit on the couch across from them, and Lachala sat between Ax and me with a wink in my direction.

Axel answered first. "We wish to know if there is anything you can tell us about what is to come. Kaizer Curran believes there to be an artifact that can help him wield all the elements. A scepter."

Sartho looked over at Makali, raising her eyebrows as Lachala sat back and crossed her legs. "We may know something about that," Makali muttered.

"You know we are neutral in these matters of mortals. We can't interfere in any significant way," Lachala explained.

"We can offer knowledge, but that knowledge comes with a price," Sartho added.

"What would the price be?" I asked.

Lachala hummed and ticked her finger on her chin a few times before she stood and joined Makali and Sartho. "What do we want, sisters?"

"I want to see your power," Makali exclaimed.

"My power?" I questioned.

"I can feel our sister on you. Show me."

I stood and unlatched the top half of my leathers. Manifesting my wings came without too much thought, and they unfurled from my shoulder blades. My skin flickered, and I begged it to listen to me and not cause any embarrassment. The colors shined brightly, rushing beneath the surface of my skin, and I asked, "The goddesses are your sisters?"

Lachala scoffed. "Mortals and their incorrect histories."

All three sisters stood and inspected me before Makali said, "We were all born from the same energy. Zalvoh, Naom, Cama, and Coab were born first of the elements they wield. We came a little later, born of the same essence Naom wields. We have no parents like mortals. We simply are. But we are all ethereal beings, forever linked to each other by that fact."

Sartho ran her hands over my wings as Lachala grabbed my hand and turned it over to watch my skin sparkle. "Why did she bestow so much on you?"

"I thought you knew everything," I muttered.

"We know of this world, but what the other ethereal beings do and why is not something we have access to," Sartho answered.

I peeked over my shoulder to find Axel still on the couch, his eyes sparkling the way they always did when I was in this state. Part of me felt like he'd be threatened by it at some point, but it wasn't his way.

"So you know *who* she is now," Lachala said, with her gaze directed at him.

"I do."

"And you know who he is?" Lachala asked me.

I nodded.

"What if the price was the love that will be between you two?"

"Then we'll find another way," Axel said before I could even open my mouth to speak.

Something about the fact he'd let this world turn to rubble before he lost me had my gut tightening.

Lachala chuckled and looked at me with a smirk. "I knew that would be the answer. Just thought others should hear it."

"What do you want for the information?" I asked, trying to stay focused.

Makali crossed her legs and placed her hands on her knee. "What do you take from someone who has had so much taken from them?"

"We could ask for entertainment," Lachala said with a grin.

"Oh, I like that option," Sartho added.

"Are you really so bored?" Axel questioned with obvious annoyance.

"I think she's strong enough," Makali said to her sisters, much more seriousness in her tone than them.

"Just because she's gotten more than the others doesn't mean she's *that* strong," Sartho responded.

Goddess, I hated when people talked like I wasn't in the fucking room.

"Strong enough for what?" I asked.

Makali sat forward. "When the goddesses created the stones and the Piedra before going to rest, they trapped us here. The least populated area in Iteria."

"They bound us to this forest. Zalvoh had already enchanted it, but Naom was the one who made the barrier. Makali thinks you might be able to break it."

"Why did they trap you?" I asked.

"With them going away, they thought it would be best for us all to go as well. We didn't agree, but they didn't give us much of a choice."

"Well, I can try, depending on the information you give," I offered with a glance at Axel.

Makali nodded at Sartho. "The artifact Kaizer speaks of was something we made—all of us, with the Creators."

"I'm sorry, what?" Axel sneered.

"When they made the stones, yes, they took some of the power from the world and imbued them with it. But they also gave a way to remake the world, should that ever be something that the mortals wanted. You all were never supposed to be separated; it was supposed to be a live ecosystem, with creatures living in the day and the night. But you all turned on each other, and I think that our sisters wanted the world to have the opportunity to go back to how they originally formed it," Makali followed up.

Sartho leaned closer, her wine sloshing in her cup. "We did it in secrecy, and it had been lost to time. Nobody knew about it for ages. It was never documented or written for your knowledge. But if the world started to heal itself, the pieces were supposed to make themselves known."

"Until. . ." Lachala trailed off.

"Before Dusra's war with Sanjry, a vampire and a fae found us. We were. . . particularly restless that day and thought we could break free from this forest if we had the scepter. We gave the vampire what he wanted, and he was supposed to go and find the pieces on this side of the wall. The fae, on the other side, was to do the same. They never came back."

"So we're in this predicament because of you?" Axel quipped.

Lachala shrugged. "Do you blame an animal in a trap for how they react to it?"

"You're a bit more developed than a mere animal," Axel responded.

"The pieces would have been found, eventually. They were always supposed to. We just. . . rushed it. Anyway," Sartho said as she rolled her eyes. "We obviously needed to get our hands on the stones as well. So, we needed to get someone from each of the elemental sanctions. The magic in this place is different from where you are. This dark forest stretches farther than Dusra. We can't leave, but there are entrances. The one here and one on the other side of the Piedra."

"I don't know about you, but I feel like this is leaning pretty heavily into 'interfering with the mortals,'" I whispered.

The Triori ignored me.

"People knew of us. While many people thought we went to rest with the Creators, there were some who thought we were still around. The only stone not in Malva was the earth stone, and the fae who we'd asked to find the scepter pieces said they'd speak to their king. We never heard from him again, but we could see that he made. . . other choices to benefit himself," Makali spat.

"And the vampire?" Axel asked.

"He brought us his stone, the firestone." Makali snapped her fingers and the sliver of stone appeared in her hand. Like ours, it was no regular rock. The colors within it moved, magic radiating from it akin to the pulse of a rushed heartbeat.

"It is all we have. He died before he was able to bring us anything else," Lachala advised.

"Shouldn't you have seen that?" I asked.

I was confused before, but every word they spoke only added to the confusion. And to the anger.

"Once he interfered in ethereal affairs, his future was murky." Makali's brow furrowed like it was an unexpected part of the plan.

The firestone was here, that was the only plus in this entire situation. I found it interesting that Kaizer wasn't looking for that first, or maybe he had no idea it was gone. There was one part that I still couldn't quite wrap my head around.

"What about the essence part? We were told that the essence would need to be pulled from someone who could wield each element."

"A small sacrifice, yes." Lachala shrugged. "They wouldn't have died, necessarily. But they would have lost all access to their magic. Something *we* could have performed, but we aren't the only ones anymore."

"Mhm," I responded. The timing of me getting this power when *this* information was coming out. . . it felt a little too on the nose. A little too much like fate or even purpose.

"I find it hard to believe this is all happening now because the world is healing. It is quite the opposite out there," Axel said with his hand rubbing his chin.

Sartho took a sip of her wine before saying, "Somehow, this information must have been written down, or the story told. Maybe by the ones that we contacted all those years ago. The Creators are resting. They would be the only other ones who know of the scepter."

"I saw Naom," I blurted.

Axel swiveled his head in my direction, and I bit the inside of my cheek. "I saw her when I died. I don't think the theory that they used so much magic that they fell into their final rest was accurate. I'm not sure what they can and can't do, but they're still there somewhere."

"Still, they would not bring forth the scepter given the state of unrest. Both here and in Bonda," Lachala looked to her sisters.

"There are more than just us," Sartho said with a tilt of her head in Makali's direction.

Makali closed her eyes and took a deep breath. "We don't speak about him, Sartho."

I thought through my history teachings, the Creators and the Triori were the main ethereal beings that we were taught. There were other minor ones, but the ethereal beings that I could remember were all women.

"I don't think we have a choice, sister," Sartho responded. "You can feel the ripples in the essence the same as me."

"The god of Chaos," Lachala's voice shook.

Great, that's fucking fantastic. Chaos. That's what we need more of.

"Chuah," Axel mumbled as he snapped his head back up toward them.

"You should not know that name, nor should you speak it," Lachala said with far more seriousness in her tone than she'd spoken with thus far.

"How do you know of him?" Makali asked.

"My mother used to sing this song when we were kids. It always felt like nonsense, but he was part of it. Chaos Chuah strews, the god of all untrue. I thought she was rhyming random words."

"Amara was always too smart for her own good," Sartho mumbled.

The urge to confront the Triori about Ishani's deal with them was strong, but I couldn't do it in front of Axel. I wasn't sure which details he knew and what he didn't, and the last thing I wanted to do was break Ishani's trust.

"Who is he?" I asked.

Makali flicked her wrist, and the old house around us shifted into a cave. I knew something was off about this house; it was as alive as we were. Black glyphs and pictographs were stark against the pale stone, and I stepped closer to inspect them. Sartho snapped her fingers, and the etchings took life, moving as if they were sentient.

"As we said, our sisters were born of the elements they wield. Naom came first, which is why we believe she had the ability to manipulate beyond the elemental magic the others received," Sartho explained. The markings on the wall shifted again, the delicate shape of four women sprouting and wielding their element. "They found this realm untouched. So they gave it life."

"Found? Where did they come from?" I asked.

The sisters glanced at each other. "We call it Hada, but it is not a *place* like Iteria is a place. It exists in a. . . realm above everything. This universe is not flat and singular, it is many things overlapping each other at once. The physiological rules of this land are simple, things are mostly as they seem. But Hada is different—it is the universe's very top 'layer.' It is simultaneously clouds and mountains, just as it is sea and river, desert and sand. It is where we believe they are resting."

Our world, the whole of Iteria, stretched across the stone. Four women rose from each section of the land, their elemental power moving with each step they took. "They spread their gifts across the land, creating the mortals, animals, plants, and all the living beings you know now."

All forms of life popped up across the stone, the world growing more populated by the second. "We were born of essence, the purest form of energy in our world, this one, and every world in between. Our sisters brought us here, to Iteria, after they created all the creatures of sorts. A world made of the same thing as us but different. Essence was vital in the creation of beings, a connection between each mortal, the very ground you walk on, the flowers you pick, and the animals you hunt. Because we came from that, we are able to see things. We can dig deep into it and feel those connections."

Three more women burst to life at the center of our world where the Piedra now stood. A vast system, like veins, ran through the Triori and into the world and from the world back into them. "But other ethereal beings are not connected to this system. We cannot see into their lives." The four Creators moved about the world, the veins flowing through everything else and not touching them. "What none of us were expecting was Chaos."

A crack through the center of Malva burst open. Creatures crawled out of the fissure, monsters even bigger and more lethal than the ones we knew. They ran over the land, killing any living beings in their path. "Chuah. The god of Chaos appeared from that dark place. Wherever he came from, whatever he was, was the opposite of essence. He was not from our world, and we could not see him coming."

The images flickered, shifting back into their state etched into the wall before Sartho cleared her throat. "He rampaged Iteria. Destroying so much that we had worked on building. Chuah's stronghold pulled the essence right from the land, leaving it dull and magicless. What the mortals refer to as the Inbetween."

The color in that space faded completely, and the ever-flowing rivers of essence recoiled from the dark area. "The Creators worked together to bestow a spell around the land so that the Inbetween could not grow further than it already had."

Sartho pulled back into the full worldview of Iteria, and I trailed my eyes across the land. "It stretches all the way into Bonda," I mumbled.

"Yes," Sartho answered. "Chuah could take the form of any being, any man, any animal, and make those around him do the darkest things. Even with our gifts, with the Creators' gifts, we could not find him. We could only find the streams of mayhem he left behind. He would appear, wreak havoc on a village, and then be gone into the night again. We assumed he went back to the Inbetween to hide, as we couldn't venture into that space without its connection to the essence of our world. It was practically another dimension."

"At first, it was small, little villages, small groups of people he influenced. Then it grew larger, and half of Malva's vampires were infected by him. Chuah is the reason the world is now separated. He is what caused those vampires to go into the night and hunt innocents. One small seed of Chaos sewed, and it grew like weeds. He got cocky, and the Creators were able to lock him inside a zone within the Inbetween. He is unable to escape, but he has been known to lure people close enough to communicate. The Creators are resting and can't do anything about it now. Neither can we, as we can't even access the space he's in. Barrier or not," Makali added.

Sartho closed her fist, and we ended up back in the living room where we had started.

"So he thinks the scepter can be used to break his own barrier?" Axel asked.

"Possibly," Makali answered.

"Where is he located?"

Lachala bit her lip and looked at Sartho. "The Piedra runs over his prison."

"He's within the rock?" Axel asked.

"In a way, more under it than anything," Sartho answered.

I'd lived my entire life beside the Piedra, never once did I think an ancient god was trapped beneath it.

"So he would want to destroy the Piedra to be set free and to ensue mayhem between the beings of Malva and Bonda?"

"That is what we think. Especially because the Creators are not here to fight back now," Lachala added.

"But we don't know how many he may be in contact with," I said as I bit the inside of my cheek.

"Chuah's influence has shielded them from our view," Makali confirmed.

"It wasn't a *what*. It was a *who*," I whispered. Naom had said that I had to stop what was coming, but she meant Chuah, the destruction he'd bring.

"You said this forest stretches into Bonda?" Axel asked.

"Yes, but the barrier between here and there still exists."

"Kaizer believes the scepter is here in Dusra. That's all we have to go off currently," I said.

"There may be pieces in Dusra, but the whole thing will not be found there," Makali responded.

"We have given you what you asked for. Will you break our barrier?" Lachala asked me.

"All I heard is that this is your fault. If I find the scepter, I will try to break the barrier, but right now, I think we have more important things to figure out." I stood, and Axel followed my movement.

"Too desperate to escape that you didn't solidify the payment," Axel laughed. "Played by your own game."

Lachala stood and rushed toward me with vigor, but I kept my chin raised. "This is not a game, child."

"You barely gave us anything to work with!" I yelled. "You don't know the location of the items or who else is involved. You didn't hold up your end of the bargain. Give me something more."

"We gave you what we could," Sartho offered genuinely.

Axel tensed, but I pushed forward before he could stop me. "Tell me how to save Zuri."

Sartho ran her tongue over her teeth. "Zuri Furaha, another pretty one."

My jaw ticked, even though I knew she was clearly baiting me. "Tell me how to save her, and I will do as you wish."

"It is a small piece of knowledge," Lachala responded, her gaze on her sisters. "Zuri will be needed to retrieve the grimoire. It must be all three of them."

"My family's grimoire?" I asked, but Makali cut me off.

Makali nodded and stepped forward. "We cannot say more. You took a prisoner from Sanjry recently, yes?"

Axel cleared his throat, and I avoided eye contact. "Yes."

"Trust Paxx. He will be the one to get the information out of him."

That wasn't exactly helpful, but if they were telling the truth, I knew we were on the right track.

"I will come back. I will set you free. As soon as I have something to return to," I stated firmly.

"Thank you, Dayanara," Makali responded as her sisters' shoulders sagged.

"Don't you know, girl, you already have everything?" Lachala added.

"Everything and nothing. Full and empty. Scared and confident. Two ends of every spectrum wrapped up in a pretty little bruja," Sartho followed up with a wide grin.

My eyes narrowed on her, but I turned and walked toward the exit. Axel brushed his hand against my lower back before stepping ahead of me and opening the door.

"Do send someone for us to play with!" Lachala yelled as the door slammed shut behind us.

Chapter Eighteen

Dayanara

"So," I started as we stepped through a portal back to the palace. "Were you one of the few Lachala didn't kill?"

Axel ran his hand down his face. "Many, many, years ago."

"How was it?" I inquired.

I had a pretty active imagination, and the few short moments of attention from Lachala had my mind reeling with possibilities.

"That feeling you got when she touched your arm? It's meant to lure and bring pleasure, so. . ." Axel laughed out.

I sighed. "Enough said. I'll need all the details at some point. Should have let me at least *try*."

"I'm sorry, are the two people in your little circle not meeting your needs, Daya?"

"Have you not heard the phrase, 'the more the merrier?'"

Axel laughed to himself as we stopped at the courtyard before going straight inside. I took a deep breath as I went over everything the Triori explained to us. Knowing what Kaizer was going after was great, but the fact we had no real leads as to the location wasn't ideal.

"The good thing is we have two of the stones," Axel said.

I closed my eyes and shut off the connection he used to enter my mind. "What did I tell you about reading my mind unprovoked?"

"You were thinking *very* loudly," he responded.

"Well, stop it." I leaned into him. "But yes, we have two of them. The Triori has one. So, thankfully, the only thing we really need to worry about is the scepter itself."

Axel nodded. "Even with the scepter, he'd need all four of them to do anything. We can figure out next steps."

It could be seen as poetic, that the Creators wanted to give us another chance at life the way they imagined. The fact that hope was being used to potentially cause more damage was more on par with what to expect from mortals.

"Can you believe that they are probably the cause of all of this?" I asked.

"I feel a sort of relief that we aren't at fault. I worried I just didn't look in the right places. We could have read every page of every book in that library and come up short. But, no, I can't believe that the Triori are the ones who tried to use it for their own purposes."

"There has to be information somewhere about..." I paused and whispered, "Chuah."

"There's nothing in any of the histories I've been taught outside of that song from my mother. But you're right. Erasing him completely could not have been true."

"What were you taught about the Inbetween? The reason there was no magic?"

"We were told it was there when Iteria was created."

"Same," I responded. "The creatures that live there, though. I did always wonder why they were *so* monstrous, lacking hearts, some lacking eyes. They didn't seem of this world."

I wanted to bring up what he'd told me, but I didn't know what to say yet. It felt inconsequential compared to the absolute disaster we'd just been made aware of. We pushed through the doors of the castle, heading toward Axel's office. Akari and Ishani turned the corner the same way we did, both of their faces turning serious as they realized we were back.

"How did it go?" Ishani asked, her gaze dragging over every inch of my body with worry.

"We didn't make any deals that will cause harm," I offered and Ishani nodded her head rapidly. I swore tears welled in her eyes at the proclamation.

"But?" Ishani asked, always hearing the things that *weren't* said even more than what was.

"We're going to need to call an inner council meeting. It's. . . a lot," I responded.

Ishani and I stood outside of the council room as everyone filtered in. I knew she was worried about us going because of what happened when she went to the fates. But I did my best to reassure her.

"Nothing bad is going to happen. Not because of them, that is. I didn't make a deal. They actually need *my* help."

"Why would they need your help?"

"They think because of the power Naom gave me, I can break the barrier she put around the forest. I'm honestly not sure I can, but at this point, we're using it as leverage."

Ishani nodded as she peeked back into the room. "And Axel? He didn't make any deals, right?"

"Nope, none." I made sure I held her eye contact so she could hear the truth in everything I said.

"Okay, let's go ahead inside," she responded, and we entered through the doorway.

Paxx, Xavier, Axel, and Akari were already inside waiting for us. Axel had started telling them some of the details about when we first got there, and Ishani and I settled into the seats beside him.

"It's still such an odd place. Did you want to share what happened, Daya?"

I shook my head. "No, you go for it."

Axel continued to tell the story in such a way that I forgot that I was there with him when the events happened. Maybe in another life, he could have been a storyteller. The details he remembered, the vivid imagery he used while explaining the cave, I was in awe of him. I sat there with my chin on my fist as he finished the story and they all turned to me.

"So, basically, we're fucked," Ishani grumbled.

"Essentially." I shrugged.

"Kaizer has to be keeping this information close to his chest." Paxx scratched his beard. "He's being very deliberate."

"I find it hard to believe that they would know more about the location of anything in our kingdom better than us," Ishani added.

"If this all happened at the time the Piedra was created, that's before even your mother lived. Before her mother, her mother even. If someone wanted that information to die out, the thousands of years would have helped," Xavier responded.

"Even if they were to get all the pieces of the scepter, whoever used it would have to be extremely strong. I imagine that much power coursing through any one person would kill them," Axel stated.

"I agree," I said. "Kaizer is strong for a vampire, probably because of his lineage, but I don't imagine he's strong enough to do that. I think the only people who could do that and not die are in this room."

"You think Athena might know anything else?" Xavier asked.

"It's possible. Otherwise, the next best thing will be going into Sanjry. . . or the Inbetween," I responded.

I *loathed* the Inbetween, but if that was where this all started, where Chuah was located, it might have been worth the risk.

"We have to think about the ramifications of something like this. For the whole of Iteria, not just in Malva. For anyone to wield all the elements, we'd need someone from the earth district," Axel said.

"Do you know anything about the tunnels that were said to be built by the humans?" I asked Paxx.

He nodded once. "As far as I know, they're rumors. I've never had any proof provided."

"Us either, but I'm curious," I responded, biting one of my nails.

"If this happens. . ." Ishani trailed off.

"We were separated for a reason. If the wall comes down, there will not only be war, not all of us would be coming out of it alive. I imagine only one side of the Piedra could truly win. Regardless of the intent of the Creators," Axel responded.

"I have no interest in the light of the sun," Xavier mumbled.

Ishani perked up, but when her eyes fell back to Xavier, her shoulders drooped slightly. She was itching for an adventure, for something new, and it didn't seem like she hated the idea of the Piedra coming down. Outside of all the imminent death, of course.

Akari sat forward. "It would be the end of the lobos, I have no doubt. We barely survived before."

"We won't let that happen," I responded quickly, another lobo on my mind. I'd never allow her to face that.

"Dusra is the last line of defense. We have no choice but to be successful, Kaizer must be stopped," Xavier said.

"Even if he falls, another may take his place. We need to get to the root of the problem," Axel responded.

"To the. . . God of Chaos," I whispered.

"I don't even know where to start with that," Ishani breathed.

"The Triori said he was in the Inbetween, on our side or Bonda's, I don't know. But he's extremely dangerous. There's a reason no one speaks of him anymore, I'm sure," Axel said.

"But your mother knew of him," I said, looking between him and Ishani.

"A song, but I don't know how much more she knew," Ishani responded.

"Did she grow up here?" I asked.

"She spent much time here, but she grew up everywhere. Her being a lobo and a witch, she had family across all of Dusra," Axel said.

"You think there's some sort of hidden knowledge we haven't yet found?" Ishani asked.

"I find it hard to believe he was completely eradicated. There has to be more," I replied. "You said the forest on the island was the oldest place in Malva, yes? The cave they took us to, do you think that's a place we could find?"

"It's possible, but I'm not sure. Let's keep that in our back pockets," Axel responded.

"And the Amapola grimoire is the oldest book known to the brujas. We should get that as well. But finding Zuri is my first priority. Lachala said she would be needed when retrieving it."

"All right. We should probably go check in on the training," Xavier said with his gaze directed at Ishani. They both stood, Akari following them, but I stopped Paxx before he left.

"How's the questioning going?" I asked.

I wasn't sure if it would interfere with. . . fate. If I told him I knew that he'd be the one to get the information from the prisoner. But it was eating at me, knowing it was just a matter of time.

"I'm getting close. This one is breaking faster than any of the others. As soon as I know something, I'll find you. You have my word, Dayanara."

That same sense of trust felt like it was running through my veins. "Okay," I responded. "And call me Daya."

Chapter Nineteen

Dayanara

It took massive effort not to become Paxx's shadow. I wanted to watch him get the information out of the soldier, but I didn't want to interfere with it either. So, I decided to eat my feelings instead. I was the only one in the dining hall, but evidence that a few of them had already come through was left behind. I knew that Axel and Paxx were on the coast, but I wasn't sure where everyone else was.

Sitting down, I inspected today's lunch. A yellow rice, rich with the smell of turmeric. I'd used the root in a spell a couple of times, but we'd never thought to cook with it. It was delicious, with flecks of coriander leaves throughout, adding some color and a fresh floral taste. I almost felt bad about eating the cute little lambs I'd seen out on the surrounding farms. *Almost*, because those little fuckers tasted delicious.

I heard someone coming but didn't immediately recognize the footsteps. Xavier paused at the doorway, his eyes bouncing to me and then the empty seats around the table. He cleared his throat and nodded before sitting at the other end of the table. Someone brought him a plate of the same food I was eating, and we ate in silence until I grew too bored not to speak.

"We've never really clicked, have we?" I asked.

Xavier coughed, his fist raising to his mouth while he seemed to have choked on some of his rice. "No, we haven't."

"Do you still worry about my intentions?"

He sat back as if the question was one for philosophers, pondering and staring me down as his jaw moved side to side. "Intentions, no. Reality of what is to come, yes."

"You think that reality is what exactly?"

His response was simply, "Destruction."

"Ishani did say you were a pessimist," I mumbled. "I think all of this would have happened with or without me."

Or, at least I'd like to think that was the case.

"Yes, but to what extent is unclear."

His long hair glistened in the light coming from the windows, those hazel eyes so much like Axel's studying me in a way I wasn't too fond of.

"I care deeply for your king. I wouldn't do anything to jeopardize him or his kingdom."

"And the last king you were with?"

I stood abruptly, my power sparking across my skin. "How could you even ask that?"

"That." He pointed to the magic dripping from my hands. "That response is what I'm worried about. You're too quick to react."

Biting my lip, I pulled my magic back in and knocked my knuckles on the table. "You don't know enough about the things I've endured to create such a reaction."

"I know what Axel has told me. I don't dislike you, whether you believe it or not. Your resilience is admirable, how much love you have for Axel and Zuri. But someone who has had everything taken from them is dangerous."

I shrank back from that word, *love*.

"What do you take from someone who has had so much taken from them," I uttered, the words one of the Triori had spoken to me before. "I've heard that before."

"If it means anything, Ishani is quite fond of you. I trust her more than anyone. But Dusra's safety and longevity is above all. If you are to keep us safe, I am by your side. If you would bring us danger, I would not be. I will not always be here, and it would pain me to leave it in such disarray."

"You and Ishani are. . . different," I said with my head tilted.

"Everyone says that." The smallest smile pulled at his lips. "She is bright where I am dark, full where I am empty, free where I am not."

"If there's anything I know, it's that we're always evolving. Changing and becoming what we need to when we need to. That, and that life is too short to fight it."

"That is very true. Sounds like something she'd say, actually." His eyes softened..

I smiled. "So, are we friends now?"

"Friend is a bit extreme. I'd call us acquaintances." He smiled back.

"So close to having all the inner circle as best friends." I clapped before he could respond. "See you later."

I could have imagined it, but I swore I heard him laughing for the first time as I drifted out of the room and out into the courtyard. A piercing pain ran up my side, the sensation sharp from my hip to my armpit. All of my breath left me with a whoosh, and I doubled over with my hand pressed firmly against the ghost-like pain. Sweat beaded on my forehead, and my breathing came in heavy pants. Then, a hand on my back pulled me out of it.

Akari glared down at me with her brow pinched. "Are you. . . okay?"

I swallowed and sat up straight, the pain waning by the second. "I'm fine."

"What happened?" She pointed to the spot I was holding.

"I don't know, I just had a pain run up my side. I have no idea what caused it."

If Akari hadn't seen it happen, I would have thought I had imagined it entirely. There was no dull ache left behind; it was as if it had never happened.

"Verdaji," she whispered as she scanned me again.

"What?" I couldn't have heard her correctly.

"Verdaji are linked in a way that causes one to feel the other's pain."

The fact this wasn't the first time I had this suspicion was unsettling. I didn't think I deserved it, there were plenty of people out there better than me. Ones who hadn't done the things I'd done to people I loved.

"How do you know that?"

"The last pair in Dusra were lobos. We know much about them."

"Recently?" I asked.

"Last few hundred years," she responded.

That was the first time I'd heard of someone alive knowing about the spiritual connection.

"But that's after the goddesses left."

"It is. The spirits of Verdaji are said to connect life after life. The goddesses are not needed for them to exist."

But still, there hadn't been many. One set was an anomaly, not proof that it was widely possible. Not to mention that we were split from half of our population in Iteria, the chances that someone's Verdaji was actually on the other side of the Piedra was likely. Even if there was. . . proof, it didn't explain one thing.

"And they can exist in. . . more than two?"

"I've never heard of that. Not to say it isn't possible."

"Interesting." I rubbed my hand down my side. "When we met with the Triori, they said something about Zuri."

She stepped closer to me, those lobo tendencies not having a drop of personal space. "What did they say?"

"They told me that Paxx would be the one to find her location. That she would be needed to get my family's grimoire."

"Did you tell Paxx?" Akari scanned the area as if she'd find him among the flowers.

"No, I didn't know if it would change fate. I don't know how that works."

"That is probably best. I wouldn't want to put that to the test."

I was partially relieved that she said that. The chances that I'd convince myself I *should* tell him went down substantially.

"Me either." I paused, looking out into the shifting grass around us. "Did she talk to you about me. . . before?"

I wanted so badly to feel connected to Zuri, to know how she felt about me before she was captured. There were a lot of conflicting emotions, but the one above all was the simple *need* for her.

Akari smirked and motioned for me to walk with her. "My cousin has had many challenges, as she filled you in on. She was born as one thing but meant to be another. We both have the blood of the First, but neither of us wanted what came with it. Much like you."

"I didn't even know she was royalty," I mumbled.

"Hm," she sounded. "We never wanted it. Our people are. . . low in numbers and only getting lower. My uncle was hopeful, and they turned on him. It took me decades to return to our land. But Zuri, something fell over her that day that never rose again. Not until you."

I flicked my gaze over to her, and she turned her head toward the path ahead of us. *Not until you.* The words replayed in my head until she continued.

"When we came to Sanjry, I saw it. The lightness in her eyes. I didn't know what it was then. I thought she'd had enough time away from it all. But she told me that you were the cause. It was difficult for me to hear, as her family, that we weren't enough to bring that back out of her. Although, I couldn't help but be grateful. I could also see the battle she was fighting on what to do about it."

"When we were in the Inbetween, I could tell she wanted to tell me something, but I didn't push." I'd thought over it so many times now. She was nervous, and I'd thought it was just about being in the magicless land. Even before at the Ritual, she'd seemed ill at ease. Zuri had told me she planned on telling me after and that everything spiraled from there. But I wondered if I'd missed signs or if I'd ever shut her down and not realized she was trying to confess. Akari turned her nose up to a breeze flowing through flowers, contentment, and peace coming from the scent.

Dusran plants and flowers were beautiful, but not quite as beautiful as Caldera, in my humble opinion. But the smell that wafted through the air smelled *so much* like Zuri. A scent that I tried to pin down before, but she smelled exactly like this flower. One I'd never seen before. I picked one up and studied the delicate petals. I realized they weren't as delicate as I thought. They were sturdy. Where many petals had soft round edges, these formed a point at each tip. The edges were dark pink, as if they'd been dipped in ink, fading into a white at the center.

"That is a lily found in Arkhia, the lobo land." Akari pointed at the flower. "But yes, she wanted to tell you before Dusra left. To bring you with us, but we were worried about the repercussions for the kingdoms."

"And when we were here?"

"She knew it was likely too late. But she was hopeful for the future."

Before I could stop it, I asked. "Do you think I was wrong for my anger?"

I wasn't sure I'd ever asked that question before. There was never a care given toward how people felt about *my* emotions.

"No." Akari shook her head. "Not at all. I was worried she'd slip back into a dark place. It was easier for me to be angry at you. I do apologize for that, the efforts in which you're fighting for her now, I see how wrong that was of me."

"And you haven't sensed. . . " I trailed off.

"She is alive. I have no doubt. It's not something I'd miss."

Her stare was powerful; it nearly sent shivers up my spine. Akari, much like me, did not beat around the bush. She didn't seem to have time for comforting words, and now I knew without a doubt I could believe her about Zuri being alive. I wondered what it would have been like for Zuri to be so in tune with her family—with her parents—that she would feel their death.

"You felt it when her parents died?"

"That's why we went out there in the first place," she answered solemnly.

"Oh." I swallowed before switching subjects. "Were you on your way somewhere?"

"I was looking for Ishani but couldn't find her."

"Yeah, I didn't know where she was either."

Axel's magic filled my mind. *"Get to the coast now. Interrogation Room Three."*

"Axel just said to get to the coast." I snapped open a portal, and Akari followed without me having to say another word. I'd rarely heard Axel's voice filled with so much demand, and it had me moving as quickly as possible to get to him.

The building was busy with bodies, and we cut through them to get to the interrogation room. The soldier we took from Sanjry was splayed out on the floor, blood leaking from his body and down into a drain. Paxx stood above him, a dagger in both hands, dark red splattered across his body. Axel was at his back, blood across his legs with a dark look in his eyes.

"Go get Athena from her cell," Axel commanded from someone I hadn't even noticed was in the room.

My gaze bounced around the room, the sheer amount of blood from one person daunting. "What happened?"

"They've been moving her like we thought. He said that they were in Kaizer's old home the day before we got there."

"So where is she now?" Akari asked.

"He said that Zuri told them you were in the desert and that they were dispatched to Caldera before we took him. They took her back to somewhere near the volcano."

Athena stepped into the room, her hands behind her back in cuffs, but still as clean as the last time I'd seen her. Her gaze roamed the room, falling on the man bleeding out on the floor. She didn't react, simply turned to me in expectation of why she was here.

"Do you know where they would be holding Zuri at the volcano?" Paxx asked.

"I might," she responded with her nose tilted high.

I twisted, grabbing her by the neck and pushing her onto the wall. My other hand found the dagger on my thigh, and I brought it up to her neck. Blood trickled down to her collarbone, and her eyes widened.

"Tell me now," I said through tight teeth.

"I'd like to be released from my cell." I pressed the knife deeper, blood now gushing, and she gasped. "Okay, okay. Just remember that I helped you."

I dropped her down to the floor, and she pressed her hand against her neck, the bleeding slowing down and vanishing after a few moments. "South side of the volcano. They take people there to sweat them out."

"Why didn't you tell us this from the start?" Paxx snapped.

"I didn't know that's where she was. You'd be surprised how many spots there are around Sanjry where they keep prisoners."

I knew it was misplaced, but the urge to tear her head from her shoulders almost overcame me. She should have told us every single place that she knew.

Axel pressed a kiss to my forehead before lifting my chin. "Handle it how you see fit."

Stupid fucking agreement. I still had Paxx and Ishani to help, though. Even if I did prefer Ax.

"How many would we need to take the site?" I asked Athena.

"Not many." She paused and tilted her head in anticipation.

"If this pans out, you can be released," I said, looking to Paxx, who nodded.

"I don't want to return to Sanjry," she replied.

The fucking nerve on this bitch.

"I literally can't deal with this right now." I snapped my fingers at the soldier who brought her in. "We'll talk when we get back. Take her to her cell."

Athena pulled away from the soldier and walked out of the room herself.

"Can you get a team together?" Paxx asked Akari.

"I'll have them ready in less than an hour." She turned and left without another word.

It was happening. It was actually happening. My heart was beating so hard that it hitched my breath. I didn't want to get ahead of myself, but deep down, I knew that this was it. We were going to save her. I was going to save her.

"Are you coming?" I asked Paxx.

Paxx tossed his bloodied blade to the side. "No, I need to stay here. I'll be ready when you get back."

"Know anything about the volcano?"

Kaizer had never said anything about it. Even during our lessons about Sanjry, it had never come up. I wondered if that was on purpose now.

"I have a map in my office. I'll get it to you." He lifted his hand to wipe some of the blood off his face.

"Thank you, Paxx. I can't thank you enough."

"Did you doubt me, Daya?" he said with a smirk.

I shook my head. "Weirdly enough, I didn't."

Chapter Twenty

Dayanara

Akari put together a team in under a half hour. She wasn't playing any games. One of the soldiers was moving too slowly, and she sent him back to the coast with the promise of pain. Damon, one of the vampires who went to the desert, was with us. Two other soldiers and Ishani joined us as we crossed the grass. We had no idea what state she would be in, so Paxx went to the infirmary to ensure they were ready for her. The rose quartz necklace hung around my neck, and I'd used the dye again to make my hair black, in case we were there longer than we expected. I also pulled it back into braids to be double sure I couldn't be identified.

I left a note for Axel, letting him know that I was going to rescue her—without specific location or details. As his magic filled my mind, I assumed he'd just read it, and he said, *"I'll be waiting for your return. Be safe."*

"I will."

I grabbed the map to remember where I'd portal us to, it was close, but not close enough. We'd most likely have to make a couple jumps across the land.

"Is everyone ready?" Ishani asked, a determination in her features.

"Our *only* priority is Zuri, do you understand? We are not going for anything else. We'll fight anyone we need to, but do not go looking for problems," I said firmly.

They nodded, and I took a deep, centering breath. Like the last time, this would drain me, but Ishani could portal if needed as well. This was it. I'd been ready for this day since she was taken, but suddenly, nerves festered in my gut. What if I wasn't fast enough? What if they saw us coming, and they killed her before we got there? Nerves were not something I was used to, but something about Zuri and Axel had that feeling surfacing. All around losing them. Ishani stepped into my eyeline, conveying through her gaze that she was there for me, and the racing thoughts ceased.

I opened the portal with my weapon ready, clearing the surrounding smoke. We'd decided on this location due, one, to the fact I knew it well enough to get us here, and two, that it was fairly deserted. Paxx had contacted a spy to confirm, and they were supposed to be heading toward where we thought Zuri was. He'd given me one of his communication stones, and I kept it in my pocket for now. Thankfully, nobody was around, and everyone already spread out to survey the area.

There was a certain. . . dead quality to the air that I didn't expect. Sanjry was always off-putting, but something felt even more off.

"Daya," Akari called over.

I met her at the edge of the field, and the smell was so pungent it burned my nostrils. Finally, I stepped up to where she was standing, cutting through tall grass to find everything around us saturated with blood. Flies buzzed around us, hopping from carcass to carcass of what may have been sheep at one point. It wasn't the sheep or the blood that had my body on high alert. It was the beast between them all.

A sword cut through its neck, not completely beheaded but pretty damn close. The man wielding the sword lay beneath him, the body of the monster weighing him down. He was dead as well, seeming to give his life to take the monster's. I pulled my dagger from my thigh holster, listening for anyone—or anything that might have been close.

"What is it?" Ishani asked as she crouched down beside the crime scene.

"A creature from the Inbetween," I mumbled as I poked at the thick scales running down the back of the beast. Just like the one I'd fought, it had no eyes, tentacle-like. . . things extended from the tip of its face. One of them moved, and I stabbed it quickly.

"How did it get out?" Akari asked.

"No idea." I toed the long dagger-like claws that appeared to be the vampire's cause of death. "But it doesn't mean anything good."

We weren't that far from the edge of the Inbetween, but they should not have been able to get through the barrier Naom created. It had withstood thousands of years, and its magic wavering now wasn't only concerning. It would be deadly for our world if it completely vanished.

"Let's move," Ishani said.

I could see the very tip of the volcano in the distance, but not well enough to guarantee I wouldn't portal directly into the mouth of the structure. Part of me wanted to take off into the sky and get her myself. It would probably be easier. I toyed with the buttons on the back of my leathers to let my wings free, and Ishani smacked my hand away.

"Don't even think about it." She leveled me with a look.

My jaw ticked, but I opened a portal instead to the furthest point I could see. We were in thick trees, stopping me from seeing any further, so we had to travel by foot at least until we were out of the forest. Akari and the soldiers took the lead, leaving me and Ishani to fall back slightly.

"Do you think this has something to do with what the Triori told you?" she asked.

"About the god of Chaos?" I questioned.

"Yes."

"It could. I think it might be the only thing that makes sense. These are his monsters."

"I would have appreciated none of this happening during my lifetime," she responded.

With no clear trail in the dense trees, we had to cut our way through. I ducked below a branch hanging low and held it to the side for Ishani to get through. "You and me both. We can't fight two enemies. At least not successfully."

"Let's focus on this task first." She bumped my shoulder. "Do you know what you'll say to her? Are you still upset?"

"I don't know. It's hard to be upset with someone who's being actively tortured. Regardless of the past."

"But not impossible," she said knowingly.

"No, not impossible. It does make me feel guilty though. I don't know. I just keep trying to put myself in her shoes. Would I have made the same decisions as her? Would I have thought that the lie was justified for my people?"

She held back a few thick vines. "Would you have?"

Yes.

"What did you see?" Akari asked.

I pulled my wings back as we hid in the tree line. We'd portaled over a couple of the ravines, but stopped in these trees for coverage. "I didn't see her, but there were a few worn down spots on the south side, like Athena said. I'd assume it was somewhere around there."

"Should we portal or go by foot?" Ishani asked.

"If we portal, it would need to be you. I'm not sure they would have left her out here without a detection spell for my magic."

"Let's go by foot," Akari said, tilting her head for her soldiers to follow her.

I could feel myself shifting into a violent head space, so close I swore I could hear Zuri's shallow breaths. Smell her warm floral scent. Ishani squeezed my arm before we powered the rest of the way, all of our heads on a constant swivel since we were much more in the open now. We'd been gone long enough that we should have been tired or hungry, but none of us made a sound as we got closer and closer to Zuri.

Akari raised her fist, and we all stopped. She lifted two fingers on her right hand and pointed across the field, then lifted one on her left hand and pointed in the other direction—two on the right, one on the left.

"I've got the left," Ishani said.

"I've got the right," I said.

Ishani disappeared into a portal, but I blasted the ground with a burst of air magic and sent myself into the sky. Not as high as I would have gone with my wings, but high enough that I had time to grab my sword from my back before I touched down to the ground.

"Surprise." I smiled.

The first soldier didn't have time to draw his weapon before I pushed mine through his belly. That gave the second one time to draw his, but I welcomed the fight.

Our blades slammed together, and just like I had done with Kaizer, I let him believe he was stronger than me for a second. The bastard smirked as if he had me, and I pushed with all my strength, sending him tumbling back. I feigned to the left, nicking him in his heel.

He groaned, and I chuckled as I took to the air again, twisting in a barrel roll as he swung his sword out in rage. I landed, pushing the sword through his heart and sliding it out as he died.

Ishani crawled up the rocky hill ahead, peaking over to see what was beyond. Her mouth dropped open, and her chest heaved, her bright magic burning in her hand. I didn't remember moving, but I found myself standing atop the hill, consequences be damned. Because I knew. I knew that whatever Ishani saw had to be bad, and it had to be Zuri.

My eyes fell on her battered body immediately. She lay between two tall trees, her wrists, and feet in chains. She wasn't moving and didn't even look to be breathing from this distance. So much of her skin was exposed, tatters of what remained of her clothing. And she was burned, not merely burned—incinerated. Her whole entire side where I'd felt that pain was covered in welts. Terror filled me to the brim, it spilled over the edges and numbed every single one of my senses.

Two guards faced away from us, but by the time they turned around, I was already holding their hearts in my hands.

PART TWO

"In the flush of love's light, we dare be brave. And suddenly we see that love costs all we are, and will ever be. Yet it is only love which sets us free."
— Maya Angelou

Chapter Twenty-One

Zuri

The wind blew from the volcano, sending hot gusts of air over my body and shifting my threadbare clothing. I groaned as I forced myself to my unmarred side, and the trail of burns screamed in agony. They hadn't healed, not even close. Otto had only added to them the last time he questioned me. Kaizer took the bait about the desert, like I knew he would. He'd said it made sense for her to go somewhere she'd told him she hated. Otto, however, said I needed to be reminded I was still a prisoner. He'd come back without Kaizer, extending the burns from my side, across my hip and to my inner thighs. I was sure that only the fact that a witch came back to portal him to the castle stopped what he wanted to do. The same one that had given me the healing potion before. She'd told him there was an emergency, and he left reluctantly. Not before she turned back to me with tears in her eyes.

I'd started to get used to not seeing clearly. With my condition, and the heat blaring from the volcano's vent, my eyes were dry as sand. To the point that blinking was painful and difficult. I tried not to think about it. I tried to let my mind drift to anything but all the alarms going off within my body.

A hallucination of Daya cresting the hill below me sparked, and it was so real that a single tear fell down my cheek and into the dirt beneath me. The one tear was all the moisture I had left. It wasn't the first time my mind tried to comfort me in my despair. I wondered if my father was truly with me before, or if it was all in my head. Daya's braids moved in the wind as she got closer. My guards for today groaned as their backs arched and they fell to the ground.

I closed my eyes just for a second, and when I opened them, she was directly in front of me. Gods, did I love this woman. Her gaze snapped between sad and pure anger as she fell to her knees. The hallucination was so real; I felt the dirt brush over my skin from the impact. Her hair was different. I wasn't sure why my mind conjured her up with black hair instead of purple.

"Zuri," Daya whispered.

I moaned at the sweet sound of her voice and closed my eyes again, wanting to remember that sound, let it play on repeat in my mind. The way she said my name like a claim, like each syllable was hers.

Something warm fell on my skin and I opened my eyes again to find Daya's hand resting on my cheek. Akari came up behind her and chopped my chains into pieces. This couldn't be real. This shouldn't be real. Otto or Kaizer could come back at any moment. But I couldn't help the relief coursing through my body.

"Daya, is this real?" I sobbed. "Daya, are you really here?"

"It's me, Zuri. It's real, it's real, it's real," she repeated as if she couldn't stop herself.

My heartbeat sped, and every thud hurt. Every breath I took felt like I was drowning in the volcano I was so close to. This couldn't have been true. It had to be my mind tricking me. I closed my eyes, squeezing them as much as I could just as my body was lifted off the ground, and I screamed at the pain. I looked up to find myself in Daya's arms as she cradled me against her chest as carefully as she could.

"It's real, Zuri. I'm here. You're safe," she whispered as her eyes got wide and I realized Ishani was there too.

"She needs blood, Daya. She needs blood now, s-she is so close to—" Akari stuttered.

Daya shifted my weight and slashed her wrist, bringing it to my mouth as I shook my head. "No, Daya. I don't need it. It's okay."

"Fucking drink, Zuri!" she yelled as she pressed her wrist firmly against my mouth and my fangs elongated to their full wolf length the moment her blood hit my tongue. I sank them into her. I drank deep and felt the air shift as bright smoke surrounded us and the heat of the volcano was replaced by the smell of the sea. I closed my eyes as I kept drinking, hoping I wasn't taking too much, but not able to stop myself.

"Paxx!" Daya yelled as she ran over to him, the movement jerking me around, but I kept my hold on her wrist.

"Fucking help me! Someone fucking help!" she yelled again.

The electric sensation of Daya's magic flared over my body and I watched it spark in her hands as strong arms tried to pull me from her.

"No, I'm not letting anyone take her," Daya growled.

Paxx made some sort of sound I couldn't quite place, but his arms pulled back. He directed us to follow him and Daya squeezed me too hard, so hard that my already pain-riddled body screamed, but I didn't think she even realized it.

"Healers!" Paxx yelled.

I heard the shuffle of bodies as Daya sat on a bed and positioned me between her legs, leaning my back on her chest.

"Ma'am, let us take care of her," a woman reasoned.

"Do your job!" Daya screamed.

I peered up at the healer, who subtly glanced at Paxx and he shook his head. Daya pushed my matted hair away from my face and I rolled my head onto her shoulder.

I needed her to know that I didn't betray her, that I didn't utter a word of her for the entire time I was there. "I didn't tell them anything. I didn't tell them anything. I didn't betray you. I promise, Daya. I promise."

The healer laid her hands on me, whatever she did, making me more conscious of some of the pain that was just surface level before. I shrieked, I shrieked so loudly my throat felt like it was closing up as my eyes rolled back and everything went black. The last thing I heard was Daya whispering, "I know, Zuri. I know."

My eyes flitted open, and the brightness in the room had me squeezing shut. I slowly opened them, and the room came into focus. Axel was sitting beside me with a book in his lap, and I groaned as I tried to sit up.

"Stay still," Axel said as he put one of his hands on my stomach. His healing magic lapped over my skin and sank down to my bones, and the pain subsided. My eyes darted around, searching for Daya, and Axel chuckled. "I just convinced her to go and take a shower. The healers kept you sleeping for nearly a week. The damage was. . . " He gulped and averted his eyes, shadows running over his gaze as his jaw ticked.

I was sure I looked similar to how he had when he returned from Sanjry. I wasn't even born then, but I'd heard the stories, the recollections of how fucked up he had been.

"Well," I started and sat up fully. "I'm feeling worlds better."

His eyes softened, and he sat back. "Obviously, we'll need to talk about what happened. Whenever you're ready, let Paxx know. He's been as diligent in finding you as Daya."

I let that sink in. Daya had probably figured out that me and Paxx had a past, and I wasn't particularly looking forward to learning how that went. The fact I was back in Dusra and Daya was okay was enough for me right now. Axel sat back and picked up his book, and I wondered why he was the one waiting with me. We didn't get along, and I was sure he'd never want to see me taken and tortured, but I would have expected Ishani or Akari to be the ones waiting at my bedside.

"You don't have to wait," I said.

Axel didn't lift his gaze from his book. "I promised Daya I'd wait until she got back."

The air was tight between us, the knowledge that we both wanted her in the same exact way. Axel peered up at me from under his brow as he seemed to be thinking the same thing.

I cleared my throat. "So. . . how are things with—"

"Zuri!" Daya's voice boomed from the entrance as the door slammed behind her and purple smoke filled the bed as she portaled directly to my side.

"You're awake," she said with both her hands on my cheeks. She scanned my face up and down, lifting my garments as if Axel wasn't right beside me and checking every inch of my body. "They couldn't stop some of the scarring, but most of the cuts and bruises are healed. Everything looks good."

Axel cleared his throat and stood, rubbing Daya's lower back. "Let me give you guys some time. I'll check on you a little later."

Daya smiled up at him the way she'd smiled at me countless times, and I couldn't watch it. I listened to Axel's steps retreating and Daya gripped my hand. We just stared at each other. So many things to say passing between us, but none of them seemed to be the right thing to say at the moment. I'd hurt Daya. I'd lied to her and betrayed her when everyone else in her life was doing the same. She said she'd forgiven me, but she certainly wasn't over it the last time I saw her.

"I didn't tell them anything. Daya, I really am sorr—"

"I saw it all," Daya said before looking away from me. "I saw the burns, the cuts, the bruises. I stayed while they healed them, while they inspected you. You needed four healers, four *gifted* healers, to get you where you are. Every day for four days in a row. They kept you asleep for an extra two to give your body a rest." Her sad gaze turned angry as she looked me in the eye. "I don't want to hear the words 'I'm sorry' come out of your mouth. Do you understand?"

I shook my head, opening my mouth to protest, but Daya gently gripped me by my chin. "Not. A. Fucking. Word. The things you endured. I saw the burns running up your thighs. I know what they were so close to doing."

"I did it all for you," I said as tears streamed down my face. Daya scooted me over in the bed in one swift movement and leaned her head against mine.

"We have things to figure out, that's for sure. But we'll do it, we'll talk through it all," she said.

I leaned against her, partially wondering if this was all some sort of sick dream still. I survived what I did for her, not knowing if I'd ever really have her again. If she'd ever even consider taking me back. The piercing pain I experienced was gone, but dull aches emitted from my side and my hip. Without having to say anything, Daya shifted her hand to the exact spot that hurt and healed me, leaving only phantom pain.

I wanted to cry. I wanted to scream. I wanted to kill something—anything. My body knew I was safe now, but my mind felt like it was still back on that volcano. I rubbed my fingers together, needing to touch something to get my mind to understand we were okay. Daya wrapped her fingers around mine, and she squeezed. She didn't squeeze once, but every couple of seconds. I didn't know how she knew I needed that constant reminder. But she did.

When I wasn't with Otto or Kaizer, the only thing to keep me company before was my heartbeat. Sometimes the fluttering of a bird's wings, the rustling of a guard's boots in grass. The noises were overwhelming. People walking, healers shouting, soldiers coming in and out and slamming the door. I tried to focus on my heart beat to ground myself. But it wasn't just my heartbeat I heard, it was mine and Daya's thudding in sync. Everything around me slowly faded as I concentrated on the rhythm of our heartbeats and her squeezing my hand. I nuzzled into her, allowing her scent to be the third thing to calm me. I'd never lose her again. I didn't care what I had to do.

Chapter Twenty-Two

Dayanara

I watched as Zuri slept. Her face relaxed and no longer covered in blood, dirt, and open wounds. I'd been through some atrocities, some truly terrible things, but I'd never experienced the pure terror I felt when I saw Zuri laid out on the dirt. She was so still and leaking blood from so many places that I thought she was dead initially. I closed my eyes and saw it all over again. Heard how slow her heartbeat was, how fast it picked up before she'd passed out from the pain. It was debilitating, my mind winding back to that place over and over again.

The things she went through because of me when I saw those burns so close to. . . the healers said there was no sign of that sort of assault, but it was evident that's where it was going. I knew she was telling the truth when she said she didn't give them anything. They'd turned to some creative vices of torture, the only reason they'd do that was to get her to talk. I knew it. I'd done it myself. Zuri's burns were so bad that they'd scar. She'd forever be marked and reminded of what Kaizer had done to her.

But I'd done it. I saved her. After weeks of restlessness and guilt, we got her. That guilt didn't go away. It still slammed into me like a tidal wave. But the constant barreling, the feeling of drowning, and the frantic scrambling to survive ceased. I hadn't been on the other side of this before—the one caring for the tortured. When I was young, Ximena would take care of me. She'd remind me that I was alive, pull me back into myself. So, I tried to do the same for Zuri. I sensed her spiraling every so often. I'd hear her breathing quip, and her eyes start scanning for a threat that wasn't there. The need to protect her was overwhelming. Every person who looked at her too long or lingered near her bed was at risk of death. I knew that it was wrong, that these people were meant to help, but it was an instinct I couldn't suppress. I supposed that went back to the guilt I felt. For being the reason she was there. I squeezed her arm harder than I meant to, and she woke up.

"What's wrong?" Zuri asked sleepily.

She rolled over to face me, and I shifted in her direction. "You're going to need to tell me what happened. I need to know who did what and how I should pay them back for every mark they left on you."

"I'll tell you all everything, but I'd rather do it with everyone so I don't have to say it more than once," she replied as she closed her eyes.

I couldn't tell if it was hesitation or pain coming from her. We needed the information, but I could give her another day or two if necessary.

"We can wait if we need to," I said.

She shook her head. "I want it all behind me, and I want us to start our plan against them."

I nodded and closed my eyes to find my connection with Axel. His magic sparked, and I said, *"Zuri is ready to talk. Get everyone into the council room."*

His response was quick and simple, *"On it."*

"I can portal us to the council room," I said as I helped her out of bed.

She was finally back in her own clothes. She'd been in the gowns from the healers for so long that her appearing this normal was a relief.

Zuri stood straight and shook her head. "No, I need to start moving again. We can walk."

I wanted to fight her on it, but she was right. Her movements were choppy and stiff—she really did need to get reacquainted with her body. We were moving slowly. The stronghold on the coast reminded me a lot of Caldera, just one long level. The infirmary was on the south side, and the council room was on the north, so we had quite a bit to walk. I held her hand tight, and Zuri looked at me with a small smile.

"You don't have to hold on that tight. I'm not going anywhere," she chuckled.

It was sort of incredible that she was able to laugh. There was a strength in that I wasn't sure I had. Resiliency was one thing, but smiling in the face of what she'd gone through was. . . something else.

"Sorry," I said quickly, loosening my grip on her.

She would have to do some work to get back into shape. The healers did their best on her, but she wouldn't be on any battlefields for a few weeks. The healers said letting her drink from me may have saved her life, but I didn't give any thought to it at all. It's like my body knew what she needed and helped her without me even having to give the command. We made it to the council room, and I could hear all the heartbeats of everyone waiting for us inside already.

I turned and grabbed Zuri by both of her hands. "If it gets to be too much, you can tell me. We don't have to do this all at once."

"I'll tell you, but I'm fine, I promise."

Zuri let go of my hand and pushed into the door. I had a feeling she wanted to walk in on her own strength and had to restrain myself from trying to help. Ishani, Axel, Paxx, Xavier, Akari, and Nia, the leader of the lobos, all sat at the long table. Everyone wore the same devastation on their faces as they watched her shuffle into the room.

"She's *moving well on her own,*" Axel spoke into my mind with his gaze on Zuri. I nodded once in recognition and sat beside her.

"Tell us what you can," Paxx said.

Zuri looked down, shame written on her features, and I reached under the table to hold her hand. I squeezed it, hoping she knew I was telling her it was okay, that this wasn't her fault.

Zuri took a deep breath. "Um, I'm not really sure where to start. They wanted to know where Daya was. That was what they asked me during each. . . session. They moved me a lot. They knew Daya would be searching for me. I spent a few hours at the volcano almost daily this week. They were trying to sweat me out. I was pretty close to the edge where Daya found me. Otto seemed to be the ring leader of the torture, but Kaizer was there and participating. Kaizer wants you because he loves you, but there's something else driving him. He never quite explained. I didn't give them anything, didn't say a word, and it pissed them off. They took me to Kaizer's old home a couple of days ago, and I told him you were in the desert to buy time. They burned me, cut me, beat me, starved me for blood and food. They nearly..." Zuri paused and looked over at me. "All of it doesn't matter now. I just know he wants you."

Every word was like a dart directly in my chest. I felt my skin flicker, my Acna power trying to stop the threat. I bit my lip so hard that blood spilled, and my leg was bouncing under the table so hard the surface shook. The last thing I wanted was for Zuri to comfort me. For *her* to tell me that it was all okay. It wasn't okay. What she'd gone through was not okay. Only the thought of Kaizer's and Otto's heads on a pike calmed me. There was something I could do about it now. I wasn't helpless. I'd repay them for all of it.

Everyone else was completely silent. Ishani had tears running down her face, and Akari was about a second away from breaking her teeth due to how tight she was clenching her jaw. Axel was a little hard to read. He stared at her, unblinking. Paxx, for once, wore his emotions on his face and looked like he was ready to jump across the table and hug her. If anger and grief were tangible, this room would have been thick with it.

"You don't know why they want me?" I asked.

Zuri shook her head. "They said something about balancing the elements, about needing your power, but they didn't seem to know how strong your powers were. Kaizer fought you, but you didn't really use your Acna power in the fight. He only saw the wings."

"We went to the Triori," I started, and Zuri's head whipped over to Ishani.

"Did you make a deal for me?" she asked with panic-stricken features.

I answered quickly, "No. But they did tell us what Kaizer is looking for. Some scepter that he'd be able to use to manipulate all four elements."

"He'd need to go across the wall," she said.

"Exactly," Axel responded before me.

Everyone sat for a moment, still digesting and figuring out where to go from there. We hadn't focused much on what we'd do next until we knew we'd get Zuri.

"Did they figure out you were a lobo?" Nia asked.

"No, you know how hard it is to detect. They didn't have any idea."

"Any knowledge about their plan of attack?" Xavier questioned.

"They don't know Daya is here or that I'm Dusran, so I don't think they plan on attacking yet. Not for her, anyway."

"They're bound to figure it out at some point. There's only so many places to go," Axel reasoned. "And last we heard, they are still scouring for that scepter. We don't know anything about it."

"We have Athena as well," I said.

Zuri's eyebrows shot up. A piece of information I had forgotten about since we'd rescued her. I hadn't even been to see where Athena was because my focus had been on ensuring Zuri would be okay.

"We. . . ran into her a little while ago. Figured she might have some information." I shrugged.

Zuri smirked and nodded, the familiar tilt of her lips nearly making my heart skip a beat. Something she'd done a thousand times when we were in Sanjry, especially when I was up to something.

"She's in the dungeon here on the coast. Feel free to pay her a visit. She's been quite mouthy, I'm told," Xavier groaned.

"Anything else you can think of that might be helpful, Zuri?" Paxx asked.

"They were pretty focused on the torture aspects of my stay with them. Always the same questions about Daya's whereabouts. Kaizer is. . . .more bedraggled than he was before. When he took me to his family home, it seemed important to him."

"Yeah, I have some information about that," I said before explaining what Athena had told us. About who Kaizer was before he became king and how he found himself on the throne. "There was a painting there of his family. His mother was the only unmarred one. I wonder what happened there."

"Fuck, I was so busy being annoyed with Athena I didn't think to look any further into her when I was in Sanjry," Zuri replied.

"I'm sure it was part of the cover," I responded. "Anything else?"

"No. Nothing else that would be of use," she said.

Everyone watched her again like she'd disappear if we took our eyes off her.

"I'm close to going over to Sanjry myself; none of my people have any helpful information." Paxx stood from his chair. He stopped at the end of the table and put his hand on Zuri's shoulder. They glanced at each other, and Zuri gave him a tight smile before he left the room quickly.

"Thank you, everyone, for working to find me," Zuri said as she trailed her gaze down the room. Ishani got up and came around the table, gently wrapping her arms around Zuri and kissing her head.

"I'm so sorry, Zuri," she sighed.

Zuri smiled as each person got up and left the room, leaving me, Ax, and her at the table.

Ax knocked his knuckles against the hard wood surface. "I have a particular. . . understanding of what you went through. I know that saying sorry doesn't help, so I won't say that. I will tell you that we'll repay them for what they did. I'll also remind you that it's over, and when those nightmares come back to haunt you, remember that you made it, and you're still here."

He didn't allow her to respond, just floated out of the room with a single brush of his hand on my cheek.

"You okay?" I asked Zuri.

"Yeah." She sat back in her chair. "I didn't have to get into the specifics, so that helped. I won't be able to hide some of it. When Ishani and Akari see the true extent..." She shook her head. "I haven't even seen it all yet."

"I can be there when you do," I said.

Zuri stood from her chair and plopped down into my lap. "Not yet. But when I do, I'd like that."

I brought my forehead to hers, relishing in the feel of her warm skin against mine. I'd already seen it all, and I was selfishly thankful for that because it was hard to see, especially fresh. I wouldn't have been able to hide my facial reaction.

"You've got one more day left in the infirmary, right?" I asked and offered her my hand.

She nodded as her slim fingers grasped mine. "Then I'm back to the palace. Hopefully, I can get back into training by next week."

"I'm sure Akari already has a whole entire training schedule for you to get back on track," I laughed.

I opened the door, and she slipped her arm into mine. She was using me for more support than she had on our way here, and it didn't go unnoticed. A door opened a few feet ahead of us from one of the underground halls, and a Dusran held a torch lit with fire. Zuri jumped back from the flames, and I sent a burst of air for the torch to extinguish them.

"Hey!" the Dusran shouted.

"Get fucking lost," I snapped at them as my nails extended, and they quickly turned away to run down the hall.

Zuri was shaking behind me, her hands grasping her side—the place where the burns were most prominent. I grabbed her and opened a portal to the beach just outside the walls. Our feet hit the sand, and Zuri fell to the ground, her fingers reaching for the abundance of water. I moved us closer, sitting on the wet sand as the water lapped over our still-clothed bodies. She stared at the sea, unmoving. The only indication she was awake was a slow blink every few moments. After a while, the slow blinks came with small beads of moisture. We sat there as each tear fell into the water, disappearing and becoming one with the tide. We didn't speak. I didn't try to pry or offer her any kind of comfort outside of my presence. I knew better than most that sometimes the scars on the soul were far worse than the ones on the body.

Chapter Twenty-Three

Dayanara

I walked behind Zuri as she slowly moved into her room. The healers had cleared her today to move out of the infirmary. She was moving a little better than before, but not well enough for me not to worry. We had so many things to talk about, so many things to go over, and I wasn't sure when she'd be up to the discussion. I was partly worried that once we started, I'd get pissed at her all over again, but it wasn't going to be avoidable for long.

I pulled down her blankets and freshened up her bed, fluffing up her pillows and situating them the same way they were in the infirmary.

"I'm not going to sleep," Zuri said as she moved into her closet.

"You said you were tired," I responded with my hand on my hip.

"I did. I don't want to sleep anymore. I need to keep moving."

I followed her into the closet. "Zuri, if you need rest, rest."

"I'm not dying, Daya. Well, not anymore." She laughed.

"That's not funny," I said as I took the folded clothes out of her hand and placed them on a top shelf.

Zuri shrugged. "Ugh, lighten up. It's not like you haven't had a near-death experience before. Morbid jokes come with the territory."

"Zuri, talk about your death one more time, and I will lose my shit," I growled.

She rolled her eyes and chuckled as she walked out of the closet and sat down in one of the chairs. I straightened up her closet. I was in such a rush the last time I came in here. I had been just trying to grab anything I could while she was in the infirmary and left quite a mess.

"Daya!" Zuri shouted. "Can you please come out here and stop fussing?"

"I'm just trying to help," I offered as I sat in the chair across from her.

"I've never seen you clean this much," she joked.

"Me either," I laughed. "Are you hungry? Thirsty?"

"Let's go for a walk," Zuri said as she stood.

I bit the inside of my cheek, wondering if that was a good idea, but Zuri peered over her shoulder at me and batted her lashes. Goddess, I forgot how beautiful she was.

"Fuck," I grumbled. "Fine."

Zuri smiled smugly, and I tucked her arm into mine, even though she didn't ask for support. We walked down the hall, and everyone we passed smiled gently at Zuri, like they'd heard about what had happened.

"I'm tired of people looking at me like that," Zuri sighed.

"This is your first day back. You'll probably receive a lot of those looks," I replied.

Zuri leaned into me a little more, and the soft orange glow of the sky filled the end of the hallway. We pushed the doors open to go into one of the courtyards. Thankfully, it was pretty much empty. If anyone so much as made Zuri flinch, I might have killed them, and that wouldn't have been a very good look for me. I led us down one of the paths filled with flowers and plants, and we watched as they bent in the breeze, snapping back upright when the wind stopped.

"I know you have a lot you want to talk about," Zuri said as she glanced over at me briefly. "You don't have to wait until I'm all the way better. Just ask."

"I don't know, Zuri. I don't want to add to your problems right now."

It was the right thing to say. I *absolutely* wanted to add to her problems. I wanted answers to everything—immediately.

Zuri pursed her lips and tilted her head. "Daya."

Ah, she knows me well.

"Fine. Yes. I have a lot I want to talk about."

"I'd rather us get it out of the way now. I had a lot of time to think while. . . well, you know."

"I don't even know where to start. When did you take me off the suspect list?" I questioned.

That was the question that kept bouncing around my mind. At what point did her mission shift, and when did it become a real genuine connection?

"I could tell that you didn't want to be there the moment I met you. But when you opened up to me about your concerns, I knew you couldn't have been in on it with Kaizer."

That was pretty early on.

"What did you tell them about me?"

Zuri tucked her hair behind her ear. "Nothing specific about you. Only the things that had a potential threat to Dusra. The joining armies, the concern around the old magic, things like that."

"When Axel came to visit, is that why you were missing that morning?" I asked.

"Yes. I stayed up late with Paxx, planning the next moves."

My jaw ticked, and I shuffled a step, causing Zuri to stop and turn toward me. "Nothing happened. We had to figure out where to go with you combining kingdoms."

That checked out too.

"When you pushed me to find Axel, what was the game plan?"

"No nefarious plan. I wanted you to be happy because you were miserable. Talking about him was the few times you lit up. As much as it pained me, I thought it was what you needed."

We kept walking, watching as the clouds rolled through the sky, and we sat on a bench on the outskirts of the courtyard, facing the shoreline far out in the distance.

"Were you really going to tell me who you were?" I asked.

Zuri grabbed my hand and put it in her lap. "I swear on everything I love, I was going to tell you. I just didn't. . . " She paused, biting her lip. "I didn't want to lose you. I know that's selfish. But once you found out who I was and what I was doing there. . . the thought of you not wanting to continue whatever it was we were doing? That hurt too much. The entire trip to Dusra, I was trying to come up with the words, but then I was worried that if you knew, you wouldn't go to Axel. You didn't have any other options for safety, I didn't want to take that from you. When I went to Sanjry, Dusra was all I had. I was so lost, I found purpose in trying to ensure my kingdom was protected. Every day was a battle over what I should do, whether to follow my heart or follow my training. It paralyzed me sometimes, the constant worry of who I'd hurt at the end of it. I'm sorry, Daya. I wish I would have told you the moment I knew who you were, the moment you saw me for everything I was."

I digested her words. If we could turn back time—if I knew who she was, how would I have reacted? Would I have been angry with her for lying still? I'd kept things from her over our friendship too, was that any different? My suspicions of Kaizer, my initial meeting with Axel, those things I had told her eventually, but not initially. What was the worst part of Zuri's betrayal? What was it that had me wanting to rip her throat out when I found out?

"Everybody has lied to me, Zuri. Almost everyone of significance in my life, at one time or another, lied. Not small omissions, but big, life-changing betrayals. I never expected it from you, from the one who took me as I was and didn't try to change me. From the one who I told my deepest darkest secrets, and you didn't look at me with judgment after. Exposing myself to the level I did and being burned for it. . . that was painful."

I regretted my choice of words as Zuri's hand shifted to her marred thigh, but she held my gaze. "I know, Daya. I know. I can't redo things. I can't take back the decisions that I made. I can show you every day that I would never do it again. I never lied with malice in my heart, never with the intention to hurt you. It will *never* happen again."

"I believe you. If you weren't trustworthy, you would have given Kaizer information. You held true for over a month. I'm not worried about you lying again."

Zuri smiled and leaned her head on my shoulder. It felt good to get everything off my chest, to get complete closure. At first when we'd discussed it I forgave her, but couldn't find it within me to trust her. I trusted her now.

"Can I ask some questions?" Zuri asked.

"Go for it."

I knew what the questions would surround—who they would surround. If we were here, might as well keep the intense conversation going.

"Axel," she said.

"Yeah, that's where I figured this was going. . ."

"What's the deal with him? With you? With us?"

I put my arm over her shoulder and held her closer. "The deal is. . . I want you both. I know that's hard to hear at first, but I do. I need you both. The more serious aspects of Axel's and my relationship are obviously newer than ours. But I feel in my gut that you're both meant for me."

"Why does it have to be *him,*" Zuri sighed.

I chuckled. "For the same reason it has to be you, it just does." I paused. "Wait, you don't have a problem with the fact I want someone else, only that it's him?"

I'd thought that the idea of sharing me would have been the bigger deterrent, but I could work with that.

"I'm a lobo. We're pack animals. My dad had more wives than my mother. They didn't make it to the. . . end. But I was surrounded by love. I don't see a problem with it. I don't see how it would work with him and me, though."

"Didn't you say you had a brother?"

I remembered it being one of the few things she had said about her childhood.

"I did. He died when I was young. Zuberi was his name. He was from my dad's other wife. My dad's third wife didn't have any children before she died."

I nodded and looked back out in the distance. Zuri sat up, gazing at me with intent. I didn't really acknowledge what she said about Ax. Hearing that she had more family took over my mind a bit, but I knew she wanted more answers.

"He's not a bad person, Zuri. I don't understand why you don't like each other."

"He's so arrogant, cocky, he always thinks he's right. And he *knows* he's attractive and powerful. He's used that to his advantage for as long as I've known him."

"Well. . . that sounds like me. . ." I trailed off.

"Shit." Zuri laughed. "I haven't connected those dots yet."

I shrugged. "I'll say that he doesn't seem like that person anymore. Well, to a certain extent."

He was still sure of himself, of course, but this pompous arrogant version of him wasn't who he was.

"You haven't had to hear people gush about him for centuries. *Axel is so handsome. Axel is so good in bed. Axel is sent from the goddesses, blah blah blah.*"

"I don't know what the answer is yet," I sighed. "But I know that I want to figure it out with the both of you. Will you at least try?"

It wasn't like I had a blueprint here. I had absolutely no knowledge of how a relationship of three people would work. We barely did them with two people in Caldera, but I knew. I knew that we were all connected.

"Try what, Daya?"

"Just to get along, spend time with each other, I don't know, not growl and snarl every time you have a conversation."

"We have years of this. It won't be easy."

"But?. . . " I raised my eyebrows.

"I'll try."

I squeezed her close to me—the most positivity she'd used toward the situation.

"Hey, I said I'll try. Don't get your hopes up," Zuri said with her cheek squished against my chest.

All the possibilities of what this meant for me, for all of us, were swirling in my mind. There were still some bigger things to figure out, but it was a step in the right direction. Not to mention that we still had to deal with Kaizer and whatever he had planned for Malva, and all of Iteria. My love life wasn't exactly the *most* important thing at the moment. But just having them both close, and somewhat willing, made me abundantly happy.

"How are you feeling? Physically?" I asked.

"Better. I'm going to start conditioning with Akari tomorrow. It's going to take a minute until I can help any, but I'm starting the journey at the very least."

"Maybe put in a good word for me with Akari," I laughed. "She is still a little skeptical."

"You really came in here and shook things up, didn't you?"

"Wasn't my intention." I threw my hands up. "Just taking what life is giving me."

"Well, I'm thankful life gave me you," Zuri whispered.

I picked her hand up and kissed it. "Me too."

And it was the goddess-blessed truth.

Zuri had been standing in front of her window for longer than expected. I'd been keeping the fire low, just enough to give her room some warmth. It being too cold in here wasn't ideal for her healing. A screen covered most of the glow, but I wondered if she was staying over by the window to avoid seeing the flame. I leaned back in the chair far enough to see her reflection without alerting her. Her hand was pressed against her side, her eyes on the moon. The glow caught in a tear sliding down her face. I slowly joined her at the window, sliding my hand under hers and the other around her body. The healers said her bandage could be removed before she took a bath today. With the skin no longer being raw, it needed to breathe.

"You haven't looked yet?" I whispered into her hair.

Zuri's only response was a small shake of her head. I realized then that she was trying to hide her crying. Her chest heaved as she let the dam free, and all her emotions flowed out like a river. I held her as her knees buckled, trying to control my own emotions and watching her fall apart.

"I don't want to see it," Zuri said as her cheeks dried. "I don't want to see it."

I turned her to face me. "I told you I would repay them for it all. I'm here. We can do it together."

"I don't want you to see me as—"

"Do you see me any differently due to my scars?" I pulled my shirt off my shoulder.

"That's not the same. You're strong, you became something through your pain. I'm still. . . " Zuri whirled and looked back out the window.

I moved in front of her and took both of her hands into mine. Placing a kiss on her forehead and then on the tip of her nose, I guided us over to the mirror and stood behind her. Zuri sniffled and wiped her tears as she made eye contact with me. I watched as the soft edges of her eyes hardened in determination. I offered all the strength I could, hoping she could feel it through my hand on her back.

She slowly lifted the hem of her shirt and untucked it, her throat bobbing but movements staying steady. Every snap from her buttons boomed in the quiet of the room. When she reached her collar, I took a deep breath. I'd watched the healers replace her gauze dressings. Each time was like the very first time, but I needed to be strong for her. Zuri shrugged off the shirt, but her gaze dropped with it. Her fingers fumbled for the ties on her pants, and I quickly fell to my knees and took over for her.

She didn't look at me or the mirror, but out the window once again. Zuri assisted me with her pants, shimmying her hips until they fell into a pile with her shirt. The gauze was held down with medical tape, and I carefully peeled each edge.

"Zuri," I whispered, but she kept her stare toward the moon.

The skin was sheen, still some fleshy pink spots between the lighter brown marks. It stood out against her smooth sepia skin. There was no doubt about that. I ran my finger over her hip bone, testing to see if it was painful to the touch. When she didn't flinch, I pressed my lips to the flesh on her inner thigh—the lowest point of her scars. I felt her tighten, but I kept going, traveling up to her hip, then her waist, and leaving kisses behind. Zuri finally turned her gaze to the mirror, and her mouth fell open into a gasp. Once I made sure every inch of the burns was covered in my love, I stood behind her and settled my head into the crook of her neck.

"What are you thinking?" I asked.

"It's bad."

"It is."

Zuri blinked slowly, and she ran her hand along the welts. "Why did you kiss them?"

"Why wouldn't I? There's nothing that would stop me from kissing every inch of you."

I lifted my gaze, finding Zuri staring at me now. Her lip wobbled, and I got ready to console her, but instead of a sorrowful cry, she spun toward me and wrapped her arms around my neck. She cried, but not in the same way she had done before. These tears held her relief.

"Hey," I said as I embraced her back. "I really hope you didn't think I'd have any other reaction."

"I don't know what I expected. I just prepared for the worst." She smiled weakly.

We stared at each other, and I thought of all the moments that I wanted this. To hold her, keep her safe in my arms. Zuri looked to be recollecting, too, but I didn't want her to think too much about her time in Sanjry. I tipped her chin up and kissed her, her body relaxed in my arms, and I walked us back toward the bed. Everything in the room went blurry, the only thing I wanted to focus on was her. My beacon of light, my Zuri.

The band holding her hair popped, and her curls spread out as her back hit the comforter. Silver still lined her eyes, and I crawled over her body to wipe the tears with my thumb.

"I've got you," I whispered.

She smiled. "I know."

Zuri ran the tips of her fingers up my arms before she wrapped her hands around my neck and pulled me closer. The softness of her lips always took me by surprise, such a confliction to the passion she kissed me with. I pulled the strap of her camisole down with my teeth and kissed across her shoulder and down to her chest.

"This is perfect." I kissed her breast. "This is perfect." I kissed the contour of her waist. "And this is perfect." I kissed the top of her scar beneath her other breast. "I'll kiss your scars every day if you need me to."

Just being able to have my hands on her again, to feel her skin beneath mine, was enough to make me *feel*. I ran my fingers all the way down her sides and to her hips, sitting back to hold her leg. Her soft thighs against my cheek sent sparks down my entire body. I kissed her pussy through her underwear before climbing back up and cuddling her.

"Is that perfect, too?" she asked.

"Yes, but you already knew that."

Zuri grabbed my hand and placed it back between her thighs. It took me by surprise. I only meant to comfort her, and wouldn't have expected this. She was moving better and healing, but the time we'd spent like this thus far had been more about existing in each other's presence, nothing beyond.

Zuri's eyes pleaded, her lips barely moving as she breathed out, "Please."

It wasn't just a plea for sex, it was a plea for intimacy. To feel like herself again. For that out-of-body sensation that turned your mind off completely. If this was what she needed, I'd give it to her without question.

With most of her clothes off already, it was easy to slip her out of her underwear. I turned her away from me so her back was lined up with my chest, trying to keep as much contact with her as possible. My hands shook, and I wasn't sure if it was nerves or anticipation, but Zuri leaned her body closer to me, and they steadied. I ran my fingers down her scars again, into the dip of her waist and across her hips. Sliding my hand back down her thigh, I pulled her knee back to give me the access I needed. I made sure her entire body was lit with the electricity left behind from our contact. My touch was feather light as I made it to her core, caressing her lips.

I kissed the column of her neck as I slid through her wetness and teased her entrance with one finger. The breath that left Zuri was the most relief I'd heard from her since I brought her back. Another finger had that same sound escaping her, with the softest moan accompanying it. I took one more glance at her, making sure she was okay, and the clamp she had on her lip reassured me.

I pulled my fingers from her, letting Zuri see how wet she was before I sucked it off my fingers. "Just like I said, this pussy is perfect," I whispered into her ear.

Zuri's back arched and I brought my hand back down to rub her clit, feeling her full body reaction to every swirl. My body reacted as well, my panties soaked and pussy throbbing. Bringing her pleasure was just as good as getting my own. Her body writhed, hips undulating as I dipped my fingers back inside her. I leaned up a bit so I could watch her take control. She moved, and I matched her speed, feeling it build like a crescendo until she burst. A single tear trailed down her cheek as her mouth fell open and she caught her breath. The pure satisfaction—of delight and contentment—on her face, fuck, it had my heart clenching.

Zuri turned her head, pressing her lips to mine softly before whispering, "Thank you."

As her eyes closed and her breathing evened out, I swore that I'd do everything to keep her in this state.

Chapter Twenty-Four

Dayanara

For once, I actually did want to talk to my mother. The fact that I could fight against her the last time definitely helped. I decided that, just in case, this time, I would do it outside of the palace. One, not to alarm the entire palace, and two, not to almost kill Ax again. Also it was nighttime, no people were out and about in the courtyard. I made a small sleeping potion, enough to get me to fall into deep sleep but wake up within twenty minutes. I tossed back the potion. It wouldn't take long for the effects to hit me, so I lay down in the grass and closed my eyes. I felt myself drifting, and instead of fighting it like I had before, I let it take me.

My eyes flicked open, and I immediately jumped up into a defensive stance. It was completely dark, and my mother wasn't anywhere to be seen.

"Mother!"

No response.

My magic flashed over my skin. "Lupe Amapola!"

A flicker in the distance.

"Lupe Amapola, I summon you!"

A cloud of green, paler than before, expanded before me, and my mother stood with her arms folded and her chin high.

"Don't feel like torturing me today?" I sneered.

She looked away from me and tapped her finger against her arm. I knew it for what it was.

I barked a laugh. "You're scared, aren't you?" I took a step closer. "What I did the last time. You weren't expecting that, were you?"

She didn't stumble a step or flinch, but her fear was potent in the air. "Why did you summon me?"

"So I can do that, summon you? Is it only you that I can summon?"

Her eyes went wide for the slightest moment, I would have missed it had I blinked. I didn't have a lot of time until the potion woke me up, but I stored that reaction in the back of my mind.

"Did you give Kaizer the spell for magic suppressant? Our grimoire?"

She tsked. "No. The man couldn't have performed it even if he wanted to. He was arrogant enough to think he could, so I gave him the location of the seraphinite. Plus a little activated suppressant to sweeten the deal."

"A bit bold?"

She shrugged. "I didn't think he'd survive long enough to be a threat."

"Was that your plan? Kill me, kill him, take over Malva?"

"Something like that."

The way she leisurely said it. . . I wanted to kill her all over again.

"Did you know about the journal?" I asked.

She tilted her head. "Journal?"

I studied her, searching for the lie, but it seemed Kaizer wasn't as dumb as she thought he was. Squeezing my hand tight into a fist I pulled at her essence, holding it in my grasp like I did before.

"Let me sleep. Do not try to come after me; do not try to hurt me, or I will return here. I will summon you and send you to a death outside of any spirit realm," I growled.

Did I know if that was true? No. Did it sound good? Yes.

She gasped for air, and I could see her trying to keep her knees strong enough to stay standing. I smirked with the knowledge that I could end her once and for all. That she'd have to stay wherever she was, worried that I could pull the essence from her.

"Be gone," I snapped.

She went up in smoke, and I sat in the silence of this dream realm for a few more minutes. There was a certain calm here without her. There was simply nothing.

I closed my eyes, letting the darkness, the stillness soothe me. My potion waned right as glowing purple eyes popped up across the space, but my own eyes opened to a wide moon ahead of me. I wondered what those eyes were as my breathing came in easier, knowing my mother wouldn't be a problem any longer. It was a win that I needed, and I could only hope that my luck would continue.

I had a plan. It was a bad plan, but a plan nonetheless.

We had to go get the grimoire, and I needed to get Zuri *and* Axel to go with me. What better way to get them to bond than a life-threatening journey to retrieve a book full of dark spells? Zuri was cleared completely yesterday. She moved about without any pain or problems and had done Akari's training for the last couple of days. So, she could get back into the swing of things with me and Axel. I made sure that I was the one to make all the decisions around entering Caldera. Even though it was playing dangerously close to breaking the agreement. I had to trust that the Triori were right when they said all of us going to get the grimoire was necessary. Axel was simply along for the ride. The first step of my plan was to soften him up, so I waited for him to do his morning check-in. I freshened up my hair and washed my face, applying a little makeup before pulling on one of the slinkier nightgowns in my closet. I got back in bed, knowing it should be any second now that he'd contact me.

"*Good morning, forceful,*" he muttered into my head, the gravelly voice he used making this even easier.

I let him in, moaning in my head, which was something I wasn't sure I'd ever done before.

"*Daya? What are you doing?*"

"*Why don't you come in here and find out,*" I answered.

Axel came barreling into my room in his tiny shorts, and a shirt half pulled onto his body. I pretended to climax and stretched my arms with a grin across my face.

"Too late." I shrugged.

"You only came once. Surely that's not enough," he said as he prowled toward me.

I got out of bed and walked past him, swaying my hips and shifting the hem of my nightgown. "No time. But. . . If you agree to what I ask of you, then we can both come a few times. Later."

Axel sighed and pushed his boner down, but it just sprang up, and he kept his hand there. "You cruel creature. What is it?"

"I want Zuri to come with us to get the grimoire." I smiled drastically.

"Only the three of us?" he questioned.

I nodded. "Mhm."

"You said it would be dangerous with too many people."

"I did. It is, but three people isn't too many. I meant that it can't be a bunch of soldiers with us. Plus, the Triori said we'd need her."

I could see him trying to figure out another excuse, but he settled for, "Should she be doing something so dangerous?"

I quirked up an eyebrow. "Worried about her well-being, are we? The healers said she's good to go yesterday. She's got to regain her fighting skills, but she's no longer in pain. Think of it as on-the-go conditioning."

Axel groaned, looking away from me, and I sauntered over to him slowly, toying with the strap of my gown and letting it fall down my shoulder. I reached up on my tiptoes, grabbing his face and bringing his gaze back to mine.

"I'll make it worth it."

Axel licked his lips and closed his eyes. "I once said you'd ruin me. I wasn't wrong. Fine."

I crashed my mouth into him, and he chuckled onto my lips before pulling back and shaking his head as he walked away. "I'll be expecting that payment!"

The door slammed shut, and I celebrated my victory with Axel. I just had to do the same with Zuri. She was going to be a little more difficult. I wasn't entirely sure Axel would say no to me ever. Zuri, on the other hand, might. She was still trying to get us back to where we were before, so as much as I didn't want to guilt her into it. . . The outcome of us spending time together would outweigh that.

I pulled on my leathers and walked down to breakfast, trying to calculate how to go about this. Zuri turned around the corner, her mouth pulling into a smile the moment she laid eyes on me. I watched as she moved as if she had never been injured and wrapped my arms around her shoulders.

"Good morning," I said, pulling back and taking in her witch leathers and new hair. "You look good."

Akari braided Zuri's hair yesterday into long braids much like hers. Zuri's were thicker than Akari's slim braids and suited her very well.

"So do you," she laughed as she squeezed my ass.

The leathers I chose today had a scale-like texture, akin to the water dragons we rode to the island. The buckles along the sides cinched my waist, and there were enough straps to carry twenty weapons at once. The smell of breakfast made it over to where we stood in the hallway, and we pushed into the dining hall together.

"So, is there a big cultural difference between here and where the lobos live?" I asked.

I hadn't had the chance to ask too many questions about it, but I was very curious. Especially because not only was Zuri from there, Axel's mother was as well.

"Arkhia, that's what it's called," she said as she took a seat at the empty table. "We've adopted a lot of things from each other. We're all Dusran at this point, but there are some slight differences. There's a lot more color in Arkhia, similar food and spices, but we have a few different things that are more specific to us."

"Do you go there often?"

Zuri shook her head. "I haven't been in years. I've actually only been back once since my parents died. It's hard."

I squeezed her hand as Ishani came through the door with Xavier on her heels, and she sat directly across from me. "Where is everyone?"

"I saw Axel this morning. I thought he'd be down here by now," I said right as he walked into the room.

He sat at my side, sandwiching me between him and Zuri. The fact that they were both so close made my chest warm.

"We're, apparently, all going to retrieve the grimoire," Axel said with his gaze on me and Zuri.

"I didn't ask her yet," I grumbled.

"Who is all?" Zuri asked.

"Me, you, and Axel," I answered.

Xavier laughed, trying to hide it with a cough as Ishani's eyes sparkled with what I was sure were plenty of comments to piss the both of them off.

"That is. . . an interesting plan," Zuri whispered.

"A plan it is," Ishani said with a laugh. "When are you leaving?"

"I'd like to leave as soon as possible," I replied.

"What do you need to take with you?" Xavier asked.

"We'll all need a few weapons, but that's really it. Shouldn't take more than a few days, and I'll portal right back."

"And what is that you'll be facing when you get there?" Ishani asked.

This part wasn't going to put their minds at ease. . .

"I actually don't know what the specifics are. I know the location, and once we get through the traps, I'm the only one who can open the book. It's designed to get any witches who think they can get to the book to turn away if they figure out the location."

"Are you sure you should only take two people with you?" Xavier asked.

I nodded. "The one thing I do know is that it's difficult to maneuver with lots of people. It's super rocky and narrow once we're inside. Three people is probably the max. It's possible with maybe a couple more, but it would make it more complicated than helpful."

Akari and Paxx walked in, the lights glistening off the sweat beading their foreheads.

"Early training?" Zuri asked.

"Yeah, Paxx needs the additional help. He's been stuck behind that desk doing his little spy work too long," Akari said with a push into his shoulder.

"I'll be missing my next couple of training sessions. I'm going with Daya and Axel to get the grimoire," Zuri said.

Paxx's eyebrows rose. "Should you be doing that?"

"As fun as this is having *everyone* question whether I'm well enough to do *everything*, I can assure you all that I'm good as new. The only thing left is to brush up on skills, just like if any of you went a month without training," Zuri answered.

I smirked at all of them, even though I was one of those people questioning her up until today. They all looked away from her and continued eating their food. *Good girl, Zuri.*

"This isn't going to be worse than half the things we've faced in our lifetimes," I blurted as I stood from my seat. *I think, anyway.*

Ishani watched Zuri and Axel stand and move to the door with a smirk. "Good luck."

I was going to need it, that was for sure.

Chapter Twenty-Five

Dayanara

Zuri trailed behind me as I exited my closet with all my favorite weapons strapped to me. I tapped each one, making sure none of them were left behind.

"You know, my side is hurting a little." She grabbed her side, pulling a very fake pained grimace.

"Zuri," I said with a tilt of my head.

She blew air between her lips and plopped down on the chair. "Fine. I'm okay."

"Let's be open-minded here. Who knows, you two could end up liking each other as much as I do," I said as I grabbed the satchels of supplies I packed.

"Doubtful," she replied as she stood up, and her braids shifted with the movement.

"Well. No time like the present." I clapped my hands. "We're meeting Axel in his courtyard."

I snapped open a portal into his courtyard, and Zuri grumbled as she followed behind me. Axel was already in his courtyard waiting with all of his weapons, staring out into the distance as if a way out of this was floating in the air.

"Ready, Ax?"

He turned and looked at Zuri, then back to me before nodding once.

"All right, I wish I could prepare us more, but unfortunately, I don't know much. We're going to Caldera near the Piedra. The entrance is in a forest directly next to it. After that, we'll be figuring it out together," I said as I opened a portal.

The rocky mountainside of the Piedra came into view as my purple smoke cleared, and I had to think back to the directions I'd received from my mother as a child. Part of my training was to prepare me for the role of Acna, and while my mother apparently never thought I'd make it to this point, she did tell me about the grimoire. There had been a few other times I'd been here, but it had been over one hundred years since then.

"Feel any impending doom?" I asked Axel.

"No, nothing. I think we're okay."

Excellent. The Triori must have been right. I looked around for the field of Flor de Maga trees that marked the grimoire's location. The entrance sat in the center of the field, cloaked with magic. The vibrant green trees sat behind us, the wide rounded petals of the red flowers spread sporadically. I ran my finger over one of the branches hanging low, the pistil of the flower tickling my finger.

I almost forgot Zuri and Axel were with me as their boots scuffed the dirt at my back.

"They're beautiful," Zuri said with her gaze on the flowers.

"Some of my favorites. It's kind of one big tree. They have grown around it. The center is the entrance."

Axel and Zuri nodded as we weaved around the interconnecting trees, some of the limbs hanging so low we had to dip our heads to get through. I followed my instinct, the feel of my family's magic pulling me toward it. We dodged one last tree, and the vast Flor de Maga came into view. It was a breathtaking sight during the day, but at night, it was even more spectacular. The flowers here glowed with my family's magic, the glittering pollen blowing with the breeze as the trinkets hanging from its limbs clang together in a soothing tune.

"All the women of my line have something hanging from this tree," I said with a look over my shoulder. "Even before the first Acna, the Amapola line has hung things of significance once we came of age, helping feed the magic used here."

I searched for the necklace hanging from the tree I placed here with Ximena. It felt like it was hundreds of years ago that my magic manifested. Brujas were born strong, but magicless. When we came of age around thirteen, our magic erupted from us. There wasn't a better word to use for it. It burst from every crevice of our bodies, the colored essence extending from us in such a way we couldn't contain it. Girls that age were slightly dangerous to be around. Everyone who came in contact with them had an air shield ready just in case the magic decided to make its initial appearance.

My line was all given some sort of jewelry when they were born, that piece was to be worn every single day until the manifestation of our magic. There were rings, bracelets, anklets, all shimmering in the dim light of the sky. It was believed that when you kept something so close to your being for such a long period, that your soul became one with it. The essence within us linked with the item, even before we had magic. A spell from the grimoire was used to attach it to the tree. The only way to get it down would have been to pull up every root. I found my necklace near the base of the tree and clasped the wing pendant between my fingers as I closed my eyes and whispered, "Ximena."

The memory of Ximena standing out on the tree line as my mother performed the spell flashed in my mind. The smile I tossed over my shoulder at her, the pride in Ximena's eyes watching me even though her magic hadn't yet manifested. I thought we would have been together forever then. The scenario of her not being beside me now, of her dying by my hand, wasn't something my wildest dreams could have conjured. I swallowed and looked back. Zuri's eyes were soft. She knew who Ximena was, what I'd done. That conversation hadn't come up with Axel yet, and he took a step closer like he wanted to question it. Zuri placed her hand on his arm and shook her head. His brow drew together, but he didn't say anything.

I looked away and pulled myself together. "This is where we'll go in. Stand back a bit. It's going to get a little crazy."

They both moved back to the same spot Ximena had stood all those years ago, and I shook my head before turning back. I closed my eyes again, grabbing the bloodstone out of my bag and placing it in my hand before turning my palms up. The spell was complicated, a mixture of air magic, bruja magic, and the bloodstone. I opened my eyes as the wind picked up around me, swirling around the tree as my hair blew. My family's tokens glowed brighter as they moved with the gust. My violet magic let loose, thick streams of it joining the wind in a tornado of my combined magic. I levitated the bloodstone between my hands and muttered the spell. The bloodstone vibrated before bursting into millions of particles, but staying between my hands. I took a deep breath and blew all the tiny pieces of bloodstone onto the trunk of the tree as I pushed more magic into the wind around me. The tree glowed with all of my family's magic, the last piece of the spell, pulling from the essence of the trinkets and allowing me entry. The trunk hollowed out in the blink of an eye, my magic and the wind dying in an instant. My hair fell back around my shoulders, and I took a deep breath, feeling that connection to my family, a reminder that I was the only one that remained of our line.

"You okay?" Axel asked as he came to stand beside me.

"Yeah, took a lot out of me," I said as I grabbed the glass jar of goat blood in my bag and drank half of it.

"So. . . we just go in there?" Zuri asked with her gaze at the dark, empty tree.

I chuckled as I screwed the top back on and put it in my bag. "Yeah, no idea what's in there. Stay alert."

My reserves tingled as I stepped into the hollowed out trunk, and the moment Axel and Zuri crossed the entryway, the tree closed up behind us, taking any light with it. I sent up an orb of my magic above our heads so we could see, finding us at the top of a spiral staircase. My foot hit the first step, and streams of multicolored light rippled like water. I felt my family's essence in the colors, lighting the way and guiding me. I vanished the orb above my head as the magic glowed bright enough that it wasn't needed anymore. We descended deep underground, and a soft hum rang around us.

"You guys hear that?"

Zuri shook her head, and Axel looked around for a moment before shaking his. I tried to home in on it, but I couldn't focus enough to decipher what the sound was. The stairwell ended, and the essence from the steps moved with us into the hallway, stripes of all the colors extending into the dark space. I ran my fingers over it, spotting Mariana's deep violet that matched my own. Axel grabbed my shoulder, and I stopped abruptly as the ground dropped off into a dark abyss. The essence on the hallway walls continued ahead, darting out at the sides and lighting the area ahead of us. Stalactites hung from the ceiling, my ancestors' bruja magic pulsing between them. The walls were made of rough stone, the ground so far below us that the light of the essence didn't illuminate it. The other side of the hallway was at least one hundred feet across the deadly drop.

"I'll just float us over," I said as I twisted my hands together to form a gust big enough for the three of us. It would have been difficult to hold both of them if I used my wings. Instead, I whirled the wind around us, and our feet lifted from the ground as I floated us across the space quickly. Out of curiosity, I threw a ball of bruja magic down to where the ground should be, and it was still descending as we made it to the other side. The essence lighting the walls followed us into the hallway, but it barreled against a dead end. It vibrated as if it was trapped and ready to be set free, almost feeling like a warning.

"What the fuck," Zuri whispered as she ran her hands on the walls.

"*Daughter of the Amapola line, Acna of the Brujas. Welcome, Dayanara,*" a combination of voices spoke, the essence pulsating with each word.

I glanced over my shoulder, eyebrows raised, not sure if I was supposed to talk back or what.

"Hello?" I responded with a tilt of my head.

"*You come for the grimoire.*"

I ran my gaze around the hall. "Yes."

"*All parts of you will be tested. Should you pass the tests, you will be granted access.*"

The light retreated, and the floor dropped from beneath our feet. My heart fell into my stomach as I reached for Axel's and Zuri's hands and softened our landing with air. The space was completely dark, but it felt familiar as if my soul recognized it even if I didn't fully. The sound of Axel pulling his sword from his sheath came from behind me as he and Zuri formed a line at my sides. I threw up an orb of my magic to light the space, and my gut tightened. It was the place I'd seen my mother in my dreams.

I moved in a slow circle to figure out the first test, and the space glittered as it transformed into the dungeons below the palace in Caldera. Axel and Zuri looked around, and I touched Axel's sleeve to make sure he was still real. "You all can see this, right?"

They both nodded, and the whimper coming from one of the cells made my knees buckle. *It's not real. It's not real. It's not real.* I moved closer, finding a woman rolled up in a ball, her body covered in bruises, cuts gushing blood into a puddle beneath her body.

"Ximena," I gasped.

Chapter Twenty-Six

Dayanara

She lifted her gaze to mine, her long dark hair shifting from in front of her eyes. "Why'd you let her do this to me?"

I grabbed the bars and pulled them apart to get to her. Falling to my knees, I clutched her body close to mine, pushing her hair back and staring into her brown eyes as my voice wavered. "I didn't know."

"It's your fault." She flashed her gaze down toward her chest. "You did this."

The dagger I used to kill her protruded from her chest, and I yanked it out and pressed my hand over the wound to try to heal her. "Ximena, I'm so sorry. I'm so sorry," I repeated as the wound continued pouring out blood. I could stop the bleeding. I could save her this time.

I glimpsed up, but instead of Ximena, Zuri's wounded face looked back at me. Her clothes were singed off, the burn marks running up her side fresh and glistening. The smell, goddess, the smell of her burning flesh brought tears to my eyes. The bars of the cell snapped back into place, trapping me for good. The real Zuri and Axel were nowhere to be seen.

"You hurt everyone who cares about you," the wounded Zuri said as she pulled from my arms. "You don't deserve love."

My chest heaved as I reached for Zuri, but her body went up in flames, and Kaizer stepped through the fire. "I'm what you've earned. I'm the only one who can love you the way you deserve to be loved."

Kaizer stepped toward me and put his hand around my neck, lifting me off the ground and pushing me into the wall. "Nobody else cares about you. I'm all you've got," he growled.

Ximena and Zuri reappeared, leaning against each other along the wall as their blood mixed and their eyes slowly closed. I screamed, the sound muffled by Kaizer's grip on my throat. Maybe I did deserve to end like this. Ximena died because of me. Zuri was captured and tortured because of me. My kingdom was displaced and taken over because of *me*. It was only a matter of time before I brought down Axel and Dusra. Before Zuri realized that I was the one who didn't deserve her. I closed my eyes as Kaizer's grip tightened, and he pushed his forearm into my chest. It would be better for everyone if I just went away.

Something sparked behind my eyelids, and Axel's magic burst to life. If he was speaking, I couldn't hear him, but the caress of his magic brushed up against my senses. The cool feel of it brought me out of whatever attack my mind was having on itself. My eyes flicked open, the purple glow of my pupils shining on Kaizer's face. His face went slack as I wrapped my taloned fingers around his heart, and his body dissipated into a cloud of smoke.

Ximena and Zuri vanished, the bars of the cell dissipating as I blinked. Everything went blank, and I braced myself for my mind to attack me again. Ximena reappeared, and my stomach grew tight. I didn't want to do this again, didn't want to see her get hurt. But no cell reappeared, and no blood was smeared across her skin. She looked older. The soft delicate lines of her face I remembered now replaced with high cheekbones. I didn't know if it was real—didn't care. She smiled, and I searched for the slight dimple in her chin she got with the movement. It appeared, and I crossed the space between us. She wrapped her arms around me, and I felt her warmth as I tried to squeeze a century of embraces into her.

"I missed you," I said.

"And I missed you," she replied as she gently pulled me back by my shoulders. Her gaze ran over my face, over the tattoos that I'd gotten since her death. It settled back into my eyes, and I wanted to stay here for a little longer. Even though I could sense my body somewhere else, and I could tell that this part of the trial was ending soon.

"I'm sorry, Ximena. I've never been able to tell you that. I don't know if you're really here. But I am. So, so sorry." My lip quivered.

"I'm glad it was you, and I don't blame you. You took care of the real reason for my death." She grabbed me by the face. "I am incredibly proud of you. Make those fuckers pay."

Before I could respond, Ximena zapped out of existence, and I was left on the floor with Axel and Zuri hovering above me.

"Are you hurt?" Axel asked.

"What happened?" Zuri questioned.

I stared into the dark abyss as I tried to pull myself together. It wasn't clear if that was real, if Ximena really forgave me, or if it was just a trick of my mind. *Mind.*

"All parts of you will be tested," I whispered. "Mind. Body. Soul."

Zuri moved closer. "Huh?"

I got up quickly, realizing that the next test was probably going to be coming any minute now. "They said all parts of me will be tested. We're made of three things: mind, body, soul. The first test was mind, next will be body."

"What did you see?" Axel asked.

I shook my head. "I'll tell you later."

Zuri's eyes narrowed on me, but the ground shook again. All three of us immediately shifted so our backs were lined up, and we moved in a small circle. Something big was coming, if not multiple big things. Every shake of the floor got increasingly more powerful, convulsing us almost to the point we lost our footing. One of the walls of the odd cave we were in vanished, and beasts that belonged in the Inbetween came pouring into the space. There were too many. Our best bet was going to be fighting separately. The walls all dropped into the ground, creating an elevated arena with the monsters.

"Zuri, how you feeling?" I shouted.

"About to piss my pants, but other than that, I can fight," she answered.

I didn't have to ask Ax. His magic was already rolling off him as the three biggest monsters circled us. The others prowled around the outskirts like they weren't all allowed to attack us at once. I took a deep breath and charged the one closest to me.

The awareness that Axel and Zuri both moved toward the others quickly vanished by the mere size of the thing I'd been tasked with killing. The odd lizard from the Inbetween that attacked Zuri and me seemed like an easy job compared to this thing. Its body was three times the size, its head so far above me I had to strain my neck to see. The body of the beast was covered in thick skin, little patches of wispy hair sporadically sprouting between the joints. Thick armor around its eyes gave the illusion that the monster was wearing a mask as it dipped its head toward me and snapped its powerful jaws. The beast's thick barbed tail swung around, barely missing me as I rolled to the side and looked back over my shoulder at Ax and Zuri.

Zuri ran under her monster's legs and covered the ground in ice, and Ax was on his monster's back with his dark magic extending from his hands. I snapped my gaze back toward the monster trying to kill me and sent out a tendril of air to wrap around the thick leg closest to me. Yanking on the rope of air, I pulled until the monster stumbled, and I ran toward the next leg closest to me, repeating the movement. It bucked onto its back legs and snapped my restraints, sending me flying onto my ass. The latch of my bag snapped and flew down into the deep ravines around the border of the space. I softened my landing with a burst of air and set my feet back on the ground.

"All right, looks like we're going to have to get creative," I mumbled.

I unbuckled the top half of my leathers, allowing my wings burst from me, and took to the air in one powerful jump. Letting my bruja magic gather in my hand, I formed a large orb, the swirling colors of my Acna gift moving within. I let it grow bigger than I normally did, testing my power as I floated above the beast. I pushed the orb, the power of the movement shooting me further toward the ceiling, and watched as the orb flew straight through the monster. A gaping hole was left behind in its neck, dark blood and gray flesh pouring out onto the ground. I tucked my wings in with my sword in hand and slashed through the remaining flesh with one grand swipe. The head fell to the ground, and I watched Axel run to assist Zuri. She had some blood dripping from her arm and her forehead, but otherwise, she was holding up.

Axel twisted his hands, moving them in a snake-like motion as his dark magic exploded from his palms. The two streams of magic formed a lasso around the monster's neck, and Zuri sent a river of water out. She let it ice over for Axel to run on as he tightened his hold on the lasso. Zuri created a cyclone of water, heaving the monster's head into it as it tried to buck out of the powerful suction. The pull of her magic was too great, and Axel made it to the neck of the monster. A dark blur caught my attention, the monster's tail whipping around to try to get Axel off his back. I lifted my hand to stop it, but Zuri flicked her wrist quickly, piercing it with an icicle into the rock behind them. Axel took both of his swords and plunged them into its neck, dragging them outward, leaving open flesh in his wake. Zuri kept the cyclone moving and pulling, her knees buckling as she pulled the beast's head from its body, and it fell to the ground in a mighty thud.

Axel hopped down and put his hand on Zuri's shoulder, and I couldn't help the smile stretching from ear to ear as they fought and protected each other. The smile was quickly thwarted as the small beasts darted toward all of us. Small wasn't entirely accurate. Compared to the others, they were smaller but still stood heads above us.

Rather than the sporadic patches of hair that the other beasts had, these had thick coats of gray, wiry fur. Their legs seemed to have an additional joint in them, bending at odd angles as they walked a circle around the three of us. My magic was reflected in their four milky eyes, tall, pointed ears flicking around with every noise we made.

"They're blind like the other one," I said to Zuri. "I'll make an air shield around us, that way they can't hear us coming. Get as close as you can to at least one and take them out. We'll have to fight out the rest after."

There had to be at least eight of the monsters, but taking out three would leave less for us to fight individually. They readied their weapons as I created an air shield and floated each of us closer to the beasts. Their ears twitched as if they were trying to figure out where we went, and I used the opportunity to break the shield.

"Boo," I whispered as I brought my sword straight through its jugular. It yelped an ear-piercing sound as the other two Axel and Zuri fought and made a similar sound.

One sat back on its haunches, pouncing toward Zuri, where she fought another. I sent a stream of witch magic toward it, which didn't do much, but enough to distract it and head my way. Just as one of its friends turned toward me.

"Oof, you stink," I grimaced.

The essence of Axel's magic pulsed through the air, surely shifting into some beast to match these. *These* beasts didn't give me the chance to find him, as they both charged with foam dripping from their loose jowls. They worked together like pack animals, caging me between them as they both nipped at either side of my body.

They were close—my daggers would be a better option to fight with than my long sword. I slid them from my thigh holsters, tossing them in the air and catching them by the hilt. No heartbeat emanated from their chests, which still felt immensely unnerving.

They charged me again, switching sides, and I plunged both my daggers out and sliced the back of their legs. Dark blood poured from them as they tried to right themselves, limping but still moving too fast. I pushed my magic into the ground, leaping high, and both of them followed. Wrapping air tendrils around them both, I forced them to crash headfirst together. I came down, my blades aimed for their skulls, and sank them deep to the hilt. They fell, and I looked back at Axel and Zuri.

Just as I thought, Axel was in another form, scales replacing his skin, his massive jaws snapping a beast in half. Zuri pulled her blade from the remnants of one, the head separated from the rest of it.

Goddess, I love it when she's murderous.

"All right," I started, but before I could finish my sentence, the bones around us rattled. "What. . . "

All the remnants shot across the room, linking together like magnets to form a monster bigger than the ones we'd fought initially.

"Fuck," Axel breathed.

"Let's not let it finish!" I yelled out.

I grew a ball of bruja magic and pushed it into the center of the bones, keeping the connection and pouring into it. The bones fought against my power, and I tried to feed in my Acna magic, but the stream remained purple. Axel put his hand on me, feeding me his power, and his black magic twirled around mine as they combined and doubled in strength. The bones slowly separated from each other before they burst apart, some of them turning into a fine powder. Zuri stepped in front of us, sweeping the remains into a massive wave, and froze them before they could try again.

The raised arena we were in lowered back down to its original height, and we held onto each other at the sudden stop. A door manifested in the wall we faced, my ancestors' essence once again flowing and sparkling around the entry. We moved as one, and the door closed as we stepped into another room.

Chapter Twenty-Seven

Dayanara

The next test was soul, and I wasn't entirely sure what to expect. The surrounding walls changed again, glowing so brightly we all had to shield our eyes. The light dimmed, clouds and fog rolling in and encompassing us. My magic reserves depleted immediately, a painful emptiness in my chest that had me doubling over and nearly retching. Zuri and Axel both leaned in closer and put a hand on my back. Or at least I thought they did. I couldn't feel it as both of their hands pushed through my body.

"What's wrong?" Zuri asked.

"It's your magic, isn't it?" Axel said.

I nodded. "It's gone. They emptied me out completely."

Light footsteps were coming toward us, and I tried my best to straighten, but Zuri and Axel immediately moved in front of and behind me.

"Dayanara," a powerful voice spoke.

The clouds around us parted as Mariana, the first Acna, pushed through them. She was stunning, an exact real-life replica of the mural in the desert I loved so much. The grace she moved with was mesmerizing, her long, curly violet locks moving in a breeze I didn't feel. Her golden honey skin seemed like porcelain. Zuri and Axel stared at her in awe, and I found a string of my essence drawn between my chest and the two of them. She waved her hand, blinking Axel and Zuri out of existence.

"Oh no," I started to panic, but she grabbed my wrist.

"They are back in the cave. They are okay," Mariana reassured with a small stroke of her thumb on my arm—her I could feel.

"My magic," I said as I rubbed my chest. "It's gone."

"Yes, this last test, as you figured out, is soul. You're down to just that, no magic, no body." She gestured to my chest.

A light emanated from my chest, my body slightly translucent. It was as if I was dead again, back in this realm with Naom. I didn't like it one bit.

"What do I have to do?"

Mariana's chuckling put me at ease. "I've always loved your eagerness."

I tilted my head to the side. "Always?"

"We've all watched you as you've grown." She turned, and all the clouds around us dissipated. Dozens of bodies stood around us, their eyes glowing in different bruja magic.

"All the Acnas?" I asked as I stepped toward them.

"Mhm. And the Amapolas even before then," she spoke from behind me. "Well, all but one. Your mother hasn't joined us here yet."

I scoffed. "Won't find me missing her."

"Passion runs deep in our line. While her methods were not what I would have chosen, she thought she was doing what was best for the brujas. We've all made our fair share of mistakes in the name of the coven."

"Hmm," I said as I turned back. *That's an understatement.*

Mariana was smiling as she shook her head. "She has not joined us because she knows we will not approve. She can't remain outside of this realm for much longer, though." She cleared her throat. "But we have watched you. We have watched you overcome time and time again, no matter what the circumstances. You're resilient, Dayanara."

"It's resilience or death. I haven't had much of a choice."

It always felt odd when people called me resilient. It wasn't exactly a compliment—or it didn't feel like one. To be resilient, you had to go through something terrible in the first place. Was the reward from my strife just. . . persisting? I'd rather skip the bullshit completely.

Her mouth straightened into a line as her eyes softened. "It is the way of our world. It saddens me."

"Me too," I whispered.

"But look at your soul." She pointed to the light in my chest. "How strong it is. We'll never know if we're making the right choices in the long run. We merely have to lean on our soul, on our hearts, and hope that everything will be fine in the end."

"Naom told me that I wasn't a singular thing. That things weren't as black-and-white as our world thinks. The vampires in Sanjry have separated everything into very harsh columns of right and wrong, and that has caused so many problems."

"Indeed. The brujas have been seen as ruthless, but our way of life isn't wrong. It is right for us."

I glanced out into the group of women that came before me. Some of them I recognized, having been taught about them as a brujita. Sometimes, I felt alone, like I was the only one with the weight of the world on my shoulders. But being here with them, it was clear that I was part of something. All of these women had protected the brujas during their time. Their presence was familiar, and I rubbed my barely there chest.

"My Acna power—it's all of yours, isn't it?"

She smiled. "It is. Your entire ancestry flows through your blood and now in your magic as well."

"It's difficult to control sometimes. The wings I've mastered, but the other magic is. . . more difficult."

"It is not meant for you to use like your bruja magic. It's meant for times that your people need protection—that you need protection."

Admitting to my idol that I wasn't in control wasn't easy. But thinking back to the moments it was easier to manage, it was when I needed protection, or someone I loved needed it.

"Even when I can summon it, it just feels unruly?"

"You have the rage of every Amapola before you, unruly it should be."

I chuckled as I took her in. She'd gotten me through more things than she knew. I'd go out to that mural on hard days to feel something other than rage. I didn't know if it was hope, but something about her always comforted me.

"Can I ask you a question?"

She tilted her chin ever so slightly. Outside of the possibility I'd see Naom again, I wasn't sure who else to ask this question.

"What do you know about Verdaji?"

Mariana contemplated for a moment. "What is it you wish to know?"

"What is it really? Can there be more than one for someone? Are. . . Axel and Zuri mine?"

"I am not a goddess, and I cannot tell you for certain if this is what you have. I can say there have been more than a pair before. Verdaji compliment you in every way, complete you. You're destined to find each other in this life and the next."

"Does destiny take away their choice?"

The thought that they were tied to me against their will. . .

"No. You are free to choose to be with your Verdaji or not, but I can't imagine a scenario in which you wouldn't want them."

I paused, wondering where to go next. "So, what do I need to do to pass this phase?"

"Nothing further. I've seen your soul, your being when you're stripped of your magic, of your weapons. What remains is still strong." She tilted her head. "You have access to all of us, to the Acnas and Amapolas before you. Should you need advice, you can come to this place, summon us, and we will help you."

She snapped her fingers, and I opened my eyes to find myself at the top of a stone staircase chiseled directly into the cave wall. I caught my balance, grabbing onto the large podium to find my family's grimoire levitating above it in my ancestors' magic. Its translucent wall surrounded me, and I could see Axel and Zuri at the base of the stairs. They were eagerly waiting, and I nodded to them to let them know I was okay before turning back to the grimoire. My ancestors' magic lapped up my skin as I reached into the pillar of it to retrieve the book. It formed tendrils around my arms, a comforting sensation sinking down to my bones. I still didn't have any magic in my reserves, but theirs tingled up and down my body until I pulled the grimoire out and the magic shot back into the surrounding walls.

I knew that the grimoire used blood magic. I'd need to cut my hand to even open the book, but I decided to go down and meet Axel and Zuri first. The staircase was incredibly narrow and so far up that it was disorienting as I kept my footing strong and my hold on the tome stronger. Both Zuri and Axel stood with one of their hands angled like they were ready to grab me if needed.

"You got it," Axel breathed out.

I ran my hand over the dark cover of the book. It was leather-bound, in what had to be the oldest leather ever created. Spirals of air, flowers, and vines were engraved into it, my family name in script in an arch on the top half of the cover. Two thick buckles sealed it shut, and sharp golden rivets sat on each corner. My fingers moved on their own accord, my pointer finger extending and pressing into one of the razor-sharp points. The golden rivet glowed, and I watched as my blood pulled from the point of contact and drained into the deep wells etched in the cover. The buckles vibrated and unlatched, and I slowly opened the book. My blood spread across the pages, the words appearing as if they were inked with the red substance.

The warmth of Axel and Zuri on each of my shoulders had me peeking over at them. I nearly forgot they were with me. "Can you see it?"

"Yeah, I can." Zuri nodded as Axel did the same.

The first page was a spell to return the book to this place, so if I took it with me, it wouldn't be in danger of being lost. I flipped through, the blood seeping from page to page and all the spells and content came to life. "Okay, let's get back. This is the part I wasn't sure about, if I was able to take it with me. But, looks like we're good to go."

Just like before, essence pulsated on the walls, leading us out of the twisting turns of the cavern. I wasn't sure what to expect when I started this journey, but it definitely wasn't coming in contact with Mariana. The connection I felt to that mural solidified. Feeling her magic, her essence, was unreal. We made it to the steps, not having to cross over the same path as before. The tree trunk vanished as we pushed into it, finding ourselves back in the forest of Flor de Maga trees.

"How are we going to get back? You're out of magic," Zuri said.

"And my bag fell. I don't have any blood." I sighed.

"We aren't exactly out of blood. . . " Axel trailed off.

I looked away and into the flowers surrounding us. The glow of the sky was fading. It would be nightfall within the hour. "Let's find some food and somewhere to rest for the night. We can figure that out later."

Zuri went on a hunt and found a large enough deer to feed all three of us. I found a cave nestled in the Piedra, and Axel started a fire for us to stay warm and cook the deer. Zuri got closer to this fire than she did before, but still stayed somewhat of a distance from the flame. I found some herbs out in the forest, as deer were not all that great without some sort of seasoning.

Neither of them brought up the idea of drinking from them yet. The deer could have been an option, but I would have needed to drink every drop. For whatever reason, not every animal was as potent as others. Goat was the closest to a person's magic levels, but even then, we drank consistently to keep up our reserves. This time, I was completely empty; drinking from them was the best option. I wasn't necessarily against it. I'd been on the receiving end of a few bites now, which had me somewhat curious as to what it would be like. However, I wasn't sure how to pick which one of them I should drink from. They'd turn it into a competition, which was the opposite of what the trip was about.

Zuri handed me a chunk of the deer. Axel handed me a cup of fresh water, and I nodded my appreciation for both of them. "You guys fought well together today."

They peered at each other before they both looked away and grabbed their portions of the meal. *Ah, got to love bonding time.* The deer Zuri brought back had massive teeth marks in it, surely brought down in her wolf form. I hadn't had much time since she'd been back to learn more about the lobos from both Zuri and Axel.

"What did you say the land the lobos live on is called again?"

"Arkhia," Zuri responded.

"Do you ever go, Axel?" I asked.

He nodded. "Nia handles pretty much everything there, but I do go every so often to make sure they know we still support them."

"You said you'd been back once, Zuri?"

"Just for my parents' funeral." She swallowed hard.

Axel's eyes softened as he cast his gaze back into the fire with a face that felt like regret. Zuri was the one to kill all those lobos, but it was because of the royals that they rioted, and her parents had died. I wondered if that was why she hated him in such a way, if it was easier to blame him for their death than to sit with the grief. She and Ishani were close, and she was of the same royal bloodline, but Axel was who sat on the throne when it happened.

"What exactly happened before they died?" I asked.

"There was some unrest around the land. One of the families, not either of ours, wanted to be separated from Axel's rule. My parents reminded them of the protection that the Vohras offered us when we were at our lowest numbers. The family said that we were now strong enough to stand on our own. My parents still didn't agree, and they died for it," Zuri responded.

"The issue didn't even come to me before they died," Axel mumbled.

"And what would you have done? Relinquished control of a whole section of your land?" Zuri snapped.

"That's exactly what I would have fucking done," Axel growled. "You think I wanted them to die? That I rejected some proposal and am the reason for what those bastards did to them?"

"I don't know what to believe. I wasn't there," Zuri quipped.

"I loved your parents like family. If they had asked, I would have found a way to do it."

I watched as they fought, wondering if I should have kept my mouth shut. I'd never seen Zuri so angry, even when she told me what happened she merely spoke with sorrow. But now, I could see the wolf in her trying to escape. The beast pressing against her skin, her eyes flickering with the glow of her lobo magic.

Standing up between them, I put both of my hands out to stop them from continuing. "I'm sorry I asked. I just wanted to know that side of you both better."

Zuri's eyes were still burning with fury, but Axel's shoulders slumped slightly before he reached for his water and took a sip. Zuri bit into her deer with a lot of gusto, and I walked over to the edge of the cave. The moon was high, and I reached my hand toward it, feeling its pull on my soul. Stars sparkled, ribbons of blue and green stretching as far as I could see above my land. I missed Caldera more than I could express. The urge to say fuck it and stay here, even with the risk of Kaizer or the brujas that followed him finding me, was extreme. This was the land I was born to rule, the kingdom that Naom put my family at the head of. I lost it all. The grimoire would be helpful, but it wasn't time to do any celebrating yet.

"What are we going to do about getting back?" Zuri asked from behind me.

I sighed and turned around. "It would be too risky to travel back by foot. I'm... I'm going to have to drink from one of you." Both of them perked up and opened their mouths to speak, but I held my hand up to stop them. "I haven't decided who. I'm going to flip a coin."

Especially after the fight they had, I wasn't going to make the mistake of choosing one over the other right now. I fished the emergency coin I kept in a hidden pocket of my leathers out, breaking the stitching that held it in place. "Heads or tails?"

"Tails," Zuri spoke quickly.

"I'll take heads," Axel sighed.

They both watched me as if I was the answer to every problem either of them had ever had. I stepped closer as I threw the coin in the air, and it spun in slow motion, feeling like it had tumbled through the air for minutes. All three of us had our gazes on the coin, the sound of it hitting the ground loud in the silence. Bending down to pick it up, I lifted it in the air. "Heads."

Zuri's nose twitched, and she sat back down. Axel smiled so smugly that I almost told him to cut it out. "We doing this now?"

Chapter Twenty-Eight

Dayanara

I flicked my gaze over to Zuri and then back to him. "Might as well."

Axel sat on a rock in the cave and opened his arms wide in invitation. I straddled his lap and heard retreating footsteps as Zuri left the cave. I turned my head, but Axel grabbed my chin. "She'll be fine."

"You're enjoying this win a little too much."

Axel shrugged and turned his head to the side to expose his neck.

"I've never done this before," I said as I trailed his flesh with my finger. "I bite here?"

"Yup, not much to it," Axel responded.

Leaning over, I opened my mouth and brushed my fangs against his pulsing vein. I didn't have any venom like the vampires, so I wasn't sure if it would be all pain for Axel. Without thinking about it too much, I sank my canines into his flesh.

My eyes went wide at the first taste of Axel's blood across my tongue. I'd had plenty of animal blood in my time, but *fuck* was his blood delectable. It was rich, like his magic, and so potent my reserves were already tingling with the first mouthful I swallowed. I may not have had the aphrodisiac vampire venom, but the evidence that Axel was enjoying this pushed against where our bodies met. He moaned, and his fingers trailed down my back as I continued drinking from him. His hands cupped my ass as he pulled me closer, encouraging me to drag my hips against his hardened dick.

I blinked open to find Zuri standing at the mouth of the cave, watching us. The anger was no longer in her eyes as she ran her gaze up and down my body and bit her lip. I'd almost forgotten she enjoyed this, watching me. It seemed like she couldn't help herself, even with the man she was just fighting with being the one beneath me. Axel's head was turned away from her. It wasn't clear if he knew she was there. If he did, he apparently didn't mind the watching because his hand slid over my pants, finding its way to my aching core. He rubbed his fingers back and forth, my body convulsing with the pleasure from his blood and the promise of more from his hand. I moaned with my mouth still around his neck, and Zuri let out a sound of her own. Axel's hand stopped for a second at the sound before he picked up speed.

My fangs pulled out of his neck as I gasped. It had been decades since I'd been completely empty, and my reserves weren't full yet. Even so, I couldn't get myself to keep drinking. He sat up quickly, captured my mouth with his, and dipped his hand into my pants. His fingers slid through all the wetness waiting for him, plunging straight into my pussy.

I fucked his hand, staring directly at Zuri, my mouth hanging open and moans escaping me as she leaned against the wall. I screamed as I came, and Axel picked me up and sat me on my feet, pulling my pants the rest of the way off my body. All of a sudden, Zuri was behind me, her hands on my waist as she spun me toward her and gave me a bruising kiss. Axel growled, and I was pulled away from Zuri.

"Wait, just wait." I turned back to Zuri. "Lay down. I still need blood."

Zuri's gaze bounced from me to Axel a few times before closing her eyes and letting out a deep sigh. She did as I asked, laying on her back slowly as I climbed on top of her on all fours. I kissed Zuri, feeling the tightness in her shoulders relax as I nipped at her bottom lip.

"I'll get more blood from Zuri, and you fuck me while I do it, Ax. Everyone okay with that?" I asked both of them.

They nodded eagerly, and I settled back over Zuri. I trailed kisses from her mouth down to her neck, licking her before I sank my fangs into her the same way I did Ax. She gasped, and I tried to see her face. It might have hurt, but her face was full of pleasure as I began pulling blood. Zuri's blood was different, sweeter than Axel's. It sent sparks all over my skin, still potent with power. Axel grabbed my hips as he straddled Zuri's legs beneath me, the head of his cock pushing at my pussy. His hands gripped the back of my neck to keep me from moving as he slammed to the hilt.

"Oh, fuck," I mumbled around Zuri's neck.

Axel stayed there for a moment, not pulling out but moving slightly inside me as I drank. Zuri moaned as I continued drinking from her, and Axel pulled out slowly all the way to the tip. I pushed my hips back onto him as much as I could to avoid ripping Zuri's throat out, and he understood what I was asking. His grip around my neck tightened as he began to fuck me the way I wanted him to.

There was a light touch on my arms, far too gentle to be Ax. Zuri ran her fingers up my arms, unbuckling the straps holding my top together and pushing it off my shoulders. I ripped the garment off, and before I knew it, Zuri licked her fingers and started rubbing circles around my nipples. She pinched them, earning a moan from me as Axel took this opportunity to pick up the speed of his thrusts. I figured Zuri needed a little more attention, so I reached down and stuck my hand in her pants, finding her just as wet as me. I rubbed her clit as I drank, feeling the last of the space in my magic reserves fill as she arched her back into me.

I yanked my fangs from her neck, pulling my fingers out of her pussy and into my mouth. My eyes rolled back before I brought my lips to her ear and mumbled, "I want to taste more."

The question in my words—Is it okay that I do this in front of him?

Zuri's answer was in the lift of her hips as she pulled off her pants. If she was going to do this, we were going to *do* this. I slid her out from beneath me, flipping onto my back with Axel still inside me. I grabbed Zuri, pulling her and having her straddle my face. Even with her top still on, her burn scars were exposed. She looked back at Axel but then back down at me before she brought her pussy right to my mouth. I could still taste her blood on my tongue as it mixed with her arousal. The combination of that and Axel throwing my leg over his shoulder and hitting a spot deep inside me almost made me come immediately.

I put a hand on each of Zuri's ass cheeks, pulling her closer to me so I had access to every bit of her. My tongue ran up to her clit, circling as I took two fingers and pushed inside her. Zuri moaned as I didn't let up, pulling my fingers out and replacing them with my tongue. Axel's thumbs dug into my hips as he pounded into me relentlessly, and Zuri dragged her hips against my face. The noises they made mixed together, and it might have been my favorite fucking sound.

Zuri came on my tongue, the rush of wetness cascading over my face as I came right after her. One more thrust of Axel's hips had him grunting, the feel of him pulsing inside of me forcing me to squirm until he pulled out. Zuri pulled off my face and rolled over as Axel fell backward.

I wanted them to bond, but I couldn't have guessed that this was where we would have ended up on this trip. My chest heaved as I caught my breath, sitting myself up on my elbows as I peered at the both of them with a smile I couldn't keep from my face if my life depended on it.

"Well, I feel fucking fantastic," I gushed.

They both raised their eyebrows like they couldn't believe it either and I sat up fully and wiped my mouth with the back of my hand.

"You know you two can touch each other, right? It doesn't have to be *all* about me. I don't mind. Honestly, it's encouraged."

Axel looked over at Zuri, and she averted her eyes quickly.

"We'll work up to that." I shrugged. "Thanks for the blood, *lovers*. Let's get some rest. We can leave in the morning."

I chuckled as I sat up to find my pants, and they both got dressed quickly as if all three of us weren't on full display mere moments ago. There was no hiding that they both thoroughly enjoyed it, and I caught them glancing at each other like they were trying to figure out how they felt.

I set a protection spell at the mouth of the cave before I laid on the comfiest looking spot among the rock. One of them put out the fire, and they both joined me on the floor. Sleep called the moment the warmth of both of their bodies joined with mine, and I let it take me.

I'd been awake a few minutes, but I couldn't get myself to wake up the others. My cheek was pressed against Axel's chest, Zuri's body was lined up with mine, her arm over my waist as they both slept like the dead. Even after last night's activities, I didn't think either of them would be transformed into best friends today. So I kept myself as still as possible until Zuri grumbled and rolled away from me, stretching her arms out as she woke. I sat up, the movement waking Axel.

"Good morning, you two. We should get going. Light just broke. I don't know of any patrols out here, but let's stay on the safe side," I said as I vanished the protection spell on the cave.

Zuri and Axel both stood, coming over to either side of me as I snapped open a portal to Dusra, and we stepped through together. I brought us to the courtyard outside of the front gates and cleared out my purple smoke to find Ishani.

"Axel said you guys were on your way back," she said as she stepped forward. "Everything go okay?"

"Axel's mind-speaking works that far?" I asked.

"We're twins. Our souls are linked. He can contact me much further than others. How'd it go?" Ishani responded.

"Well, we got the grimoire."

Chapter Twenty-Nine

Dayanara

I stepped out of my bathroom, the steam escaping into my room with me. Axel and Zuri had gone to rest, both of them still a little awkward from our time in the cave. I wasn't getting apprehension, but I was thinking the idea of all of us together and us actually *being* together might have been a bit different for them. Especially after the talk they had about Zuri's parents. That was a difficult thing to maneuver. At the end of the day, no matter who was to blame, her parents were gone. Like Axel's and mine were as well.

Either way, I wanted some time to go through the grimoire before I had to do it in front of everyone. It wasn't necessarily that I wanted to hide any of the information, but that it was always meant for my family. If there was anything that would damn us, I wanted a heads-up. The grimoire not only held our family spells, but there was a section dedicated to each of the Acnas. Their accomplishments, their downfalls. The Acna typically wrote it at the time, but there were some instances when the next in line had to add the information due to their sudden deaths.

I flipped through, landing on one with the header 'Lupe Amapola' and scanned the text. She hadn't finished. It didn't look like she'd put anything in here in a couple of decades. The war we'd fought in was listed, small things she'd done around the kingdom, but her plans for the future weren't listed. Tapping my finger on the wooden table beneath the book, I debated whether I should update her page with what actually happened. Or was it worse to leave her 'accomplishments' completely blank? This would be handed down my line to my potential daughter or to another powerful family should I not have a child.

"Everyone is going to know who you really are," I whispered as I filled in the space with the truth of who she was and what she'd done. That she'd tried to sacrifice me all in the hopes of more power. Because of a vision she didn't truly understand. I let the ink dry, humming with content before flipping through the pages. The book was still pristine, thanks to all the spells and enchantments.

A feeling I couldn't quite pinpoint overcame me as I held this book that had existed since the first bruja. That had withstood centuries upon centuries of battles, and goddess knew what else. I needed to see if there was any information about this god of Chaos. A chill ran up my spine at the thought. The goddesses weren't necessarily seen as being perfect beings—they weren't seen as pure good or evil. But this god, wherever he came from, wherever his beasts came from, they were pure evil. I knew it down to my bones. Something repulsed within me with the knowledge.

Scanning the pages, I tried to see if anything stood out to me through the Amapola women even before there was an Acna. Our line had always been the most powerful, the ones who led since the start. From what the Triori had said, the god wasn't here at the very beginning. Just the Creators and the other ethereal beings. They weren't clear about when it happened, only that the crack in our land appeared, and the monsters came through while the magic was sucked from our world.

The word *chaos* had me stopping on my ancestor a few before Mariana—Valentina Amapola. She spoke of the fissure, of the beasts attacking the coven, and how they were unlike anything they'd seen before. The bloodshed they'd spread across the land, and it dawned on me then that these beasts may have been part of the reason the people of Bonda thought we were the ones attacking, too. She wrote about an odd being who didn't seem to be part of our world, who spoke with a voice that was one and many. Wore different faces like one wore different clothes.

This was what I was looking for. Valentina said that he was unstoppable, and that many were lost while trying to defeat him. There was a time when all the beings of the dark tried to band together to stop him, which I thought was interesting given the state we were in now. The god's name wasn't written. From what I could gather, they didn't know who he was yet. They referred to him as the scorpion, but it wasn't clear why. Valentina fell while trying to protect the coven. The next in our line had more to say about him, but a knock on my door had me listening for who it might have been.

One of the heartbeats that matched the beating of my own. I closed the grimoire and felt the magic seal across the cover. Zuri stood in my doorway, a haunting visage in her eyes.

"What's wrong?" I said, scanning the hallway for the source of her pain.

"I'm just having a bad night," she said. "Can I stay with you?"

"Of course," I responded as I pulled her into the room and closed the door.

Her steps were heavy, dragging across the stone floor. She flinched at the crack of an ember in the fire, and I swept the flames out of existence.

"Hey," I said before grabbing her arms and doing a once-over.

"It's not always like this," she whispered with her eyes on the ground. "Some days feel harder."

"I understand," I responded and pulled her into my body. "I understand, I promise."

"How do you live?" she asked on my shoulder.

Goddess, if I only knew. There wasn't any one answer, no combination of words that would vanish all the pain and anguish. But I still tried.

"We don't let them win. They tried what they could to break us, and they couldn't."

"But what if I *am* broken, Daya? What then?"

"Then we'll put the pieces back together." I lifted her chin. "They took something from you. Sometimes you don't get it back. But we'll make new pieces to replace what you lost."

She nodded, and I couldn't help lifting her off the floor and putting her in my bed. My Zuri. I wanted to rip the world apart to get back who she was before. Wrapping my arms around her, I tried to offer her some of my strength. I'd pull it out of my body and put it in hers if I could, but I gave her what I was capable of until her heavy breathing filled the air.

Whispering woke me, but the two voices had me lying still and listening. Axel was in the room now, on the other side of my body, caging me between them. They didn't seem to realize I was awake, their whispers continuing.

"When I came back, I didn't leave my room. I locked myself in there for days, only let Ishani in the room with me. Everything. . . scared me. It got better, though. Just took time, and knowing that, well, it got better."

"I don't have proof that it'll get better," Zuri responded in hushed tones.

"We have Daya. Don't think it'll get much better than that."

"I don't want anyone to see me as weak."

"I know she doesn't." He paused. "Neither do I."

Silence rang between them, and I felt both of their bodies push closer as they cuddled me and fell back asleep.

Axel's thumb brushed small circles on my hip, Zuri's hand under my shirt and cupping my breast, still sleeping. I tipped up my chin, finding him already looking down at me with a smile.

"Morning," I said, my voice cracking with sleep. "When'd you show up?"

"Middle of the night. Wanted to see you, but you were both already asleep. So I just laid down."

I relished in the feel of their warm bodies against me, a cocoon of security I wanted to stay in forever.

"This feels nice," I said.

"It. . . it does, actually."

He seemed confused by the declaration, but I knew this was only the beginning.

I rubbed my cheek against him. "We should use your bed next time. It's bigger."

"Next time we sleep, or next time we. . . ?"

"Eager are we?" I squeezed his arm.

Zuri groaned awake, stretching her arms with a soft smile. She appeared to forget where she was, her eyes widening after landing on the both of us and setting back down. "I haven't slept that well in a while."

"We can do it nightly." I sat up, my nightgown shifting. Both of their hands lifted to touch my exposed skin, and I laughed at their mirroring instincts. "I slept great, too."

I could feel the tight air, even after the bonding they'd seemed to do last night. Instead of feeding into it, I stood and walked over to the bathroom, looking back to find both of their eyes on the hem, just grazing the cusp of my ass. Leaving the door open, I freshened up and heard shuffling in the doorway.

"I'm going to go get ready," Axel said.

"Me too," Zuri followed up.

I opened a portal to her room—that way she didn't have to walk across the palace—and she jumped in. Axel turned to leave, but I stopped him with a hand on his wrist.

"I heard some of what you guys talked about last night. Not all of it, but just. . . thank you."

"We've all had our fair share of pain by the Sanjryans. We'll get revenge for it all."

I nodded and smiled, and he kissed my forehead before going back out to his room across the hall. There wasn't a better way to wake up, and I really hoped that this could become our new normal.

The grimoire felt like it called to me. So much power emanated from it that I was surprised I couldn't see it in the air. What I read confirmed some of what the Triori had said, the beasts, the magic pulling, the shape-shifting. I wanted to know if there was anything else that could help us understand who he was and what his powers were.

After the meeting, I'd send the book back to its safe location and use the spell to retrieve it going forward. I was lucky to be able to trust Dusra's inner circle, all of them earning it and more since I'd been here. I was even more lucky that they'd all seemed to trust me now, too. Even if I wasn't quite used to it. My mother trusted me, but not in the same way. She trusted that my fear of her would be above anything else. But these people truly wanted what was best for me. I hoped I wouldn't fuck it up.

I made my way down the halls, not hearing Axel in his room when I left. The grimoire was heavy under my arm, and I squeezed it tighter as I almost dropped it when Ishani popped up beside me through a portal. That was pretty common growing up in a coven of brujas, but something about the possibility I'd be the first one to fuck up the grimoire had me a bit on edge.

"Good morning," she said, taking a whiff of the air. "You smell interesting."

"I can't tell if I should be insulted or not," I responded.

"Not a bad smell. You smell like old power and lovers."

"Hm, sounds hot. I'll take it." I stepped into the room where we were meeting. It wasn't the normal place where we ate breakfast every morning, but I was assured there would be food.

"Akari won't make it, she had to go to Arkhia. Everyone else should be here, though," Ishani said as she took a seat.

I placed the grimoire in the middle of the table, in front of my seat, and Ishani tilted her chin toward it. "Have you looked inside yet?"

"Yeah, I scanned the lineage journal. He's mentioned in what I've seen so far."

"Any hope?"

"Yet to be seen," I said.

Everyone filtered in, Xavier immediately taking the seat next to Ishani, Zuri, and Axel by my side again, and Paxx between Xavier and Axel. I could never thank Paxx for what he'd done, but I hoped that whatever I'd do with the information would help protect him and the ones he loved in return.

CHAPTER THIRTY

DAYANARA

Everyone had gone for morning training after we ate, but I stayed behind to read through more of the grimoire. I could bet the little I had that my mother didn't expect me to *ever* get my hands on this. The knowledge inside was overwhelming. Not to mention the fact there were new spells that would be helpful come war. Some were too dangerous to practice for the first time in this room. Footsteps were coming toward me, and I twisted to find Paxx in the doorway.

"We got a bunch of this when we raided Sanjry. Figured you might want to try out the spell," he said as he handed me a chunk of seraphinite.

"Thanks, Paxx. I want any leverage possible."

Something inside of me recoiled at the chunk of stone, it was raw, not activated, but my body knew it. I set it down, hoping Paxx didn't catch on.

He pointed to the grimoire. "How do you feel after that?"

I closed the book and snapped it into the holding place. "There are so many secrets in here. I'm almost worried to keep reading."

"What are you worried about?"

"We've been seen as the villains for a long time. I haven't cared much. As long as we were safe, but now? What if there are things in here that could put us at fault for all of it?"

"It's the past. You'd be righting it now in the present."

If we were successful.

"I suppose," I said as we left the room together.

I liked that Paxx was comfortable in silence. Not everybody was. I was even guilty of filling silence with unneeded words, but with Paxx it was easy quiet.

"Axel and Zuri seem to be getting along," he said.

"A bit forced but I'll take it," I laughed. "You haven't given me your thoughts about it like everyone else."

"Dusra is my priority. I don't think it would negatively impact our kingdom. Axel and Zuri are. . . the most important people in my life. If they're happy, I'm happy."

I held the door into the training wing open for him. "Ya know, other than Zuri, I haven't heard anything about your romantic life."

"Don't really have one. My work is all-encompassing."

"You haven't been with anyone since Zuri?" I picked up a sparring sword. Zuri and Ishani were sparring across the yard, and Axel and Xavier were nearby.

"I'm not saying that." He swung his sword. "Nobody of permanence. Never felt the urge."

"I was like that for a long time." I ducked, blocking and absorbing the impact of his blow. "Gets lonely eventually."

"I don't know. I wouldn't say lonely. There's an entire group of people here I can go to should I need support."

"There are other things that need. . . fulfilling."

"Have no problems there, Daya."

I don't doubt it. I'd seen women whispering about him as we walked by, him and Axel, but one growl from me had put that to a stop pretty damn quickly. Left all the ogling to Paxx as no one would come close to Xavier because of Ishani. As a completely subjective party, I could see what Zuri saw. He was tall, very handsome, all those muscles had to be good for something. . .

"Um." Paxx stood still.

Forgot he had that weird aura-reading thing. Might be worse than the mind reading. "Hm?"

"Nothing." He shook his head.

I swiped his foot and pushed him to the ground with a blast of air, tipping his chin up with the end of my sword. Axel and Xavier clapped from where they stood, and I chuckled as I helped him up.

"Distraction is not a fair fighting technique," he said.

I shrugged. "Fair is overrated."

After a more thorough training than I thought Paxx was expecting, he went and downed an entire jug of water. Everyone else finished, and we stood on the outskirts of the courtyard.

"I'm going to get ready for the festival," Ishani told Axel, and he nodded before turning to Zuri.

"Are you going to the festival, Zuri?" Axel asked.

She bit her lip. "I'm not sure."

I could feel her apprehension. A festival seemed positive, but the way Zuri reacted had me going into protection mode.

"What festival?" I asked, stepping closer to her.

"It's a festival in Arkhia the lobos have once a year to celebrate our ancestors, the people who have passed since the last one. I haven't been in..." Zuri shook her head. "I haven't been in a long time."

I understood the apprehension then. But I was still curious.

"What does it entail?"

"It's a big celebration. Lots of dancing, lots of food. Where you took us in Caldera, Cape Coven, we have a similar place to that. The dead can visit us on this day. This is the one time they're allowed in this realm," Zuri explained.

"Do you normally go, Ax?" I asked.

"It's been some time."

The tight air around Zuri seemed to relax as she explained what the festival was. She still seemed hesitant, but there was something else under that.

"Why don't we go? At least for a little bit?" I suggested.

Zuri's fingers tapped gently against her thigh, a nervous tick I'd noticed in Sanjry when we first met, but it had been missing for a while.

"I don't want to push. I just. . . who knows where we'll be in a year after the information we got. We have to take advantage of every opportunity we can," I followed up.

Tears rimmed Zuri's eyes as she nodded. "My parents. . . I haven't seen them." She shook her head. "No. You're right. I can do this. With you, I can do this."

I thought back to what Akari had said, that I brought something out of Zuri that died with her parents. It felt really fucking good to be the one to get her to this point.

Axel let out a deep breath through his nostrils before saying, "Okay."

"How do we get there?"

"There's a portal door similar to the one you used to get here from the border. It's on the coast, so we'll need you to portal us there first," Axel responded.

"All right, let's do it." I clapped my hands.

"Um," Zuri started. "We're going to need to change."

"Into?" I trailed off.

"We're supposed to be colorful. It's a celebration, not really a mourning situation." Zuri gestured to all three of us in all black.

"There's a dress in your closet that should do," Axel said. "Lots of color, lots of beads. You can't miss it."

I wondered if that was one he'd seen me in from the visions from the Triori. We still hadn't discussed it, with us rescuing Zuri right after. I knew I wasn't necessarily upset that he'd kept it from me. I had them both now, I just wanted to move forward.

"Okay, everyone meet in the courtyard in twenty?" I asked. Zuri nodded, but the tightness in her shoulders hadn't waned yet. "Actually, why don't I portal to your room first and we can grab what you're wearing. We can get dressed together in my room, and then we'll meet you in the courtyard, Axel."

Axel nodded before exiting the room, and Zuri sagged slightly. "Thanks. Going to need to work myself up to this. I'd be lying if I said I hadn't thought about going all day."

She joined me where I stood, and I snapped open a portal into her room. She hurried over to her closet and grabbed a dress hanging on the very end. Her arms were full with the garment, jewelry, and shoes by the time we portaled into my room and she set it all down.

"So, can the dead speak to you today?" I asked as I went over to my closet.

"Yeah. That's the problem. My parents are going to want to talk to me, and I don't know what to say to them. I know they've seen that I haven't taken the path they wanted me to."

My gaze trailed up and down my closet until I found one dress that looked similar to Zuri's in color and pattern. The dress was heavy, so much intricate detail that I was still staring at it as I made it back into the room.

"You don't think it'll feel good to at least be able to speak with them?"

Zuri ran her hand down her face as she stepped out of her leathers, and I tried to focus on the very serious conversation at hand and not the fact she was naked.

"It probably will. The possibility that it won't, though, that's what's been holding me back." Zuri pulled her dress on and turned around for me to help.

I stepped over to her and pulled at the strings to tighten the dress. "I get that. Either way, I'll be there for you. I promise."

Zuri turned around as I finished and threw her arms around my neck, pulling me into a kiss. I took my time with returning the gesture, hoping she felt the truth in my words. She pulled back and relaxed into my chest, and I took the opportunity to run my hands down her back in comfort until she sighed and stood back up fully. I was really starting to like being the one to console.

"Okay, I wasted enough time. Hurry up before Axel is in a mood because we're late," she laughed out and wiped a few stray tears.

"He'll be fine," I responded as I quickly changed.

The dress wasn't nearly as heavy as I thought it'd be once the corset strings were tightened. It was beautiful, with oranges, yellows, and a deep navy blue pattern I didn't think I'd ever seen before. The rows of beads shifted as I moved, and Zuri slipped a couple of bangles onto my wrists before sliding a hairpiece into my hair as well.

"Perfect. You could pass as a lobo right now," she said with a chuckle.

We made it into the courtyard where Axel was waiting, wearing the most color I'd ever seen on him. The hem of his tunic was a bit longer than the others he'd worn, with a similar pattern and colored fabric as mine.

"Let's get to the coast," Axel finally said, and I realized I'd been staring for an abnormal amount of time.

I opened the portal and stepped through into the halls of the coastal stronghold. The sound of blades against blades caught my attention from beyond the wall, but Ishani stepped into the hall wearing a gorgeous gown.

"Oh, you guys look amazing," she gushed as she moved toward me and ran her hands down the fabric of my dress.

Ishani was always beautiful, but something about the confidence she had in this traditional dress of her mother's people gave her something extra.

"It's my mother's," she mumbled with her eyes on her dress.

"You're beautiful," I said with a smile.

Ishani turned to Zuri. "How are you feeling, Zuri?"

Sometimes I forgot that Ishani and her were close, that there was a possibility that she knew Zuri in different ways than me—in more ways even.

"I think it's time, you know?" Zuri answered.

I wrapped my fingers around hers and squeezed her hand. "We're all with you."

Axel led us down the halls, to the other side of the building and opened a door, the same swirling pattern of bruja magic as the one by the border.

"I never asked. Is the doorway made of moonstone?" I questioned.

Ishani nodded. "It's Maeve's magic."

"That makes sense," I whispered as I dipped my hand into it, now recognizing her essence since I'd met her.

Putting one foot through the portal, I turned back and grabbed Zuri's hand, and Ishani squeezed her shoulder as we stepped through. I wasn't sure what I was expecting, but the other side of the portal putting us out in the middle of a field of multicolored trees wasn't it. They shot up so far I couldn't see the tops, big, thick leaves covering long branches of so many hues I couldn't keep up. They reminded me of home. The trees lining the capital in Caldera were much smaller with jewel-toned leaves, but there didn't seem to be a single color missing from these. There was a gentle humming, a serenity that made me want to lie down in the grass and close my eyes. A strong hand jerked at my arm, snapping me out of the haze.

"It's the trees," Axel said with his gaze on the swaying branches. "They have a siren song of their own, a small thing from the other side. You can go mad out here if you stay too long."

"That's. . . dangerous?"

"It doesn't affect the lobos. I don't know why, but they can stay within this forest in their lobo form perfectly fine. Almost feels like a sort of protection," Zuri said, her hands brushing up and down her legs nervously.

"Our ancestors used to lure people out here. Let's get Daya out. She doesn't have a drop of lobo blood," Ishani chuckled.

The soft hum from the trees faded as we moved, the sound of a celebration replacing it completely by the time we exited the tree line. We crested a hill, hundreds of people dancing and celebrating until one person spotted us, and every single one of them went quiet. Head after head turned to us, the music stopped, and waves of people dropped to a knee with their eyes on the ground. Zuri took a step backward, but Axel put his hand on her shoulder and shook his head.

"This is for you, not me," he said.

Zuri looked up at him, a crease between her brows as she raked her gaze back over the sea of people. Someone started beating on a drum, words I couldn't make out being sung in hushed tones as she descended the hill.

"This is her family's song," Ishani said with a smile.

Someone in the back of the crowd moved forward, light brown braids shifting as they picked up speed. Akari parted the people, her mouth open as she ran to her cousin. With each step she took, the crowd sang louder until Akari wrapped her arms around Zuri. We stayed a few steps back, letting her have this moment to rejoin her family. Akari pulled Zuri by her hand to a raised altar where Nia sat upon an intricate throne.

Nia stood, her arms open wide, and Zuri shook her head, trying to stay in the crowd. She looked over her shoulder, her tear-lined eyes locking with mine while I shook my head and pointed to where Nia sat. Akari waited for her to make her decision, and with a small smile, Zuri stepped onto the altar, still holding Akari's hand. The pride that shone across Zuri's face was nothing short of incredible—no, contagious. I felt it ripple off her to every single person around. It hit me like a rock, and damn if it didn't have the biggest smile possible stretching across my face.

"Zuri has returned!"

Chapter Thirty-One

Zuri

My heart was racing, the rhythm booming in my ears as the scents of my home filled my nostrils. So many smiling faces peered up at me. Some I recognized, some too young for me to remember. My people started dancing again, the music even louder than it was before.

"I wasn't expecting you." Nia smiled.

"Me either," Akari added.

"I didn't think I was going to until. . . " I trailed off.

Daya was in the crowd with Axel and Ishani. Her back turned to me as someone introduced themselves.

"Daya convinced you?" Akari asked.

"She just pushed me hard enough," I answered.

Akari had been trying to get me to come for years, and I made an excuse each time. Being separated from everyone in Sanjry for a few years was almost a relief, not having to face this. But I was ready now. Night was coming, and the spirits would start crossing over into this realm. Everything was set up the same way I remembered it all those years ago. The dancing, music, and flowers peppered throughout to guide the spirits to our altars. I looked at the one I stood upon, the biggest of the altars covering the space. The one for my parents.

A painting of each of them was propped up, and the constraint on my throat, I thought I shook, came back. My father, his dark loc'd hair hanging down past his shoulders, the roots of them twisted tightly the way he always liked. His smile stretched across his face, framed by the facial hair he'd had all my life. The painting captured the exact way his angled eyes sparkled, the smooth texture of his dark russet skin, his wide nose. He was a beautiful man, only rivaled by my mother.

My mother was the type of woman that people stopped and stared at no matter where we were. She wasn't only outwardly beautiful, but had a heart that radiated kindness. People always wanted her attention, wanted a piece of the warmth that she always brought with her. I took after her in many ways, her deep caramel skin, those golden freckles splattered across her nose and cheeks. Even her light brown hair that fell in ringlets down her back. I had my father's eye shape, but their dark gray color came from her. Seeing myself in these people who brought me into the world, who loved me and cared for me, who were taken far too soon, tightened my chest. They'd covered the altar in their personal effects, my father's sword, my mother's jewelry. I ran my finger over my favorite of her headpieces, one she called the evening gazania. It resembled a flower, how it puckered up at night. She always wore it around her bun. Sometimes she let me wear it, which always made me feel so close to her.

Warm tears welled in my eyes, and the moment they fell, another presence moved close to me. I didn't need to look to see that it was Daya. She stayed at my back, her hand brushing the skin on my arm every few moments, but she allowed me the moment I needed. My father's other wives and my brother sat on either side of them. They hurt, remembering how much they cared for me, especially after my brother died. But the pain I felt from them was different. I'd mourned them already, had moved on while my parents still lived. I wasn't worried about seeing them.

"You okay?" Daya whispered as she turned to face me.

I nodded, pointing to my parents. "I haven't seen a painting of them since before they died. It's bittersweet seeing them like this."

"I see so much of them in you." She grinned.

"In our lobo forms, me and my mother were almost identical," I said.

What I wouldn't give to be mistaken for her again. It used to bother me that everyone assumed I was just like her. But now I'd give anything for it.

"So, how does the crossing work?"

"It happens when we transition to dusk. It's hard to explain, but you'll know when it happens. They'll appear on the altars, as themselves, but in a spirit form. When you saw your mother, did she have some sort of glow around her?"

"Yeah, she did," she responded.

"Like that. They can touch us in a way, but we can't touch them. They'll be here until the morning, then they'll be sent back to the spirit realm."

"It's only the lobos?"

I nodded. "This tradition goes back as far as our writings."

"Do you want me to. . . go somewhere else?"

"No," I answered immediately. "No, I want them to meet you. If you're okay with that."

She smiled that smile that I always felt in my core before saying, "I'd love to meet them."

It had never even crossed my mind until this moment that I'd ever be here with her. Daya had said before that she couldn't imagine her life without me, that I was a reason to keep going. But she didn't realize how much she did for me. Our relationship was like the first breath of air after drowning, after not knowing who I was, who I wanted to be, Daya, coming into my orbit. . . I could never repay her for what she'd done for me.

"It's time!" Nia exclaimed over the music.

The music shifted from the celebratory tune to something I could only describe as spiritual. The same song they played on this day every year, said to help guide the spirits with the help of the flowers to the altars. Nia hummed loudly, and I knew I shouldn't have resented her, but a small part of me did. When I made the choice to pass my title over to her, it was made by a version of me so taken by grief and depression that I couldn't think clearly. I didn't think I could lead our pack when I was barely surviving. Every day was painful. Every breath I took that my parents didn't, every beat of my heart while theirs was decaying in the ground, felt wrong.

Being in this land they loved, seeing reminders of them everywhere, I couldn't do it. Now that I was better, standing strong, and with Daya by my side, part of me regretted it. There wasn't any going back, and I had made a whole life away from Arkhia. But I couldn't help but wonder what Daya would look like on that throne beside me. Axel stepped through to the front of the crowd, reminding me that my situation was slightly more complicated than that.

We'd been able to get along more than before, but the gut reaction I had to him would take much longer to deal with. He stepped up onto the altar with us, brushing by Daya with his hand on her waist.

The air shifted, the atmosphere changing as the crossing began. There was an electric charge in the air, reminding me of Daya's magic in some ways. My hands shook as spirits popped up at altars around us. My legs wobbled slightly, and Daya wrapped herself around me, her head in the crook of my neck. I leaned into her, and my body stabilized just as my mother manifested on her throne.

I thought the painting captured their features well, but seeing her corporeal, as corporeal as she could be. . .

"Mom," I sobbed, pulling out of Daya's arms and darting toward her.

I stopped short, having to let her be the one to embrace me, or I'd go flying face-first into the throne.

"Zuri, you came," she said gently.

"My girl," my father's voice boomed from behind me.

I whirled around, one arm on my mother, the other reaching for him. He embraced me back, and I could sense their touch, but that warmth wasn't there as it had been when they were alive. But I'd take it. They were here, and they were embracing me. My father didn't shun me, my mother didn't recoil from my touch. They didn't call me a monster for what I'd done. I felt like an innocent child again, just needing their parents' comfort. I cried like one, too.

"I knew you'd be strong enough one day," my father mumbled.

"I miss you guys so much," I said, barely able to get the words out between sobs.

"We're never too far," my mother responded with a tap on my chest.

I dropped my chin. "Still."

Nia cleared her throat, and we turned to find her in a deep bow. "We have your offerings, and I'd like to give you the usual updates. But find me when you have a chance, Zuri."

"Okay." I nodded, and she gracefully left the altar.

"Valyn, Imara," Ax declared as he rose from a bow as deep as Nia's.

"Kiaan." My mother smiled.

Sometimes I forgot that Axel wasn't his true name. Everyone called him Axel or Ax, but my mother had told him that *his* mother gave him that name for a reason, and that she wouldn't use anything else.

"Ishani is around here somewhere. I'm sure she'll come say hi," he responded.

The only person on the altar who hadn't acknowledged them yet was Daya. She stood with her hands behind her back, seeming to be waiting for the moment I thought was best.

I stretched my hand out toward her. "Mom, Dad, this is Dayanara."

I couldn't help the smile that overtook me as she grinned and bowed to my parents, stepping forward to stand right beside me.

"I'm so happy to meet you," she said, her tone so warm and genuine.

"You as well," my father said, his eyes bouncing between us and over to Axel, who stood mighty close to Daya. "Who are we meeting, Zuri?"

"She's my. . ." I started before looking over to Axel. "Our. . ."

How in the world did I quickly explain that Daya just happened to be the center of both our worlds, that we hadn't ventured too far into relationship stuff yet because I was briefly captured by Sanjry and her psychotic ex-fiancé?

"I belong to both of them," Daya said simply.

"And do they belong to you?" my mother said with a smirk.

"We do," Ax and I both responded quickly.

Well, that was easier than I thought. It was simple, she was ours, we were hers. The declaration, the ease in which Daya said it filled me with warmth.

"Are you a witch?" my father asked.

"I am," Daya responded with a smile.

"She's the Acna," I said proudly.

My father's brows raised, my mother nodding with appreciation. There weren't too many other times people didn't know who Daya was. Taking the opportunity to gush about her was fantastic.

"It sounds like they're both lucky to have you," my mother said.

"I'm the lucky one." Daya turned to face me. "I'll let you guys get caught up. Let me know when you're ready for me to come back, okay?"

"No, it's fine," I said before turning to my parents, who appeared like they really did want a minute alone with me. "Okay."

Daya rubbed her palm to my cheek before grabbing Axel by his wrist and dragging him off the altar with her.

"You've got your hands full," my father chuckled.

"Understatement. Were you actually there in Sanjry?" I asked my father, unable to hold back the question any longer.

"I was." He nodded once. "You were very close to the edge of the spirit world, close enough that I was able to contact you."

"I didn't realize how close I was to dying," I whispered.

"But here you are." My mother rubbed my arm.

"So, my daughter, what has happened in these years since we saw you?"

I talked to my parents for hours, letting them know about me moving to the palace, doing the spy work with Paxx, going to Sanjry, meeting Daya. We talked about everything, and not a single thing stole their love for me. But there was one thing I couldn't bring myself to ask, not until this moment. The one thing that might have them disowning me.

"Before you." My voice cracked. "Before you died, did you try to separate from Dusra?"

My father shook his head. "We discussed it among our council. But your mother and I didn't think we had the numbers or the resources to fully separate."

I swallowed hard. Ax wasn't lying. I'd blamed their deaths on him for so long. Assuming that it was his arrogance that led to my people revolting and killing my parents. And to me. . .

"You thought this was his fault?" my mother asked, reaching over to place her hand on my knee where I sat between them.

"I did. I needed someone to blame. . . " I trailed off. "Do you know what I did when I found your bodies?"

Neither of them responded, didn't incline their heads or give me any sort of indication that they knew, or didn't know.

"I killed them all. Every person who seemed like they were part of the revolt, I killed them. I didn't stop and ask questions. I didn't try to reason with them. When I saw your bodies..." My throat tightened. "Leaking blood, lifeless. Dad, I snapped."

"We know, Zuri. They're with us, in the spirit world."

"I hated him. It was so easy to hate him, to let myself off the hook for killing all of those people because it was *his* fault you were gone," I practically growled.

Who was responsible, then? Where did all of that rage belong? It wasn't Axel anymore. It had to be *someone's* fault. The ones who revolted were at fault for my parents, but that only left. . . me at fault for the rest.

"It was no one's fault," my mother whispered. "Our deaths, any death, it comes exactly when it's supposed to. We were meant to die on that day, and you were meant to follow the path you did."

"But that doesn't mean I should have done what I did."

My parents glanced at each other, and it brought me back to when I was a child. When they'd have these silent conversations.

It was my mother who responded, saying, "Perhaps not. We all have to live with the decisions we make. You reacted to something terrible, and you grew from that. Would you have left Arkhia if we hadn't died?"

"The love you have for Dayanara, that is no small thing. She is who you were meant for," my father added.

"That's not fair. I shouldn't have had to lose you to get her," I said.

My mother smiled gently, pulling me into her chest for a hug. "There is no fair, my love. There is only life, fate, love. Your father and I had many good years, and now we remain together."

I sniffled. "Wait, where are Lena and Nova? Zuberi?"

I had been so wrapped up in my parents, I didn't realize my other moms and brother weren't here. My parents were the ones I was most worried about, because their deaths were what set me away from the path they wanted.

"They wanted to give you some time with us. I can bring them forward now?" My father asked.

I nodded. "I want to see everyone."

Chapter Thirty-Two

Dayanara

I watched as Zuri flitted back and forth between her family members. They all squeezed her and pulled at her curls, inspecting every inch of her. The smile she wore. Fuck, that smile was something I wanted to get tattooed on my body. Her brother was the spitting image of their father, his body thicker, whereas their father was leaner, but still very similar. He had Zuri in a headlock as they tussled, and she laughed as she tried to pull out of his hold.

Other lobos were starting to come up to the altar and try to get time with her parents, and she sat beside them, listening to whatever the lobos were telling them. Looking very much like a princess.

"I haven't seen her this way since before they died," Ishani said, startling me.

Axel had gone to catch up with Nia, so I was sitting on the outskirts. Perfectly content to watch all the familial love from a distance.

I turned to Ishani as she plopped down on the ground beside me. "I like it."

"Me too."

It was a beautiful thing, watching the living spend these moments with their dead loved ones. A spectrum of feelings was represented—some crying, others dancing and laughing. They only got this moment once a year, and I wondered how they prepared themselves for it. What things they thought they needed to share with their family that were gone. *Wait, family.*

"Is your mom here?" I asked.

"Axel told you about the barrier, right? She gave up her soul for it. There's no realm where she exists, nowhere we can talk to her."

"We keep her in our hearts. That's the only place she exists," Axel said as he joined us.

To give up her soul to protect her family. . . that was an extreme love. I wondered if it had to do with Ishani's deal with the Triori, but I couldn't ask that right now. All three of us peered back into the crowd, a howling going up in the distance.

"What's that for?" I asked.

"It's time for the run." Ishani beamed.

"Everyone shifts and runs through the forest," Axel elaborated before I could ask.

"Even the spirits?"

Axel nodded. "Even the spirits."

Something about this excited me. I'd seen lobos at the palace, but not this many in one place, and definitely not them running as a pack. Axel and Ishani had never shifted together either, and that would be a sight.

"Do you guys shift into your other forms?"

"We do," Ishani responded as she got up and stretched.

It was interesting the way that their gifts split between Ishani and Axel. Ishani could shift into a lobo like Zuri, but Axel could do so much more. He could maneuver essence almost in the way I did, guiding it into other forms. I had a feeling that in this scenario, he'd shift into his lobo form, though.

The earth shook around us as everyone shifted, heavy paws hitting the ground one after another. Ishani's beautiful black lobo darted from behind me, bounding toward Akari and tackling her. They were such powerful beasts, but watching them play like pups was hilarious.

The hairs on the back of my neck stood on end, an awareness rushing through me with a blast of dark magic rippling past my shoulders. Axel, in all his strength, in all his power, stood behind me, choosing a massive lobo as his shifted creature. So much like his sister's, but somehow. . . more. His fur shifted, flickering in shimmering black and silver, but the same hazel irises stared me down. Just as they did when I'd seen him in his water dragon form.

I reached my hand out to run it down his powerful jaw, and he flashed me his fangs before nuzzling his head into the crook of my neck.

'Ride me,' he said into my mind.

'Not in that form.' I winked before hiking my dress up and jumping onto his back with a blast of air. I squeezed his strong ribs with my thighs and grasped his hair to hold on tight right before he threw his head back and howled. The sound boomed around me, my eardrums shaking with my proximity to his head. Another howl went up, and more consecutively, until the entire tribe of wolves was echoing his command.

Nia bolted over to where we stood, her legs extending in massive pounces until she reached where Axel stood. Zuri came next, Akari, Zuberi, and her parents behind her. That same soft glow encompassed their lobo forms. A cold nose rubbed into my side, and I found Ishani lined up with us.

Axel turned his head to Zuri, and she turned hers to Nia. Nia fell back on her haunches, and I could feel the ripple of shock course through Zuri. It was quickly covered by pride as she stood taller, letting out a howl that rivaled Axel's before turning into the forest.

Her family trailed her as each of us moved to run, the rest of the tribe crowding around us. We dodged fallen trees, weaving around the ones still standing tall. The love and innate belonging they all felt while together was astonishing. It was heavy in the air like a thick fog, a deep affection for those lost over the years, for those still in this mortal world.

Was this how a nation was supposed to be? I'd grown up with the brujas, never felt like we did this incorrectly, but I definitely never felt anything remotely close to this. Wolves nudged each other's side, playfully nipping at each other as Axel picked up his speed.

He shot to the front of the group, tossing a challenging glance over at Zuri. She looked up at me on his back, and I swore if a lobo could smile, she would have. I knew she missed this, regardless of what she had said previously. A cloud of dirt kicked up at her back feet as she pushed faster. Akari and Ishani were now at the front of the line with us. Each of them pushed the other faster, Ishani nosing to the front. She whipped her tail across Axel's face as she took the lead out of the trees, and he yelped, stumbling a step before his body began to vibrate.

'Hold on,' Axel's voice boomed in my mind.

The fur on his body dissolved, shifting into hard scales as his torso elongated and wings sprouted from his sides above where I was sitting. His long neck turned, and golden dragon eyes now stared back at me. He let out a roar, so different from the howl he had let out before, and sliced through the open air.

We left everyone in the dust behind us. No way they'd be able to keep up with him in this form. I lifted my chin, letting the air wrap around me and toss my hair, the beads on my dress rattling at our speeds. This was different from when I'd flown. There was freedom in not being the one in control, and to completely trust the one who was.

Axel landed in a bed of wildflowers as his body returned to his vampire form, his clothes not even slightly wrinkled. I still straddled him, butterflies leaping from the flowers and fluttering around us, along with a sparkling cloud. The heavy footsteps of the tribe were getting closer, but I took the opportunity to reach down and press a kiss to his lips. His hands reached into my hair, returning the kiss with even more passion.

The orange of the sky always made his eyes feel like they burned with fire, the reflection adding more amber to his already golden irises. But this time, they burned for me. All his emotions for me were concentrated into a gaze, into a stare that didn't just see me, but saw my soul.

Zuri slid into where we were, shifting in midair before she landed right beside us. Her smile, fuck, her smile burned as brightly as Axel's eyes. I wanted to stay here, to let her live in this moment of bliss. But her family only had until morning, and they'd be gone. We all sat up as everyone made it to the field, sparkling dust shifting in the air with each person running through the flowers.

Zuri's family approached us, but I hadn't met the two other women or her brother yet.

"That's Lena and Nova, my other moms," Zuri said before she bounded over to them and wrapped her arms around both the women. "And that's my brother."

She pulled her moms by their hands, stopping in front of me and leaving them to grab me. "This is Dayanara."

"She's hot," Zuberi whispered into Zuri's ear, slightly too loud so that all of us heard it.

"Right?" Zuri grinned wide.

I laughed at her brother, but Zuri's mothers moved closer. Their gaze bounced between the two of us and then to Axel, who came to stand at my other side.

"It's nice to meet you," the one on the left said.

"Nova," Zuri said before pointing to the woman on the right. "And Lena."

Zuri's parents crowded us, and all of them were far touchier than I was used to. After the second time I nearly recoiled, Zuri told them to stop acting like I was a wolf. I expected judgment, or something negative, but they just nodded and smiled before asking a million questions about Zuri. She was overwhelmed, but something told me she didn't mind too much.

Zuberi had been watching, observing, much like Paxx did. He watched as I interacted with his parents and watched as Zuri and Axel interacted with me. When Zuri stood to perform some sort of dance she made up as a child for her mothers, her brother scooted over to me.

"I missed my sister," he said without taking his eyes off Zuri.

Zuri spun and stretched her arms toward the sky, getting up on her tip toes and gallivanting across the field. She was so fucking adorable. That leisure joy she had right now, it was intoxicating.

"She missed you all," I responded.

"I wanted to be angry with her. Our parents forgave her quickly. I even had a whole speech for if she ever showed up. Ready to rip her a new one for not visiting in such a long time."

"But?"

Tears balanced at his waterline, but he quickly brushed them away before they fell. Zuri hadn't told me what happened to him, just that he died when she was young. He had a warrior's stance about him, and if I had to guess, it would have involved that. "Father told me what he saw."

"I plan on returning every bit of that pain tenfold," I responded.

"I can see it. Not being there to watch her grow up in the real world, only getting bits of pieces as she visited me with our parents. That hurt. I was supposed to be her protector, and there's been so much she should have been protected from."

I put my hand on his shoulder. "I'll take it from here."

"I'll haunt you if you don't." The twinkle in his eye, the little crease in his nose, it reminded me so much of his sister. Siblings weren't too common in Caldera, but I found myself wondering what it would have been like to even have a couple of years with someone like Zuberi as a brother.

I cursed the hours rolling by, knowing it wouldn't last forever. Zuri's parents had convinced her to take some of their personal belongings, a sword, and some sort of headpiece, which Zuri lit up about when her mother mentioned it. The sword was a masterpiece, a true craft of workmanship.

Axel lingered at Zuri's back, and I could tell he was about to remind her there were only minutes left until her parents went back to their spiritual rest. Zuri's father got up from the group of women on the brink of tears and sat down beside me.

"Can I trust you to take care of my baby girl?" he asked.

I looked him in the eye, hoping that he could hear the sincerity in my tone as I said, "I'd give my life for her."

We didn't have fathers in Caldera. Our mothers had no use for them, and half the time they didn't see another day after conception. I wasn't used to this. . . paternal energy. Even our type of maternal energy wasn't the same as the kind here. But Zuri's father radiated love for both of his kids. Her mothers hadn't stopped doting after her since the moment they laid eyes on her. It was a foreign concept for me, but to grow up like this, and have it taken from you in such a way, I could see why Zuri did what she did.

"She would do the same for you. I can feel it. Protect each other. There is unrest in the spiritual world. Something is coming," her father said.

"Does the god of Chaos mean anything to you?" I asked, wondering if Zuri had already asked him.

"Not when I was living," he answered, his gaze trying to convey something else that he couldn't say. "Be prepared."

"It's time," Axel interrupted with sadness in his voice.

Their forms were already fading by the second, half-drawn figures sprawled across a beautiful canvas of flowering fields. Fingers and feet were already gone, and the spirit world slowly reclaimed the rest of their bodies.

"I love you, my daughter." Zuri's father pressed his forehead to hers, and their family formed a huddle around them.

"I love you all," Zuri whispered.

Axel gasped, his hand clutching his chest as he placed his other hand on his knee. Zuri's family all snapped around, but their bodies were almost gone. Axel's eyes were wide, droplets of sweat spotting his forehead. I reached out to help him sit up, and his heart pounded against his chest, as powerful as the lobo paws that just beat against the earth. Zuri put her hand on my back, assessing Axel the same way I was.

"What's wrong?" I asked.

The last of the dead disappeared, leaving the living standing around and whispering. Axel's chest heaved a couple of times before he used the back of his hand to wipe his forehead.

"Kaizer. He broke the agreement."

Chapter Thirty-Three

Dayanara

The bastard fucking did it. Kaizer really broke the agreement. There was no way he did it without realizing. Both of them had been dancing the lines of the boundaries. For this to happen, it had to be intentional.

"What does this mean?" Zuri asked.

"I can't tell. I'm not sure if this means he's here or if he broke part of it," Axel said as he rubbed his temples.

"I'll go to the coast," Ishani said without waiting for a response.

"Let's find Paxx." I snapped a portal open into Dusra's head of intelligence office. We found Paxx at his desk. His head ducked down as he assessed a map of Sanjry.

"Everything okay?" he asked as his eyes bounced between the three of us. When they landed on Ax, he stood up and grabbed his weapon. "What is it?"

"Kaizer broke the agreement. I felt it. Any word from the borders?"

Paxx shook his head before one of the stones on his desk lit up. We all stood still for a moment as we watched it glow, and I stepped forward. "Where's that one?"

"Island border. I can do the spell for this one." He picked up the stone and whispered the same spell I'd use. With the distance not too far from the palace, he was able to do it himself.

"We just brought down three boats of Sanjryans," a deep male voice came from the stone.

Boats? Why would they come through the water?

"Was Sanjry's king on those boats?" Paxx asked.

"Negative. We should get more men out here."

"Sending now." Paxx set the stone down. "We need to notify Ishani and Xavier."

They were aiming for the portal door, but I opened another one in front of us. We stepped into absolute mayhem. Ishani was screaming at a guard covered in blood, but he wasn't responding to her. He only stared at her as she demanded him to speak more and more loudly. Xavier was talking to another, much quieter by the door, but that guard wasn't responding either. Papers were on the floor, their weapons both on their desks as if they pulled them out after hearing some threat.

"What the fuck is happening?" Axel caught everyone's attention.

"Athena, she's gone," Xavier responded.

Fuck. She was one of the few sources of information we had.

I grabbed one of the guards by the neck and snapped, "How did that happen?"

At first glance, I'd thought he was covered in blood, but it looked like he'd jumped into a pool of the substance. The bright whites of his eyes were unnaturally stark against the crimson crusting his skin.

"We don't. . . " he stuttered, staring at the other, less bloody guard. "I don't. . ."

"You feeling any more articulate than your friend?" I asked the one I wasn't holding by the neck—yet.

"She was there, bitching about the food, and then the next moment she was. . . everywhere," he responded.

Ishani stepped forward. "That's all I've got out of them. Let's go find out for ourselves."

We rushed down to the dungeons, Axel on our heels. Xavier stayed with Paxx to try to figure out how to handle the border problem. More guards were scurrying around the cells, one covered in even more blood than the one from the office. The same haunted expression echoed in his eyes. I could smell it before I saw it, the pure gore. It leaked from the cell that once held Athena, a river of it still flowing through the doorway.

I'd seen a lot of things, but never had I seen something like this. The walls were covered in the thick red substance, bits of brain matter mixed in and stuck on the stone. Something snapped under my feet, splinters of white gravel on the floor. I bent down, grabbing one, realizing that it wasn't stone, but was the remnants of Athena's bones.

"The agreement," Axel mumbled.

"What about it?" Ishani asked.

"Shit," I whispered, running my finger through the blood on the wall. "He must have loved her in some capacity for it to take her as the price."

"If what she said was true, she was the reason he was even in the position he was. They'd been *something* for years. Even if he was. . . otherwise occupied when you came into the picture," Axel answered.

I was just glad it wasn't me. It really went to show what kind of man Kaizer was—that the magic in charge of the agreement thought he cared about her most. The person that brought him into his power.

"So does that mean we can go to Sanjry now?" I asked.

"The agreement is null and void now that he broke it. We can do whatever the fuck we want."

"To risk this, he had to have something substantial," Ishani added.

The blood was drying in some spots, no clothes or hair, or any other remnants left behind but Athena's blood, guts, and pieces of bones. I didn't like her, but damn, was this a bad way to go. She might not have felt anything, or fate may have made sure that she knew what was happening. Did they show her Kaizer's face in her last moments? His true face, the one that decided something he loved, was less important than the scepter.

"Is it weird that I sort of feel bad?" Ishani said with her lip pulled back.

"Play stupid games, get stupid prizes." I shrugged, even though I was thinking the same thing. "We're all in this situation because of her and her father. Whether she was the one who pulled all the strings or not, she knew what she was doing."

Axel scratched the back of his head while Ishani kicked a rather big piece of muscle. There wasn't much we could do here. We left the room, and Ishani directed someone to clean up the mess. Too bad we didn't put her in the wet cell, the tide could have done most of the hard work.

By the time we made it to the island coast, it was an absolute shit show. The boats didn't make it all the way through the barrier, but they got a lot closer than anyone else had, apparently. From the looks of it, the agreement was broken because Kaizer sent them through. He wasn't among the dead or the captured. Unless he got away.

Two massive sea dragons pulled up to the coast, a vampire on one and a lobo on the other. I'd gotten pretty good at identifying between them. I wasn't sure specifically what it was that set them apart, but there was something there. Maybe because I'd been so intimate with both.

One thing I hadn't gotten used to was the sea dragons. They were beautiful, massive, deadly creatures. The one on the left blended in with the water, dark blue scales reflecting in the light of the sky. The other was a dark red, much more prominent than the blue one. Razor-sharp teeth sparkled as water dripped from the scaley mouth, its neck outstretched for the rider to get back to land.

"No casualties on our side. Seems like it was a test of the barrier," a soldier said.

"How'd you determine that?" Akari asked.

"Found this." The other soldier tossed her something with their eyes on me.

Her hands wrapped around the mass, and she lifted it between us. "Daya?"

The raw, lime-green gem took me by surprise. "It's peridot. A conduit, we use it to train witchlings."

"There's a whole pile of it lined up on the sea ground," he followed up.

"They're hoping to blast the barrier into pieces," I said. "They would need a fuck ton of this to do it."

"There's a fuck ton down there," the soldier responded.

That was the last thing I was expecting them to pull from the water. Especially from Kaizer. I expected brute force, an army battering against the barrier. For this, he had to trust the witches.

"Collect it all and discard it. Let's not leave it there for them," Axel commanded before turning to the other soldier. "How'd they transport it?"

"My guess was one of the witches helped, but there hadn't been any sightings out here since the agreement."

I wished there was a spell that tracked down traitorous witches and killed them where they stood. They must have done some sort of covert mission before. For them to portal here, they had to have seen this exact spot in the water.

"They could have been working together before the agreement was solidified," I responded. "Take me to the captured soldiers."

The soldier turned immediately, and I saw a few vampires lined up in the distance, being watched by armed guards. A long black braid whipped in the wind, water still dripping from her armor. I didn't recognize the rest of them, but I stopped in front of Quinn. I actually liked her when in Sanjry, but I wasn't there anymore, and I'd defend Axel and Zuri's land as my own.

"Hello, Quinn."

A glimmer twinkled in her eye, the slightest bit of amusement before she hardened her features into a sneer. She was on her knees, her hands behind her back. A great wall of water surrounded the captured, ready for if any of them tried to wield fire. There weren't too many vampires who were skilled enough to wield with their hands tied, but there were a few that could make the attempt.

"Bring this one with us," I said as I opened a portal to the hall near Athena's cell.

Axel, Zuri, and Ishani followed behind me while Xavier and Paxx stayed to monitor the situation at the border. A soldier pushed Quinn through, her eyes dilating and nostrils flaring as soon as she stepped onto the stone floor. The blood hadn't been cleaned up yet, and the scent was still potent in the air.

"Athena," Quinn mumbled.

I stopped at the doorway, watching as they tried to use their water magic to lift the grime. "It was. Now she's no more." I lifted one shoulder. "Not before she opened our eyes to. . . a few things."

Quinn's gaze went even wider, and I tipped my chin to the room across the hall. The soldier had to push her to get her to move, but we all filtered in as Quinn was chained to the steel table at the center. I used one of my mother's tactics—silence.

We listened as the soldiers struggled to remove Athena's remnants from the cell across the hall. I'd left the door open so we could watch—so Quinn could see. She didn't know what happened to her—if it was by our hand or by something else entirely.

"I assume this isn't the outcome you were hoping for." I smirked as I broke the silence.

She glared at me, unbothered by her current circumstances. "Always a possibility."

"And what were you hoping to accomplish?" Axel asked.

"I think that's pretty clear."

"You know, I actually liked you. You weren't nearly as uppity as the others in your kingdom. Give us something, and we won't gut you."

"What a nice offer," she said, flashing me her bright white fangs. "I decline."

A soldier through and through. I almost respected it, but unfortunately that wasn't going to do for where we were.

"We know what Kaizer is looking for. Do you?" I jeered.

She tilted her head to the side as she clamped down on her lips momentarily. "Something powerful."

"Oh gosh, he hasn't even trusted you with what that is, has he?" I asked in a voice I thought sounded as obnoxious as Athena's.

Quinn shifted her focus away quickly, and I stood from my seat. I let my bruja magic dance between my fingers as I circled her, bringing my lips to her ear and saying, "We know another secret."

Axel's magic flickered in my mind. *"Should we be giving that information?"*

"I'd like to sow a seed of doubt," I responded.

He nodded ever so slightly in agreement. I wasn't used to having to run anything by anyone in these situations. As controlling as my mother was, she typically let me go about this how I preferred. As long as the outcome was what she desired. But I wasn't alone anymore.

"You can sit in here for a bit before I let you in on that secret. Let me know if you rethink my offer." Before I exited the room, I turned to the guard. "Actually, go ahead and put her in the wet cell. Easier clean up should we have another Athena situation."

Quinn didn't make a sound, but I heard the guard struggle to remove her as we went to meet Xavier and Paxx.

"How does that stone they found work?" Ishani asked.

"It's a conduit. We use it to train witchlings when they get their powers. When our magic emerges, it's volatile and hard to control. The stone absorbs some and extinguishes it without doing any real harm. The way they were using it, I'm assuming they hoped to absorb enough of the magic in the barrier that they could get through."

"It wouldn't have been enough to bring the whole thing down, though?" Axel asked.

"No, I don't think so. They were just testing a way to get in momentarily."

Paxx and Xavier walked toward us, and the heads of the captured rolled to the ground with a thud. Something about the sound of the hard flesh hitting the ground in that way solidified what this was. We were out of time.

"Anything?" Ishani asked Xavier.

"Nothing. Who was the one you took?" he asked me.

"Quinn, one of his generals. We didn't get anything out of her yet. I'd like to tell her about who Athena was and send her back."

"Make him doubt himself," Paxx said.

"Exactly."

"Are you ready for him to know where you are? That's the last leverage you have," Zuri added.

I'd been hiding long enough. It was time for Kaizer to be reminded of who I was. A weapon, a monster, and his destruction.

"It's time."

Zuri clasped her hands and brought them to her chin. "So this is it."

I gripped my dagger. "This is war."

CHAPTER THIRTY-FOUR

KAIZER

My advisers and I stared at each other. Something wasn't right, but neither of them seemed to want to be the one to tell me. I was losing my patience. These days, I barely had any to spare as it was. They saw that I was close to losing it, my hand tapping against the surface of the wooden desk progressively faster with every second we sat in silence. Finally, Otto spoke.

"They haven't returned, Your Majesty."

"None of them?"

Abel shook his head. "None."

"It's safe to assume they were not successful," Otto asserted.

"We should not have sent Quinn with that battalion," Abel said under his breath.

"Well, it's a bit too late for that now, isn't it?" I grumbled as I stood at the window.

Zuri had been taken, and she was my last hope of finding Daya. Her lead of the desert was still being looked into, but I feared it was a ploy to buy her more time. Without her, I'd have to move forward in the fight with Dusra. If we took over those lands, I could find the scepter. Trying to get in with the barrier in place was far too difficult.

"Do we know if the test was successful?" Abel asked.

"I said no one returned, didn't I?" Otto snapped.

Otto was getting increasingly restless as we moved forward. Especially after Athena was taken. Which Abel seemed more concerned with than Otto. He'd searched for her the most, but Athena was not the key to it all. Daya was. I did love Athena at one point, maybe even still did in some ways. She had been integral to getting me to where I was, even if I didn't admit it. There was a part of me that hoped she was at least safe. Regardless, I needed to find Daya and the scepter.

"What's our next move?" I asked.

"If the Dusrans know what we were trying to do, then we can consider our war officially started."

"They know." I rubbed my chest, that dull ache still there from when the agreement was broken. Even knowing that it was coming, after sending the battalion out there, I wasn't prepared. That was a pain not meant for mortals. I would have chosen to have my limbs slowly pulled apart than to go through that again. I had no idea what the price was or if I'd paid it yet, but I knew Axel was aware of what we'd done. The only way for it to be completely broken was for me to send someone there or vice versa. We couldn't wait any longer. Breaking down the barrier was the first step and was worth the risk. Or at least we thought.

"Then we need to prepare," Abel said as he stood and waited for Otto to insert the comment he surely had.

"We've been preparing for years. It's time to act," Otto added.

"Anything else from the journal?" Abel asked.

I shook my head. There hadn't been anything since Daya left. I wondered if whatever power controlling the journal was punishing me for failing in the task they deemed most important.

"So we get the army into position," Otto said.

A banging on the door startled all three of us. We stood with our hands on our weapons just as Quinn pushed through the doorway with the guards on her heels. I waved them off, taking her in. She'd seen better days. It looked like she might have walked back from the border. Dried blood was caked into her hair, dirt and mud covering her legs.

"What happened out there?" I snapped.

"It didn't work." She flicked her gaze over to Otto and Abel. "I have a message."

"Speak," I demanded.

Quinn's lip shook as she said, "Dayanara is in Dusra. . . and Athena is dead."

Daya was in the only place I'd never thought she would go. I'd been trying to get into Dusra for decades with no luck, and she was officially out of my reach. Her siding with my only remaining enemy was going to complicate things, but I still needed her. *How* was the question. I ran my hand over the only inscription on the leather journal, the symbol for 'creation.' I opened it and thought over how to word this request from the Flame. The last four things I'd written had gone unanswered, the ink dry on the page. Abel and Otto left to take the first steps in preparing for war against Dusra, so I took the time to see if I could get any guidance.

How do I get Dayanara from Dusra?

My leg bounced beneath my desk, the liquor within the glass rippling in the movement. Again, nothing happened. The Flame answered instantly before, and right as I slid my hand beneath the cover to slam the damn journal shut, the ink disappeared.

The magic within the pages sparkled, new words appearing on the opposite page.

YOU WILL NEED TO STRIKE FIRST.

I couldn't strike first without getting through the fucking barrier.

How do I get through the barrier?

YOU WILL NOT.

"This is entirely unhelpful," I mumbled as I tossed the journal across the top of my desk.

It was still odd returning to my chamber without finding Athena there. What Quinn said of her death. . . I almost regretted making the decision to break the agreement. The rest of Malva had to be worth one life lost. It did open my eyes to just how important she'd been to me over the years. She was a nuisance at times, but she was the most consistent and significant person in my life for a long time. I wondered what they did with her remains, if I could retrieve them after I took over the kingdom.

Daya probably wouldn't have that. She wasn't going to be easy to convince, especially if Zuri found her. The things Otto did, what I had a hand in. . . they may have been unforgivable. Although she'd done things just as bad, if not worse, in the name of protecting Caldera. Maybe she'd understand. If she knew that we could have the entire nation in our control, the power of three kingdoms—maybe more—she might understand. She had to.

Quinn entered my room, the dirt and grime removed from her body, her hair now groomed how it typically was. She'd even shaved the sides the way she did before a battle.

"Something wrong?" I asked as I tucked the journal into my desk drawer.

"Can I speak freely?" she responded.

"Of course."

She took a step forward, her eye contact intense. "I don't think we're going to win this."

"We have two kingdoms?"

"You didn't see what I saw. When the Dusran king was here, he warned us that even with our joint numbers, we did not outweigh his. Daya will not join you, no matter what you offer her."

That wasn't an option. She didn't know what she was talking about.

"She must."

"Sir, she will not!" She exclaimed before composing herself and starting again. "She will not. You can feel the. . . connection between her and the king. It's like there's a string tying them together. You are playing with fate."

"Fate." I laughed sharply. "You know not what you speak."

Quinn's nose twitched. "She also told me what you're looking for."

There was no way. I'd only trusted Otto and Abel with the full extent of that information. In no world would they have betrayed me. Quinn had to be incorrect.

"She can't possibly know that," I said.

"A scepter," she replied plainly before pointing to the desk drawer. "And I know what that is, too."

My jaw ticked as I ground my teeth together. "How did she come across this?"

"Do you think she sat down and told me everything she's done since running from you?" Quinn quipped. "You are out of your depth here. I've served you well for as long as you've sat on that throne, but we will not win."

Everything was slipping from my fingers. The agreement with Lupe, Daya, the knowledge of the scepter. None of this was going my way, and I was going to explode.

"So you would abandon your kingdom?"

Quinn set both of her hands on my desk and leaned closer to me. "I will die for Sanjry. For our people. For you. But right now, I will die in vain."

"What would you have me do?" I stood to look down at her rather than up. "Don't you think this might have been why she let you return? To shake up the loyalty here."

"Athena, she wasn't even who—"

"Athena is not important." I stopped her from continuing. I didn't want to talk about her. She was gone, and I had to keep moving forward.

Quinn raised a brow and crossed her arms. "You know what. . . I tried. Who else knows about the scepter and journal?"

"Otto and Abel."

"Do you even have proof of the scepter?"

At this point, there was no reason not to give her that information. The fear that I may truly be out of my depth snaked up my spine, but I released it before it took over. Quinn was just one more person. I wasn't losing control. I could regain it.

"The magic in the journal is old magic, ancient magic. Whoever is controlling it may be the greatest seer in our existence."

"That is how you took over Sanjry," she said, not a question in her tone.

I nodded once.

"Why have you not told anyone else?"

"It's nobody else's business. Your jobs are to do as I say and trust that I'm doing what is best for Sanjry."

I meant to speak it calmly, but it came out in a demanding growl, spit flying and my hand slamming down on the desk.

Quinn clamped down on her lips, disgust running across her features. "Understood."

We stared at each other for a moment, all the years of us being more like friends than anything sizzling away with each passing second. She headed toward the exit, but not before turning back and saying, "If we continue, you will not be king of Malva. You will be king of the ashes—from a fire *you* set."

Chapter Thirty-Five

Dayanara

I'd been worried about blowing up the Dusran castle, so I'd gone far underground to one of the caverns beneath the coastal stronghold. Where the wet cells were, actually. Nobody was in them at the moment, but I passed by one nearly full of water. Whoever was down here would have needed to stand on their tiptoes to avoid drowning. Or they'd need to actively keep the water back with magic for hours. Excellent choice in prisoner interrogation.

I had the grimoire open in my lap, the chrysocolla stones all surrounding me in a circle of bluish-green. I'd seen my mother do this, but it was forbidden for anyone else to try. It wasn't something I questioned before. I figured she wanted to make sure she was the only one with the ability and that it wouldn't be used against her. Now, I wondered if, at some point, it *was* used against her, and she'd done it for that reason.

Anytime I needed the suppressant, she'd give it to me already activated, and I never saw where she pulled it from. Some space she'd conjured specifically to hide it. Regardless, I didn't want to mess up the spell. It was one of the more complicated ones, and if I fucked up, we may not have had any left to use in battle.

Soft footsteps were coming in my direction, and I looked over my shoulder to find Zuri. She was eating some sort of fruit, the rind a dark red while the flesh was a bright orange. It dripped down her chin with her bite, officially distracting me from my task at hand.

"You look *very* witchy right now," Zuri said with a smile.

The dim candlelight lighting, the stones surrounding me, legs crossed, and my hood up as I mumbled under my breath. Very witchy.

"It's hot," she followed up before walking around my circle of crystals.

"Glad you think so because I'm feeling not-so-hot about this," I responded.

Zuri stepped into my circle and joined me on the floor. "What's wrong?"

"This is all we have. I want to get it right."

"Is the fact your mother often used this on you part of the worry?"

A flashback: me in a cave similar to this one, my magic gone, and my mother trying to teach me some sort of lesson. There were a lot of them, I didn't remember which time this was. I did remember the pain that came with empty reserves, the bruises she refused to heal until I was successful in whatever the test was. I remembered my heart drumming in my ears, my eyes blinking rapidly, and my skin turning clammy as spots of lights flashed in my vision.

Zuri scooted behind me, her thighs bracketing mine and her arms wrapping around my waist. I pulled myself from the memory, thinking maybe she might have been onto something. I'd once told Axel that my biggest fear was failure. Failing in this would have big repercussions, and I'd already failed my kingdom in so many ways.

"You helped me face my family. I'll help you do this," she said into the crook of my neck.

The grimoire felt like it was made of bricks instead of paper, but I read over the spell one more time. Zuri handed me a smaller chunk of the chrysocolla stone to practice with first. This spell wasn't a quick couple of words. It was a whole paragraph. My intent couldn't waver for a moment, or the whole spell would cease. I held the intent of protection in the front of my mind, for my loved ones, for the Dusrans and true Calderans. Malice was sometimes as strong as love, depending on the wielder, but I thought for this particular spell, it would be better. I knew which my mother usually used.

I recited the spell, enunciating every single syllable. It spilled from my mouth, my tongue clicking against the roof of my mouth over the trills, my lips contracting and stretching as the soft mumble formed a powerful, sonorous sound.

The crystal glowed, my bruja magic forming a purple case around it. It sparked, stretching out into the air and rebounding back to the stone. The chrysocolla broke down, vibrating as pieces fell from it and turned to powder. I had to keep going until it was done. The activation spell wasn't too difficult, but the initial one needed time.

The purple magic encasing the stone burst open, and the powder slowly settled onto the ground in front of me. Using some air magic, I swept it all into a wooden bowl I'd brought down here for that purpose. I could feel Zuri's pride in me, where our bodies were still connected, and I bathed in it. She used to love watching me do brujeria like this before, and it was kind of nice to be doing it together again.

"Akari told me of her suspicion of us being Verdaji," Zuri said. "And Axel."

I turned around to face her, throwing her legs over mine to keep the closeness. "Did you know the last couple?"

"I remember them from when I was a kid, but they died around the same time my brother did."

"How did they know?"

"They had a mark here." She lifted my arm and drew a line from my second finger to my chest.

"It just appeared?" I asked. Mine would have to go over the other tattoos there, but I wouldn't be opposed.

"That part I don't know." She kept my hand in hers, rubbing over my skin with her finger.

"Mariana said that the souls of Verdaji find each other lifetime after lifetime. But there have been many generations since they'd been seen widely. I wonder where those souls are," I responded.

"I'm glad that mine is here with yours. . . And Axel's, I guess."

Like music to my ears.

"I told you he's not that bad," I teased.

"Could be worse."

I swore I recalled her saying that he *was* the worst person to be in this situation with, but I didn't bring it up. The cavern hummed, a faint sound of trickling water in the distance. Zuri wrapped her legs around my body and brought herself flush with mine. She pulled down my hood and wrapped her arms around my neck, toying with my hair. Every time she slept in my bed, I'd stay up and study her face, count her freckles, watch her lashes flutter in her dreams. Zuri was art. Her caramel hair seemed darker beneath the earth, less of a contrast against her warm brown skin than when in the light of day.

Those lips—I had no artistic ability, but I knew that if given the task, I could draw an exact replica. The bow at the center of her top lip, the wide curve of the bottom, and the crease down the middle, the way they were permanently set into a voluminous pout. But as much as I loved her lips, her eyes were my favorite. So expressive, and even when she was angry, there was still so much kindness within them. The slight tilt of them made her appear pleased, and her lashes curled and framed them perfectly. Those dark gray irises held flecks of silver, only visible to the ones who took the time to find them. Two precious gems made for me.

"What are you thinking about?" she asked.

"How breathtaking you are."

Zuri looked down, the lashes I was admiring nearly grazing her cheeks. I pressed a kiss to her lips, savoring this slow moment between us. The chances that I'd get used to feeling her again were slim—needing to touch her to know she was real. I unzipped her shirt, and I ran my finger over her scars. Every single time I'd seen her naked since that day, I'd kissed them. No matter what we were doing, where we were going, I took the opportunity to show that she didn't need to hide them. The ones on my back weren't a deterrent to her, and the ones on her weren't a deterrent to me. Part of it was for myself, a reminder that I'd bring Kaizer and Otto pain. Her nipples pebbled underneath her thin brassiere, and I bit down on one of them through the fabric.

I groaned as I heard rushed footsteps coming in our direction. I zipped her up, but the racing heartbeat had me on my feet, placing Zuri on the ground. With my weapon in hand, I moved to the only exit in the cavern.

A Dusran soldier stopped when he saw my blade, his hands going in the air to show he wasn't a threat. "They need you upstairs."

Zuri moved around me. "What's wrong?"

"It's Xavier, he's—"

I didn't let him finish. I opened a portal to Xavier's office and found him at his desk, Ishani with her hand on his back. He looked. . . terrible. His skin was pale, making the normal olive tones of his skin even more prominent. I wasn't sure when he'd taken such a turn. I'd seen him a couple of days ago, and he appeared to be doing great. Axel stormed through the door with Paxx, and Xavier worked to sit up straight. Ishani had to help him, and I tried to snag her gaze in mine, but she kept hers on Xavier. I couldn't read her, and I could see Axel trying to get into her mind and failing.

"What is going on?" Paxx asked.

"Well," Xavier said, the moisture clearly missing from his throat. "I'm dying."

Everyone spoke at once, trying to understand why he was saying this, but nobody let the other speak, and nobody was heard. Xavier lifted a shaking hand, and finally, Ishani looked at me and Zuri. Her lip quivered, with tears on the brink of falling, but there was also something else in her gaze: resolution.

"It's been coming for some time now. I've held it back with tonics and magic from the witches, but I have no desire to do so anymore."

"Ish?" Axel's voice cracked as he looked at his twin.

"He's telling the truth," Ishani responded, her voice steady.

"I'm tired. My body is tired, and with everything going on. . . I don't want this to happen while we're at war."

We all stared, not understanding what he meant.

"What are you saying?" Zuri asked.

"I'm saying, I've decided to die today. Ishani already has everything in place. We've. . . worked out a lot of things. I just wanted to tell you all ahead of time."

"Oh, how fucking nice of you," Axel responded.

Xavier was one of the few people who had watched Axel fully grow into himself. From being a cocky prince to being captured to being a king, other than

Ishani, Xavier was the only other person to see Axel's journey. They were like brothers, but I wondered if Xavier was also someone he looked up to, a paternal figure, even though he was younger.

"Absolutely not," Paxx added.

Paxx and Axel stood like a wall with their arms crossed and eyes piercing holes into Xavier. Zuri had grabbed onto my arm when Xavier admitted why we were here, but she let me go, and we all watched her as she slowly walked over to where he sat. She scooted a chair beside him, grabbed his hand in hers, and leaned her head on his shoulder. Zuri didn't say anything, only offered him comfort, and Ishani's tears finally broke free. Xavier placed his other hand over Zuri's and shook his head to fight back his own tears.

"You all have been the greatest family a man could know. I am immensely proud of each of you. Not only have you all overcome so much, you've leaned on each other in the tough times."

"I don't—" Axel glanced at me, and my knees buckled at the pure devastation radiating from him. "I don't know how to do this without you."

I wanted to scream, to yell at Xavier for hurting them. Especially now. But when he looked at me, I felt it. The weight of all the years showed in his eyes akin to the rings in a vast tree. The outer rings blackened by whatever sickness was plaguing him. He didn't have long, and who were we to tell him how to live his last moments. It almost felt. . . brave. To tame something as unruly as death.

"I'll still be with you, in all the knowledge I've bestowed, in your memories. But I'm ready. I know that is hard to understand, but I'd prefer to be in control of how this happens."

"How will you do it?" Paxx questioned.

Paxx's heavy stare bounced all around Xavier's head, like his emotions were coming in too fast for him to decipher one from the other.

"I have a tonic. I've been told it will be painless."

I still had the grimoire under my arm, and power rippled off it, a nudge or a reminder.

"I can perform a spell," I blurted, but Xavier simply raised his hand.

"Ishani told me of what you can do. I don't want to be a burden for the rest of her life."

"That's not how it would be," Ishani said quickly before placing her hand over her mouth.

"We talked about this," Xavier reasoned. "You are the stars and flowers. You are the sparkling over a rushing river. You are *everything* good. I would be clouds and weed, a boulder that would clog your current. I want you to live, truly live. You can't do that with me. We've already seen it."

Ishani fell to her knees beside him. "It doesn't have to be like that. You can tie yourself to me, and we don't have to be together."

Xavier brushed her hair behind her ear and placed a shaky palm against her cheek. "You will be fine without me. You all will. I've got letters for each of you to read tomorrow. If there's anything you'd like to say before then, I'll be in my chamber until dusk."

He got up from his desk, and I wondered what sort of sickness moved so quickly or what tonics had been hiding it. Axel was still in disbelief, but Xavier staggered over to him. They stared at each other for a few moments before Axel pulled him into a tight hug. I didn't know Xavier very well, and I wasn't even on good terms with him until recently. But I knew how important he was here. My heart ached for the people in this room. For what they'd lose in just a few hours. For what all of Dusra would lose.

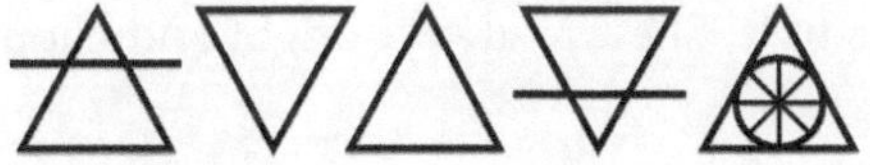

The service for Xavier was beautiful. Every Dusran soldier and even some Calderan soldiers were in attendance. People came from their homes from all over the kingdom to pay him tribute. They told stories of how he helped them, of how his time in the kingdom changed their lives. That was what he wanted—Dusra to remember him this way.

Axel stayed with him, talking until Xavier called time. He'd been the one to administer the tonic, with Ishani by his side. Healers hadn't agreed on how much time he had left, and he didn't want any of the focus to be taken from finding Zuri or the war brewing with Sanjry.

Much like Ishani on that day in the office, they all had a certain resolution around it. I hadn't asked what was in any of their letters, but Zuri read hers in silence, sporadic tears running down her cheeks until she laid down at my side. Axel paced outside as he read it, and had transformed into his beast and flown for hours. When he returned, he kissed my forehead and joined Zuri and me. Whatever combinations of words to explain must have been enough for them to accept it. Not a single one would have wanted him to be in pain, that I was sure.

I watched as the builders chiseled away in the garden, Xavier's eyes already found within the dark stone. Ishani observed, pointing out where it was wrong and where it was right. When she sat beside me, we watched them work in silence.

She'd told us just how bad it was, that he'd come to her a long time ago and made her promise not to say anything until he was ready. For us, it was so sudden, but it had been eating away at her for much longer. I knew she probably wouldn't admit to a feeling of relief, but I wondered how much of her was locked up by this.

Ishani was the type of person who never would have moved on knowing he was hurting. Even if they weren't together, the years and history still tied them together. Even in those last moments she was still trying to help him. I hoped she really did find peace in it. She was always bright and happy, but even now she seemed...lighter.

I wasn't sure if I'd know what to do or what to say, but when Ishani put her head on my shoulder and exhaled with contentment, I knew I was where I was supposed to be.

CHAPTER THIRTY-SIX

DAYANARA

"Where are we going?" I asked Axel.

"Somewhere that brings me peace," he responded with mischief in his eyes.

It was the first time we'd been alone since Xavier's passing. I couldn't tell if he had the worst or the best timing because everyone seemed to be coming to terms with it. Axel and Ishani weren't strangers to grief. They'd seen many friends die over their lifetimes. But I knew this one stung more. He was in good spirits today, so I played into whatever it was he was trying to do.

"If you told me *where,* I could save us from having to walk?" I offered.

Axel shook his head. "The walk is part of the magic."

A few days had passed since we sent Quinn back, and we hadn't heard of any movement yet. We all knew it was coming and had already given the army a heads-up that they needed to be ready to march at command. It had been exhausting. Even though we all knew this was coming, taking all the action to ignite the war was a lot.

Water raged to the right of us, with the full moon's reflection off in the distance, doubling it in size. The crashing of the waves was peaceful, but Axel turned away from the water and down a set of stairs carved into the ground. I peeked around his body, and he looked back at me with disappointment.

"Patience, my Daya. Patience."

Not something I'm known for. But I did try. We seemed to curve back toward the water, but more land met us. Axel picked up a pebble from the ground and kept his eyes on me as he threw it into the field.

"What are you doi—"

The entire field lit up, rings of bioluminescence pulsing from where the pebble landed. Each ring turned a different color as it passed over our feet, and a whoosh of static energy came with it. Small bugs shot into the air, their bodies radiating the same light as they fluttered around and illuminated another path.

Axel chuckled to himself as we crossed, and I dipped my hand in the sparkling greenery, now pulsating with every step we took. The light faded behind us, and the smell of salty water hit me again, but the ocean was still nowhere to be found. The loose dirt and sand transitioned to hard stone as we came upon the mouth of a cave. Had anyone else brought me out here, I may have been more on high alert. I didn't hear anyone nearby. But it was Axel, and my body knew I was safe with him.

The tunnel narrowed, one section so tight we had to pass through sideways, but my jaw dropped when we came out on the other side. Whatever substance was on the plants outside the cave covered the stone walls here, reflecting onto a deep body of water, a stream of it pouring down the side of the room like a narrow waterfall. A blanket was spread out on a dry area, with a bottle of wine and snacks in the middle.

"When did you do this?" I asked.

"Had to get Ishani to help," he admitted, guiding me over to the blanket. "It's been a stressful couple of days, and I didn't know when we'd have the chance to do something like this again."

Axel held out his hand for me to hold as I sat on the blanket. He joined me, pouring a glass of wine for the both of us. I watched as the water streamed down the rigid stone wall, the light behind it making the liquid resemble melting crystals.

"I came here a lot. . . after," Axel said. "The water is the perfect temperature, not like the cold of the ocean. It's a good place to recalibrate."

"How are you feeling going back to Sanjry?"

He took a sip of his wine. "You know, the first time I went back was when I met you. I was at that pub that night—even though everyone told me not to, might I add—because I was nervous. We got there a day early because I didn't want them to be a step ahead of us, but I also needed to remind myself that I was okay. Seeing you, every ounce of worry I had disappeared."

"I never would have known." The side of my mouth tilted up.

"But I know we'll get through this now. I just hope we don't lose too much more before then."

Goddess, I hoped the same. I didn't have much, but what I had left I wanted to keep. I wanted something to return to when it was all said and done, or else what was the point?

"The future you saw for us—I imagine that we survived?" I asked.

"The future is never set in stone, but yes. That is giving me reassurance." Axel paused. "Should I have told you about that before we went to see the Triori?"

We hadn't had a moment to talk, only the two of us in a while. So much had happened since seeing the Triori, but I knew it still needed to be discussed.

I took a deep breath. "I don't know. Just. . . we all have to agree that we'll tell the truth no matter how hard it is moving forward. I can't do the 'I was trying to protect you' thing anymore. But I do get why you didn't say anything."

"Agreed. With the treaty being broken now, you won't have to keep anything from me, either."

"Thank the goddesses. That was getting annoying as fuck." I tossed the last bit of my wine back. "Let's swim."

"I thought you'd never ask," he responded as he unbuttoned his shirt.

I slipped out of my clothes quickly, looking back just as Axel pulled his pants down, and his dick hardened at the sight of me. Diving into the water before he caught up to me, I saw immediately what he meant when he said it was the perfect temperature. I stayed below the surface, taking in the depth of the cenote and how the water darkened far from the light of the cave. There was a time I would have seen how long I could stay beneath the surface, tested it until my eyes darkened. But I was in control of my life now—mostly. Axel's massive body plunged in, and he used his magic to pull me close to his body.

He shot us back to the surface, and I tread water, but Axel seemed to be suspended.

"Lucky," I muttered.

"I'm sure air has its benefits," he chuckled as he let go of the hold on his magic and swam with me. "You asked me if I'm worried, are you?"

I dipped under the water before answering, feeling my hair weighed down as I resurfaced. "I don't think worried is the right word. I want this shit over with."

It might not have sounded like the truth, but it was. I wanted to create the life I'd had little glimpses of since being here. Couldn't do that in the middle of a war.

"I have an idea I haven't voiced yet because I'm not sure if it's a good one," he responded.

"What is it?"

"I think when we cross the Inbetween, we should search for the god of Chaos."

It crossed my mind, but I didn't know how it would work.

"That would be in the opposite direction? We'd have to leave the army."

"That's why I don't know if it's a good idea." He shook his head, his hair spraying water across the surface. "But if we stopped it at its source, lives could be saved."

"We don't know if his influence stretches to anybody else; he has to have someone on the other side, too," I said, thinking.

"You know what?" he said as he swam closer to me and wrapped my legs around his body. "Let's think about this tomorrow."

I pressed my forehead to his with a smile. "Okay."

We stayed like that for a moment, listening to the water and letting it take away some of the stress of the impending war. Some of the pain and grief.

"So," I said, pulling back and peering into his eyes. "Do you take all your conquests here or only the ones who were previously engaged to your enemy and you've seen visions of the future with?"

His chuckling vibrated against my chest as he grinned. "Oh, good. We're joking about it now."

I tried to swim away from him, but the water rushed away from my body, and my back smacked into his chest.

"Where do you think you're going?" he whispered into my ear, the gravel in his voice melting my body into him.

Dipping my hand into the water and behind me, I grabbed him by his hardened dick. "Here seems like a good place to start."

Axel grunted as he turned me to face him, his lips pressing into mine before I was even fully turned. One of his hands in my hair, the other gripping my ass as he ensured there was absolutely no space between us. Axel's tongue pressed into my mouth, and I sliced it with my fang, the taste of his blood covering my own. I loved the taste of it; before I just wanted blood to refill my reserves, but his blood was like dessert. He moaned as I pulled more from the cut and created an air pocket around us in the water. The ripples of water sloshed around the hardened air, the colors from the walls reflecting on the surface.

"See, air has its benefits," Axel said as he got his footing in the space and nipped at my lip.

"I suppose. Lay down," I commanded.

He did as I asked quickly and propped himself up on his elbows as he waited for me. Goddess, this man was a fucking specimen. Every inch of his olive brown skin glistened, every muscle taut beneath it. His abs and biceps being the most defined in this position. I could have stayed staring at him like this for the rest of the evening, but I decided we could have more fun.

I dropped down to all fours, climbing over his body and kissing him again. Not staying at his mouth too long, but kissing a trail down his jaw, descending to his chest and over those muscles I was just admiring until I got to his hips. The saltiness of his skin and the water coated my tongue as I ran it from his hip to the base of his cock. It jumped, his body going even tighter as a quick breath escaped him.

I teased the head at the seam of my lips, watching as his eyes darkened. Keeping our eye contact, I took him into my mouth, swirling my tongue around the length of him and pulling him back out with a pop. He moaned—the sound encouraging as I went back for more and ran my nails lightly across his legs until I reached his balls. The buck of his hips from the movement had me taking all of him, my cheeks hollowing out.

A jolt ran through me as a cold sensation caressed my nipple, and I found a stream of his magic running over my skin. It traveled across my chest, hardening my other nipple as my head continued bobbing. I tried to stay focused as it flowed down my body, leaving goose bumps behind in its wake. Axel bit his lip as he watched it caress me, his eyes flicking back to my mouth.

I groaned as he hit the back of my throat at the same time that his magic lapped over my clit. It swirled around the nerves, warming and replicating his tongue. Gripping his dick with my hand, I ran it up to the tip before wrapping my lips around it again. His magic sped up as I felt his climax building, one in me as well, at the pure speed it vibrated against my clit.

Our moans echoed off the wall as we came together, and I climbed on top of him, rubbing his cock against the evidence of my arousal. He sat up fully, kissing me and pushing fully into my pussy.

"Fuck, you feel. . . " He trailed off, his mouth open as he tried to form a word, but I dragged my hips against him, holding whatever he wanted to say prisoner.

I kept my mouth a breath away from his. "I feel like yours."

Axel closed the distance between our lips, the kiss wilder than the ones before. He flipped us, putting both of my legs on his shoulders and folding me in half as he leaned over me. There was nothing but lust in his eyes as he pulled out to the tip and slammed back in. I screamed at the sudden fullness, one of his hands on my ankle as the other trailed up my body.

"Say it again," he groaned right as his fingers met my neck.

"I'm yours." The moment the last syllable left my mouth, he squeezed, my head tingling immediately at the lack of air.

He slammed into me, every thrust harder than the last. Another orgasm was building, but he released his hold on my neck, both his hands sliding under my ass as he pulled out and lifted my hips. Axel sucked down on my clit first, and I couldn't stop the scream at the sudden change. He lapped at me until I was trembling, right on the edge again. The moment he reinserted himself, I came undone, my scream seeming to go on forever in the small room.

The smug look on his face would have been obnoxious had he not earned it. He flipped me onto my side, lifting my leg and holding it against his hip. My toes curled as the wet sheen on his skin from the water turned to droplets of sweat at his vigor. I felt him everywhere, not just where we were connected, but in the same way, I sensed him at the pub. My magic seeped from my body at the pure bliss I was experiencing, and the moment it caressed Axel's skin, his dark magic met mine. It intertwined, an electricity more than either of our magic alone could create lapped over our bodies. He slowed his pace as he closed his eyes and let it engulf us.

I'd said before I liked the rough and wild sex, but something about this intimacy, this closeness, not just of our bodies, it felt right. Axel brought his forehead down to mine, and I wasn't sure if I was thinking loudly or if he felt it, too. He caressed one of my cheeks with his hand, capturing my mouth in a slow and intentional kiss.

"One more," he whispered against my lips.

The part of me that wanted to dominate reared, but the tingling through my body had me not fighting him on it. I repositioned myself, giving him back the full access he had with both my legs on his shoulders. Our bodies slammed into one another, the knowledge that things were going to get a lot more intense the moment we left this cave heavy around us. I held my gaze in his as I felt him about to tip over the edge, his thumb coming down to rub on my clit. He moaned as he came, and I followed him just as the air bubble I made popped. Axel drifted away from me for a moment before sweeping us both up in a wave and laying us down at the edge of the cenote.

"For the record," he said as he moved my hair out of my face. "I've never done that here with anyone else."

"Hm." I kissed his chest. "Let's keep it that way."

Chapter Thirty-Seven

Dayanara

I sat with my legs crossed beneath me, my eyes closed, and my hands resting atop my knees. Focusing was difficult with all that was going on in the palace, so I left to a bordering field. One of the farms with the cute little—tasty—lambs. I had myself positioned under a vast tree, only the sounds of nature surrounding me.

Mariana said I could come back to that place within my mind and contact the Acnas before. Just had to figure out how. A part of me recoiled at the thought of it, because my mother was there, or somewhere close. My back burned with the memory of that pain, but I pushed through. I put all of my energy into making that connection. Once I was about halfway there, my body took over, guiding me to where it was I was trying to get.

I opened my eyes within the spirit world, feeling my body still on the other plane of existence. Mariana wasn't the one I was here for today, though.

"Valentina Amapola, I summon you," I said, the same words I used to bring my mother forward before.

A cloud enveloped me, two cerulean irises flashing at the center. She stepped forward, long ultramarine coils falling down to her shoulders. A smile pulled across her face as she took me in. I wasn't sure what to expect from the women in my line, but she at least appeared happy to see me.

"Dayanara, it is good to see you in this form," she said.

Valentina wasn't an Acna, but she was one of the last women in charge before Naom blessed us.

"I wasn't sure if this would even work," I mumbled.

"Self-confidence is important, young one."

"Yeah, don't know if that's the issue here," I chuckled. "I summoned you because I saw what you wrote in the grimoire."

I hadn't gone through every single page yet, but I knew she should have some information.

"About the god of Chaos?" she asked.

"Yes, how did you know that?"

Valentina tossed her curls over her shoulder. "It's the most interesting of my entries. What do you want to know?"

"When I was here last, Mariana made it seem like she couldn't answer everything?"

"We cannot interfere in any great way. We can guide you, offer you knowledge and wisdom as those before did for us."

Those before? As in all the Amapolas?

"I've always been able to do this?"

She smiled. "Yes. Your mother hid it from you. She should have guided you here, as our mothers did for us. When you were at Cape Coven, you could feel us, yes?"

Of course she did. She wouldn't have been able to accomplish half the things she did if I'd known about this ability. I didn't have time to be pissed off about that.

"Yes, it was always like a whisper, just low enough that I couldn't make out what was being said."

"The Amapolas have always had this gift, to be able to contact our ancestors. We've used it to our advantage time and time again. Your mother made sure that you never knew of this and that much of the knowledge from the grimoire was not shared. What is it you seek of the god?"

"I want to understand him. How he fought, what to expect. You fell by his sword, yes?"

An enemy unknown was dangerous. If you didn't know what made them tick, what weapons they chose, the ways they could defeat you, they were ten steps ahead. I needed to know everything.

"Something like that, yes. He was unlike anything we'd seen before, a shifter of a kind. Even when he was in one form, he could appear as something else entirely to another in the room. We didn't know how he did it, but he'd mark people with a scorpion tattoo, and he was able to control them in a way. He'd get into your mind, and if you weren't strong enough, he'd take your will. His monsters were created purely for bloodshed. They tore through our people as if we weren't warriors."

That was helpful, but not enough.

"But what is fueling him? What is his purpose? I don't understand his desires, so I don't understand how to stop him."

"He is fed by the chaos—by the fear he evokes. The power he gets from those that fall in battle is. . . vast."

Again, not enough. There *had* to be more.

"So it's just for the fuck of it?"

"There is..." She paused. "More than meets the eye of our world. Beneath the surface, a world he hopes to pull our dead to."

The Triori mentioned this. That there were worlds layered on top of each other, ones that didn't follow the same rules of physics.

"And he was unsuccessful?" I asked.

Valentina looked past my head, biting the inside of her cheek. "The Inbetween was his first step. I've already said more than I should. You must use what I have given you. Be careful who you share the information with, as you may be the only one alive who knows. Few of the other orders came face-to-face with his true self."

She disappeared, my eyes opening with the serene sounds of nature still buzzing, as if the information I received had no impact. What the god wanted with our dead wasn't clear, or where he wanted to take them. I ran my fingers through the surrounding flowers, hearing a herd of heartbeats coming my way. A petite woman walked across the field in the distance, the sheep following her like she was their mother.

Dusra was such an odd place. I marked her as a witch immediately. The only kingdom of the three where you could run into all makes of creature. There was only my own coven—and a small coven at that—to worry about originally. But the brujas here still came from my land, from Naom, and were mine to protect. As much as they were Axel's, if not more.

"Where are you?" Axel's voice filled my head.

"Out by the sheep farm. You okay?"

"Yes, we're getting ready to lead the army out. Will you be meeting us?"

"Coming," I responded before taking in the quiet peace. It may have been one of the last times I'd be able to enjoy it for quite some time.

I'd been out on the coast plenty, seen the different groups of our combined armies training. But I'd yet to see them all in one place. There were thousands, tens of thousands of soldiers at the ready. I'd portaled over and hadn't seen Axel, Zuri, or any of them yet. The sound of chatter among this many, combined with the crashing waves next to us, was so loud I needed to tune out of my witch hearing. Everything went quiet immediately, and I was impressed with myself for being able to turn it off that quickly. Just for a second, because I saw the true reason the space went quiet.

Ishani lifted herself up on a wave from the sea, floating a few feet above the crowd. She commanded a room. Everyone stopped what they were doing the moment she walked through a threshold. There was a certain authoritative energy that radiated from her, and it was not one of fear but of respect. To be able to have the same effect on this many people at once was astonishing. She wore armor somewhere between my leathers and the heavy stuff the Sanjryans wore. Hers in a golden bronze that reflected onto her deep almond skin in a way that made her glow.

The air shifted again, but I was sure it was just for me because I felt Zuri and Axel coming. The both of them, along with Paxx, turned down the line of soldiers, all of them in their own war attire as well. Ishani smiled down at them as she pulled her sword from her sheath and jutted it into the air. She let out a war cry, the sound bouncing off the ocean and across the surface, extending it as the army let out their own.

"It's been some time since we've been here all together. We've got some new faces, too. I hope you're all prepared. You fight beside the greatest army this side of the Piedra has ever seen. Probably the other side, too." She winked.

Axel and Zuri made it to where I stood, taking their spots on either side of me. Ishani moved both of her hands to the side, guiding the magic in the wave as she settled it down to the ground and sent the water back into the ocean. Her armor clinked with every step down the front line before she tucked her sword back in its sheath.

"This will be a fight unlike the others. For we will be fighting vampires of fire and witches of air and essence. Do not let this discourage you, for I have seen each of you train, and I wouldn't send this army across the border unless I had full faith in you all. We will cross into the Inbetween, and for those of you who have not yet had the pleasure of a visit, be attentive. Keep your wits. Do not venture off by yourself. The land and its patrons will take great pleasure in any pain they can cause. We may have to stay one night, but I hope that is all. From there, we will be in Sanjry, and you all know your responsibilities. We do this for freedom, and we do this for Xavier! Let's move out."

I heard Akari yell a command from somewhere in the middle of the army as Ishani jumped on a horse at the front. She was fucking incredible. I didn't have many people to look up to, but I thought Ishani might have earned that. Someone brought over two horses, and I raised my brows as I realized one of them was for me.

"Uh, I have to say I'm not too well-versed in horseback riding," I said.

"I don't think I've ever heard you speak with such little confidence," Ishani replied from atop her champagne horse. "You'll be fine."

Someone brought over a large red horse, and Axel smiled. "This is Xavier's horse. Samrat."

"Are you sure?" I looked at Ishani.

"He was the one who decided. It was in my letter," Axel responded as he jumped atop his massive dapple gray horse.

I tried not to let that hit me the way it did, but I couldn't stop it. My chest warmed, and I silently thanked him for such an honor. I watched Zuri mount her horse with grace, and she felt me watching. She subtly pointed toward the stirrup hanging on the side of the saddle. *Here goes nothing.*

My foot found an easy hold, and I may have used a bit of air magic to make the move more graceful. Horses weren't very common in Caldera, as few people had use for them. But I could see how people could get used to it. Its strong heartbeat thudded against my legs, and I swore I felt Xavier's presence. Zuri's horse came to my side, nudging Samrat with her nose.

"They're whatever the horse version of a couple is," Zuri said, pointing to the horses we sat atop with a chuckle.

"Well, then, that's fitting." I smirked.

Axel was staring out across the water, a countenance to his features I couldn't determine. *"You okay?"* I asked within our mind connection.

Before he could respond, Ishani reached her hand out and brushed it against his shoulder. Axel smiled at her before turning back and nodding once at me. Zuri watched it all, but Paxx came trotting over before we could say anything else.

"Everyone is ready," he said to Ishani.

He gestured for her to go, much more relaxed now, and the army slowly moved down the coast. Large carts were peppered throughout the sea of people, carrying our weapons, food, tents, etc. They took longer to move, so our pace wasn't what it could have been. Ishani was right. We'd have to stay in the Inbetween at least one night if not two. It did give me the opportunity to do some potential digging about what exactly the Inbetween was in relation to the god of Chaos.

I took in the row of my friends, my lovers, my people behind me. Cat was at the rear. I'd have to bring her in on the update. Maybe a few others. Only those I was sure I could trust, as Valentina said. Because whatever was coming for us was not an easy foe.

Chapter Thirty-Eight

Dayanara

It felt like years ago that I stood at the other end of the bridge into the Inbetween, leaving my kingdom behind. When I found out Zuri had lied to me about who she was. Before she was taken, before everything else came to fall on my shoulders. I was pretty sure Zuri felt it too as she avoided eye contact with me, her horse just a few steps behind me rather than directly at my side like it had been.

Paxx bounced his gaze between the two of us. "We aren't moving backward here, are we?"

"Way to make it awkward," Zuri snapped at Paxx.

Axel and Ishani were with the guards at the end of the bridge, and I assumed they were talking about what they'd be doing after we crossed. Unfortunately, there was no way to get out of the conversation.

"I'm only saying we need to leave everything on this side of the border. After we cross, we are all each other has." Paxx lifted his hands in surrender.

There were no doubts about that. Outside of the Inbetween being a literal nightmare of a place to be, any miscommunication or rift between us could end up fatal. I'd moved past it, but Zuri still had so much guilt.

"It's okay, Zuri. You've more than paid for any wrong. We're okay, I promise."

Zuri smiled slightly, her eyes falling to the ground, but I sent a gust of air to lift her chin.

"That's more like it," Paxx chuckled as Ishani and Axel came racing over.

"They're going to freeze over the river, so we don't have to wait for the bridge," Ishani said as she signaled to the generals at the front line.

"And they're moving out the extra castle guard to man the border while we're gone," Axel added. "Xavier is usually the one to stay and watch things I . . ."

"The magic at the border hasn't waned, even with their attempt. Everyone has been highly trained. Dusra will be okay," Paxx reasoned.

It seemed to put Axel at ease, and we all made for the bridge. The Inbetween taunted us across the border, and even though I knew my magic would fade the moment I crossed it, I wasn't ready. It receded deep into my body, tucking itself into some part of me I wasn't familiar with. Each person jolted as they experienced the odd sensation, and it was evident who was crossing for the first time. Some of them doubled over with their hands on their chest, appearing to be struck with an arrow. Others strolled through with just a tiny flinch.

"I fucking hate this place," Zuri said as she worked through it in deep breaths.

Color faded, a distant memory as we got far enough that we could no longer see the lush shades of Dusra.

"We need to meet after we set up camp. I have some new information," I said, eyeing the front line.

"Don't love the sound of that," Axel said.

"You're not gonna like what I have to say, that's for sure," I replied.

Paxx released a breath, and Ishani shook her head as we powered through the first leg of the journey across the Inbetween.

"Tirsa, the bruja we saw the last time we were here, said we'd cross eight of the eleven zones the way we took. I'd suggest we take the same exact path, so we have some knowledge. Some of the zones weren't even populated," I said.

I'd already told them this when we were determining our plan, but I felt it should be repeated. The sensation that we were being watched already began in the last zone we crossed, and if Zuri and I remembered correctly, we were coming up to one of the uninhabited zones.

"I remember," Paxx responded as he seemed to be drawing something in the air. "Next zone is the one for us to camp out, yes?"

"Right," Zuri responded.

Ishani had gone down the line of soldiers to check in with her generals, so we hopped off the horses to survey the area better.

"When's the last time you were here?" I asked Axel and Paxx.

"Dusra hasn't had issues with the Inbetween in a very long time. We don't banish any of our people here. It's probably been centuries," Axel responded, and Paxx agreed.

"Well I can assure you it fucking sucks," I said before stretching my arms out. "This seems as good a place as any."

There was still a bit of sand from the last zone, but the land was flat, and wide enough for our people to set up camp. Nobody had a better idea, and everyone was directed in. Clicking in the far tree line had all of us turning around quickly, but no leaves rustled, so we stayed on high alert.

For an army that hadn't done this in a while, the camp was set up pretty quickly. We all had tents, and I was sharing with Ax and Zuri, which I had *no* problems with. Cooks already had the warm smell of something wafting in the air, one of the few other things we had smelled since crossing the border besides putrid death. Ishani had a more significant tent than others, one with a makeshift table in it. Which happened to be where everyone was currently staring at me with wide eyes after I told them what Valentina said.

"We're in the Inbetween now. We could go looking," Paxx suggested.

"It's too dangerous. Losing soldiers before the battle would not be ideal," Zuri reasoned.

"Doesn't have to be everyone, maybe just a small unit. They could come back and meet up before the first battle," I suggested.

"I don't like the idea of us splitting up," Ishani mumbled before dragging her hand down her face. "But I do like the idea of us possibly avoiding war."

We all looked at Axel, who beat his knuckles against his knee in contemplation. His gaze bounced from his fist up to me and then over to Zuri. "Regardless, I'm not sure if it would stop the war. Things have been set into motion that can't be undone, not easily anyway."

"We have wars waiting for us at every turn. It's not that simple either," Paxx responded.

Ishani bounced her gaze between her brother and the head of intelligence. There hadn't been any times when they didn't listen to her opinion, even if Ax did have the final say. "Who would we trust with this information? My soldiers would give their lives for Dusra, but this, this is asking much more."

"I don't think we could trust many outside of this room," I responded.

"And who are we suggesting *in* this room?" Axel asked.

"I go where Daya goes," Zuri said.

"As do I," Axel responded quickly.

"Great, you're all adorable, but that wasn't really the question, was it?" Paxx smirked.

"I think I have to be the one to go," I said. "I'm the one with the information, and I'm the one Naom seems to think will help. That's if the power she gave me has anything to do with it."

"Don't love the idea of the future of Malva being sent to the evil underworld deity," Ishani said.

"Future of Malva is a stretch," I said.

"If you say so," she responded with that knowing look.

There was far too much to think about before anything resembling that happened.

I stood up and put my hands on my hips. "So me, Axel, and Zuri? Anyone else?"

"I'll go too," Paxx said. "My skills are better served tracking and spying than preparing for battle."

"Someone should stay with Ishani," I said.

"I have Akari and the rest of my generals. I agree that Paxx is better served on this mission."

"Hard to not take that as an insult," Paxx mumbled.

"You're the one who said it." Ishani pushed him on his shoulder with a chuckle. "I'll be fine. I'm a big girl."

"If there is any problem at all, send someone to find us. Even through our twin connection, I don't think magic will work here. We'll travel with you to the border and see you through, then we'll turn back," Axel said.

"I wonder if the Triori really knew what Chuah had planned," I said.

"They're self-preserving, so I doubt it. He's not of this world," Ishani mumbled.

"I can't imagine another world outside the spirit world," I responded.

"It doesn't sound like a place we'd want to visit," Zuri said.

We all sat in silence for a beat—similar images running through their heads as mine, I was sure. What would someone want with the dead? What could Chaos benefit from? Valentina said he fed off fear, especially when someone fell in battle. Merely pulling people to whatever world she referenced wouldn't be enough. He'd probably want more.

Screams outside the tent had us ripping through the entrance and scanning the campsite. The trees across the empty space shifted, something massive moving through them and agitating the quiet. Lines of soldiers were already at the ready at the very edge of the tents, more coming from the middle. Branches snapped as red eyes glowed within the tree line, which was even more unsettling as the others we'd battled had been eyeless. Two more opened above the already glowing eyes, a long furry snout breaking through the tree line first. Its scaly lips pulled back, exposing razor-sharp teeth rotted and cracked. The beast surveyed the area as if it were deciding whether it would win a fight. I saw people reaching for their magic, realizing it wasn't possible on this land.

Everything went quiet as the monster watched us, and we watched it, waiting to see who would move first. Just as I was about to charge, it snorted and turned on lanky, spindly legs, and its two tails swished back through the trees. More movement on the other side of the camp started and stopped.

"I fucking hate this place."

Chapter Thirty-Nine

Dayanara

"Dayanara, heir of Air and Essence," a voice not of this world filled the darkness of my sleep.

It wasn't the same sensation as when my mother invaded my dreams. Something darker and heavier held me down against the force of my mind. A dark, inky liquid covered me, moving like an organism across my chest and over my arms. It slinked its way up my neck and pressed against the seam of my lips. I fought with all my power not to let it in, but I lost the fight. I gagged as the pressure moved through my mouth and into my nasal cavity, shooting out through my nostrils and leaving the rotting taste of death behind.

"I welcome you to my land." The liquid stopped, rising as if it had eyes and swaying akin to a serpent. "You know me now, yes?"

My nostrils flared as I squirmed to keep from barfing. The dark matter felt heavier, keeping me in place. "I'm assuming you're Chuah?"

Wherever we were, we didn't seem to abide by the same laws of nature. The air was thick and hard to swallow, that same lack of color in the Inbetween somehow even more pungent.

The substance purred, an appreciative hum ringing through the air. "I have not heard my name spoken in many centuries. I like the way you say it. Say it again for me."

"What do you want?" I snapped as I struggled to loosen myself from his hold.

"I want what every being of this world wants: freedom."

"But you're not of this world, are you?"

A dark chuckling vibrated everywhere the being touched me. "I am of everywhere. Born of the same molecules as anyone else in this universe. I just prefer a little more. . . chaos than most of the beings here."

"Chaos is one way to put it." I moved to sit up, and the black mass slithered backward, forming the same shape as my body, mirroring my movements.

"Well, we don't appreciate whatever it is you're trying to do. Go back to whatever world you came from and cause some chaos there."

"Oh, I have. But I want more. Surely, you understand my appetite for destruction. It feeds us. We bathe in it, don't we, Dayanara?"

"As someone who doesn't know me, you can stop talking as if you do."

The blob still moved with me, the finger I pointed at him a hair away from his mirror movement. "I may not be of Iteria, as you've pointed out, but chaos and darkness flow through everything. I know more than you think. I've spent a long time within the barrier of Naom's magic. You're as close to her as any being that has come through my borders."

Within the confines of my mind, I waged war against whatever he'd done to keep me here, but without being successful, I tried to keep him talking. "Again, what do you want from me?"

A grin formed within the mass of ink, taking a new shape of my mother. "I liked your mother too. Now, that was a being that could have fed me for decades. So many bad decisions, so much pain, destruction, chaos."

I deadpanned, growing more annoyed with the god.

"I thought she would have done it. She caused a rift between every being on this side of the wall. The disorder that would have come from that might have broken me free of my bindings."

My consciousness blinked in the back of my mind, and I stared down at my feet to focus on the sensation to escape. When I looked back up, Chuah was directly in front of my face, now taking the form of Kaizer with night-filled eyes. Void, but pinpricks of light like stars. "Make no mistake, I am coming. We will meet again, pretty witch."

I gasped awake. I wasn't even sure how long I'd slept or even what time it was as the Inbetween seemed to be in a constant state of muddied dusk. Rolling my shoulders and shuddering, I stood, not waking Zuri as she slept. I needed some fresh air. The sense that something slimy was covering my skin was still too strong.

As I ducked out of the tent quietly, I tried to tune out of my witch hearing as I passed a tent where people were certainly *not* sleeping. The deep timber of Paxx's voice from within had me moving a little faster. I forgot vampires don't have air shields for privacy.

I spotted Axel across the camp, and I tugged his ear as I made it to his side, his presence enough to calm me. "Any problems?"

Axel smiled down at me. "Nothing of note. Couple smaller beasts. Someone was taking a piss in the forest, and now they're. . . missing some parts, but the lack of self-awareness has me thinking we're better off."

"Splendid," I said.

"Typically, I'd ask you mind-to-mind what's wrong, but that's not working,"

I took a deep breath. "Had a bad dream. Don't want to talk about it quite yet."

His thumb brushed my waist as he nodded with his gaze out into the sky. "I can't believe people choose to live here."

"I said the same thing when I was here. There isn't anything that could make me willingly go without my magic."

"I think it would drive you mad." He squeezed my side. "It's about time for me to do a border check. You want to come?"

"As long as you promise to keep all your parts. I like some of them."

"Shit, me too," Axel agreed.

The snap of branches to our right proved that the border check was indeed needed, and as the creatures bounded for me, I took comfort in the swing of my blade and the spray of blood.

There had been two more attacks since I'd walked the perimeter with Ax. Even with taking turns with shifts, it had been hard to get any real sleep. Zuri didn't seem to have this problem as she snuggled up to my side. Axel had gotten a couple of hours in but was already back out on a watch. I heard the site starting to wake, enough rustling to signify that it was time to pack up.

Running my fingers down Zuri's spine, I roused her out of her slumber. She took a deep breath before rolling over and opening her eyes.

"I have no idea how you actually got rest," I said.

"I grew up around wolves. You can't imagine the amount of howling that goes on through the night." She stretched her arms the way she always did when she woke, and I loved that I knew that. That I'd been around for enough mornings that I knew she'd stretch her arms at least twice before officially getting up and that she'd rub her eyes before she put on her clothes for the day.

"We lost a couple soldiers in an attack since you fell asleep," I said as I stood. "The beast was too quick. We'll have to move through carefully because I have a feeling they might start tracking us."

"Wonderful," she said as she rubbed her eyes and grabbed her pants.

Axel came through the tent flap, his eyes flicking from Zuri and then to me. "We're moving. Ishani thinks we'll make it to the border before nightfall."

"Well, we still have a whole day here," I responded before throwing him his bag. "And if last night is any indication, we're going to need to be on high alert."

"Agreed," Axel responded as he grabbed both me and Zuri's bags and strapped them to his shoulders.

Zuri pulled her braids back away from her face, wrapping a leather strap around the base of them. We all moved out of the tent, and Axel went to retrieve our horses. Paxx stepped out of his tent, a woman scurrying away quickly over to the tent beside his, but not before we noticed. Paxx watched as she ran away before he noticed we were watching him.

"Hey, I was just comforting a fellow soldier." He lifted his hands in dismissal.

"Yeah, yeah," I responded. "I thought I heard something in the night."

From what I recalled, he was *very* comforting. Paxx shrugged one shoulder before going back into his tent, the sound of bags packing coming from within as we walked by.

"So tell me about you and Paxx," I said to Zuri.

Zuri's brows raised with a chuckle. "You know, talking about this in a place where you don't have your magic is probably best."

"Please, you know I'm just as dangerous," I said as I flipped a dagger in my hand.

"You didn't ask him about us while I was gone?"

Gone. She says as if she took a trip.

"I was focused on other things," I responded.

"Hm," she sounded. "We'd both been through some pretty tragic things at the time. I think it was nice to be with someone who understood the anger and pain, but when we moved past the trauma, we grew apart. It didn't end in any animosity."

"Your parents, but what did Paxx go through?"

She looked back over her shoulder to where Paxx was almost done packing his tent now. "He comes from a village where they were a little more. . . traditional in their ways. Similar to the vampires in Sanjry they had beliefs on how they should have kept peace. Paxx had a younger sister. She was born during a particular moon phase that was significant to this group of people. It was said to be a bad omen, and she had to be. . . dealt with or evil would come. Their beliefs went back to the time we were all one, before the Piedra—the last of their kind in Malva. They stole her in the night, and. . . it wasn't good. Paxx didn't find out until the next day. That village no longer exists. He broke it off the continent, and it now sits at the bottom of the ocean floor."

My throat tightened. I couldn't imagine someone doing such a thing to a child. I tried to scan the procession for Paxx, I wasn't sure why, there wasn't anything to be done now. But I couldn't find him. I dodged some soldiers reattaching carriages to horses, the metal weapons inside clinking in the abrupt movements.

"Axel said there'd been some issues here since the border closed, but I didn't think it was *that* bad."

"It was before my parents' death. When Ishani brought me to the palace, Paxx was already there. Axel didn't condemn him, only asked him to join his service. We leaned on each other. It was like we both needed to remind each other that we were here, the physicality of it. I don't know, it was a weird time for the both of us."

"Something I can understand," I responded.

I'd used so many people after I lost Ximena, a different kind of love, but the hurt was the same, I was sure. I understood why Paxx was quiet and reserved at first. He'd come out of his shell quite a bit, a side of him now that trusted me. A funny, comforting side I actually was starting to quite enjoy. It was hard not to care for someone who cared for the two most important people in my life this deeply.

The ground rumbled and jolted to a stop. We all searched for the source, and the beasts made themselves known.

"Let's move!" Ishani belted from atop her horse.

Axel made it to us with our horses, and we hopped on, filtering into the line moving. I tried to take into consideration where we were and if we should come back this way when we went searching for Chuah. Chills ran up my spine, and I wondered if people were onto something about not speaking his name. Merely thinking of him in this place, I had a strange awareness raking over my skin. Zuri and Axel seemed unbothered, both of them riding in silence with determination on their faces.

An unnatural breeze lifted the ends of my hair, the chills everywhere before Paxx joined me at my side, and it suddenly vanished.

"Hey, you okay?" he asked.

I couldn't help the way I saw him now. It had happened a long time ago, but things like that didn't leave us. "Hm? Yeah, why do you ask?"

He narrowed his eyes. "Something around you seemed off, I can't see your emotions right now, but something felt. . . wrong."

"I sensed it, too," I mumbled before we both looked up at Axel and Zuri.

"We can deal with it once we get rid of the army," he said, and I nodded my agreement.

Zuri's horse sped, and of course, Axel's picked up speed as they tried to stay in front of the other.

"I heard what Zuri told you," Paxx said.

I couldn't tell if he was upset about it, so I let him continue.

"That happened a long time ago, I don't want you to view me differently. We all have our tragedies that have put us on this path. We live, and we grow."

That was an understatement. I didn't necessarily believe that events like this were decided before we were born, that fate lined up these disasters for us to face.

"I understand why you observe now, why you sit back in silence sometimes."

"Intention is important to me. Sometimes that is more difficult to find between actions, words, and the plague that is mortality."

"You're a morbid one, but I think I just might like you."

The sound of a bowstring pulling tight and an arrow whisking through the air had me reaching for my sword on my back. The arrow flew past my face, the sound of punctured flesh coming from beyond the trees. A shriek, loud and piercing, moved through the air in shock waves as a beast akin to a wolf plopped down, the arrow buried deep in its forehead.

A soldier holding the bow moved out of the line to determine what they took down, their gaze surveying the trees for more animals, but none came. They fell back in line without another word, and Paxx and I both sped up to Zuri and Axel.

A massive bird flew overhead, not any bird, an owl with eyes as dark as night, lights sparkling in them like stars. Those chills came back, and I kept my hand on my weapon for the rest of the way out of the Inbetween.

PART THREE

"Love makes your soul crawl out from its hiding place."
  —Zora Neale Hurston

Chapter Forty

Dayanara

"Fucking goddess," I exasperated as I pulled my sword from the belly of a beast.

We'd almost gotten to Sanjry's border, the side closer to Caldera, where there was much less of a population. *Almost* being the key word because we'd been ambushed by a whole herd of some creatures with the faces of pigs, but much larger and with hard armored backs. Bloodied tusks pulled out of a soldier beside me, and I pushed him with all of my strength through the border into Sanjry, about twenty feet away.

"I'm regretting ever eating bacon with the look of you," I said to the creature as it charged for me.

In my peripheral, I saw Zuri exiting the Inbetween with Axel just a few feet away. I sidestepped the beast, its low center of gravity and massive body making it difficult to pivot with me. Jabbing my dagger into the crease between the plates of armor across its ribs, I sliced all the way down to the tail, blood thick as tar sprayed. The pig didn't die right away but turned its head to me slowly. Black, void eyes watched me, and I swore I saw pinpricks of light within them before they glazed over with death.

I crossed the border and while I never thought my body would be so happy to step back into Sanjry, the overwhelming feeling of *right* filled me as my magic came, tingling back to life. I hadn't given much thought to the border of the Inbetween. But now I sensed Naom's magic actively holding in whatever was trying to take over our world. My Acna powers pulled me toward it, all the essence in me recognizing her.

That sensation was quickly thwarted by the stench coming from the blood covering half of my body and a sharp sting trailing down my arm. I nearly gagged as the black blood dripped into a cut I didn't remember getting. *Fucking disgusting.*

Axel rolled his neck, his magic hitting me harder than I thought he meant as he cleaned the blood off my body. Zuri was at my back, and I bumped into her as she gently gripped my arm and healed the cut. Her brows narrowed for a second, the wound taking longer to heal than others she'd mended.

"Sorry, was a little backed up there," Ax apologized with a swipe of his thumb across my cheek.

The space we were in was a sort of no-man's-land, a sliver of Sanjryan land between the Inbetween and Caldera that nobody occupied. I could make out a Calderan forest out on the horizon, almost too dark to see, but I knew it well.

"We'll make camp there near the forest tonight," Ishani said as she flicked something very fleshy-looking from her shoulder. "You should probably stay the night here and then leave in the morning."

"Agreed," Zuri said.

"You sure we'll be good here?" Paxx asked at my back.

"Yeah, I'm sure they expect us after breaking the agreement, but nobody lives out here. We still need to keep watch, of course," I responded.

"And the trees should give us some coverage," Axel agreed.

The Piedra wasn't too far in the distance. The clouds in the sky were thick and fluffy today, so just a portion of the rock showed. I thought about the thousands of times I'd been this close and never knew what the stone was covering. That unease filled me as the memory of my dream came back to the surface, goosebumps rippled down my body, but I covered it with a stretch of my arms.

There was something enticing about Chuah in an entirely disgusting way. If he was truly the source of all chaos, of all mischief and evil, I wondered if he had some sort of influence even in the stone. For our world was full of violence even with him being imprisoned—my life alone was full of it. Were we to be soldiers in some impending war? Or destined to be pulled down into the pits of whatever his realm was. Maybe it'd be fun, a land of bloodshed and violence without anyone blinking an eye.

My limbs felt heavier, and Paxx came over and snapped his fingers in my face. "We need to talk—now."

We both smiled and nodded at Axel and Zuri as we padded across toward the tree line.

Once we were out of earshot, Paxx hissed, "What is that cloud of black around you?"

I snapped down an airshield. Being out of earshot of the vampires and lobos wasn't the same as the brujas. "You saying I don't always have a black cloud around me?"

"Dayanara." Paxx tilted his head.

"Fine," I exasperated. "When we were in the Inbetween, I had a dream, and I saw him."

"You saw. . . *him?*"

One curt tilt of my chin.

Paxx rubbed his temples. "You haven't told anyone else?"

"No. It could have just been my mind!"

Goddess, I wished that it was all in my head. That I'd made it up, simply a dream put together by the things that I'd seen and heard. But I knew better than that. I could still feel his inky touch all over my skin.

"It wasn't your mind. That cloud is him. It's like. . . splotches of tar in your aura."

I swallowed, trying to fight the shock that was taking over at the use of the word 'tar.' That was exactly how it felt. "What does this mean?"

"I don't know how, but he's..." Paxx paused, "inside you now somehow."

"Gross." I grimaced.

"Not like that," Paxx said with annoyance. "Not all of him, but a piece. You didn't touch anything while we were there?"

I shook my head. "Nothing that nobody else didn't."

We sat for a moment, just staring blankly at each other and wondering where to go next. I broke eye contact first, disbanding my air shield and heading back toward camp, Paxx's footsteps falling behind me.

"We need to tell Ax and Zuri," Paxx whispered.

"We don't know what to tell them right now. Let's wait until we know something for sure."

Paxx didn't let it go. "I know what I'm seeing. That is real, whether you can see it or not. You said you trusted me."

I did. I *do*. But whatever this was. . . I knew it was going to be bad. I rolled my sleeves up, the weather a bit warmer than I expected. Reaching down to gather logs like the others were doing—but mostly to ignore Paxx—I grabbed a few that looked good for a fire. Paxx stayed at my side. I could feel his stare boring into the back of my head, but I continued trying to figure out what to do.

"What is that," Paxx said as he grabbed my arm with caution in his tone.

A black tattoo of a scorpion stood out against the other ink on me, the black deeper and more void of color than the rest. The tail of the scorpion snapped down, and if Paxx wasn't watching, I would have thought I'd imagined it.

"This is where the blood of that beast seeped into my skin," I whispered.

"Believe me now?" Paxx said with a raised brow. "He's attached himself to you somehow."

"Fuck," I exhaled. Valentina had warned me of this.

"This is not an 'I'm Daya, and I'll deal with it' situation. None of us know what this means," Paxx said.

"Just give me a minute, Paxx. I'll tell them before we leave."

Honesty was what I had asked from the both of them, and it was cowardice of me not to tell them right away. I knew that. But I also knew that a delay in us figuring this shit out could have been worse for everyone. It was hypocritical, and I *hated* that it felt like it was the right thing to do. There was a possibility I could control it, that nobody would have to be hurt. If we didn't get to Chuah first, thousands of my people could die in this war and beyond.

I told myself it was right, even if a piece of me knew it wasn't.

My mind felt foggy. This dream I was having was different from anything else recently. Suspended in a pool of inky blackness, my limbs kicked and reached, trying to swim to the surface. It was exceedingly thick, the jerky movements exhausting me by the second. I told myself to calm down, to control my breathing to reserve energy, but it was useless. The thick tar fought against my every move, my thrashing only pleasing it as it pulled me down further. I reached for my magic, for any of my magic, but none came.

Just as my lungs started to burn, and the tar invaded my nostrils and throat, it dispersed. The black substance dripped off my body, retreating from my mouth and nose but leaving a sticky residue behind. There was a film over my eyes, the surrounding scene so similar to the one I'd fallen asleep in, everything but that hint of shimmering ethereal darkness. Axel's spot was still warm to the touch like he had just left for his shift of the night watch.

Zuri slept, rolled into a ball with her ass nudged up against me. This was the position I remembered her falling asleep in. I'd done the thing where I counted her freckles. Her time in the outside light of Dusra made them more prominent than they were in Sanjry. Her individual braids were braided into two thick braids, the tail of one of them laying across her neck. Zuri's pulse beat beneath it, the tiny hairs shaking with each thud.

"Wouldn't it be nice to make her pay for her treachery," a voice spoke from all around me.

I jolted up, Zuri not budging per usual. I saw nobody within the tent, no shadows on the canvas. Closing my eyes, I tried to wake from the dream. My palms bled from me squeezing my fists so tight, but I stayed within the dream.

"She did lie to you after all," the voice said again, this time directly into my ear. "Are you really over it? How can you trust her?"

My gaze shifted back to Zuri where she slept, my heart beat racing in my ears. I didn't remember moving toward her, but I suddenly hovered beside her sleeping form.

"She could be working with Kaizer. Wouldn't it be easier to get rid of her and ensure your safety?"

Zuri had lied. She'd been in Sanjry for years. Who knows what happened. Her loyalties could have shifted. Kaizer could have offered her something sweet just like he did my mother. Had she helped decide on this route into Caldera? Before I knew it, both of my knees were on either side of her hips, my hand reaching for my dagger.

No. Zuri was taken. I'd seen her scars. I trusted Zuri. I understood why she did what she did. She'd never forsake me. My hand froze where it was. My mind shouted, WRONG, WRONG, WRONG.

The voice wasn't interested in that.

"STOP! What did she really tell Kaizer to cease the torture? She probably cut a deal for her life."

"No, she almost died," I responded aloud.

Zuri shifted, moving fully to her back and reaching for the spot I was before.

"Exactly, *almost* died. She was there for weeks. Why didn't they kill her sooner when she didn't speak? Maybe she gave them clues they found useful. How you did with Athena."

My hands trailed up Zuri's arms, and she smirked, her eyes staying closed as she whispered, "Daya."

Something inside sparked at the sound of her voice, but whatever that darkness around me was pushed it down. It snuffed out the warmth her presence and voice brought me, leaving only cold emptiness. I wrapped my fingers around her throat, and I squeezed.

"A bit of a forceful start." Zuri's eyes opened, and her arousal turned into fear in an instant. "Daya!"

Her voice did nothing this time. I leaned closer, bearing all of my weight into her hips, and I continued squeezing her throat. My nails extended, and I felt blood dripping down the back of her neck from the motion. Zuri's eyes started to bulge as she lifted her hips to try to buck me off, but I was stronger. She gasped for air, her nails dragging down my arms and drawing blood. Zuri reached for my face, but the hold I had on her kept her from being successful.

"Daya, it's me," she huffed.

"You're going to betray me," I said, my voice deeper, an echo of it sounding and extending an unnatural amount of time.

"I would nev—" she tried to say, but I squeezed tighter.

"Finish it," the voice said, my hands squeezing and hesitating every moment that passed.

A firm hand landed on my shoulder, ripping me away from Zuri and my revenge. I bared my teeth at Axel, who reached for Zuri as she held her neck and gasped.

"Daya, what the fuck is wrong with you?" Axel yelled.

I growled, my hands tightening into fists, but Axel yanked my weapons away with a stream of water before I could do anything. He positioned himself in front of Zuri and the tent ripped open again, this time Paxx coming in.

"Fuck," he said as he put a hand on my arm. "It's invading you."

"What's invading her?" Axel asked.

Paxx turned back to me and put his other hand on my arm to hold me in place. "This is not you. I'm going to help."

His brow tightened as he focused, and the dark tint on the world flickered. I glanced back at Zuri, and she was slowly healing her neck, the bruises fading as Axel helped her, but his eyes were on me.

"This might hurt," was the last thing I heard Paxx say as pain wrenched up my entire being, and the world went wholly black.

Chapter Forty-One

Dayanara

I groaned awake, my body aching and my limbs not listening to my commands. Blinking my eyes a few times, I realized my arms and legs were tied down, Axel and Zuri watching on the other side of the tent.

"What the fuck is going on?" I asked as I pulled at the restraints.

"We'd like to know the same thing," Axel said. "You attacked Zuri."

"No, I didn't. I just woke up." I paused with a gasp. "The dream."

"It wasn't a dream, Daya," Zuri said as she gently pressed her fingers to her throat.

Fuck. Fuck. Fuck. I knew it wasn't my average dream. What I'd almost done. . .

Paxx came back in, a jug of water in one of his hands and his dagger in the other. "How do you feel?" he asked me.

"I'm confused. Can we take this shit off me, please?"

He was reading my emotions, his eyes focusing on the surrounding air before making eye contact. "Promise not to attack any more loved ones?"

I flicked my gaze over to Zuri, my throat tightening. "I promise. I'm in control."

He watched me for another moment before looking back at Axel, who nodded in agreement. I didn't miss how Axel kept his arm in front of Zuri as protection, though. Paxx removed my bindings slowly and stepped back with his arms across his chest.

"Tell them. I'll be back," he said before exiting.

I explained what had happened yesterday and how the invasion masqueraded as a dream. The way he coerced me. All as I kept my distance from Zuri in case she was scared. She nodded her head, never shrinking away from me or hiding behind Axel.

"Do you feel different now?" Axel asked as he grabbed one of my hands.

"No, not right now."

Zuri grabbed my other arm, where the tattoo felt like it was watching us. She ran her finger over it, her healing light extending and fizzling it out. "I've never felt anything like this before."

Axel's magic entered my mind, brushing up against my senses and searching for anything unnatural. "No compulsions or odd thoughts?"

"Well..." I paused and bit my cheek. "I did have a thought about whether his realm of violence would be enticing. . ."

"That's not nothing." Zuri deadpanned.

"It could have been a thought of my own, who knows? " I shrugged out of both of their holds and took a step back.

At the time, it felt a little odd. It wasn't out of my character to be violent, but wondering what his world was like, if it would be fun, definitely was.

"We should try to remove this before we go back. If he can do whatever he did while we're outside of the Inbetween, who knows what he can do inside," Axel suggested.

Our gazes bounced between one another before Paxx came back into the tent, balancing bowls of food in his arms. "Figured we could use some food."

"Thanks, Paxx," Zuri said with a smile.

"Has the part where she denies she needs help come back up yet?" Paxx asked as he spooned some food into his mouth.

"I do need help," I snapped, and he threw his hands up in surrender. "I want this shit out of me as soon as fucking possible. . . I know two people that can possibly help. I don't know if this is how their power works, but I'll check."

Everyone set their bowls down to follow me, and I turned to put my arm between us. "You all stay. I don't want to spook them."

I could see that they were hesitant to let me leave alone, but I left before they could stop me. I really didn't want to put Ishani in this situation, but if it was blood that got me into this, it was possible she could be of assistance. The other person was a bruja from my coven, one I was actually surprised was on my side after what I'd done.

Last I checked, the bruja I was looking for was stationed on the north side of the camp with the group of witches she had come to Dusra with. I'd asked Cat if we could trust her. She ran her own screenings on her and determined that she held no ill will toward me. As much as I wanted to believe that, the last time I'd seen her, she was on the brink of killing me. Plus. . . what I'd done to her aunt.

"Luz!" I called as I spotted her.

"Acna." Luz bounded over, dipping her head slightly. She was not Rosa's daughter, but fuck did she resemble her. Luz's complexion was much deeper than Rosa's, her hair a mixture of waves and curls, but those eyes were a perfect replica of her aunt's. Rosa had a younger sister back when it wasn't difficult for us to procreate once, let alone twice. She'd died in the same battle that killed Cat's mother, and I was pretty sure I never offered my condolences for it.

"Your mother and aunt told many stories of old. Do you happen to remember them?" I asked.

"All of them."

"What about the. . . other practices?" I said with my brow raised.

Her mouth fell open, her lip sputtering. "I don't know. . ."

"Please, Luz. Outside of the obvious, there wasn't too much that went on that we didn't know about. I'm starting to think your aunt knew more than she let on. I should have let her speak instead of killing her."

This wasn't the time to remind her that she was also quite the pillow talker and had let it slip one time during one of our escapades. As a matter of fact, it might have been the last time we'd slept together. The time she tried to get me to commit, and I'd banished her from the capital.

"Yes, I am well-versed in those practices." Her face softened for a moment. "And. . . thank you for saying that."

Long, dark, curly hair caught my attention, Ishani receding into the tree line behind Luz. "Can you come to my tent in an hour? I need your help."

"Of course, Acna." She dipped her head again.

I retreated with a slight nod, going in the direction I'd seen Ishani go off into. There had been doubts since I'd found out what my mother had done, and I'd wondered if Rosa was truly going after me or Kaizer. She said that Kaizer was who she wanted dead, that he would dispose of us once he got what he wanted. The cranky old bitch might have been right, but I'd been so stuck on the disrespect she'd shown to me and. . . my mother that I let it cloud my judgment.

"Ishani," I said as I found her crouched down, picking something from the grass.

"I knew these mushrooms grew in Caldera. We used to get them imported before, well, you know." She lifted the blue and white mushroom. "My mother used to love them."

I smiled weakly, knowing what I was about to ask her was not going to bring up good memories of her mother. It was the widest she'd smiled since Xavier, and I hated that I was about to make it go away.

"I have to ask something, and I want you to know I would never ask unless I absolutely had to."

Ishani's shoulders sagged, and she dropped the mushrooms into her satchel before wiping her hands on her dress. "What is it?"

"When we were in the Inbetween, I saw *him*." I paused, now knowing he was. . . inside me, causing a hesitation that wasn't there before. "He came to me in a dream with these void black eyes. They had something silver swirling in them like stars. One of the beasts had those same eyes, and when I fought him, the blood seeped into an open wound that caused this to appear."

I showed her the tattoo. She ran her finger over it with notches between her brows. "You want me to use my blood magic?"

"I want you to try. He has some sort of control over me." I shifted my focus down at my feet. "I almost hurt Zuri because of it."

I still couldn't believe it. But I needed to say it out loud to remind myself of the importance behind the ask.

"Is she okay?" she asked in slight panic.

"She's fine now. Paxx says he can see *him* in my aura like he's attached to me somehow. But it was blood that caused it. I thought blood magic could cure it."

"Daya, I don't have enough practice. I could hurt you more. . . "

"I think we have to risk it. If I go back into the Inbetween, who knows the power he may have over me."

"It could be worse than poison." She bit her lip.

The battle in her eyes—the worry—was why I didn't want to ask for help in the first place. But I had no other choice.

"Yes."

"I'll try, but I wish I had someone there with me to help."

"There will be. I've got a blood witch of my own. Be at my tent in an hour."

I left Ishani, not hearing the shuffle of her footsteps until I'd gotten out of the forest. I knew what I was asking, knew that it was an impossible ask. But I had to protect Zuri, Axel, and Paxx as they'd be coming with me into the Inbetween.

There was no more voice in my ear, no heightened desires for chaos or destruction, but there was *something* in me that I knew didn't belong. A foreign substance building beneath my skin. I looked at the scorpion, wondering how far Chuah's influence had.

Zuri had said that Kaizer was more deranged than usual. As far as I knew, he'd only been contacting him through a journal. The thought that maybe he'd had this. . . shit inside him, too, came to the forefront of my mind. Or maybe it was Joseph. His eyes always set me on edge—something about them feeling wrong. Regardless, what they'd started had gone too far to turn back. I was just happy to have people surrounding me who cared and brought me back to myself. I tried not to think of the terror I might have become if this happened to me before I met them. They were my anchors, my purpose, and I'd fight this shit until my last breath for them.

Chapter Forty-Two

Ishani

My palms were sweating, my head spinning as I sat in this tent with Axel, Zuri, Daya, Paxx, and the blood witch. I had to tell them first. I had to tell Axel what the price of saving him was, but my throat was constricted. Every time I tried to speak, the words stayed lodged in my chest. I wished that Xavier was here. He could have told them for me, taken some of the weight of it. He'd thought he would be a burden on me, but I realized how much I'd leaned on him over the years, even when we weren't a couple.

"Ish, what's going on?" my brother asked.

Tears lined my eyes. "I need you to know that I would make all the same choices again. After I tell you, I need you to know that I'd do it all again. To keep you safe, I'd do it again."

Axel looked over at Daya, who gave him a tight smile. My brother was never outwardly worried, hadn't been in centuries upon centuries. But ever since this mess started, I'd seen so much more of it. I hoped that I'd never see that crease between his brows or the panic in his eyes again. It broke my heart.

"Okay." I took a deep, centering breath, knowing my next words were not going to be easy for Axel. "When you were captured, Mother and Father weren't trying to get you back. Well, they wanted you back, but they weren't trying hard enough. They were playing politics, trying to find some sort of way around losing the war."

Axel's jaw went tight, but Daya and Zuri both leaned closer to his sides, and he let out an exhale.

"I could feel it, Kiaan," I said, using his given name. "I could feel what you went through over there. The pain. You almost died. At the worst of the worst, I felt every part of the abuse. I couldn't see what was happening. Whatever suppressant they had on you made it impossible to get into your mind. But I felt it. Even the days you don't remember, I remember all of it. It's like those scars on your own skin live beneath mine."

The blood witch watched, but I wasn't uncomfortable. She was going to see what I could do one way or another.

"I went to the Triori. They tried to talk me out of acting. But Lachala couldn't hide her worry. There was a hint of. . . something. She wouldn't tell me outright that you were going to die should you continue, but I read between the lines. I asked for power, for something to help me get you back. I was filled with anger, bearing the pain of losing you and the actual pain you were experiencing. It made me. . . It made my mind unclear."

"Ish. . ."

I shook my head, needing to get the words out before he asked any more questions. "They gave me blood magic. That's how I got you back. I brought a battalion who'd follow me anywhere and came to Sanjry's doorstep. I manipulated the blood of every soldier that tried to stop me. Some of them exploded, some of them simply burst blood vessels and passed out. I even. . . I manipulated yours when you tried to attack me. You were so out of it."

I would never forget that look on his face. We'd seen bloodlust; it wasn't common as most people had a steady supply of blood, but I'd seen it before. Whatever state Axel was in was past that. His skin had a pale hue, the white of his eyes completely red. He didn't even recognize me when I found him. He only growled and tried to attack me. Manipulating his blood while trying to keep him alive was harder than killing the hundreds I cut through.

"What was the price?" Paxx asked.

"Our parents," Axel uttered. "The accident."

"Yes, I don't think it was a real accident. I think they were the price."

"Wait, you don't know for sure?" Daya asked.

"The Triori did not tell me after they took the price, but I'm pretty certain."

It happened so soon after bringing Axel back, after getting the blood magic. They were strong, no real explanation as to how they ended up that way. It looked like a freak accident, but I knew better.

"How have we never seen you use it?" Zuri asked, pain written in her features. I was focused on how hurt Axel would be by this that I didn't think about how one of my closest friends would feel about me hiding it from her.

"I rarely use it. It. . . it takes from me when I use it."

Axel folded his hands, bringing them up to his chin as he watched me with uncertainty. "You shouldn't have done that for me."

"You'd be dead," I whispered.

"But you wouldn't be. . ." Axel searched for the right word. "Cursed."

"I told you I would do it all again for you, my twin."

And I would. Again and again. A few moments of silence passed as they all watched me with varying emotions and facial expressions. Paxx stood and put his hands on his hips, his eyes narrowing and relaxing.

"I don't see anything in your aura," he said.

"It's not something that can be seen," I offered with a flat smile. "But now, I may be able to help Daya."

"And that brings me to our other friend." Daya turned to the bruja in the room. "This is Luz. Her aunt was Rosa. She's an old. . . friend."

Zuri's brows rose in shock, but none of us knew why that name held any significance. The friend part had Axel's eyes narrowed on her, too.

"Blood magic may have been outlawed in Dusra, but it's been used in Caldera. Not in the same way of controlling it, and not for a long time. It has been such a long time that it was suggested that nobody attempt it, as there aren't many who know the ins and outs of it. Rosa was an elder. She did not tell my mother or me that she knew the ways, but we were aware."

"So what do you do if you can't control it?" I asked Luz eagerly.

"We use the blood itself for runes and incantations. Different runes can tell us different things, glimpses into the future, protection. . . cures." She turned to Daya. "What exactly are we looking for?"

"There's something in my blood that shouldn't be there. It entered through here." She pointed to the tattoo.

Luz brushed her finger over the scorpion, the tail of the arachnid moving as if to pierce her.

"I need you to try to get it out, Ishani. I need you, Luz, to figure out its purpose or if there will need to be a cure," Daya explained.

As if the tattoo heard what Daya's intentions were, she fell to the ground, convulsing, her eyes going black as the scorpion moved from her forearm up to her shoulder. Axel dropped to his knees, grabbing her head and trying to wake her up, but she mumbled words none of us understood. Zuri's hands lit with healing, but the scorpion zapped every attempt away.

"Ishani, do whatever it is you came to do," Paxx said, the only one semi-calm.

I grabbed the dagger from my side and cut open the original cut. A black tar-like substance seeped from the cut, so much thicker than her regular blood.

"That's what I see all around her," Paxx said.

"Okay." I nodded, hoping I didn't accidentally blow Daya's head off her shoulders. "Here goes nothing."

"That's not very encouraging!" Zuri yelled as she continued trying to use her healing magic.

I closed my eyes, drowning out everything around me. It would have been great to have had some practice in recent years, but the ability was part of me as much as water. Reaching for the connection to Daya's blood, to the water within, I opened my eyes before I took my pointer finger and laid it right on the open wound. I pulled back, taking the substance with me. A stream of it connected from my finger to Daya. Daya's back arched, her chest heaving in short pants.

Stay focused. The odd matter in her blood stuck out like a rock in an ocean, but it was much further than just her arm now. The scorpion had moved over to her neck, and I realized that there was a large mass of the tar right beneath it, a trail behind it. Wrapping Daya's blood around the foreign substance, I guided it down her arm, the color of the scorpion tattoo fading by the second.

Just as I was thinking that this was easy, the tar seemed to take on a mind of its own. The scorpion flickered and fought against my hold. I pulled, and it pulled back, shooting further into Daya's body than before. She stopped convulsing and went so incredibly still that I had to make sure that blood was still flowing through her veins.

"Ishani, is it working?" Zuri asked.

"It's fighting back. I'm trying," I said as I focused, sweat beading on my brow.

"Can we power share?" Axel asked.

"I don't know if it works for this magic, but you can try." I nodded rapidly, hoping and begging that it would work.

Axel took a shaky breath, his eyes on Daya. He placed his hand on my shoulder, and I felt his power feeding into mine. I wasn't sure if it helped the blood magic specifically, but it did help offer me strength. The cut on Daya's arm widened as I pulled the big ball of tar out, wishing I could have figured out how to make it fit through without further injuring her.

Daya's eyes shot open, her mouth agape in a silent scream, and Zuri moved closer to her head. "Is it all out?"

"There's remnants." My mouth twisted as I went back in for more.

Luz dipped her stick into the mixture of Daya's blood and whatever the other substance was, drawing in the dirt swirls and symbols I didn't quite recognize. I turned my focus back wholly on Daya.

"Come on." I kept pulling at it, the little pieces floating around much harder than the big mass I'd already pulled out.

I felt my body weakening and my gut turning, but I let Axel's magic help keep me going. Just a little longer. Daya appeared to be in less pain now, the shock of it wearing off as she sat up slightly, and Zuri slid behind her exactly as Daya had done for her once before. I closed my eyes again, visualizing exactly where those pieces were.

"Kinda wish you would have stayed passed out," I whispered before making small cuts where I sensed the remnants.

"Couple cuts won't hurt me," Daya said with a small, pained smile.

She ate her words shortly after as I dipped my finger into the wounds to guide the rest of the poison out. Daya groaned, throwing her head back into Zuri's chest. I searched around for more, and I could feel small fragments, but too little for me to pull the same way I did without her losing too much blood.

"I think we got it," I said.

The scorpion tattoo showed as a barely there outline, proving there were some tiny pieces that I wasn't able to get. Axel took his hand off my shoulder and fell to his knees, inspecting every inch of Daya's body, ripping her clothes off, and baring her to us.

Paxx's eyes widened, but Daya just smiled and winked at him before her head fell back again, and she passed out.

"I don't see anything else on her skin," Axel said.

"Me either," Zuri said as she frantically inspected the same way he did. "That's good. You did good, Ish."

My knees buckled, but kept myself standing strong, even with the nausea rising in my throat. I did it. Without killing her and hopefully saving her life.

Luz cleared her throat. "I've written a few runes. I don't want to complete the incantation until she wakes back up."

"Can the runes wait?" I asked.

"Yes, they will hold, but I have a feeling she's going to need to see whatever they reveal."

"Very well," Axel said as he ran his fingers through Daya's hair.

I smiled, interlacing my fingers. "I'm going to go find someone to give me blood."

"Thank you, Ishani," Axel said. "For everything, thank you."

"Anything for you, brother."

Xavier would have been proud. I tried to keep myself positive, to always raise my chin and see the bright side, but this ability never felt light or positive. Not with what I'd done, with what I felt when I stormed Sanjry. Feeling the sheer amount of blood one body—not to mention hundreds—held was unsettling. Xavier said I punished myself for it, that it wasn't the magic but my mind. Today, I used it for good. To protect someone I loved. I walked out of the tent, passing only two more before I started retching. My skin was clammy, and Paxx's hands on my back were the last thing I remembered before I fell unconscious like Daya.

Chapter Forty-Three

Dayanara

I took a bite of the bread Axel had brought me, washing it down with some water as he watched me with worry. I'd been out for a bit after what Ishani had done. She said that she got most of it, but she thought there may have been some small remnants, nothing like it was before. She was resting now, thanks to the toll the magic took on her. The scorpion tattoo was almost gone, nearly invisible if you didn't know to look for it. It was interesting that this was the symbol he chose, something that very much existed in our world. Maybe he was their creator. They bled the same black blood as the other creatures. If parts of him had lasted this long outside of the Inbetween, I wasn't looking forward to what would happen should he escape.

"That was fucking terrifying," Axel said.

"Didn't feel great either," I mumbled, my gaze falling to the series of runes Luz had drawn with my blood. It was dark, nearly black now that it had been out in the oxygen for this long and that it was mixed with that shit.

"I really almost hurt her," I whispered.

Axel wrapped his arms around me, and I let myself melt into him while it was only us. He kissed my forehead and tilted my chin up to him. "Are you still worried that you can't trust her?"

"No, I'm not worried at all. It was all him. Every time I justified something he said, he had something else to add. What he does, it clouds your mind and forces you to see things his way. I understand why he was so dangerous. An army of people led by him, they'd be unstoppable."

"Ishani got almost all of it, but if you feel weird or off, you let us know *immediately*. Not trusting us with that information is not an option." Axel pulled back, ensuring I saw how serious his face was.

"I know."

I knew I should have told them right away in the first place. Zuri came back with Paxx and Luz, and the blood witch bowed her head before going over to the runes.

"I didn't want to finish the spell without you, Acna."

"I appreciate it." I motioned for her to start, my body feeling mostly back to normal now.

"The first one I inscribed was to understand where the source of the substance in your blood was from. The second for a cure, and the third to see any glimpse of violence in your future due to it."

Luz hadn't asked many questions, and we'd only told her that it was something foreign from the Inbetween. Brujas weren't prone to sticking their noses in things, especially when it could come back to bite.

"I'll start the incantation. You might want to put up an air shield," Luz said as she rubbed her hands together.

I did as she said, just as the temperature in the tent dropped low enough that clouds of our breath appeared on every exhale. This was the first time I'd seen blood magic used. It was volatile and touchy; one small thing could ruin the magic, and the repercussions were said to be extreme. It was understandable now as I watched her hover her hands across the runes, her dark pink bruja magic extending from her fingers and wrapping around her wrist.

She muttered something in a language old and lost to our time. I recognized some of the words from other spells, but this was something as old as our world. The same language that was scribed onto the elemental stones that we deciphered with Kaizer's book. This was dark and devastating, and it was beautiful.

The first rune sparked, the dark color of the etchings fading by the second as her magic filled the wells. Once the first rune was completely lit with pink, she moved over to the second and the third. Luz sat back and finished the last line of the incantation. In an instant, the lines of each rune broke and created new lines of writing. I stepped closer, the language the same as what she spoke.

She pointed to the first bunch of words. "The source, it says—"

"Creation," I interrupted, recognizing one of the symbols.

"That's not how the Triori told the story," Axel responded.

"It reads." She slid her pointer finger beneath the lines of symbols. "Creation is the source, as is chaos, as is darkness, and anti-essence. From the pits of our world, and the pits of every world."

"How comforting," Zuri muttered.

Luz bit her lip. "Moving to the second. This one is inconclusive. This typically means the cause is something above us, therefore the cure is out of our reach."

"Or below us," I whispered. "The third?"

"This one." She looked up at me and back down. "Violence is imminent."

"Pretty much expected that answer," I said.

It validated what we thought, and what the Triori said. Chuah, wherever he drew his power from, wherever he came from, it wasn't here. We wouldn't find any solution in this land. Ishani couldn't use blood magic on every single body potentially infected. We were on our own.

"I can do another test on your blood now if you like," Luz said.

"Sure." I held out my arm and sliced big enough for her to be able to get a sample.

Luz drew this rune directly on my hand. "This will also offer some protection."

Her magic sparked across my skin, the blood not turning pink with her magic like it did before but darkening into black. She said the incantation before licking the blood off her finger and waiting a moment. Axel's body went tight where he stood, but before he could say anything about her consuming my blood, she spoke.

"There's barely anything left now. I don't think you need to be worried. This rune will give you a barrier of protection from him, but tread carefully, of course."

I felt the protection barrier rush through my blood, around my bones, and over my skin. Unlike other magic or protection from crystals, this seeped into every cell in my body and became one with me.

"Thank you, Luz. How many others from your sanction with these abilities joined us?"

Luz wiped any remnants of blood off her hands. "Only a handful. My aunt didn't trust many."

"Rightfully so. Should we need you when it is time for battle, I will find you. And I'm sorry about what happened between us before. I was. . . not in a great place."

Luz smiled softly and bowed her head before she left quickly. Paxx hadn't said much during it all, but he stepped forward to look back at the inscriptions left from the runes.

"What I felt in your aura and how I felt watching this be performed were eerily similar," he said as he rubbed his hand over the runes.

"This magic is ancient. Come here, Zuri," I asked, and she hurried to my side. "Doesn't this look similar to what we saw in Kaizer's books? I'm pretty sure it's the same ancient alphabet."

"It does. His obsession with old magic. I wonder if he has any idea about what we've found out? I find it hard to believe he actually thinks it's the Flame," Zuri agreed.

"My sources have definitely said he's less religious than any of the other kings prior," Paxx said.

"Oh, we got a glimpse when we took Athena." My mouth turned down in disgust.

Barf.

"So what do you all want to do?" Axel asked.

"We still need to go to the Inbetween," I said definitely.

If there was anything we learned, it's that we'd have to go to the source for answers. We were fucked regardless.

"We can wait until tomorrow. Let you rest for the day," Zuri said, lifting her hand when I went to object. "Not up for discussion, even if you think you don't need it."

"All right. We can leave first thing in the morning. I'm going to go check on Ishani," Paxx said.

"I'll go with you," Ax added.

Leaving just Zuri and me in the room together, I crossed my arms over my chest. "Zuri, I'm sorry."

"It's okay, Daya. I promise. But," she said as she looked down at her feet. "Do you still have doubts?"

"No," I said immediately. "I don't. It was all his influence."

"I wish there was some way for me to prove it to you."

I understood why she was worried, but I didn't know how else to explain it to her with words. If I could cut myself open and expose the truth to her I would.

Lifting Zuri's hand, I kissed her knuckles. "I don't need it."

"It will always be there, hanging over our heads," she mumbled.

I glanced down at the runes, a memory sparking. "There is something that could be done."

Chapter Forty-Four

Dayanara

I would have never asked Zuri to do what we were about to do, but I knew clearing her name would be as much of a relief for her as it was for me. So before we went into the Inbetween, I asked Luz to come back to our tent tonight. While I wasn't an expert in blood magic, I knew about this incantation. I'd read about it in my family's grimoire. An Acna, many centuries ago, used to have all of her closest brujas perform it to ensure they meant her no harm. It felt. . . meant to be that I'd stumbled across this information and that I just so happened to have a need for blood magic already.

"This incantation is not like the others. It is a little more complicated and certainly. . . more intense," Luz said as she stood at the center of our tent. Axel had taken Ishani her dinner and advised that she mentioned feeling much better using the blood magic this time.

"That's fine," Zuri said with a nod of her head.

"It is meant to determine whether there is any ill will toward the other." Luz grabbed a vine of twisted vervain from her satchel. "You each will cut into your palm and bring them together. I'll wrap this vervain around you and perform the incantation. Should there be any ill will between you two, the vervain will turn black."

"We're ready," I said.

Luz drew a circle around us, staying outside of the border as she nodded for us to cut. I dragged my dagger across my palm and reached for Zuri's, waiting to make sure she still wanted to do this. She grabbed the dagger from me and cut, taking my hand with a determined force.

Luz wrapped the twisted purple flowers around our hands, catching a drip of our combined blood and dropping it into the circle around us. She started the incantation, her magic picking up the drop of blood and filling it through the wells of the surrounding circle. A magnetization pulled me and Zuri toward each other, both of us gripping the other's shoulder as our hands melded together.

The chant fell into a whisper, or so I thought, but the circle had encased us with magic, creating a sound buffer. It felt as if it was only Zuri and me, our eye contact intense enough that a tear fell from her eye. She tried to move her mouth, but the force of the magic was too much. I brought my forehead to hers, letting the warmth of her skin combine with my own. I focused on that as our entire past seemed to play through my head. Zuri's eyes were closed as if it was doing the same for her. I thought about the first time I saw her, but the point of view was different from what I remembered.

I wasn't seeing through Zuri's eyes as I watched the two of us come together. It was as if I was a goddess, watching it all happen from above. Our memories played, and I watched myself fall for her. I watched her fall for me, the smiles all genuine and all-encompassing. It showed me Zuri in her room alone, looking as if she was mentally battling herself. I saw when Axel came, her meeting with Paxx and her telling them she wasn't sure if she could continue lying. I watched as she opened and closed her mouth so many times when I wasn't looking. How she watched me as I slept when we were in the Inbetween. The warmth of the magic suddenly retreated, the magnetization gone, but Zuri and I still held each other tight.

Peeling my eyes open, I had only an inkling of doubt around the incantation. For it to be spelled out in black-and-white was terrifying, as we didn't live in a black-and-white world. Zuri's mouth pulled into a radiant smile before I saw the flowers. Each and every petal was still in its beautiful purple hue.

Luz smiled, extinguishing her magic and backing away from us. "There is no ill will."

"Thank you, Luz," I said, dismissing her with my eyes still on Zuri.

"I love you, Dayanara. I can tell you that now, and you will know without a doubt that it is true. I've been scared that you wouldn't believe me. But I tell you now, Daya. I love you with every fiber of my being, with every beat of my heart, and every breath that I take. I'd endure it all again, if I knew that at the end of all of that pain, was you."

My chest fell with a deep exhale. Not having heard those three words in such a long time, I wasn't even sure they would ever be directed at me again. Pulling back our hands, I healed my cut, and then hers, before I pulled her by her waist and kissed her. A kiss that rivaled the well of power within me, so much passion behind it that we both fell to our knees. The dirt around us clouded, and I held the back of her neck, fearing she'd want to break the contact. I needed more. She didn't try to pull away. She only met every pass of my lips with one of her own. Her tongue slipped into my mouth, that unique taste I'd tried to understand the first time we'd kissed running over my taste buds.

Zuri's arms wrapped around my neck, not letting an inch of space between our bodies. Placing a hand on the small of her back, I lifted us in a sweep of air and laid us down on our bed rolls. Zuri's desperate breaths brushed against my ear as I kissed down her neck and across her collarbone. Her back arched into me, and I hoped she had more clothing options packed as I tore her top in half. Zuri's perfect breasts shook with the force, her nipples pebbling in the air. I stopped, hovering above her to take it all in. Zuri's freckles were enveloped in a deep blush, her lips full and eyes low. Her braids splayed around her head, a crown fit for her.

I felt it then, the impact of those words coming from this person. *I love you.* From someone who had loved deeply and from whom just as much had been taken. She'd seen all of me. The vulnerable parts, the violent parts, the vicious parts. Zuri had seen more than most people, maybe even the most of everyone. And she loved me. It didn't feel like that love was in spite of those things but because of them.

"I love you too, Zuri," I said as I brought my lips down to hers.

Zuri's body quivered, not in the same way she did when I'd kissed down her collarbone. But a whole body shiver—one of relief.

"I mean it." I kissed her again. "I think that's why I was so hurt before. I felt it then. I didn't think I could experience this anymore, and I. . . " I felt it two-fold. Not only for her but for Axel as well. But this wasn't the time. It wasn't clear if Zuri knew where I was going, but it just felt so damn good to be able to say that aloud. That I was loved, that *I* loved.

"I know." She smiled, a genuine one.

Slipping my hands under her back, I slid them down to palm her ass and lift her hips up. I kissed her pelvis through her pants before pulling them off and going straight for the soft skin of her inner thighs. Zuri's fingers gripped the blanket beneath her, clenching the fabric as I traveled higher. I got close enough to feel the warmth of her right on my lips, and she tightened, bracing herself for my mouth, but I rose back up to her hip bone.

I wanted to savor every squirm of her body. The frustrated exhale that left her only encouraged me more as I swirled my tongue over her hip and to the sensitive place above her pussy as I traveled to the other side. Her fingers left the blanket and pinched at her dark, rosy brown nipples, but I wanted it to be me. I smacked her hand away, replacing her fingers with mine as I clamped down on them. She pushed her chest into me, writhing as I took delight in the pleasure I knew she got from this. Making sure she got even more, I took one into my mouth, sucking before squeezing with my teeth. Zuri moaned a little louder than she had before. She slapped her hand across her mouth, and I created an air shield around us.

"Get as loud as you want," I said as I moved back to her pussy.

The evidence of how much she loved nipple play leaked from her, dripping down to her thighs and onto the sheets. She took me up on my suggestion, an even louder moan bouncing around the air shield as I made sure none of her juices went to waste. When her thighs were wet with just the spit from my tongue, I finally got to where I'd been wanting to be this whole time.

Her scream and my moan mingled as I spread her wide and flattened my tongue against her pussy. No matter how many times I'd tasted her, I never got tired of it.

I'd bottle her up if I could. I slid my finger into her as I closed down around her clit, sucking and flicking my tongue against it. Zuri's hips undulated, telling me exactly where she wanted me, and I let her. I let Zuri take everything she wanted from me. Inserting another finger, I pumped them in and out at the tempo of every surge. Her core was swollen, gleaming, and soaking as she held my head against her. I feasted, feeling just how close she was, and I didn't let up until she screamed—until she stopped squirming, and her body fell limp.

I rose on all fours, licking between her breasts and taking great pride in precisely how hard her chest rose and fell. Placing my pussy directly onto hers, I dragged my hips, letting her see how wet I was. Energy surged through her, the orgasm waning as she gripped my ass, and the laxness of her limbs disappeared.

"Get back on your knees. On the edge of the bedroll," she demanded, and I listened, loving it when she got like this. Zuri moved behind me, and I felt her hand between my shoulder blades as she pushed me down and forced my ass into the air even higher.

"Good girl," she said, and I could hear the smile in her tone. I bit my lip, but with my face pointing toward the tent wall, I didn't see her coming. She buried her face in my pussy, her hands holding each of my ass cheeks. Zuri repaid every swipe of my tongue with one of hers, the sensation of her moans against me having my body shivering with need. She rubbed two fingers around my clit, slowing her pace down from the zealousness she started with. Her fingers separated, running down my lips before plunging back into me.

I turned my head to try to get a better look at her just as she hooked inside me, and a groan escaped my mouth. Zuri smirked as she kept pumping, her other hand gripping me and guiding me to push back on her fingers. I did as she asked, sending my hips back and fucking her hand.

Zuri slapped my ass, and I felt the sting of the welt as it rose, the pain so fucking sweet. I was close, and Zuri must have known, because she pulled her fingers from me and flipped me onto my back, saying, "I want you to come on my tongue."

My knees rested on her shoulders, and she wasted no time in getting me right back to where I was. My hips rose, and she kept them elevated as she sucked down on my clit, her tongue running from my entrance and back up to the nerves. She coated her thumb in ice, dragging it slowly from my pelvic bone, around my navel, and between my breasts. The sensation had a different type of shiver running through me, but it only heightened the pleasure. She ran the ice over my nipples, and they got painfully tight.

"Zuri," I moaned.

"Daya," she said against my pussy.

Her fingers practically vibrated against my clit, her tongue working in tandem. Zuri's gray eyes flicked up to mine, and my orgasm burst through me. I screamed, dragging my hips against her face until the tingling sensation spread throughout every part of my body. My head spun in the best way, my eyes rolling back into my head as I let it overtake me.

Zuri plopped down beside me, her lips pressing into mine as our tastes mingled. I placed my hand on her cheek and kissed her back slowly. We stayed there, our lips grazing each other as I disbanded the air shield. Not even the war tent—a reminder of what we'd have to do tomorrow—could bring me down from this high.

Chapter Forty-Five

Kaizer

I watched as Joseph performed the death ritual for Athena. We had to use a different body since hers was not in Sanjry, and from the sound of it, her body wasn't *really* anywhere. Abel had found someone that matched her description. How, or where, he didn't tell me, but with the mask covering the cadaver's face, nobody could tell it wasn't Athena.

Joseph was normally a wall of stone, performing his duties around the dead without issue. But today's ceremony was getting to him. His eyes were rimmed in red, his words sputtering every so often.

After I took Athena out of the dungeons, and after Daya left, Athena had gone to the temple to repent and become anew. She was seen with me around Sanjry, and we had to ensure the people didn't see me as weak or going back on my word.

She had a way with the people—the leaders, not the civilians—and many of them were here grieving her loss. The stand-in body went up in flames atop the altar, sending it into ashes as the acolytes hummed and sang. I knew those auburn locks didn't belong to Athena, but watching as they burned and turned black, curling and crisping before becoming a crown of ash around an ashen skull. . . it made my stomach turn. I bowed my head, pretending to be in prayer rather than watching the rest of the ceremony.

When I felt the room clearing, I lifted my head and opened my eyes. Only Joseph and a few of his acolytes were left in the room, so I joined him at the altar. The head priest's hand shook as he scooped the ashes left into an urn, one of the women in robes coming and taking it from him.

"Joseph, I've never seen you bothered by this," I said.

"Or you, sir," he responded quickly.

Yes, but I knew why I was reacting in such a way. The woman finished up, and the others cleaned off the stone slab until nothing remained.

"Did you know her. . . the way I did?" I finally asked.

Joseph's face crumpled into a grimace. "No, you know that is not permitted."

"Doesn't mean it doesn't happen. . . from time to time," I responded as his eyes went back to the altar. "Just seems like you knew her well."

"We had crossed paths here at the church over the years." He stepped down and brushed his robes.

"Okay," I said, but there was still something off. "Did you need to push our meeting?"

"No, I am fine."

We walked back to the red room in silence, a few sniffles from Joseph, but by the time we got there, he was back to his stone demeanor. I closed the door behind us, locking both of the locks. The lock that only I had the key to, not Otto or Abel or any of my other high-ranking staff. The bell rang in the temple, and Joseph moved into the corner of the room to do his afternoon prayers.

My advisers weren't typically invited to these meetings with Joseph, and if they were, it wasn't unless we had already met in private prior. For many reasons, one of them being that the journal was something they knew of, but they had not witnessed the magic of it. The other was because sometimes I did want to repent my own sins. I didn't completely buy into a lot of it, but there were times when getting things off my chest was beneficial.

Joseph had been there when I slew my cousin and his wife—had been part of the planning for it. It was worth it, and I didn't regret it, but that fell heavy on my soul in the aftermath. That was something I talked through with Joseph, and he advised that sometimes violent acts were needed to please the Flame, as long as we didn't take any joy in them. The part where I could make decisions and then obtain forgiveness later was also beneficial.

Being chaste and sober was not a part I felt was necessary. But it was also why I was a king and not a priest. My own father was religious, but in many of the ways that I found solace in it. He was a man quick to anger and quick to violence, even though he didn't show that side to many people. But my brother and I saw it. However, Declan was always the softer of us. I saw my father and wanted to be him, but my brother wanted to be anybody but him. In the end, I was the one who survived.

Maybe had he taken more lessons from our father, he wouldn't have died early. However, I was glad that he wasn't there when I came and destroyed my family and town. The only death that really impacted me from that day was my mother's. She was a stupid woman, sticking by such a violent man in the name of love and duty. But she was my mother. She was kind, even if she never stood up for Declan and me. A death with my father was the best thing I could have given her. To kill just my father and leave her as a widow would have pained her more.

I couldn't have any rivals to my spot on the throne. The Flame demanded it. For me to maintain my stronghold, everyone else had to go. I was the only remaining Curran, and if I was not successful, I would be the end of my family's name. There were other noble families in line, but none from my bloodline. It was also why this was important. I had this—I had Daya and Malva—or I had nothing.

Joseph finished his prayers, silently moving to the seat across from me and pouring himself water. It usually took him a few moments to come out of the intensity of his prayers, and I let him finish the entire glass before starting.

I cleared my throat. "Has the Flame spoken to you at all?"

There were times when Joseph said that the Flame spoke with him directly and not through the journal. I was a bit wary of those proclamations since I wasn't sure how it all worked, but we'd gotten this far with the amount of trust that was between us.

"He has been unnervingly silent, Your Majesty."

"Did we misinterpret something he said? Do you think he is upset with us?"

There had to be a reason. After this many years of assistance, and that stopping now, something felt off.

Joseph folded his hands in his lap. "I do not believe so. I think we are still on the path that was set out for us."

"I know that war was very likely, but it is definite now. If Dusra was not already on the verge of attacking, this may have tipped them over."

"War is a necessary evil to achieve things of this magnitude."

People and their regimes had to be broken and vanished before I could build my own. The fact that we've been split, worshipping different beings and interested in only our own cultures was part of the problem. If we were unified, under the Flame, and under me, all would set itself right again.

"Quinn believes that this is a mistake. She said with what she saw, it was unlikely that we would win," I said.

"Quinn should repent for speaking against the will of the Flame," Joseph spat.

"I'll let her know," I mumbled.

That was a sure way to get her back to believing. Tell her she's wrong and repent, and then everything would be okay. We didn't live in those times anymore. She'd seen too much.

"Are your loyalties wavering, My King?"

Sometimes, I'd forget to keep my mask up. I'd let it slip there without even realizing it. The uncertainty in the Flame, and Joseph was not one to miss something like this.

I slipped my mask back up. "They are not. I did ask him how we can get Dayanara from Dusra, and he said we would need to strike first."

"You should not doubt him. Has Dusra been spotted yet?"

"Not yet."

We figured they would be on their way, if they weren't already. The chances of them hiding behind their barrier were slim. Especially with Daya there.

"Well, we should send out battalions to find them if you believe them to be on their way. If he says we should strike first, we should strike first," Joseph suggested.

"I'll have to speak to Otto. The last I heard, the armies are ready for whatever direction we give them."

"Good. Is there anything we wish to ask today?"

I pulled out the journal from the locked drawer in my desk and set it between us. The old magic radiating from it was damn near suffocating. I'd been around enough artifacts and ancient items that it didn't affect me as much anymore. The satchel I kept it in was spelled so that nobody could feel it should someone get curious, as well as the drawers I kept it in.

"Our questions have been too broad. We need to be specific," I said, grabbing the pen from atop my desk.

"Something like a location?" Joseph offered.

"Precisely."

I wrote slowly, always making sure to have very clear handwriting should the Flame not be able to understand what I was asking.

Where will the first battle take place?

We both leaned in slightly, waiting for the ink to dissolve and reappear. If there was an answer, it typically happened in a few moments. But nothing happened. I flipped the page, realizing that we had more unanswered questions than answered ones, as nearly 75 percent of the journal was inked pages.

When will the first battle take place?

Again, we waited, watching as the ink dried, the silence between us significant enough that I could hear my own heartbeat in my ears. The ink disappeared this time, dissolving and reappearing on the next page.

ONE WEEK

"We know when. We just don't know where," I said.

"The Flame gives us what we need. He will not give us everything. We must use our own resources to determine the rest," Joseph said as he stood.

He bowed, not saying anything else as he left. Which was uncharacteristic; he typically stayed around and asked for something for the temple or asked me to repent. I was certain he got off on knowing everyone's dark secrets, but he left swiftly. That left time before Otto and Abel joined me, which I wasn't expecting.

I pulled out my shirt that Daya had worn that day when my people rioted. Or a piece of it. The rest of it was covered in blood that wasn't hers. Zuri had stripped her clothes and sent them to launder, but I intercepted them before they got there. It was one of the few pieces of her that I had. Because of her... sudden leave, many of her things were left behind. But she hadn't brought much, and her things were all kept clean and tidy. On this piece of fabric, I took a deep sniff of it, our scents mingled. Our individual intimate aromas, the uniqueness of them combined.

My cock ached as I remembered what I did to her to get this scent to stick to the fabric so fervently. I unbuttoned my pants, taking it into my hand and fisting it as her name left my lips on a groan.

"Daya."

Chapter Forty-Six

Dayanara

I sent Cat to get another healer, even though Ishani said she was fine. She even reminded me that she'd used the gift to take down a couple hundred soldiers, and a little blood from my body wasn't anything compared to that. She was right, but we still were worried. The healer crossed over to her tent, where I heard Ishani yell my name, but I grabbed Cat by the wrist and dragged her away from the wrath of Axel's twin.

"I'm going back to the Inbetween," I said after putting up an air shield.

"For what?" she asked, a crease forming between her brows.

I filled her in on what happened in the Inbetween and what we'd come to find the true evil was. Cat was always very calculated. She didn't grow shocked or worried, but I could see that she was trying to think through the next steps for our people.

"I've been working pretty closely with Akari and Ishani. I'll make sure everything is handled here with the brujas," she said before shaking her head. "But I don't like this."

I looked out into the forest, into my home, the place I was supposed to protect. The trees shifted in the wind coming off the Piedra, the branches bending and leaves whistling as they rattled. "I don't like it either. Keep an eye on Ishani. There's typically a lot more of her people around."

"Of course. What do you hope to do?"

"If *he* is the source of whatever is trying to get to Kaizer, maybe we end it all by getting to him first. If it's too dangerous, we'll return, hopefully before the first battle, but I think it's worth a shot."

Cat nodded as she patted her pockets. "You have any amethyst?"

"Yeah," I responded, twisting the bead on my bracelet.

"I don't think we'll be able to contact you there." Cat grabbed the bracelet as her magic wrapped around the stone. "If this glows, battle is close. If it turns to ash, the battle is already here. I just hope it works there."

"Good idea. I was actually going to try to re-up on crystals before I left. Can you have someone drop me off a little of everything?"

"Of course. I'll make sure anything else is handled. Be safe," she said with a smile.

I put my hand on her shoulder, squeezing and returning the smile before I had another thought. "Thanks, I will. Also, can you see if we can find any seers?"

"There's one. . . but your mother practically eradicated the strong ones," she responded.

"I know, but we need all the help we can get."

Cat nodded and turned. I knew my people were in good hands with her. They were in good hands with Ishani, too, but Cat knew exactly how we operated. There was a chance the battle could start before we got back, as we couldn't portal from within the Inbetween, but I really hoped it didn't. I didn't know how to prepare for him either, and I wished I could use some sort of crystal to block Chuah from my mind. The rune would help protect my body, but with his magnitude of strength, I wasn't sure how much. As far as I knew, nothing like that existed, but I knew who to ask.

Making my way into the woods, I made sure nobody was nearby. The state I had to reach in order to contact my past Acnas required me to be completely at peace. As I'd only done it once, I wasn't sure what threats to my body would do while I was there. Finding a space I thought was safe, I nestled myself between two wide trees and sat.

I closed my eyes, trying to will myself into the state, but nothing happened. Frustration bubbled up in me, and I fought hard to push it back down. That was probably part of the problem. *Deep breaths in, deep breaths out.* Words my mother had once spoken to me: *Ground yourself with the beat of your heart.*

Focusing on my chest rising and falling, I felt myself drifting into the state in which the Acnas lived. I tried to memorize the path my consciousness took. It seemed like it was turning in on me, diving deep into the center of my being. The thump of my heart was the only thing that transitioned from the world I left behind, and I stood in a room of clouds just as before.

"Zerlina, I summon you," I said, waiting for Valentina's daughter. Zerlina was the one who filled in Valentina's death, so she might have had more information about what exactly happened. A bruja with brown skin and ringlets of pink hair crowning her head in a halo stepped forward.

"My mother mentioned you might be summoning me," she said, a demeanor to her I couldn't quite determine.

"Yes, I spoke to her a few days ago," I responded, trying to smile warmly, but I wasn't particularly well-practiced.

The side of her mouth ticked up in a small smirk. "This is the most action our side has seen in quite some time. Your mother wasn't too fond of us."

"I'm sure she knew you wouldn't approve of what she's become." I paused, thinking over something Mariana said. "Is she there with you now?"

"She's created her own space within our realm, not coming too close to any of us. What you did to her, it was impressive." She tilted her head in appreciation.

Good. She didn't deserve to be around the rest of them, and I certainly didn't want to share any sort of eternal space with her whenever my time came.

"I wasn't sure if that was real. I'm still getting used to all of this."

"What is it you summoned me for?" Zerlina asked.

"I'm trying to remember my bruja history, but you were the last of our line before Naom blessed us, yes?"

I'd never been tested so much about our history. I was glad that education was important in Caldera. It didn't seem pertinent at the time, but it may eventually be our saving grace.

"I was."

"Were you there when they imprisoned Chuah?"

"I was."

Witch of many words, I see.

"Is there anything that can block his influence?"

Her eyes narrowed slightly. "You are going after him?"

"That's the plan, yeah."

"That is not wise."

Boy, did I know it. Unfortunately, all options left were unwise.

"Wise or not, it could help avoid war," I stated.

"That is true. There is nothing I know of that could block him. The Creators were only able to imprison him because he got cocky. If you are inside the Inbetween, you have no access to your magic. You could try some old brujeria, crystals, or potions. The ones that don't need magic."

There used to be a saying, centuries and centuries ago, that we should never rely on our magic alone. But this was the first time there was ever a threat to that, and we'd grown very comfortable in our use of it from day to day.

"That's what I was thinking, too."

"I know what it takes for you to ask for help. I commend you for your effort with us," she said before disappearing into the clouds.

When I opened my eyes, Axel's form stood before me, facing away. I rolled my neck and shifted where I sat, the sounds of the leaves having him turn around.

"Acna communication?" he asked, offering me a hand to help me from the ground.

I placed my hand in his. "Yeah, I always feel like I'm going to get more from them than I do, but being able to ask for advice and know it has been tested is nice."

"You ready?"

"As ready as I'll be," I responded. "How mad is Ishani?"

"She'll get over it," he said. "But maybe we just see her when we get back."

There was a hint of teasing in his tone, but also a bit of seriousness that had me thinking maybe it was a good idea. Taking a longer route around Ishani's tent, Zuri and Paxx were out on the border packing our supplies for the trip to the horses. Grabbing my sword from the pile, I brushed Zuri's side and made sure to strap all my weapons to my body.

"Only two horses?" I asked.

"We'll move quicker, and there's a chance we'll have to leave them somewhere. These are two that don't have owners... anymore. Not to mention, we could have to leave them behind somewhere," Paxx answered.

"Well, that's sort of sad," Zuri said as she brushed the mane of the darker horse.

"Reality is sad," I responded.

Zuri leveled me with a look, but I shrugged and hopped on one of the horses. Axel was faster, jumping on behind me and forcing Zuri to ride with Paxx. He helped her onto the horse, out of politeness, because she could probably jump higher than all of us without magic. I blew her a kiss, and she smiled as we pushed away from the camp and back toward the fucking Inbetween.

I glanced back, wanting to remember the trees in the forest of my home, the smells of the earth and the plants. Stepping into Sanjry was jarring, but I knew the step into the Inbetween would be worse. I took a deep breath, preparing for my magic to retreat from my body, and it still hit me like a brick wall. My body jolted, an instant emptiness, and Ax put his hand on my leg, even though he went tight as he crossed in too. Zuri and Paxx's faces twisted in pain, but we all adjusted after a few minutes.

"Keep an eye out for those beasts," I said. "If you see anything with black eyes, tell me."

Chapter Forty-Seven

Dayanara

I'd forgotten how oddly normal some parts of the Inbetween were. There was no magic, no laws, but some of the zones were more similar to Malva than the rest. This one, with a pub in it, was probably one of the most normal. The building looked like it had been here for centuries, with strong stone at the center of it and additions in wood sprouting from the sides. There was no known number of people who called the Inbetween home, but judging from the building, it had grown. I'd been to this pub before and had barely gotten away. I wouldn't make the mistake of underestimating any of the patrons again.

"Remember to avoid engaging with anyone. Just listen for if there are any ideas of where we should go," I said as I tied the horses to a wooden beam.

The Triori had told us that he was within the Piedra, or under it, but gave no other information. We didn't have a lot of time, and from what I remembered, this is where the leaders of the Inbetween came to do deals. The parts we'd passed through with the army were selected because of their lack of population, but this time, we needed it. We pushed into the pub with Zuri beside me and Axel and Paxx at our backs.

It was loud—louder than anywhere we'd been since we left Dusra. Clinking of cups, heavy boots against creaking wooden floorboards, and too many voices speaking over each other, it was hard to decipher anything. I pulled the hood of my cloak low on my forehead, avoiding eye contact as we found a table in the back of the space. Paxx's gaze bounced from table to table, and Axel and I were scanning for other exits.

"If my magic wasn't so far out of my reach, I might have forgotten where we are," Zuri said.

Someone burst from one of the additions we'd seen, a crazed look in his eye, his skin moist and pale. His arms wrapped around his body as his nails dug into his arms, blood dripping down his elbow and onto the floor. He mumbled words I tried to focus on, but everyone within the pub didn't acknowledge his odd behavior.

"Gotta go back, gotta go back," he said over and over before his gaze stopped on the door. He bolted, not bothering to dodge any of the bodies and opting to run right through them. The door to the addition swung open again, a larger man surveying the room and running toward the one losing his mind. He dragged him back to the space he'd made a run from, legs kicking and arms reaching out to break the hold the larger man had on him.

A raspy female voice said from behind us, "Not everyone is made for the Inbetween. Magic withdrawals. I remember how bad they were. I'm sure you all do, too." She stepped around the table and into our sight. "Can I get you anything to drink?"

Wasn't expecting table service.

"Four of whatever the house ale is would be great," Zuri said, the warmest of the bunch of us.

Everyone else at the table's body relaxed after she left, and we went back to looking around the room in silence.

"My guess is that the woman in red at the front and the man in furs to the left are some sort of leaders here," Paxx broke the silence.

I'd clocked the same two. The woman—a bruja—at the front was covered in shades of red. A wine-colored dress hugged her shapely form, and her blood-red gloves wrapped around a cup much fancier than the rest of the pub's patrons. Her table was lined with armored men, a young woman sitting directly across from her. She looked to be pleading with the woman in red, her fingers lifting to her eyes and coming back down, damp with tears. The bruja in red listened, not making any kind of response other than offering her some very intense eye contact. She peered at one of the men next to her and nodded once. Her soldier stood and lifted the young woman by her arm. She followed, offering thanks to the witch, and she looked away as her soldier left into a hall.

Her gaze landed on me immediately, as if I'd called her name from across the loud room. She didn't blink, only watched me with intrigue in her gaze until the next person sat down in front of her.

The other man, a vampire significantly bigger than most, sat at a table across from the bar. He had fewer men with him, a couple who appeared less serious than the woman in red. All of them were covered in the same thick furs, wind burns on their faces.

"They must live by the Piedra," Ax whispered.

Our waitress went over to his table, and he pulled a smile far more charming than he looked capable. Even if his thick auburn beard had foam from his beer. He watched as she walked away, and it was then I noticed the scars of bite marks on her neck. It was possible more than beer was on the menu here. Without the factor of consuming blood for magic, I wasn't sure what it would be for. Probably one of the few things they were able to do and feel like they weren't trapped in this land. She went down the same hall that the woman in red sent her soldier, and I turned back toward my table.

"I think the witch owns the pub," I said, turning my head so that no one could see my mouth. If she was truly a witch, she might hear our conversation. It was extremely loud here. It was unlikely, but not impossible.

"The waitresses seem to be in her employ. They're all regarding her with a mixture of fear and awe," Zuri noted.

"I'll deal with her." I moved to stand.

"One of us should go with you," Axel responded as he stood.

"You've got bruja blood, but not enough. She's more likely to be open with me. I won't be far if something happens. Wait at the bar," I said.

He looked like he was about to fight me on it, but I raised an eyebrow, and he gave in. We weaved between the patrons, and a memory played in my mind.

"This feels familiar." I smiled.

"My intuition says some of those events may repeat." He chuckled.

"You said you were looking for a woman with a penchant for violence. You got one," I said with a wink. "But I'll be on my best behavior."

I watched the soldiers at the table conversing with one of the bartenders, who had blonde hair that was nearly white at the end. She seemed to be the one who was sending people to the bruja in red. After ordering another beer for both Axel and me, I continued watching to ensure I was correct. Someone else came up to the bartender, handed her a piece of parchment, and sat as she read it. The blonde woman nodded, motioning for her to go over to the table.

"You stay here," I told Axel.

He stayed but turned his body enough to see what I was doing while still appearing inconspicuous. Continuing to survey the table and my surroundings, I made my way down to the end of the bar. Before I could open my mouth, the bartender smiled and said, "La Madama would like to talk to you as well."

"La Madama?" I asked, finding the witch in red's gaze on me.

"Mhm, you're next," the bartender said.

It was odd trying to determine someone's power level in this land. Their essence was blocked, but that didn't mean they didn't still have the physical strength that came with it. La Madama was most likely strong, or she'd been here for long enough that she had enough of a standing with these people. Looking closer, I could see how people revered her in a similar way they did my mother.

"She'll see you now," the blonde woman said.

The weight of my blade at my thigh comforted me as I felt all the eyes of her soldiers turn in my direction. I touched the tips of my nails as I sat across from La Madama and peered up at her from under my hood. She was beautiful, as all my kind were, her hair a shade of black so deep it seemed to absorb any light around us. Her eyes were even darker, black pits that had seen more time than her lack of wrinkles would imply. A tattoo crept across her neck and up her jawline, vines so similar to the ones on my arms that I was nearly taken aback. Her lips stretched into a smile—a knowing smile.

"Acna, didn't think we'd see you here for some time," she said. "I'm Lucia, but they call me La Madama here."

Lucia, why is that not familiar? A witch of this age, of this power, had to be someone that I'd known. Or at least my mother was aware of. She watched me as I thought this over and picked up her wine to take a sip. The overhead flame above us reflected off her golden chalice as she set it down between us.

"Would you like a drink?"

"I've had a couple already," I responded, gathering myself.

"I saw," she replied.

I decided I'd be as bold as she was. "What is a bruja of your magnitude doing in the Inbetween?"

She sat back and shrugged one shoulder. "I'm not good at doing what I'm told. Something I'm sure you understand. Who is it that's here with you? Your Sanjryan lover or one of the Dusran lovers?"

My hand slid to my dagger, the coolness of the hilt digging into my palm.

"That won't be necessary. If I wanted to hurt any of you, I already would have done it. Are you here to gather more for your army that passed through?"

She couldn't be a seer. Her gifts wouldn't work here. Just a very well-connected witch.

"No, I'm here to slay the maker of this land," I said.

Lucia tipped her head back and laughed, the others at the table joining in with her. When she noticed that my face was still as hard as a rock, she tilted up a brow. "You can't be serious?"

"As serious as your love for the color red."

Her tongue ran along her teeth, and she looked across the room at the bartender. She nodded once, disappearing into the hall.

"You can bring your friends. No need to have them watching you from across the room," La Madama said as she stood, holding her arm out to point toward the corridor.

With a tilt of my head, all three of them came to my side, and we followed the woman. Many sounds came from the rooms; without air shields, it was hard to hide much. Sounds of pleasure, sounds of pain, anguish. It was overwhelming the journey of emotions we walked through. We made it to a set of steps with a single door at the base, and La Madama's men stayed at the top of the stairs. We descended, the temperature dropping and the smell of earth replacing the carnal scents we'd passed through.

"Please, have a seat," La Madama said as she situated herself behind a desk.

"I meant what I said out there," I replied.

"I know, which is why we are here and not in the room full of eager ears. You know not of what you speak."

"I do. I read my family's grimoire. I think I may be the only one who knows," I said.

"And your friends? They know everything you do?" she asked.

"They do."

La Madama reached into a drawer and pulled out a pipe, lighting it with a match and blowing a cloud of smoke that enveloped her head. She sat forward, pushing through the smoke. "If you truly know everything, you know that what you're trying to do is impossible."

"Making the impossible possible is sort of my thing," I replied.

That didn't seem to give her an ounce of reassurance.

"It took four goddesses, and you are one bruja."

"She's more than that," Axel asserted.

La Madama ran her gaze over him in a way that made me want to rip out her throat, but she brought it back to me. "It is pointless. Not to mention the Inbetween thrives because of him."

"We just need to know where to go," Paxx said.

"And what do you have to offer for that information, pretty one?" she winked.

They stared at each other for a moment before she sighed and pursed her lips. "It's not information I'm privy to. Many have gone searching for him but have not been successful. The people here don't know who he is. Just that there is a powerful being somewhere in our land."

I surveyed the items on the desk between me and her, a black leather-bound book with the words *Death Log* scribbled across the cover. The book had additional loose papers stuffed into it, like there weren't enough pages.

"You sure you're thriving here?" I asked, my lips pointing toward the book.

"*I am.* It's why I'm here in the first place. People come to me for resources and protection."

"I thought the whole selling point of this place is that nobody is in charge," Zuri said.

"Nobody is in charge, per se. But some find their lives easier with my help. There are zones beyond this one that are free for all, monstrous animalistic behaviors within their bounds. We're a little more. . . organized here. That's all."

"We saw an Inbetween monster in our land. I imagine their numbers are picking up here for that to happen?" Paxx inquired.

The first sign of shock from La Madama. Her eyes widened ever so slightly, air passing between her lips. She grabbed the book and shoved it inside of a drawer.

"What you're asking is impossible. But. . . there has been an instability here as of late. The very ground feels ready to split open again, and the beasts have multiplied. Thousands of them now roam, and they are no longer as easy to kill. It's like their life force—whatever it is—has been amplified."

I sat forward. "Chaos is coming, and you all will be the first to join his army of the unwilling."

Smoke billowed from her mouth. "Give me a couple of minutes."

Chapter Forty-Eight

Dayanara

The man in the furs was Bastian, and as he stared me down, I realized he was used to fear. He awaited a sign of it from me, but I gave him nothing. La Madama brought him to her office, and he sat beside her. The wood had creaked as he sat, a hulking form next to her. His red beard was free of beer foam now, and that wind burn on his sandy brown skin was even more evident up close. We'd told him what we wanted, and he hadn't said a word since.

"My ancestors spoke of humans getting through the wall many centuries ago. They logged the way the humans said they came—allegedly. They spoke of a darkness within the heart of the mountain. That is where we think he is," he finally said.

"Okay, well, give us that," I said.

He laughed, a sound that traveled from his belly and boomed around us. "You are funny, little witch. The bunch of you could not traverse the Piedra, no matter how invincible you may think yourself."

"We can take those chances," Axel replied.

"You say your armies are on the move now? This journey would take a month for experienced mountain men. For inexperienced, double it, maybe even triple."

The statement hit us all like an arrow to the chest, knowing that this journey had been pointless. There was no saving our armies, no taking out the head of the serpent. We would have to fight, and people would have to die. As if the universe wanted to take one more blow, the bead on my bracelet from Cat glowed, an indication that battle was close. I'd told my companions what it meant before we left, and their shoulders dropped even more.

"Look," La Madama said as she watched the defeat written on our faces. "The land here is giving omens, ones that indicate something bigger than all of us is coming. Should you defeat your enemies in Sanjry, we will still be here."

"You will guide us to him?" I asked Bastian.

He peered at La Madama, unspoken words bouncing between their gazes. "I will."

And with two small words, a sliver of hope.

La Madama was right. There was an instability in the land of the Inbetween I didn't quite notice at first. A certain level of energy that felt on the brink of snapping, or exploding, really. It set me on edge, but the others didn't seem to sense it. Paxx tended to a fire in a spot we picked not too far from the pub, somewhere hopefully fairly safe for the evening. We could make it out of the Inbetween tomorrow morning. Then we'd have to find where the armies were.

I wasn't completely sure how far off the battle was. The glowing of the stone meant that it was close. Could be days, a week, or it could be hours. Zuri and Axel were setting up the tent, bickering about the correct way to do it. I'd take this sort of petty argument over how much worse it could be.

"I'm going to grab more wood," I said, but neither of them acknowledged me. Paxx didn't seem to hear me either as he took long strides toward where they were, snatching the tent from them and saying something under his breath. The tree line wasn't too far off, and before I knew it, the glow of the fire was just a soft ember over my shoulder.

My internal clock told me it was nighttime, but the forest was still awake. The normal nocturnal creatures that made the trees their home always seemed to be prowling the earth. Seeing normal birds, squirrels, and deer void of the odd skin and eyes was comforting. I bent down to grab a branch, but it was wrapped in black vines sprouting from the trunk of the tree. Pulling a bit, I decided to grab another branch as it was stuck.

With an armful of more wood, I pivoted back toward the camp. Eyes like the night sky met me, my feet sinking into the ground that was once firm. The branches went flying from my hands as my arms flailed for anything to grab, and the world turned upside down. Darkness invaded every crevice of my vision, and I extended my nails to their longest length. I swiped at anything and everything around me. There was a resistance to each slash. Small lights sparked above my head, illuminating enough for me to see which way was up.

Every kick of my legs burned, the ability to see cluing me in on exactly where I was. The surface of the thick liquid didn't break as my face pushed into it. More effort and another clawing from my nails punctured it, and I stuck my arm through. My shoulder and then my face came next, a gasp of painful air as I used the leverage to pull myself out and stand atop the sea of black.

That goddess-damned chuckle vibrated through the substance all around me, and I reached for my dagger at my thigh to find it missing. No longer wearing leathers, a black silk fabric was draped across me in a similar fashion to the garments of the Triori. A form started to take shape in front of me, not like the last time when he mimicked the silhouette of others.

It started at the crown of his head, standing several feet above me, even taller than Axel. Straight, long hair formed, flowing in a non-existent breeze as eyes dark, round, and dead glistened. The rest of him took shape quicker, a straight nose, full lips, broad shoulders and long legs. In the blink of an eye, the black substance dissolved, and he stepped through, so corporeal that a burst of fear ran up my spine.

Skin that looked as if it had been trapped beneath a mountain for centuries wrapped around taught biceps and forearms. The same silk fabric draped over his body as mine. Although the inky blackness his body was formed with was gone, that same black swished behind his pupils. A pang of pain sprouted from my shoulder, and I rubbed it with the base of my hand, realizing it was where his mark remained on my body.

"Mmm, Dayanara. You're back. Are you here to be my queen?"

I sneered, my fangs exposed and my nose curled. "I already own that title, so no thanks."

"I must have misread. But you got my gift?"

"Is that what you call poisoning me?" I snapped.

"Poison is such a strong word, Dayanara," he purred. "I had to test if some of my. . . abilities still work. Plus, I wanted you to keep a little piece of me inside you. Stay connected."

"Hard pass."

Where I once was curious, thanks to his influence, I had no interest in being a part of the destruction of our world.

He took a step toward me. "This is your last chance to join me, for the end as you know it is coming."

This might have been my chance to understand how to fight him.

"Is Kaizer the start of that?" I asked.

"He is but a pawn. Kaizer has no clue about the other players on the board. I gave him the location of some old ashes from the Forest of Incen, and he believed me to be his deity. A mind easily molded, easily convinced. Not like yours." He flashed a smile far too beautiful to be coming from such a man. "And I revel in a challenge."

"I'm not a challenge to be won," I said.

"Maybe not. But you will either join me, or you will bow with the rest of them. Rest assured, I will get what I want. For every realm before this has crumbled beneath my boot, but none of them had a being as pretty as you."

I gave no fucks about the flattery. "How are you doing this right now from your prison?"

He took a deep breath, as if smelling flowers in the air. "The bounds placed on me are weakening. My reach is intensifying. I'll be with you soon enough."

I jutted my hand out, expecting it to pass through his body like it had in that realm I was in. This time, he caught it with a force so hard my bones shook, pulling me closer to him and bringing his lips to my ear. "What do you say?"

"Why me?" I asked, morbid curiosity getting the best of me.

"I told you before, Chaos is in your blood—in your bones. A witch with the power of a goddess and the darkness of a god, you're the perfect person to join me. I thought Kaizer would bring you to me, but you found me all on your own. Be my queen."

There were plenty of creatures on this side of the wall with darkness, with violence, but I supposed I took the cake.

"Over my dead fucking body." I tried to pull from his grasp, but he held strong.

"Very well." An otherworldly darkness fell over him, the muscles in his face tightening into a snarl. "Think about this moment when you're crumpling beneath my army. You better get back to your friend." He sniffed the air. "Oh, you may be too late."

His eyes fell on the symbol on my hand, now burning and smoking. He quickly released me, and the moment I was free of his grasp, the sea of black swallowed me. My body thrashed as the world turned once again. I gasped a breath just as my feet landed back on the hard surface of the forest with the branches still in hand. The scorpion on my shoulder itched so badly it burned, and I scratched it wildly as I ran back to the camp.

"We need to move. We can't stay the night here," I said.

Zuri whirled around. "What happened?"

"He got a hold of me again." I swallowed. "But this time was more intense than before. Someone is in danger."

"Who?" Axel said.

"I don't know," I said as I racked my brain. I only had but so many fucking friends. *Fuck.*

"How did he get to you?" Zuri packed our things back into a satchel.

"He said the bounds on his prison are waning. He pulled me into the ground, but it was like he pulled me through the earth to where he is. He touched me."

Axel snarled, and Paxx quickly took down the tent they'd worked hard to build. The fire was doused, and I felt eyes on me from somewhere. I twisted, trying to find the source, and my gaze fell on a shadowy figure in between the trees. Everything blurred except the hard lines of the dark eyes.

"What are you looking at?" Zuri asked.

"You don't see that?"

She shook her head and wrapped her fingers around my arm. "No, let's get out of here."

Our horses kicked up dark, dry earth as we made for the border into Sanjry. No creatures of this land attacked. They only watched from afar as we bolted past them—some glowing eyes, some dark. We didn't stop for a break or water, and the moment we pushed through the border, my magic hit me, and the amethyst stone on my bracelet crumpled to ash.

The hours of pushing without stopping wore on us, and we paused right at the edge of the Calderan forest. My stone was gone, and that meant that war wasn't only close, it was here. Paxx pulled out his spy stones, and Axel rested on a log as he tried to connect with Ishani. I could still feel Chuah's grasp on my arm, like his touch was welded into my bones, not only in the tattoo with his poison.

"They're at the river between kingdoms," Axel said as he rubbed his eyes with the back of his hand. "She said they have eyes on the Sanjryan army, but no moves have been made on either side yet."

"They say why?" Paxx asked.

"He wants to talk to you," he responded with his gaze on me.

"Fucking men," I ground out. "No offense to the two of you."

Zuri muffled a chuckle with her fist, and the men I wasn't *trying* to offend shook their heads. But what the fuck was going on with their species as of late? I wish I knew. Since we stopped, I had been expelling magic to get the pressure of it beneath my skin to wane. The portal jump would be a big one, so I did need blood. Instead of going through the drama of the last time, I chose the body closest to me. Zuri gasped as my fangs dug into her neck from behind, and she reached up to hold my head as I pulled. The taste of her blood washed over my tongue, and I moaned as she pushed her ass into me. Axel and Paxx both watched, and when I flicked my gaze up to them, Paxx averted his eyes, but Axel kept his stare locked in mine.

"I'm going to do. . . something," Paxx said as he shuffled away.

I shrugged a shoulder because it didn't bother me either way. But the way Axel's nose twitched told me that the scent of both of our arousals was wafting through the air. Paxx could probably see it like a big horny cloud around us too. Zuri's blood tingled through my body, and I knew I should have stopped. We all needed to fill our reserves, but the pleasure I was feeling through her had me going a little longer.

I licked the wound, and she ran her fingers over it to heal it, but left the scar this time. Axel looked just the tiniest bit jealous, but if he wanted one, I'd give him one too. Later.

"How did Ish sound?" Zuri asked Axel.

"Confident, but I'm sure she'll feel better when we're all there."

"All done turning the forest into an orgy?" Paxx said as he came back.

"Please, you haven't seen anything yet." I winked, and he mumbled something under his breath.

I rubbed my hands together, picturing the river, and snapped open the portal. "Shall we?"

I made sure that we were a bit of a distance from the river, just in case I opened a portal in the middle of the camp. Bending down, I stuck my fingers in the soil of my land, this very field somewhere I'd been often. I focused as I tried to feel for the connection I always sensed, peace running through my veins.

"There they are," Paxx said as he pointed toward the river.

In the distance, we could see the Dusran army, along with the parts of the Calderan soldiers that had joined our side. It was vast, taking up more space than I had imagined. People bustled around the camp, the sound of clinking from training coming from one side and tents taking up the other. Across the river, barely visible, was the Sanjryan army. I didn't see Kaizer right away, but I swore I could feel his gaze on me the moment I turned around.

Trekking across the tall grass and through the flowers, I remembered why we were here. To get my kingdom back. And damn if I let anything stop me from that.

Ishani's tent was at the center like before, but she wasn't inside when we stopped. Axel said he sensed her near the training, so we moved in that direction. Everyone looked to be in high spirits thus far, soldiers moving about and tilting their heads to us, some nodding. The true effects of war hadn't hit yet. There were no wailing soldiers too injured to be healed, no piles of corpses to be burned, and I hated that we didn't find a way to prevent it all.

We found Axel's twin watching the soldiers train, and they all moved as one, completely in sync and ready to fight.

I opened my mouth to tell her we failed, but Ishani beat me to it. "Axel already told me. We knew it wasn't guaranteed. Still, good information to be used after."

We could get Caldera back from Kaizer, but that didn't mean whatever influence Chuah was wielding wouldn't take it right back.

"You're right," I responded. "Everything looks good here."

Ishani nodded. "Going great, no real problems. A couple of squabbles, nothing we couldn't handle."

"You're feeling okay?" Zuri asked as she ran her fingers through Ishani's thick hair.

"Right as rain. Recovery wasn't too bad this time," she responded.

I watched for any signs of deceit, but it seemed to be the truth.

"We have one of their messengers. I'll let them go back and advise that you're here," Ishani said, and Paxx followed her.

I paced back and forth, my hands flexing into fists and my magic sparking from me.

"Are you nervous?" Zuri asked.

"I'm fucking livid," I replied. "This is the part of the job I don't like. I should be able to stab him when we meet and end it all."

"You could, but Otto would just attack in turn," Axel said.

"And if I kill him too?"

"Save it for the battlefield," he said as he squeezed my side.

A Sanjryan horse rode away from the camp, a rolled up parchment attached to the rider's hip. I watched as he crossed the river and as he galloped toward the center of the camp.

"I've got more than enough for the battle."

Chapter Forty-Nine

Kaizer

She was here. Dayanara was close enough that I could smell her scent, see her purple hair waving in a sea of Calderan and Dusran soldiers. The messenger we sent rode back toward us, hopping off his horse before stopping and darting toward me.

"Here, Your Majesty," he said as he kneeled.

I snapped my fingers at Abel, and he sent back the Dusran messenger we kept. Sliding my fingers down the edge of the rolled parchment, I popped the wax seal and unraveled to see what was within.

"They agreed to meet," I said to Otto and Abel as we moved back into the council tent.

"They met all of our asks?" Otto questioned.

I rolled up the parchment and handed it over to him. "Neutral ground, minimal soldiers, this evening."

Quinn's jaw ticked, her shoulders tight. She still hadn't agreed with what we were doing since coming back from Dusra. Not in a way that made her insubordinate, but I could see that she was still unhappy.

"And if they don't surrender?" she asked.

"Then we will fight as planned. If I can get Dayanara to join me—join us—we will be double as strong before we take down the Piedra."

Joseph quietly entered, his footsteps always light and difficult to hear. He stopped suddenly, his eyes on the ground. Otto and Abel both looked at him with confusion, but I knew him well enough that this was how he acted when he believed he was receiving some sort of vision or message. My advisers were believers, but there was always a certain leniency offered to the elite members of society, and they took advantage of it. They nodded to Joseph with respect as he passed them by and stopped before me.

"Have you spoken to the Flame?" he asked.

"We are on the right path," I said, a lie—an omission.

I could not risk asking now. Not when Dayanara was close. Should I be punished for it later, then so be it. Joseph watched me cautiously but asked no more questions.

"Quinn, get the alpha unit together. Advise there should be no violence unless told otherwise."

Quinn turned and left quickly and without a word. Otto bounced with anticipation, that cruel smile on his face I'd seen more recently than before. Abel was just as ready, but there was another wave of caution coming from him. I wouldn't be asking what they thought now, either.

For I now had in my possession something that would change everything.

The neutral ground they chose was directly between our campsites, slightly on the Calderan border side. Although both Sanjry and Caldera were under my rule, I understood why Daya wanted to be on her soil. I'd allow it if it made her more likely to hear me out. Joseph, Otto, and Abel all trailed behind me as we crossed the bridge, finding a tent set up with Dusran soldiers at the entrance.

One of them yelled something in a language I did not recognize, and there was movement within the tent. They remained still, their eyes boring into us, a promise of violence in their dark gazes. The tent flap pulled back, Axel's figure taking up the space behind the soldiers. He ducked out, and I took stock of the weapons strapped to each of his limbs. He wore dark leathers—witch leathers, I realized—the fine garments he'd worn in Sanjry before now long gone.

"Kaizer," he said, formalities long gone as well.

"Axel. You've got a lot of weapons for a meeting we both agreed to."

He stepped forward into my space, and every Sanjryan soldier shifted toward me, but I held up my hand. The king of Dusra looked down at me, blocking out the lights from within the tent. His hand slipped to the dagger on his side, and my fist tightened at the reflex to do the same.

"We had an agreement before, and we see how that went," he spat.

"You stole my bride."

"Let me be perfectly clear." He leaned closer, so close I felt his breath on my face. "She is not yours. She will never be yours, and if I detect a hint of discomfort from her, I will kill you instantly." He retreated from my space. "And that would be a kindness because I can assure you a death by her hand would not be quick."

I made sure my shoulders were square and my chest extended. "She will choose me in the end."

Axel bared his teeth, but the aggression waned as his lips pulled further into a smile, a. . . laugh vibrating between us. "Let them in."

Dusrans. The air left my chest as my gaze fell on Daya, as beautiful as ever. Maybe even more beautiful. Definitely more beautiful. She had a color, a vibrancy about her now that had been missing in Sanjry. Her hair was twisted into braids, sparks of her magic jumping from her hands atop the table. Even with the ferocious tightness of her lips, the lowness of her brows, and the fury burning behind her pupils, I *needed* her.

Zuri, the fucking traitor, sat beside her. I'd only ever seen her as meek, even unnoticeable, but she had a presence now I couldn't quite decipher. Her gaze was not on me but on Otto. She leaned a little too much into my fiancée's space, Axel now taking up Daya's other side. The threat of his words was now back and evident in his features. Every single one of the Dusran council seemed to care for Daya, as the same look of disgust was on the faces of the others at the table.

"It is nice to lay eyes on you once again, my bride," I said with a smile.

"I'll pluck your eyes out of your fucking skull," she seethed.

My smile only widened, but it retreated quickly as both Axel and Zuri placed their hands on her arms in what looked like an attempt to calm her. Too much familiarity, too much closeness. I growled, my fist tightening as smoke billowed from my nostrils. This seemed to bring Daya joy as she smiled and relaxed.

"You are the one who requested this meeting," Axel said with his eyes on me. "Speak what you intended."

"You all should remember my advisers, Abel and Otto. I also have Joseph here, my head priest."

Daya sat forward. "How's your daughter?"

Joseph's eyes narrowed, a chill running through his body. "I have many sons and daughters of the Flame."

"You know which one I'm talking about, specifically," she said with a tilt of her head.

"Your Majesty, please proceed," Joseph said tightly.

I didn't know what that was about, but I was too eager for the next part of the conversation to ask any questions.

"Before I accepted your hand in marriage, under a magically binding agreement," I started, and Daya lifted her hand where the tattoo no longer remained. "I was on the search for something. An ancient relic."

"The scepter, yes," Axel inserted.

I needed to find out how they got that information. As far as I knew, I was the only one the Flame was conversing with. Regardless, I knew they were not aware of my next statement.

"I found it," I said.

All of them leaned forward, exactly what I thought they'd do.

"Bullshit," Daya said.

"It is in pieces, and I have found the biggest piece," I said, and both Otto and Abel nodded.

It took longer than I would have liked, but with the agreement holding back both us and them from attacking, it bought us time. Time for us to plunder places long abandoned across both Sanjry and Caldera. The Calderan soil had been left almost entirely untouched compared to my kingdom. Vast stretches of land where no mortals had dug up and created homes, and there, left alone and damn near one with the rock beneath the soil, was part of the scepter.

"Having a single piece without the others means nothing," Daya said.

I tipped up my chin. "How long do you think it will be before I have all of them?"

"Depends how long you live," Daya said as she crossed her arms. "You don't even realize you're merely a pawn."

I was not a pawn. I was a king. I had authority—I chose what to do.

"The Flame works in mysterious ways, but always to protect us," Joseph inserted.

"You think the Flame finds the people of *Sanjry* superior? That the world should be under *your* rule?" Ishani snapped.

"If he didn't, I would not be in this position. Many things had to go right for me to be here with the power that I have," I responded.

"Or severely wrong," Zuri seethed.

Her gaze burned through me before bouncing over to Otto. She wasn't supposed to get away, not before I could return her wholly to Daya as a gift. But she'd gotten away when she was still so injured, having just witnessed the worst of me. My own stare fell to her side, where I knew the worst of her wounds lay etched into her skin. With the smirk on Otto's lips, he didn't regret it one bit. I might have been too callous in my methods, but I thought Zuri would eventually lead me right to Daya. I could have apologized and explained, but now it was too late.

"You are not talking to the Flame," Daya growled. "You're talking to an ancient being you have no business trusting."

"People will try to sow doubt on our journey, Your Majesty. Do not let it grow within your mind or your heart," Joseph quipped.

I nodded but looked back at Daya. Daya was many things, but she was not a liar. Not when she was confident in her ability to fight.

"You are speaking to the god of Chaos, and he is *using* you," Daya said.

"The Flame is not real. The goddesses made our world, but this god came from somewhere else. He wants to pull all of Iteria into his grasp, starting with you," Axel quipped.

"These are *lies.*" Joseph stood. "How else would we have found the scepter? Put you on the throne? The Flame has guided us to this very spot. Do not backslide now."

"Joseph is right. I stand firm in what I've said," I spoke unwaveringly, even if there was still some doubt.

"The point of this meeting is to find a resolution to avoid the battle," Axel added.

Wrong.

"The point of this meeting was for me to confirm that you have my wife and that she was well. I will have all the pieces of the scepter soon, and this war will be pointless. Join me now, Dayanara, and I will not kill your. . . friends," I finished.

Axel and Zuri stood, their chairs flying behind them and crashing into each other. There was an empty seat beside Zuri now, and I felt a presence behind me that wasn't there before. Paxx, I believed his name was, loomed behind me, a blade pressed to the base of my throat.

"Say it again," his deep voice came from behind me.

Blood trickled down my neck, and without moving, I peered at Daya while keeping Paxx in my peripheral. She was still as a statue, only the constant rising and falling of her shoulders evidence that she was still breathing. She stood with quiet, calculated movements, her hands placed firmly on the table between us as she leaned forward.

Something shifted in her. "You thought you'd come in here, wave an ancient piece of crap around, and I'd magically become yours?"

An energy so intense it radiated in my gut, booming as her skin changed from her golden brown hue to. . . every hue. It ebbed and flowed like her body was merely a cage for every color in our world, and it could barely contain it. Her eyes glowed, and the air in the room felt as if it was removed with her magic. Massive wings spread from her shoulder blades, the length of them wrapping around the people on her side of the table.

My gut tightened, an uncontrollable reaction to the pure power she exuded. Otto had a hand on each of his swords on his hips, and Abel was going to be blown from his chair at any moment. I glanced over my shoulder with wide eyes at Quinn, and she only shook her head, her lips mouthing, 'I told you.'

Slowly turning my head back to Daya, I tried to calm myself. The fear I tried to push down grew and bent until it felt less like fear and more akin to. . . desperation. Daya's face pinched together, her fangs sharp and exposed.

"I don't care if you have the goddess of fire herself in your pocket. Hear me now and know I mean every word. You will die for what you did to my people, for what you did to me, and for what you did to Zuri. I don't care if it takes my last breath. You will never know peace. You will never wield the power you seek. Vengeance is coming, and I will be her vessel."

Chapter Fifty

Dayanara

There was something calming about the beat of the war drums, of the heavy footsteps running to and from parts of the camp. I knew Kaizer was delusional, but the *level* of delusion was not something I expected. I wasn't sure how he found such a significant part of the artifact, but I did know that being in such proximity gave us the opportunity to steal *both* the journal and the scepter.

"They could attack at any moment now," Ishani said.

All the Dusran inner circle and my trusted brujas, minus Paxx, were with us, surrounding a large map of Caldera and Sanjry. He surprised me with his outburst at the meeting. He said that he would protect Ax and Zuri's happiness, and he wasn't lying. He was out blowing off steam but said he'd join us shortly.

"Getting into his camp unnoticed wouldn't be easy," Zuri said.

"Damn near impossible," Axel agreed as he scratched his beard.

"We have to fight, we win, and we take everything," Cat asserted.

"Have we found any seers?" I asked Cat.

"We found one, but she is. . . unstable. We're trying to determine if she is trustworthy."

"Unstable?" Axel questioned.

"Um..." Cat paused. "She's just a little. . . kooky."

Wasn't entirely sure what kooky or unstable meant in this context, but a seer was a seer. There weren't many left, so I'd take what I can get.

"I'd like to meet with her," I said.

"I'll arrange it," Cat responded.

Paxx came through the tent entrance, much calmer than when we left him. He sat between Akari and Ishani, and she put her hand on his arm with a smile.

"We were trying to determine whether we could break into his camp to get the journal and scepter," Akari said.

"My spies say it's tight. Their witches are at the borders. Ours said there are definitely detection spells up. I don't see you getting in," Paxx responded, his eyes on me. "But once the battle starts, I think they will need all of their soldiers on the field. We outnumber them vastly. They won't be able to reserve any bodies."

"So we have a team move in once they are distracted," Ishani replied, nodding her head.

"I'll lead it," Paxx said. "Lend me whoever you think will be helpful."

"Cat, I think you'll be best there. Grab another soldier," I commanded.

Just looking at the map pissed me off. The fact that it was no longer separate, and no longer mine. I had to remember to use it, to let it fuel me, but not let me make any rash decisions.

Axel rubbed his chin as he stared down at the map. "This will not be a prolonged war. We have one shot at defeating them completely."

"And then we have a whole other issue with the god of Chaos," Zuri mumbled.

"One step at a time," I said as a blanket of determination fell over me.

Zuri's eyes glazed and her hands balled into fists. "And I want Otto."

Paxx flinched, and I didn't need the ability to see emotions in order to feel the rage and pain pouring from her. We were all intent on making sure Otto was delivered to Zuri, but it was Axel who placed his hand atop hers, snapping her out of the trance.

"He's yours," Axel reassured.

Zuri's lip wobbled, but the line of tears vanished as she held his gaze.

"Everyone is ready," Akari said tightly. "All the units know where they should be. Once the fighting starts, I think you guys should go through the north side of their camp. We've determined they're mostly setting up toward the south, so eyes won't be there."

Paxx looked down at the map between us. "I can do that."

"We have the upper hand in almost every avenue here, but let's not allow that to make us too confident. Keep your heads on a swivel. We took most of the suppressant, but if they have more, that could be a factor."

Axel was more conscious of that than the rest of us. Brujas knew it as my mother's choice of weapon, but a reminder that it could now be in their hands was evident. She said that she didn't give them the spell and that if they did, they couldn't perform it, but I wasn't counting anything out anymore.

"We aren't taking prisoners. I want nothing left of Kaizer or his supporters by the end of this," I said.

Everyone agreed, and the bell for dinner rang through the camp. Everyone shifted out of the tent, and I left with Axel and Zuri at either side of me. My brujas were fierce, and every single one I passed was ready to kill. It wasn't an oddity to have quarrels or fights between brujas, but the fact we'd be fighting our own on such a scale fell heavily on me. This wasn't our way. It was the coven above everything. Our people above everything.

The traitor witches thought whatever Kaizer promised them would come to fruition, but it wouldn't. There was no place for disloyalty as we moved forward into what Malva would be after this. I wouldn't rule with cruelty, but I wouldn't allow this sort of uprising again.

I thought I'd feel nerves from Zuri, but she moved with a power she didn't have before. The ability to take back what was stolen from her was right at her fingertips. Even if all of it couldn't be restored, I'd help deliver that to her just as Axel would. As if she could sense my protective thoughts, she looped her hand in my arm as we moved toward the cook tent. The main cook saw us and guided us to the table they'd set out for us.

Paxx appeared, taking the seat beside Axel. "I'm sorry for my outburst."

"No need to apologize. If it was up to me, I would have told you to slit his throat," I said as I grabbed the bowl from the cook and set it down before me.

I realized then he wasn't apologizing to me but to Axel. No matter who I was, Axel would always be his king, the one he held in high regard and the one he owed.

"I could see the pure degeneracy radiating from him. As well as the truth he spoke with, the desire to take Daya and kill you both. I was up before I realized what I'd done."

"You did what I would have in your position," Axel reassured.

"He was never going to agree to surrender. The direction in which the rest of the meeting went wasn't your fault," Zuri added.

Paxx looked like a weight was lifted from him. We ate in silence, all of our gazes bouncing around the soldiers surrounding us. Some hadn't stopped fighting for decades, and others had never seen a true battle. Knowing that many of them would die, I offered up a plea to Naom that this would not be their end, but it would be their beginning.

Kooky was a polite way of putting the state of the seer Cat had found. The witch was absolutely deranged. And not in the way I typically enjoyed. She didn't feel tethered to this world, not keeping her gaze on any one thing for more than a second or two. Her hair was a wild matted mess, her skin paler than brujas typically were. She didn't look familiar, and I wondered if she ever left her home before she was forced out of it by Kaizer.

"She was part of the last round-up in Caldera. She didn't want to come, but we told her nobody would be protecting her. Name's Yadira," Cat said as she watched the woman flit about, rubbing her bare toes over the blades of grass.

"You're sure she's a seer?" I asked.

She didn't seem to be. . . all there. Not enough to relay any visions.

"Pretty sure. She told us herself. We've seen her eyes glow, too. I didn't think she was reliable. I marked her file when we were doing our screenings, but she got. . . weirder. So she's been on a watch."

"Weirder?"

"A lot of what she says is incoherent, riddles, unnatural patterns of speech. But she's all we have. Anyone else who may be a seer is too scared to show themselves."

"I'm not my mother," I said through tight teeth.

"You were her weapon for a long time. You killed some of the seers yourself," Cat said, giving me a straightforward stare.

I looked back at Yadira rather than respond to that. She was right. Most people respected me for it, but there were some who might have seen me as no better than her. I'd have to show them I was different, no less ruthless, but not the same.

"I almost suggested she stay back in Dusra, but she insisted on going. I can't remember what she said, but she was persistent," Cat stated.

"Yadira." I stepped toward her.

She continued playing with the grass, dropping down onto the floor and running her finger over it now. It wasn't clear if she even heard me, her gaze still bouncing around as she stroked at the grass like she was playing an instrument.

"Yadira, we need to know if you've seen anything," Cat said.

No response again. She started giggling, but the sound wasn't laced with any sort of joy. It sounded uncomfortable, unnatural. Yadira's gaze snapped up to me, the smile still on her face but the laughter ceasing. She held my gaze as she stood and as she slowly glided toward me headfirst. Her smile dropped when she entered into my personal space, the tip of her nose only a few inches from mine. Her eyes glowed white, reminding me so much of Ximena. There wasn't any space to let the sentiment bring me down as the strands of Yadira's hair lifted and encased me in a gust of air.

"The light burns! It's breaking through split and cracked rock. You aren't the only one he wants. There's another, far, too far. I can't see her."

I stepped back. "Are you talking about the god of Chaos?"

"Too many outcomes. Too much pain. It all hurts. His heart may be stone, but it can still be pierced," she prattled.

"Who's heart?"

"She is pretty. Pretty things must be kept safe. Cherished. Even ones with scars."

"Zuri?" I snapped.

This was only pissing me off.

Cat put her hand on my arm. "Daya, I told you. It's all like this."

Yadira was still staring into my eyes. They flashed white sporadically, her head nearly vibrating with every vision that came to her.

"Vengeance, retribution, power, death," Yadira said, and I stilled. Those exact words were whispered in my ear when Zuri was taken. She moved closer, her lips a breath from my ear lobe. "Death brings power, but power brings death."

Yadira cackled, spinning around so the hem of her dress lifted into the air before she plopped back into the grass. Chuah said that one of my friends would die.

"Do you know if one of us will die?" I asked.

"Tsk, tsk, tsk. No power without death," Yadira responded before she began humming.

Cat looked back over her shoulder at Yadira. "My mom used to say that some seers went insane from the constant visions. Unable to tell the difference between now and then. I think that's what happened to her. Was any of it helpful?"

"Not entirely," I mumbled.

"What now?"

"We move forward with our plan."

CHAPTER FIFTY-ONE

AXEL

I knew I'd be back in this moment again. As much as I wished I wouldn't, it was inevitable. War was another part of life for mortals, and no matter how much power I had, I was still just that. A mortal. I felt better knowing that I was on Calderan soil and with Daya. As well as the rest of my Dusrans. Ishani had barely left my side since we'd gotten back from the Inbetween. She tried to be nonchalant, but unfortunately for my sister, that was not one of her strengths.

"Ish," I started, and she immediately threw her hands up in surrender.

"I'm not doing anything!"

"You have been glued to me since I got back," I said flatly.

She opened her mind to me as she eyed the surrounding crowd. *"I'm worried."*

I cleared my throat. "Leave me and my sister, please."

The soldiers around us left, and I sat down beside the fire. Ishani joined me, handing me a cup of ale and staring into the flames.

"When I told you about the blood-bending, I told you that I felt it all. You were able to overcome it, sit with it, and conquer all of those feelings, but I still feel it. I still remember waking in the middle of the night as if someone was cutting into me. No matter how hard I try, it's always there like a phantom pain."

"I know the feeling," I said.

I remembered just as much, but I understood how it was a different experience for her.

"Thinking about it happening again, I—"

I cut her off. "It won't happen again. I'm not that young and naïve soldier anymore, and I can't be used as a pawn."

"I know it wouldn't. I just want to make sure you're okay. That it's not starting to bother you. Reactions to trauma are real, even for us."

"I'm okay, I promise. I won't lie and say that it hasn't. . . brought up some poor memories, but I'm fine," I responded.

Seeing Kaizer smirking across the table with that fucking white hair, so similar to his cousin, damn near had me seething. Seeing the Sanjryan sigil across all of their armor and their weapons was almost too much. But then I remembered those visions the Triori showed me, and I remembered that she was now with me. That I'd seen our life beyond this point. They say the future is always changing and that one small decision could change it all, but something told me it wasn't the case this time.

"How are you feeling after Xavier?" I asked.

We hadn't talked about it much. We read our letters, and not shortly after, we were moving with the army. I typically could sense her emotions, but it was hard to decipher this time.

"I carried the weight of his secret for a long time. . . Relief isn't the right word, but. . ."

"I don't think that's wrong," I reassured.

Ishani's face twisted in grief. "We weren't this great storybook love, you know? But we were there for each other. What we had was real and constant. He wasn't my destiny like Daya is for you. Our pieces didn't fit seamlessly, but *not* having him here hurts. I hated what he wanted to do at first, but the sicker he got, I understood. I just want my. . . I don't know. Every sentiment I have around it feels incorrect."

It wasn't the first time someone we loved met their natural end. Our lifespans were long, and at this point we'd already lived the average vampire's life and a half. I remembered the first time Ishani lost someone she loved this way. It took a lot to pull her out of it, and it didn't seem the same this time. I could see how that would make her think her emotions were incorrect.

"These lives we live are seen as a gift to many." I put my hand on my sister's. "But we know that it doesn't always feel like one. The way I see it, we're given more chances. More opportunities for pain, sure, but more opportunities for love, too. You are going to get *everything* you desire, Ish. I know it. You only have to wait for that opportunity to present itself."

"You're right. Why are you always right?" she laughed, but tears streamed down her cheeks as she moved.

"I've been through a lot to get here. I know if I get my happy ending, you will too. Even after all of it."

My twin was the better of the two of us. That was undeniable.

"All of this to say that I'm here, okay? I know you have Daya and... Zuri?" She questioned, fishing, and when I didn't give her any answer, she kept going. "You have us all."

"I've never questioned that," I said with a smile before pulling her closer to me and squeezing her.

"But seriously?" She nudged out of my arms. "Is it like the lobos? They typically have a hierarchy with someone at the center. You guys seem all connected."

I stood and chuckled. "You know as much as I do. I'm taking each day as it comes."

Which was the truth, even though it sounded like I was trying to evade her.

"Not a bad way to live, brother," she responded.

"Speaking of..." I said as Daya knocked at the door of my consciousness. "I've got to go."

"Say no more." She clapped her hands and portaled somewhere else.

I answered Daya's call, saying, *"Yes, forceful?"*

"Where are you?"

"Just leaving Ishani. Over on her side. You okay?"

"I'll be better when you get back to the tent," she said, the seduction in her voice quickening my steps.

Paxx and Akari were coming toward me from across the camp, but I ducked away and avoided them. I had somewhere to be. Paxx shouted after me, but I waved my hand in dismissal over my shoulder without looking back. Outside of us currently being attacked, I couldn't think of anything more important than getting to our tent.

A light glowed within the canvas, but the fabric was too thick to be able to see any shadows. My hope that she was already waiting for me naked was thwarted as I walked into Daya and Zuri, flipping through the pages of the Amapola grimoire.

"Oh," I said, hopefully hiding my disappointment.

"Hey." Daya turned back a few pages. "Look at this."

"What is it?" I asked as I sat beside Daya and placed my hand on hers.

She smirked before pointing with her other hand. "It's an illusion spell."

"How does it work?" I asked.

"The one that lasts longer is to disguise an item as something else, but this one would practically be taking over someone's mind," she responded.

"Something you might actually be good at," Zuri added.

I wasn't sure if that was a compliment, but I'd take it.

"I'm so far removed from my witch side. I haven't done a spell this complicated in. . . a long time."

Probably not since my mother was alive. She always pushed us to stay connected with all the orders within us, but I'd mostly leaned into the lobo and vampire. Not for any particular reason. It had just been mostly what I was surrounded by. The three of us—my sister, my mother, and I—were one of a kind. Oddities that couldn't quite be explained. Nobody else around us had to balance between so many orders, so we set the rules and expectations for our peculiar magic.

"Do you want to try?" Daya asked.

The fact that this was a spell from her family and that she wanted to share it with me wasn't missed.

"Don't laugh if I fail," I said as I read the guidelines in the grimoire.

"So, are all of these solely your family's spells?" Zuri asked.

"Some of them, only a few of them, were protected and not shared. Ones that my ancestors thought could become dangerous if in the wrong hands."

"I don't know how I feel about that," Zuri mumbled.

Daya tilted her head. "Hm?"

"Who gets to decide what's safe and what's not? Seems like something that shouldn't be decided by one person," Zuri responded.

I continued reading the spell, trying to focus on getting it right, but I was actually curious about Zuri's question, too.

"I guess I never really thought about it that way," Daya responded. "I always assumed it was done for protection, but who knows? Guess I could ask."

"Okay," I said as I rubbed my palms together. "I think I'm ready."

"What are you going to do?" Daya asked.

I whispered the spell, trying to home in on both Daya and Zuri's consciousnesses so they'd both experience the illusion. It took far more effort than simply speaking in someone's mind, but I continued the spell, feeling a bead of sweat roll down my forehead. The pieces of it came together slowly, and it blurred slightly. The fabric of the tent vanished and was replaced by vast trees. The sky was no longer a fading orange but a deep blue with stars sparkling far above the trees.

Zuri grabbed Daya's hand as they wandered around. The surrounding scene was no longer hazy, but clear and vibrant. A creek rushed to the left of us, bright patches of flowers flourishing between the trees, blanketed in moonlight.

"Where is this?" Daya asked in amazement.

"Nowhere in particular," I said. "Just felt peaceful."

Zuri bent down and picked a flower near our feet. "I can even feel the flower."

"This is really good, Axel," Daya said with so much pride I almost came in my pants.

"I didn't think it'd work." I chuckled as I adjusted myself. "Feels a lot like the mind-speaking, just making a picture to communicate rather than words."

"So you had a bit of a head start," Zuri teased.

Shrugging a shoulder, I ran my hand through the water of the creek. It was cold, shockingly cold. I almost forgot that it was an illusion. The drips fell from my fingers, creating rings of movement before they were swept away with the current.

"Can you make something you've seen before?" Zuri asked.

"What do you want to see?"

"Try my bedroom in Dusra," Daya inserted.

Thought about that one plenty. I closed my eyes, recollecting all the small pieces of her room. The vanity, the faint crack in the ceiling, her bed, the pillows, the slippers she left by her bedside.

"Oh, nice," Daya said as her clothes were replaced with a silk night dress she'd worn before we left.

Zuri groaned in annoyance to find herself in a buttoned top and shorts I'd seen her in before, but it made Daya laugh, so I was okay with it. Daya flopped onto her bed and rubbed the velvet pillows.

"Feels perfect," she said.

"Are we wandering in the middle of the camp, or do we stay where we were before you started the illusion?" Zuri asked.

I kept my focus on maintaining the magic while trying to lift it enough from my point of view. All three of us were still in the tent, looking frozen in time.

"We're still safe and in the tent."

Dismantling the illusion, I let them see that we were indeed safe. I wasn't sure that if there was a bodily threat we'd feel it or if the vision would take over completely.

"We didn't need a seer. We just needed to be able to control what *they* see," Daya said as she lifted to her tip toes and kissed my jaw. "This is perfect."

"Did it take a lot out of you? Could you hold it up for a longer period?" Zuri questioned, always the thorough one.

"I feel like I could, but I'd have to test it. It didn't pull from my reserves at all," I responded.

She nodded, her thumb and pointer finger on her chin as she seemed to be contemplating. Not as easily impressed, apparently.

"We can practice the object illusion too. That could come in handy as well," Daya said as she closed the grimoire and sent it back to its safe place with a snap of her fingers.

My Daya. She'd had an air of defeat around her since we got back from the Inbetween. It wasn't her fault we couldn't stop it all, but with the power she'd received and the interest from the god of Chaos, she felt like it was. But she was coming back around, even if nobody else noticed the hint of chagrin. I was more than happy to be the one to help her get to where she was now.

Daya's gaze bounced between the two of us, and I felt the whoosh of an air shield going up around our tent. She laid back down on the bedrolls we'd pushed together, her hand lifting to her zipper. Zuri raked her gaze over Daya with heavy lids, squeezing her bottom lip between her teeth. We both moved toward her, but she lifted a finger with a tsk.

"Let's agree to some ground rules."

"Rules?" I questioned, my dick already hard.

"We can start with a safe word." She smiled. "I told you I want us all to be together. Neither of you have seemed against it." She waited for us to make some remarks, but neither of us did. "So, if there's a problem, say. . . 'rose petal,' and we'll stop."

"Stop what?" Zuri asked.

Daya's smile grew wide, her tongue running over her teeth as she nodded her head toward me. "Kiss."

Zuri glanced over at me, a look I couldn't quite read. It wasn't discomfort I felt. Zuri was a beautiful woman, but there'd been a lot of derision between us. Much of it we'd been getting over recently, but this was a step further. It wouldn't be the first time we'd shared Daya, but it was the first time we'd share each other. If she wanted. I wouldn't have been offended if she used the safe word, and I wasn't going to pressure her. So I stood firm, with a boner, as she appeared to be debating what she wanted to do.

Zuri looked at Daya one more time, the question of if this was really okay bouncing between them. Daya nodded eagerly, and Zuri finally turned fully toward me. I let her come to me, worried I'd scare her off if I moved too quickly. My gaze met Daya's with a need for reassurance that I wasn't overstepping. She didn't back down and certainly didn't seem like she was changing her mind as she sat up and watched us with her nail between her teeth.

I didn't speak mind-to-mind with Zuri often. It was a peculiar sensation when she opened her mind to me. *"This doesn't mean I like like you."*

"Mhm." I smirked.

She rolled her eyes, but pushed up onto her toes as I brought my lips toward hers. The energy was always charged between Zuri and me, typically with sneers and snide remarks, even when we were on good terms. It was part of our relationship for her to be a little mean to me, at the least. But as I brought my lips to hers, it felt bizarrely *right*. The sound of Daya moaning as if she was the one between us certainly helped. Zuri pressed deeper into the kiss, her lips soft and supple.

She hesitated for just a second, and I reentered her mind, asking, *"Are you okay?"*

I was partially worried. Like me, she'd do anything for Daya, and I worried that it wasn't actually what she wanted.

But contentment filled my consciousness as she reassured me with a short, *"Yes."*

"Come on, we can do better than that," Daya teased.

My hand shifted to Zuri's lower back, and I brought her flush with my body, or as close to flush with her short stature. Zuri's tongue teased at the seam of my lips, and I let her in, realizing that it wasn't truly the first time I'd tasted her. I'd tasted her on Daya's lips plenty of times before. Her fingers brushed through my hair, and I wondered if she'd watched Daya do it before because she pulled the exact way I liked it.

"There we go," Daya said. "Let's move over here."

We did as she asked, slowly lowering down onto the bedroll with her. Zuri and I stayed knee to knee, with Daya sitting on the other side of us. We both waited for some sort of direction as she was calling the shots thus far. Daya, as expected, was really working on the anticipation between us.

"Take his clothes off," she commanded Zuri.

The authority she spoke with had my dick painful, and Zuri didn't wait this time. She did exactly as Daya asked. She pulled the hem of my shirt with her small hands, unfastening the buttons holding it together. Before I knew it, my top half was bare, my chest moving with my heavy breaths. Zuri stilled, taking in the large scars I'd earned from my own torture at Sanjry's hand. Her gaze slowly fell to her own side, a feeling of distance pushing between us, but I grabbed her hand and placed it on the most gnarly of my scars.

"I'm not ashamed, and you shouldn't be either," I said.

I'd already seen them, whether she remembered or not. Our time in the cave had escalated so quickly that I didn't think she really was conscious of them. But now, in this slow-paced. . . intimacy, it was hard to tuck these things away in our minds. Zuri came back into herself, the confidence she moved with prior returning. She poked her finger into my waistband, a trail of warmth left behind as she slid it toward the zipper. Only the sound of our breaths and heartbeats filled the tent as she relieved the pressure against my cock. Her eyes went wide as it was set free, my pants around my knees.

"Good girl, Zuri," Daya said as she pulled my pants the rest of the way off. "Your turn, Axel."

Zuri ran her tongue across her bottom lip before exhaling. I moved slower than she did, making sure that each motion was easily detected. She nodded as I pulled her shirt over her head before I lifted her by her ass to pull her pants completely off. Settling her back down gently, I grazed my hands up the sides of her body. She shivered, and I kept my hands at her waist.

"You both have no idea how much I've fantasized about this," Daya said, her cheeks flushed and lips dark. She pulled off her own clothes, her breasts bouncing as she leaned back on the pillows and opened her legs, showing us how much she was enjoying it. "Continue."

Both Zuri and I were still entranced with Daya as she dipped her fingers down and circled her swollen clit.

"I only keep doing this if you two keep going," Daya said as her mouth fell open.

We crashed into each other immediately, our lips pressing together and hands exploring all the exposed skin. That familiarity, but the both of us seeing the other in a different light. Her fingers ran down my abs, her thumbs dipping into the ridge of each muscle until she reached the last one. I cupped her ass just as she gripped my dick, and Daya moaned, her fingers deep inside herself.

It wasn't the first time I'd been with two women, but it was all so carnal before, solely for our own pleasure. This time, I felt a pressure to make sure we all got what we wanted. Not a pressure, but a desire to show them both satisfaction unlike they'd had before. To be between these two, spinning on the same axis as a woman as powerful as Daya, as strong as Zuri. . . it was a privilege I didn't take lightly.

I groaned as Zuri fully grasped me in her hand, sliding down to the tip and rubbing her finger through the pre-cum gathered there. She leaned over to Daya, sticking it in between her lips, and she sucked it off fervently. As soon as Zuri righted herself, I took one of her nipples into my mouth, squeezing it between my teeth and flicking with my tongue.

She arched into me, and I took that as an invitation to take it further. I shifted her quickly, laying her on her back right beside Daya. She took the opportunity to pull Zuri into a kiss, and I fisted my dick as I waited for them to pull back. They both looked over at me with swollen lips and anticipation in their gazes. I made sure they were close enough that I could reach them both, but Daya tasked me with Zuri, so I returned to her.

Zuri didn't try to hide this time, letting me settle down between her legs as Daya sat up to watch. Her scars ran so close to her entrance. I took my time running my hands over them, kissing each welt and indentation, and showing that I meant what I said before. Zuri relaxed further, knees falling to either side of her as I fully nestled between them. I flattened my tongue against her, running it up to her clit. She was soaked and ready, and I pushed a finger inside her and then another until she was tight around me. Zuri moaned, and even though Daya had set up an air shield, she swallowed the sound with her mouth, now on all fours beside her.

I pumped my fingers, learning what made her squirm, what earned me moans. Daya sucked on Zuri's nipple, pinching onto the other before trailing kisses up to her neck. Zuri arched again, and I had to throw an arm over her hips to keep her in place. I kept at it, lapping and rubbing my thumb over her clit until I felt a rush of wetness, and I licked every bit of it up. Daya rushed over to me, running her tongue over my mouth and chin to taste Zuri.

Zuri pushed onto her elbows, her skin sheen with sweat. But Daya apparently really had fantasized about this, because she knew exactly what she wanted next. She positioned Zuri on her side, lifting her leg and handing it to me before I even realized what she wanted me to do. I quickly caught on, lining my chest up with Zuri's back and situating myself at her entrance.

"Go on," Daya said as she bit her lip.

Zuri turned her chin to me, catching my mouth in a kiss. *No going back now.* I pushed into her fully, feeling her tightness encase me. She felt. . . amazing. Different from Daya, but no less perfect. We adjusted to each other, our chests moving in the same exact cadence. Zuri's toes curled, and she pushed her hips further into me in invitation. I took it, pulling out to the tip and thrusting back in. Zuri screamed as I picked up speed, and Daya moved closer. She laid down beside Zuri, her face pressing into where we were joined.

The heat of her tongue ran up my dick every time I pulled out of Zuri, and I felt her tighten each time Daya sucked down on her clit. Zuri reached her hand over, making sure Daya wasn't left out of the mix, and pushed two fingers inside her. We all worked in tandem; every push met with a pull, and every moan echoed between the three of us. I felt a pulse of constriction around me, Zuri close to orgasm. The vibration from Daya moaning seemed to tip her over, and I kept my pace as she came all over my dick, and in turn, Daya's tongue.

Zuri rolled over, and Daya found my body like a magnet. Her hand guided my dripping dick straight to her pussy as she pushed me onto my back. Daya was possibly the wettest I'd ever felt her, and I slid in without any resistance. She rode me, and I lifted her up, driving into her fast and rough. Zuri watched us move with her lips slightly parted, but Daya grabbed her wrist and dragged her toward us. Daya bore down on me as she placed Zuri where she wanted. Which happened to be on my face. I was sure I was in some sort of paradise or that I was going to be awoken from a dream. But I knew it wasn't a dream as I felt Daya drag her hips and as I sucked down on Zuri's clit to make her scream. *Still sensitive, noted.*

Zuri leaned forward as Daya pulled her into a kiss, which only opened up Zuri's hips more. Every lick had her twitching, and she moaned a throaty sound when I pressed my thumb against her clit. It was like second nature to please both of them simultaneously. I continued matching Daya's movements, and Zuri abandoned her lips in favor of sucking Daya's breasts.

Daya took over, and I let her use me exactly how she wanted. Zuri moved to sit back fully on my face, and I positioned my fingers so that she'd sit on those, too. Her body tightened as she came and rolled off my face to the pillows, but Daya pushed into the free space quickly. She licked my chin before pressing her tongue into my mouth. I knew I wouldn't last much longer, and we gave everything we had left, our bodies slamming together and Daya's nails digging into my neck. We came together, falling onto the bedroll, and we both reached for where Zuri was still panting.

I had absolutely no quarrels with this being the rest of my life.

Chapter Fifty-Two

Dayanara

The waiting had always bothered me. Waiting for the first strike, for the initial waft of death in the wake of battle. I always preferred to be the first person on the field, but it wasn't up to me alone. There was an entire team of people who needed to agree. As much as that annoyed me, it was also sort of. . . nice. To know that there were people who had my back not because of blind loyalty, but because they truly believed in me. I certainly wasn't the emotional type, but if I was, it could have warmed my cold little heart. Might have made me shed a tear.

But alas, I was who I was. It was the thought that counted, I was sure. We'd gone over the battle plan, nitpicked every single thing that could go wrong. But the ones who had seen battle knew you could never think of everything. There were always surprises, always things that you could never conjure in your craziest of thoughts. Like the explosion that put me on this path. There was always a chance that Kaizer had found something else, that Chuah had given him the location of some other ancient weapon lost to time.

I wondered how far his influence had dug into Kaizer's and Joseph's minds. If it was like me, where I felt him, where I saw him, or if it was mere words on a page. The flash of doubt when I told Kaizer who he was really speaking to—that his faith was misplaced—I wanted it painted on a fucking wall. Even if he didn't fully believe me, or Joseph didn't allow him, I knew it had to be eating at him.

Silently chuckling to myself, I found Paxx standing alone at the very edge of the camp. He stared out into the distance as if he was imagining all the pain and turmoil he'd be seeing in the air.

"Do you experience the pain?" I asked, and he turned as if he knew I was coming. "Do you only see it, or does it affect you?"

He let out a deep breath. "It's hard to explain to someone without the gift. I don't feel it like my own, but it does weigh on me. All the emotions in the air encompass me. I can't ignore it."

"What do you see now?" I asked as he returned his gaze to the field.

"There's a lot of hate and greed. Some nerves, some confusion. That's pretty typical, though."

We sat in comfortable silence for a few beats. The stars were brighter today, as if they leaned closer to see what would happen on this battlefield. Watching, judging, probably taking bets on the sad mortals that lived here.

"I've been fighting practically every minute of my life. This is the first time I'm fighting for myself, though, for people I care about, not just the idea of a kingdom. It feels different," I said, opening up just a little bit.

"Fighting for a purpose and to protect." Paxx nodded. "I know what you mean."

"Can you promise me something?" I asked.

"I don't like where this is going," he said.

"If something happens to me. . . take care of them."

"That's what I figured you'd say." He ran his hand over his face. "Nothing is going to happen to you."

"I have this feeling. I don't know. I was marked as a sacrifice long ago. Maybe it was always meant to be. If it means that everyone else will be okay—"

"Respectfully, shut the fuck up," Paxx cut me off.

"I'm just saying—"

"Axel saw your future. None of them would let that happen."

"Things change. I wouldn't willingly do it. Something feels different than before," I responded.

I wouldn't have given my life for much prior to being here with the Dusrans. Some may have even said I was selfish, but I had to be. I took the small things I was able to control for myself without question. But now, there wasn't much I wouldn't do for these people. I wanted to be here with them to experience the joy of victory and to continue the fight; there was no question about it.

"I think that comes with being part of a family." Paxx smiled. "There's more to lose, more to gain. More all around."

"You might be right."

I didn't think about it that way. The rustling of our camp was loud, and I turned to face the lines of tents. I watched as people zipped around, some eating and drinking, others sitting alone in silence.

"Do you have a prewar ritual?" Paxx asked.

"You mean bruja shit or me alone?"

Paxx led us back toward the camp. "Just you."

"I think that's part of what feels different. Typically, I'd be consulting with my mother on the things I was allowed to do. What I could decide on my own. I'm usually sitting on the front lines, huffing and waiting to fuck someone up."

"Well, let's see about making a new one," he responded as we headed toward Ishani's tent.

His dark eyes twinkled with mischief, and I followed instead of asking any questions. If there was one thing about Paxx I knew, it was that he could be as tight-lipped as he wanted to be. Laughter came from the tent, warm light radiating as Paxx entered, and all of my favorite people were found inside. Cat was already here, sharing a deep belly laugh with Zuri. Axel and Ishani were in a heated argument, but in that fun twin way, they did where they both found it hilarious.

"We're all here now!" Ishani exclaimed, grabbing everyone else's attention. "We can start!"

Axel left Ishani with a playful push on her shoulder, bending down to kiss me. "I was just about to see where you were."

"What are we doing?" I asked.

He glanced at his sister, and her smile turned even more joyful than typical. She dumped out a crate and stood atop it, assumingly for impact, because everyone was able to see her perfectly fine without it. "You have only heard the stories of this, as it's been so long that most of you weren't even a thought in your mother's mind yet."

She and Axel laughed, and I held back the desire to make an old man joke when I saw how purely happy he was. His dimples were deep and the slightest crinkle at his eyes from the size of his smile. He looked down at me with a question, but I only leaned into him before returning my attention to Ishani.

"Many centuries ago, my grandfather started a tradition before battle to lift the spirits of his soldiers. The leaders would get together like this, and they'd give each other well wishes for the fighting. We draw names, and that is the person you have to give a blessing. You'll also give them their war paint. He believed that by holding that intention for blessings and marking them into the skin of someone you love, you were protected."

"The army should be doing something similar right now. We'll go out and celebrate together when we're done," Axel added.

"I've always wanted to do this." Zuri beamed as she rubbed her hands together in anticipation.

Paxx made a big show of shaking the bowl with the names on it as he handed it over to Ishani, who jumped down from the crate. She started on the other side of the room, and I watched as each person held the papers close to their chest until all the names were dispersed. I dipped my hand in, only a few names left, and made sure that Axel didn't see who I got.

Ishani finished with the last name and pulled out small jars of paint. Tucking away the piece of paper in my pocket, I hopped up and held my hands out for her to hand them to me. She narrowed her eyes, but handed them over. I grabbed one of the stones from my bracelet and turned it into a powder in my palm. The spell fell from my lips as I mixed the powder into the paint, and it glowed before returning to the black, red, blue, and white hues.

"It'll last longer now," I said as I handed them back.

The pride and appreciation had me retreating back to Axel, who regarded me exactly the same.

"What? Nobody wants the paint to peel before we even get our blades bloody," I said as I avoided eye contact.

"Sure," he responded with a twinkle in his eye.

"Okay, everyone, look at the names!" Ishani shrieked with joy.

"I got you, Ishani," Zuri said as she jumped up and down.

"Paxx!" Axel called out.

I finally read the writing on my piece of paper, finding Cat's full name scribbled across it with a tiny heart above the 'i' in Catalina.

"This seems fitting," she said as we sat together on the ground.

"We've been doing this together for a long time," I agreed.

She set the paint down between us. "But I don't think we've ever done anything like this."

"We haven't."

If I would have gotten to pick someone to do this with, it would have been Cat. As much as I would have enjoyed putting Zuri or Axel's war paint on, Cat was the one I was meant to do this with. My friend who had been there for me since we were children, even when I didn't deserve it. The one who stepped into her position of warrior without question. When it all came down to it, I was doing it for the coven, but Cat was *my* coven. We both surveyed the others, every one offering protection to the other, expressing their love and admiration. Zuri already had streaks running down from her brow to her jaw as Ishani, very expressively, wished for her to return whole.

"These sorts of emotions haven't been a witch forte." Cat laughed. "But I like it. I like the Dusrans. They've shown that we can be ruthless but vulnerable."

I dipped my finger into the paint and smeared the red pigment in a line below her right eye. "I hope that you fight with the ferocity of a bruja and that none should fell you."

Catalina dipped into the black, painting a line from the base of my lower lip to beneath my chin. "May your blade swing true, and all of your ancestors offer their strength."

Repeating the same streak under the other eye, I said, "I hope that your mother's warrior spirit flows through you."

Cat's lip wobbled slightly. She was one of the lucky brujas who had the real love of a mother. They didn't always agree, but I was envious of the obvious love between them.

"I'm proud of you, Dayanara," Cat said as she had me close my eye and swept paint on the lid, and repeated it on the other. "You've always had my loyalty and support, but seeing you now, sometimes it's hard to believe how much you've grown."

"Me?" I questioned as I connected the two lines over the bridge of her nose. "I'm proud of *you*. I couldn't have done this without you. Especially when. . . " I trailed off and peered at Zuri. "You kept the coven together when it shouldn't have been your job. There aren't words to express how grateful I am for you."

"It wasn't a burden. I believe in what we're doing, and I'm happy to be fighting on your side."

She finished my war paint with a streak of white down my forehead and nose and three red dots below each of my eyes. I ran my pinky across the edge of the red already there and added two thin lines on her chin. We watched each other with care, holding that true intent of love and protection in our hearts. Ishani brought us a mirror, and we looked in it together; tears welled at Cat's waterline, and I pulled her into a hug. Not one like the last time, where I wasn't sure of the embrace, but one that I hoped conveyed that every word I spoke to her was true.

Everyone finished, and I took in their paint, specifically how fierce Zuri looked. She lifted her finger and traced the paint as if she was offering her own protection, and I held her hand to my chest.

"You are so beautiful," I said.

"Have you seen yours?" she chuckled in deflection.

"I have."

"You both look perfect," Axel chimed in as we stepped out of the tent and into the camp.

Everyone, vampire, witch, and lobo alike, was painted in different variations. My people mingled comfortably with the Dusrans, genuine camaraderie between the kingdoms. Each step I took felt more empowered, every beat of my heart more intense. By the time I made it to the center, I was overcome with pride and determination.

These kingdoms, both Dusra and Caldera, were my people now, and I would not fail them.

Chapter Fifty-Three

Dayanara

The air was crisp, breezing between our soldiers, a sign from Naom that she was watching. The line of Sanjryan soldiers were stiff, the atmosphere stagnant. Kaizer wasn't on the front line yet, but Otto and Abel were. For them, this battle was all or nothing, and it was evident in the way they watched us. The gaze of people who knew they were being sent to slaughter for nothing more than their king's desire for power.

The tension between Otto and me was tight, my lip twitching into a sneer with every passing second. He broke the eye contact, facing his army and speaking to them. Axel joined me on the front line, Ishani beside him. Zuri wasn't at the front but with Akari toward the flank. I expected Ishani to be the one to give the speech as she did in Dusra, but she nodded for me to go ahead. I didn't prepare anything, but I was pissed off enough to wing it.

"If you would have asked me a year ago where I'd be today, fighting for my kingdom beside Dusra would not have been my answer. I thought I knew what was to come, even thought I was prepared. But that was unbridled confidence. I had no idea what plans my mother had for me and for my coven."

I paced across the front line as Axel continued watching the Sanjryans across the field. "I don't ask you to fight for me or even my kingdom. I've recently realized that land is not what makes us who we are or even the magic it offers. I don't ask you to risk your lives for rock and soil. I ask you to fight for your right to exist as you see fit. I ask you to go out there and demolish Sanjry, to tell their king that there is no place for his bullshit. Tell Kaizer that he can't have us, that he can't have our power. That he will never be fit to rule all of Malva. I, Dayanara Amapola, Acna of the brujas, ask you, vampire, bruja, and lobo alike, to give everything you have to protect the lives we've curated. The peace we've found, for I no longer think that land is what made me who I am, or that these gifts I've received from the Goddess Naom is who I am."

I stopped and looked back at Axel. "No, I know that to be truly alive, truly happy, is to know the love, admiration, and respect of an army as great as this one. I know that they can never take that from us no matter what they do. For he rules in fear, but we live in pride! Pride for knowing that the person beside us shares our values in freedom. Pride in the mutual respect I have received from every single one of you. So I ask you to rise, Dusra and the *true* Calderans! Rise and fight! We will be victorious, and we won't allow this issue to arise again. We take no prisoners. We leave none of Kaizer's supporters alive. Let's show them exactly how we feel about their Flame fuckery!"

The crowd roared, and I saw Sanjry's front line jump back a step at the sound. It wasn't the shout of a desperate army. It was the bellow of one that knew they would win. I peeked through the lines of soldiers, finding my Zuri atop her horse toward the back. She smiled, lifting her sword and yelling with the crowd.

"Part of me hopes there's another battle so I can top that," Ishani joked.

"Don't think this will be the last one we ever see," I responded with a breath of laughter.

"You incredible, vicious creature," Axel said, pressing a kiss to my lips that had our armor clinking against each other. I wore a hybrid between the witch leathers and Dusran armor, the shoulders, chest plate, and forearms in their hard bronze metal with my impenetrable leathers beneath it. Axel had pushed for me to be in the full armor he wore, but I wasn't used to it and didn't want to take any chances. He settled for the vitals being covered. . . only after Zuri also agreed it was best. I tested the sword she'd made me in my hand, the first time it was seeing real battle. It glimmered as my magic sparked in my hand, and I dragged the blade across the air.

Something felt heavy on my chest, not in an unpleasant way, but in a comforting one. An invisible embrace. I closed my eyes briefly and sensed my ancestors pouring their love into me. The sensation of all the Amapola women lending me their power, just as Cat had wished for me. My skin sparked alive, and I watched their power wrap around me like a blanket.

Axel took a step forward, and the army silenced. He reached his hand back for me, facing the Sanjryan army, his sword in the other. Hand in hand, we pierced the sky with our blades and charged forward together.

Our boots beat against the hard Sanjryan soil, and a cloud of dry dirt encompassed us as brujas used their air magic to hide us. We'd studied this land, knew the pits and falls enough that we wouldn't have to see. The sound of the Sanjryan army charging us grew closer with every step we took, and once I felt us descend the final hill, I threw a ball of bruja magic forward and gave the signal.

"Air shield!"

Everyone on the front line joined, creating a thick air shield that shot high into the sky. The cloud of dirt hit the shield hard and dissipated, but the impact of the magic suppressant bomb boomed against the other side. The ground shook, and the shield vibrated, but it stayed strong. They played dirty with a bomb that turned everyone into dust in the last battle, so I had no quarrels with matching his crazy.

They all screamed as they inhaled the powder, and their magic reserves fell empty, blocked from their access. It didn't reach everyone, but enough to give us an edge. We waited for the suppressant to vanish and disbanded the air shield. My gaze locked in Otto's, pure rage seething from him as no sparks or flames formed. His hands balled into fists, his jaw tight and ticking as he turned back to his soldiers. I didn't care if he had magic or not; Zuri would take his life, and Axel and I would help her.

Blood splattered across my chest as I pulled my sword out of another Sanjryan vampire. The brujas were avoiding me, almost all of them moving to either side of the battlefield and away from the center where I was. I wanted to take them down, and they must have seen it on my face. Scanning the field around me and throwing my dagger over my shoulder to hit the soldier approaching, I tried to find Zuri. The soldier at my back fell to the ground, and I retrieved my blade, finding her still fighting beside her cousin. Her caramel braids whipped in the air as she twirled and stabbed a witch, and I smirked as I felt someone else coming for me.

My smile may have been manic, but I didn't care. I let my witch magic loose from my hand, striking the vampire in the neck and making him jolt and thrash. Ishani jumped across us, slicing him through the throat just as I pulled my magic back.

"Have you seen Kaizer?" she asked.

"No, I haven't," I responded as the fighting raged around us.

Two more soldiers stormed toward us, and I forced air onto the ground to flip and position myself behind one.

"You picked the wrong side," I whispered in their ear as I realized they were of my coven.

I hadn't taken the time to be so gruesome in my fighting thus far, but now, the first traitor witch to fall, I took the time. I severed her head from her shoulders and lifted her by the hair as blood sprayed from the cut vessels. Spinning around, I screamed, hoping that the rest of them nearby knew that I wasn't showing them mercy. I tossed the head into the fighting and moved with even more speed. Tearing through body after body, everyone fell in my wake. My hair was dripping with blood, the ends nearly black. I tossed it over my shoulder, and the drenched curls hit my back with a heavy smack.

I lost track of Zuri. I knew she had experience fighting, but not like Axel, Ishani, and I had. She was confident and had enough anger fueling her, but it didn't stop my worrying. A battle was something I could do with my eyes closed at this point, but it did take some of my focus away from what I was doing. That brought me back to a memory of my mother, advising me that I shouldn't get attached to things when I needed to be fully present for our people.

There was nothing that could make me regret my feelings for Zuri. Even as I turned right into a soldier. He had stumbled back while fighting a Dusran, and I took the opportunity to hold him still while the lobo cut him down. The lobo nodded his appreciation to me, and as soon as he moved, I found what I'd been hoping for. Across the field, Axel and Zuri fought back to back, and fuck did it make my heart sing. I could see where Axel was slightly overcompensating for her, but he kept up his speed and precision. She twisted, ducking low to avoid the swing of a blade, and her own sword found its mark on the attacker.

Someone was charging me from the back, but I took an extra minute to admire how they moved together. How beautiful they looked in blood, sweat, and their war paint. Turning quickly, I pulled a throwing knife from my leather corset and tossed it at the attacker. It landed in his eye, and he screamed, as expected. A blast of air expelled from my hand, pushing the knife in further and killing the man. It was slightly too deep to retrieve the blade, so I left it within the man's skull as he bled out beneath the feet of his fellow soldiers.

I still hadn't seen Kaizer, which wasn't exactly surprising. He didn't often fight in his kingdom's battles, but I thought he would fight in this one. He was up to something or a bigger coward than even I thought. The sensation of someone watching me had me swiveling my head to the left. Across the field, in a window between fighting soldiers, I saw Quinn. She was tall, her head an inch or two above the others, her general armor marking her as someone with authority. There was something hard to read in her gaze. When I sowed the doubt into her and told her what was really happening, I saw that it hit her harder than Kaizer or his advisers.

When she was captured in Dusra, she watched us with the intent of a spy, and I clocked her as she seemed to put together that she was fighting a losing battle.

We stared at each other, neither of us moving until she took long strides across the field. The fighting seemed to stay an arms-length from her as she made it to me. She sheathed her sword, her hands nowhere near her weapons.

"I told him this would not end well," she admitted with her gaze on the fighting.

"So did I," I responded, not entirely trusting her and resting my palm on the hilt of my sword.

She held devastation in her gaze. "Who is coming, truly?"

"Chaos. No one good."

She humphed, reaching for her sword. "I have no desire to see it from this side."

My brows pinched, wondering if she was asking me to end her.

"Make no mistake, I will not make it easy. But falling at your sword? One of the greatest warriors of our time—a female." She nodded. "That is a worthy death."

She didn't wait for me to respond. She only swung her blade quicker than I'd seen her do in Sanjry. I dodged, deciding to fight her as she intended. Quinn was one of the few Sanjryans I could stand, but war was war. I blocked the next jab with the armor on my forearm. There was resolution in her eyes, and I didn't quite know what the Sanjryans believed of death, just that they returned to the Flame. I wasn't sure if there was paradise or torture in her future, but I gritted my teeth as I pushed her back.

Our blades clinked together, locking as we both pushed our bodies into each other. I won, forcing her to stumble back and drop her sword. Sheathing mine, I lifted my fists, and she smirked. Quinn had the height and reach advantage. I had to be fast. Her left fist cut through the air, aimed for my jaw, and I spun, using my elbow to hit her in the side. The impact through the metal of her armor had her exasperating a breath, but she didn't stop.

She used her heavy boot to kick my shin, and I jumped back as the force reverberated through my bones. I caught the elbow she tossed toward my head in my hand, having enough of this. Quinn didn't pull back her strength. She didn't give up. The only Sanjryan general who didn't judge me like the others held strong until I slid the dagger from my thigh and held it to her throat. Only then did she show any sort of change to the fierce demeanor.

She closed her eyes and whispered, "May the Flame take me."

I gave her what she wished: a quick death at the hand of a warrior. She slumped to the ground, unmoving eyes with an unseeing gaze in the clouds. Bending down, I closed her lids and turned to the next soldier nearby.

Chapter Fifty-Four

Paxx

Nobody had laid eyes on Kaizer yet. Axel's magic retreated from my mind with the update, and I turned to the group with me. We'd kept it small, needing to move as quickly as possible without being seen. Me, Cat, and one of my spies, Selina. She had been stationed in Sanjry for a while, but I'd pulled out all the spies once we started moving the army. I trusted her, one of the few I trusted, actually. Outside of our inner circle, which now included Daya, I could count the others I trusted on one hand.

Selina was someone I'd been vulnerable with, a vampire I let get close against my better judgment. Neither of us had any of our blood family left, and we'd found comfort in not having to explain our overall demeanor. Both of us were cold, reserved, preferring to stay back and monitor than be part of the group. But we'd found a certain warmth with each other, particularly in the night. It didn't stop us from working together, and I knew she'd give me shit if I tried to tell her she couldn't go on this mission with me. We'd go months without seeing each other, but that comfort always stayed. Neither of us had a desire to take it any further, not wanting that permanent attachment.

It was the hardest part of this kind of work. Not allowing anyone past a certain point. Regardless, we knew what we were getting ourselves into and agreed it was for the best. Her dark eyes narrowed on me, the outer corners slightly upturned. The wind blew the black hair I'd had wrapped around my fist last night across her supple cheeks.

"Still no sight of him?" Selina asked.

Cat finished putting away the journal we'd created as an illusion for Kaizer—a contingency just in case he wasn't killed at the end of the battle. I scanned the battlefield, seeing what was once purple hair, now darkened black with blood shooting across.

"No, but we need to do this before the fighting spreads out. They won't keep it on that side for too much longer. Now is the time to move," I responded.

Getting whatever piece of the scepter Kaizer had was vital, as was the journal. We needed to ensure that power was harbored and didn't fall into the wrong hands. I gathered that he didn't trust many other people with the information. It was likely that anybody with the knowledge would fall on the battlefield today. But I didn't like leaving things to chance. Especially when so much hung in the balance.

"Moving," I advised Axel.

He confirmed he heard me with an affirmative grunt, and we skirted around the field. Cat put up a tight air shield, and we moved as one unit. Cat had been particularly helpful while Daya was. . . indisposed. She handled any issues within her coven with grace and authority. The brujas of Caldera were a bit different from ours, and Maeve had quickly defaulted to her.

I held no judgment for how Daya handled Zuri being taken. It was a situation nobody was prepared for. Including myself. Zuri had been someone I leaned on, more than just a friend or colleague, but certainly less than what she had with Daya.

A swell of water rose from the river in the distance—the diversion. We watched as it swept all the soldiers close to the bank into the current, and our soldiers used their own magic to avoid being pulled in.

"Perfect," Cat said as more soldiers ran to the battlefield near us.

Daya had done a lap above the camp after the meeting with Kaizer and advised us of the overall layout. We'd drawn a route we thought was safest and memorized it. I still was so embarrassed at my lack of control in that meeting. Axel and Daya hadn't seemed to mind, but something about Sanjry's king grated under my skin. Between that and the threat to the ones I loved, I couldn't help myself. The sad part was that if Daya had told me to take his life, I would have without question. Consequences be damned. Axel and Zuri were finally where they were meant to be, with who they were meant to be, and I'd protect that with my last breath.

Cat held up a fist, slowing down our procession through the tents. She opened her hand, her fingers winding as she focused on something. The heavy silver helmet of a Sanjryan soldier rolled to our feet, and she stopped it with her foot. He looked like he was sleeping, but I knew he was gone. Whether she did some witch shit or suffocated him with her magic, he surely didn't see it coming.

Just as Daya said, Kaizer's tent was toward the back of the camp. I tapped into my empathic abilities, feeling for any emotions within the tent, but there were none.

"Let's move," I said.

Cat fell back and let me take the lead, placing Selina between us with what I assumed was her instinct to protect. Two soldiers were posted outside his tent, and before I could advise the women, Cat and Selina were bounding forward around me. Cat held Selina's hand, blasting them both into the air and coming down on top of the soldiers in complete silence. By the time I'd gotten to the tent, both of them were dragging the dead bodies inside. We stood at the entrance, trying to determine whether there were any traps. There wasn't, but there also was barely anything inside. Only a bed sat within the vast tent, not the abode of a power-hungry king.

"Where is all his shit?" Cat asked.

"How long has the camp been here?" Selina asked directly after.

She kneeled on the ground, a straight line of dead grass parallel to the lone bed roll.

"They were here before us, but not too much earlier," I responded.

Cat bent and picked up a piece of a white button-up shirt. "This has Daya's scent all over it."

"The man has a few screws loose," Selina offered.

"Well, there's nothing else here. The scepter and journal have to be somewhere else," I said.

"Hold on," Cat said.

Cat's cerulean magic spilled from her hands as she whispered. It moved like a snake searching for prey. It bound up the walls, nestling into the corners of the tent. It pooled at the edge of the bedroll, and she swiped her hand where it gathered.

She shifted the roll over, the grass beneath it lusher than the rest. "Whatever witch set this spell didn't add a degenerating aspect to it. The grass shouldn't look like this."

Cat took time breaking down the spell, and the grass disappeared, a deep hole appeared. It was empty, but she lifted the dirt in her fingers and rubbed it into the palm of her hand. "This is where it was kept. I can feel the magic, but it's been moved."

"Can you track it?" I asked.

"I'm not sure," she responded as she appeared to be trying the location spell. It took more work than I'd seen before, but a small ball of her magic lifted, bobbing in the air. It moved to the tent's entrance, and she held up a finger to stop its procession until we were ready. This time, we lined up behind Cat and let her magic point us in the right direction.

The sound of metal against metal, of dying screams, and of magic raged behind us. We just needed to get those items, and then we could join in and help the fight. I wasn't sure when we'd need to turn back, but I knew we weren't there yet. This time, yelling from within the camp had Cat's legs going stiff, boots stopping abruptly, and forcing me to run into her back. Her head turned to the side, the way I'd seen Daya do when she was tapping into her witch hearing.

"Kaizer is ahead," she said, studying her magic. "I think he has the items with him."

Just as she advised, the king bounded across the path ahead of us, Abel on his heels.

"You said it would be ready *before* the fighting started," Kaizer quipped.

"*I* didn't say anything. Joseph told me it'd be ready. I only conveyed the message," Abel snapped back.

"Get back to Sanjry and figure it out. Take this with you." Kaizer handed over the scepter staff but kept the journal in his pocket close to his chest.

Abel called for a witch nearby, and Cat's eyes narrowed on her. Loyalty had been the root of all the brujas' beliefs, and watching it be thrown away was more than painful for the ones following Daya.

"We're going to hitch a ride," Cat said.

Selina looked back toward the fighting. "Should we leave the battle?"

"If we have a shot at the scepter, yes," I responded.

The witch with Abel nodded, coming in our direction as she yelled out to another witch that she'd be back. It was interesting. Many of the soldiers left at the camp were witches and not Kaizer's vampires. Rustling on the other side of the tent sounded, and Cat grinned a smile so similar to Daya I almost laughed.

"New plan," she said before disappearing into the tent.

A thud, the sound of zippers, and a few moments later, Cat re-emerged in a cloud of blue wearing the clothes of the other witch. She pulled the headpiece down low, tipping her chin up to wink at us and leaning in close. "I'm going to take him deep into the woods, away from the fighting. Once I make the portal, you two can jump through from inside the tent."

Lifting the canvas of the tent, both Selina and I slid underneath and waited. Cat's voice boomed, advising that the other witch asked her to take him instead. Abel grunted, not giving a response, but footsteps stopped right outside of the tent. At the whoosh of Cat's magic, we gave them both a beat to jump through, and then we followed.

"You useless witch." Abel turned to us, staff in hand. All the color in his pale face drained, leaving him gray and ghostly. His hand sparked before he remembered what he was holding, and Cat snatched the staff from his grasp.

Selina moved quickly, tucking her dagger beneath his chin, and I slid to his back, holding another blade to his spine.

"Care to share what Kaizer has planned?" I purred.

I might have been in love with Cat. Not genuinely, but damn, was she impressive. Watching her and Selina interrogate Abel was straight out of some sort of fantasy I never knew I needed. We'd brought magic suppressant with us, figuring it would be a good last resort if we needed to escape. None of us thought we'd be using it to try to get information from one of Kaizer's advisers, but hey, it was a turn of events I didn't mind.

Selina had tied his hands after we suppressed his magic and quickly scaled the tree to force him to hang by his wrists. Cat shook her hand after the last blow to Abel's jaw, the skin on her knuckles splitting. I hadn't needed to step in yet. Only watched the two ladies work with my arms crossed. Cat tilted her head for me to come forward, and I listened.

"You're not tired of this yet?" I asked as I rolled up my sleeves.

Abel spat a wad of blood at my feet before he snapped his gaze up to me in resilience. I spun his body, letting him twist until his arms were contorted and his face pinched with the pain.

"Very well. How much do you know about the other side, Bonda?"

Just a sneer was his response.

"I'm not sure which of my ancestors it comes from, but apparently, the sirens have this gift. It has to do with emotions—empathy. Somewhere along the line, someone in my family must have slept with one because I have it. I can see exactly how you feel. I see the nerves in the air around you. I see the trepidation, and I see the desire to live, wrapped around it all."

The curl of his top lip relaxed and separated from his bottom with surprise.

"Oh, do you know what I can do?"

There weren't too many people who knew of this gift, something many sirens were able to do with ease. It took me years to even understand it, and the help of Uma in the grand library on the island. I thought something in my mind was broken when it started. Many people who had extra . . . gifts got them at a younger age. But mine didn't manifest until I was well into my adulthood. There was a single book in the entire library out of tens of thousands of books that spoke about it. And within those pages, I realized it wasn't just the ability to see.

I ran my hand through the cloud of emotions around him, and I grabbed onto it. Abel gasped as I guided them to something darker, the cruelest of his fears taking hold. The vein on his temple pushed against the tight skin there. His forehead sweat, his eyes closed, and I sat back as the magic took root and twisted around his brain cells. It wasn't a visual thing. He wasn't experiencing himself drowning in water or being eaten by a monster of the Inbetween, but his body was reacting as if it was true. It didn't know the difference between the emotions overtaking him.

Selina smiled at me; I'd used these gifts for other. . . more enjoyable things fairly recently. She stepped behind me, out of my view, since she couldn't contain her smirk. Abel squirmed, thrashing as his mouth opened like a fish thrust out of water. I wrapped my hand around both his wrists and pulled back the magic before bringing his gaze to mine.

"Anything you'd like to say?"

Again, he stayed quiet. I lifted my hand, and he finally spoke one word, "Okay."

"What was that?" I asked as I moved closer.

"Okay!" He gasped. "Just, don't do it again. Please."

Abel glanced up at his restraints, the question to be released before he spoke. His magic was suppressed, and the women had thoroughly beaten him, so I decided to indulge. With a quick swipe, his body fell to the ground, and he pushed himself up on all fours with a pained huff. We watched as he righted himself, but not enough to get on his feet.

"Kaizer is not himself any longer. Whatever he's doing with that journal." He shook his head, blood falling to the ground in the movement. "The cost of what he gained was high."

"What is he planning to do?" Cat asked.

"The Flame,"—Abel used air quotes—"wants the wall to come down. He needs Daya to wield the scepter and remake the world."

"We already knew that," I said.

"You don't know that Kaizer gave the last bit of himself for a backup plan. You're all fucked, even with that useless piece of metal." He nodded to the scepter staff. "You're done for. If it's any consolation, I lost faith in my king some time ago. I knew what Athena and Joseph were doing. I should have done something. I thought what I was doing was for the greater good of Sanjry. Death is the least I deserve for betraying my kingdom."

Abel hung his head low, but Cat tucked the tip of her blade under his chin and lifted his gaze to hers. "Tell me exactly what the backup plan is, and I'll make your death quick."

Chapter Fifty-Five

Dayanara

I pulled Zuri's wrist from my mouth, making sure not to take too much blood that it would leave her at a disadvantage. Axel drank from me, while Zuri drank from him, forming a quick triangle of power to re-up mid-battle. A growl formed in the back of my throat as I realized more people were pouring onto the field, and one of those people was Adriana.

Axel and Zuri quickly noticed what I did and fell into step behind me. I heard one of them peel off, the sounds of grunts and a soldier meeting their end, but I kept my eyes ahead. Adriana hadn't noticed me yet, but the moment she did, oh, the fear in her eyes brought me more joy than I'd thought possible. A few of her sanction members were with her, and she turned to back away just as the others noticed me. If she were to retreat now, she'd look like even more of a coward. Her lips tightened into a line as she kept on her path toward me.

"Remember what I told you the last time I saw your sorry ass?" I seethed.

She lifted her chin but couldn't hide the wobble in her lip. Pointing a finger toward me, she advised the witches to attack me. The first one swung her blade, but I had my witch magic streaming toward her chest already. The moment it touched her, I slammed my knife into her ear and moved to the next. She was quicker than the first, and the tip of her sword sliced through the air, a small cluster of my blood-crusted hair falling with it.

I yelled, kicking her right in the chest and pouncing on her body as she fell. My blade went straight through her heart before she hit the ground, and I jumped off. Turning to Adriana, I smiled, hooking my finger in the air for her to come forward. Adriana had not been a warrior for some time, but she preferred a double-sided spear when she was.

She twisted it in her hand in what I assumed was muscle memory. There were some things our bodies didn't forget, no matter how much time passed. A blast of magic had her flying through the air, one side of the spear pointed toward me. I blocked her path with a shield of air. Her body jerked, but she found her footing and stood before me.

"Do you ever wonder if Rosa knew what Kaizer was doing?" she asked as we circled each other.

I did. I wondered if I should have listened, if things could have been avoided had I believed the cranky old bitch. But what's done was done, and there was no going back.

"This was inevitable," I said as I tossed my sword from hand to hand. "There will always be someone who wants more than they're given. For you to follow someone like that, a vampire, *a man*, you deserve what is coming."

My magic twisted around the hilt, extending to the blade's tip in sparks of great violet power. Adriana knew the fight was pointless, but I had to give it to her. She fought like a bruja in the end. A warrior's scream burst from her throat as she charged me, disconnecting the two pieces of the spear to hold each end in hand. My magic whipped through the air in the form of a lasso before it pierced her back. She twitched, and I threw an elbow into the side of her head. Her movements were jerky, but she still jutted one of the spears toward me. I pushed more power into the magic holding her, and she gasped as her hands flexed, forcing her to drop her weapons.

"You know, I've been thinking about what loyalty means. 'May the Acna rule long, may the brujas remain loyal.' We've been saying it for centuries. Loyalty because of fear might not be the way, but *disloyalty* because of fear truly shows who you are."

I gripped Adriana by her hair and yanked it hard enough that her jaw clicked and her eyes squinted. "I don't care if I rule long. I don't care if my true people question me with good intent. But I do care about sellouts. Brujas who care not of their own."

The indiscernible sound of bone breaking squelched as I broke through her ribs and pierced her heart. It stopped mid-beat, dark red blood pooling at the wound and dripping down her stomach. Her mouth opened, her teeth stained crimson as she made a final grunt. I yelled a guttural, primal sound as I spun to see who was next. Zuri was still nearby but fighting her own fight. The stone bracelet on her wrist glowed, something I gifted to her and the rest of the lobos for protection. Zuri's flesh melded into a beast of fur, teeth, and claws. The faint glow of yellow surrounded her, the shield spell I'd made just for them taking place. It took time to have it activated by their transition, but her body was too vulnerable. No matter how fast she moved, she wasn't protected without some sort of armor or witch leather.

Zuri tipped her caramel snout back and howled. The sound sent every hair on my body on end, made my heart flutter with the power she exuded. Heavy paws hit the ground around the battlefield, all with the same yellow glow around them. They howled back, and there was something intensely beautiful about the way Zuri was the start of this. She growled at her opponent, her ears pointing forward as she bared her teeth. Then she moved so fast I hardly recognized what she'd done. The vampire lay on the ground, neck turned at a wrong angle as large teeth marks leaked pools of blood around them.

The lobos attacked with ferocity, the Sanjryan clearly shocked and unprepared to face them. The shields wouldn't hold forever, but they could shift back into their other forms by the time they waned.

My neck prickled, my instincts warning me of something I couldn't see. I spun, nothing jumping out at me until Cat, Paxx and another woman ran full speed ahead toward me. They were yelling something, panic in their eyes, but the war raging around me made it difficult to home in on them. A cloud of blue surrounded me as Cat stepped out of a portal with the others behind her.

"We need to pull back," she gasped out.

"What's wrong?" I asked, holding her shoulders to help calm her.

"Kaizer, he's—"

A screech one couldn't forget rattled through the air, and my breath left my chest. Kaizer stood at the top of the hill, his white hair framed by that silver crown he wore in Sanjry. Suddenly, as if the sky itself went black, monsters of the Inbetween, vast in size and quantity, crested the hill.

"How?" I gasped.

Paxx handed me a bag, and I fished out Abel's head from within. "I don't know how, but I do know that it was the god of Chaos who helped."

"That one we saw in Sanjry, it must have been a test," Cat said.

Time stood still as fighting on both sides ceased and turned to the creatures. Some I'd seen before, others new, fresh and untested by time. Kaizer looked like a toddler beside them, and other witches moved between their legs to stand beside the king.

"He had them in Sanjry," Cat said. "Abel didn't tell us how they got there. Just that the witches were instructed to bring them should the battle go downhill."

"They'll kill his own people," I said.

It wasn't a surprise that he'd take a risk. He'd done it before. Kaizer lifted his hand, and the monsters pounced like they'd been unleashed. Axel and Zuri appeared beside me, and Ishani and Akari found us soon after.

"What do we do?" Zuri asked.

Magic sparked from my fingertips. "We fight."

Cutting between soldiers, we made our way to the front line, the earth beneath our feet shaking with every monster's step toward us. Lobos shifted back to their other forms, choosing to fight with blade and magic.

"Air shield formation!" I yelled.

Our soldiers were scared, and I could see it in the shaky lift of their hands and the sputtering magic. Kaizer's showed even more fear as they ran from the front line. Some beasts cut away from the herd, chasing them down instead. We could barely keep our footing by the time they'd gotten close enough for us to see their true size.

I'd seen a drill that Cat had run on the coast, one where the shields were used, only opening sporadic spaces for arrows to go through. It was genius, and I wondered why we'd never thought about it before. The air shield was tight, drowning out so much of the sound the creatures were making. They rammed into it with no concern for their well-being, black blood dripping from the crowns of their heads and snouts.

"Open!" Cat yelled.

Pockets of space opened between the shield, arrows shooting through and finding their marks. The beasts wouldn't be put down that easy, but they screeched as each tip pierced their flesh. Some of the smaller ones resembling lobos limped, the ones with minimal protection. But the ones with hides like armor kept forward. Most of these had eyes glowing red, and I couldn't help but scan them all for Chuah's dark voids.

"Forward!" I yelled, and we pushed the shield forward a step.

Axel was calculating, his eyes moving quickly from one side of the field to the other. I waited, knowing he was about to come up with a plan.

"The river," he said, drawing a line in the air with his finger. "How deep is the river at this part?"

"A little further north, and it's too deep for them to stand," I responded.

"Think they can swim?" Ishani asked.

"Not if we ice over the surface," Zuri offered.

I took count of the soldiers, we hadn't lost too many, but we might if we kept forward. We could continue pushing them, but it would take too long. Our air shields could hold, but by the time we got them out there we might have been too tired to actually fight. We needed a diversion.

"Axel, we need to lure them out there," I said.

"You mean flying?" Zuri asked.

I nodded, and all of them took a step closer to me.

"That's dangerous," Paxx inserted.

Axel agreed with me, though. "Dangerous is all we've got."

"All we need to do is draw them north, get them to the edge of where the river widens, and then you all can help push them in," I said.

It sounded easy, but goddess knows nothing has been as simple as that thus far.

"What about Kaizer?" Ishani asked.

"We'll deal with him once the monsters are taken care of. He won't be any-where near this until he's certain he's winning," I responded.

Zuri brought her forehead to mine. "Be careful."

"Please, I'm always careful." I pulled her closer into a hug.

Zuri lifted her hand, resting her palm on Axel's cheek. "You too."

He gave her a quick nod, but the smile was genuine. It made me ridiculously happy, even if I was about to fly into the jaws of a hundred beasts. They yelled for the surrounding soldiers to make space, and I called to my wings. My skin didn't change, but the wings burst from my back, heavy and strong. A crack burst through the air akin to lightning in a storm. Axel's soft skin and curls were replaced by a dark dragon, his golden-slitted eyes narrowed on me, and everyone around us screamed with shock.

Axel didn't shift into this form often. He'd said it took a lot out of him—to guide the essence in such a way. The lobo form was smaller, easier, and in his blood. But this one was vast, and he'd most likely need his reserves topped off before we fought. He screeched, and the monsters on the other side stopped their beating against the air shield. Their sporadic patches of hair stood on end, a new, bigger opponent showing up to the fight. I couldn't see Kaizer, and if I had to place a bet, he was portaled back to his camp to watch the destruction he'd caused.

A single flap of Axel's wings created wind like my magic, the second bringing his front legs off the ground, and the third, he floated in the air above the soldiers. With one more kiss to Zuri's cheek, I shot myself in the air, my wings tucked in tight until I reached the altitude I wanted, and Axel followed behind me. We backtracked slightly to avoid the edge of the airshield, and the moment we crossed over, the sounds of the creatures assaulted my ears. Too loud, too nasty, and too dangerous. Everything inside me said to run, probably one of my ancestors who had been killed by something similar. They tracked us, the ones with long necks snapping around, the more stout ones turning their bodies completely. Foam dripped from their jaws as Axel let out a roar that got the attention of the ones still trying to get through the air shield.

From here, I could see the area of the river we needed to reach, but it looked so much further than I remembered. I cut to the left of the sea of creatures, and Axel cut to the right, dipping lower to ensure they all saw him. I did the same, throwing some big balls of witch magic down to antagonize them. Some of them jumped up at me, the heights they reached a slight shock. Then we shot toward the river, the wind beat against my face, and I allowed it. I let myself feel every particle of the air around me as I moved quicker than I ever had before.

The sound of rattling between the heavy stampede caught my attention, and I glanced down just in time to see wings sprouting from one of the smaller creatures. Two more appeared, and then three and four. They appeared to be testing their wings, choppy unsure movements. I'd never seen a creature of the Inbetween fly, and I quickly cut my gaze over to Axel.

"Some of these fuckers can fly," I spoke into his mind.

He growled a response before slicing through the air closer to me. The lizard-like creatures took to the air, and I hated that they reminded me so much of the salamanders at the lake in Caldera. These were not sweet creatures spreading light across the land. They were made with one purpose—to kill. Their jaws snapped as they caught up to us, the rest of their herd still following, thankfully. I spun, flying backward to make sure I had my eyes on all of them. Three of them were going after Axel, the bigger target, but only one of them trailed me. *I'm sort of offended.*

I slid one of my throwing knives, the last one from my corset. Rolling it in my hand and taking into consideration the wind and speed we were flying at, I tossed it through the air. I added a bit of air magic to the throw, shielding it from some of the wind and adding a push. It cut through the left wing, and I barrel rolled as it lost control and spun through the sky. One of the creatures was too close to Axel, but I knew he saw it. His head slightly turned in the direction it was coming.

Suddenly, Axel stopped beating his wings and free-fell, and it passed him. He grabbed the beast in his claws, and the sound of its neck snapping made it to me over the wind. The last two seemed to understand that this wasn't going to be easy as they picked up speed. One went above him, the other below, and they mimicked every small turn Axel tried to make. I went toward the one below. My magic sparked in my hand on its own accord, the feeling of wanting to protect him coursing through my veins. The top creature dropped onto Axel's back, and I shot my magic through the air for the one beneath him.

The river bank was close, and portals sporadically popped up beneath us, a few yards from the monsters still following. They were close, but many of the vampires were still running at full speed. I watched as some of my witches offered them help, widening their portals and bringing more and more of them forward. The creature dodged my magic, and I ground my jaw as its mouth opened, exposing sharp teeth and aiming right for his left wing. I had to time it correctly, and I waited a beat to make sure Axel's pace didn't change. He kept the same speed, and I let out a breath, opening a portal right below Axel's wing and watching the beast shoot right through it, the other side of the portal opening up above me.

My sword was ready, and I sliced it in half. I watched the two sides of its body separate as it showered the ground in black blood. One-half fell atop one of the larger monsters, blinding it and making it stumble, which took out two of the smaller ones beneath their vast paws. The other half splattered across the ground, and I looked back to Axel.

He had the creature in his jaw, limply hanging and breezing in the wind. Axel dropped it atop one of the monsters following us, and the impact killed the one he aimed for. We'd made it, and we both skimmed over the water. Axel shifted back to his other form and wrapped us in a tidal wave. The beasts snapped at us from the edge, sniffing the water but not going any further. *Perfect.*

Our army lined up behind them, and I watched as the air shield was built piece by piece. I waited until it was big enough for the creatures not to be able to back up and shot me and Axel into the clouds. There was a certain peace here. No battle, no blood or violence. Just the soft orange glow of the sky and the fluffy white clouds encompassing us. There was no time to appreciate it as I aimed us back on the front line, spotting Zuri in the crowd.

Our feet hit the earth harder than I planned, a small crater forming around us. "How's your reserves?" I asked Axel.

"I didn't hold that form for long. I'm good," he responded as he wiped sweat from his forehead.

Ishani surveyed us both with a once-over before she lifted her sword to the sky and yelled, "Forward."

The creatures were rallied, not noticing their defeat until it was too late. They snapped at each other, turning with every step we took closer.

"Forward!" Ishani yelled again.

A splash sounded, the water taking one of the large beasts captive from the height of the waves rippling from the bank.

"Time to ice," Zuri said.

Ishani nodded, creating a portal and not telling us what they had already planned. Before I could ask, they were gone. Ishani's bright magic popped up on the other side of the river, and she stepped out onto the water with Zuri behind her. Ice formed beneath their feet with every step they took. Others popped up, Akari and Paxx portaled by a Dusran witch, with another set on their other side. The water raged with every beast it took prisoner, but everyone was far enough that the rippling didn't cause them to lose their footing. Zuri went far to the left, and I pushed the air shield further as I watched them all separate. The rush on the water's surface ceased, muffled by the thick layer of ice they formed. Paxx stood the furthest from them, his arms straining, but I didn't see any ice forming.

"He's trapping them," Axel said as he watched. "He's creating a wall within the water."

Fucking genius.

"Forward!" I yelled, only a few feet between us and the river's edge.

The smaller creatures scratched their thick claws into the dirt but couldn't keep their position. They screeched, a sound worse than before, and something close to fear bloomed in their eyes. We pushed the last ones in, and Axel bent down to the river's edge. He placed both of his hands atop the water, and I watched as the surface quickly crystallized. The face of a monster burst through the surface as he worked, and everyone else with water magic joined him until all the creatures were stuck in a prison of ice. A few of them beat their thick skulls against the ice, small fissures spreading like a spider web before icing over again. The current was too strong here to fight too much longer, and bubbles formed, disappearing with the impact of the hard surface until the last of them drowned.

Chapter Fifty-Six

Zuri

As if part of the plan, the Sanjryan army appeared the moment the creatures were gone. But now, our backs were to the river. I rushed across the ice to Daya and Axel to ensure they were both okay. The Sanjryan army was closing in, but they weren't close enough to engage just yet.

"Good work," Daya said with a tilt of her head to the frozen river.

"Thanks." I beamed, always a sucker for any sort of admiration from her.

Axel pulled his weapon out. "Don't get too excited."

We weaved through the soldiers, and I was still confident in our numbers. If Kaizer had any other tricks up his sleeve, now would be the time. Otherwise, the rest of the battle would be fought purely metal against metal, magic against magic.

Otto shouldered his way through his soldiers, his countenance pissed at the lack of death on our side. Both lines stood still, yet Kaizer still not on the field. We waited, getting into formation and preparing for whoever moved first. I should have known that the moment Daya saw Otto, we'd be the ones to be pushing forward.

"Let's end this!" she belted.

Our soldiers needed no extra push. We all followed her, the air tight with anticipation. I'd seen this side of Daya, but only in short windows. I hadn't gotten to witness the true weapon she was. Didn't get to see the ferocity and focus she fought with on a battlefield. The fact she was using a weapon that I crafted for her was really the icing on the cake. I watched it glimmer with her purple magic, the dark alloy of the blade like a pool of ink. It was originally supposed to be a gift for a truce, to get her to look at me and understand that I didn't mean to hurt her. Deep down, I hoped that it would be used to reclaim her land, to cut down those who wanted to oppress her. As she swung it out, I thought back to all the intention I put into it.

My father used to say that a blade that was truly made for someone could take on a life of its own—a near sentient being, becoming one with the wielder. If it was forged with love, with desire, with the hope that it would swing true, it was an unstoppable weapon. I never told her what it truly meant for me to make it for her—that it was a sacred thing among my people. I just hoped that it did the job it was meant to do.

It was pure chaos at the center of the fighting. I dodged a soldier coming for me, kicking the back of their knee and causing them to fall. My first slash was at their ankle, not allowing them to stand. My second was between the joints of their armor, through their back, and into their heart. There was no time to think, as another soldier was already upon me. I'd lost track of Axel but saw Daya a few feet away, taking on two soldiers herself with ease. I froze their feet, but this soldier must have stayed in the camp because fire burst from them and melted it immediately.

The only thing I could hear was the clink of their armor as they kept moving toward me. They swung their blade, and I blocked it with my own. We circled each other until they overpowered me, and my sword slid from theirs. The soldier moved quickly, but I anticipated the elbow they'd throw. Ducking low, I kicked out their feet, and they hit the ground hard. They gasped out a breath, and I dug my blade into their neck, not caring about the damage I'd done.

Few things would bring me back to such gruesome fighting. There weren't many people or things I cared about enough, but Daya was one of them. A presence I couldn't forget overtook my senses. One that was ingrained in my soul and in my body. He'd marked me wounds that would never heal, scars that would never go away. I hated that my side burned with the memory, that I could feel every ridge and welt like I'd just received it. Part of me would stay on that volcano and in the lower levels of Kaizer's home. Daya was right. Pieces were stolen, but the ones I'd been slowly replacing them with were even bigger than what was taken.

"Zuri, nice to see you on your feet," Otto said with a cruel smile.

Daya immediately met me at my side, and Axel wasn't too far behind her. This was my fight, but there was no way they'd let me do it alone. My hands didn't shake, my voice didn't waiver, and my footing didn't stumble as I lifted my blade in the air.

"You burned me, but you did not break me," I said.

"Pity, you looked pretty damn broken when you were naked on the ground of that volcano," he tossed back.

A pool of Daya's magic fell around our feet, and I knew she wanted to pounce. It sparked, not hurting Axel or me, but ever flowing and moving.

"Your fire forged the weapon that will be your demise," I responded.

Without another word, I attacked. He smirked, his chin tucked as he watched me without concern. They had drugged me, using whatever was the last of the suppressant from Daya's mother. They thought me weak, feeble, frail. But that was far from the truth. I was the daughter of the greatest warrior in the history of Arkhia, daughter of the most spirited woman in our tribe. I was born of love for our people, and I would not let them down.

Otto's brow raised as I spun, quick and nimble, dodging his first blow. He was large, stocky—not flexible like I was. Daya had told me before that the Sanjryan fought with their bodies, not their minds, and that they used uncalculated brute force. She was right. Otto put all of his strength into the next move, anger in the curl of his lip. He swung his blade, and I dodged but didn't see his elbow follow the movement. The impact of it on my temple reverberated through my body, and the corners of my vision darkened for a second. Otto looked pleased with himself as he circled me, and Daya and Ax stepped closer. I held my hand out for them to hold. A little knock on the head wasn't going to stop me. I'd seen and fought through worse.

I let my instincts guide me. Paxx had once said that my body knew how to avoid danger, and that I should always listen. Everything around me quieted, my heart beat loud in my ears. Not just my heart beat, two others beat with mine.

I let it push me like a war drum. I moved with every single thud, never staying in one place for long. Fire erupted from his hands, jumping from his sword and toward me. *Thud*, I stepped to the left. *Thud*, I conjured water beneath the flames, swallowing it before it reached me. *Thud*, I was right beside him. With one more beat, I sliced my sword through the side of his neck.

His hand shot up to stop the bleeding, but it was too deep. Dark red blood spilled from the wound as he stumbled. He caught himself before he fell all the way to the ground. Daya was there, kicking him back and pinning one of his arms with her sword.

"I recognize these hands," she seethed. "I've seen them in places they should never have been."

Otto gasped, but he didn't offer any remorse. Axel's hand landed on my shoulder, his presence slowing the fast and heavy breathing I expelled. Daya looked back at me, waiting for my next move. Suddenly, I was stuck. For weeks, I dreamed of this moment. I stayed up late and held onto the future in which this happened—when I'd pay him back. I'd imagined it thousands of ways. I let it fuel me, but now that it was here, my feet wouldn't move.

Daya returned her gaze to Otto, and without another word, she chopped his left hand off and then his right. She lifted them in the air by the wrist, and she poured her magic into them. Melting flesh filled my nostrils. I knew it burned, but I felt none of it. Or at least my body didn't register the pain. What was burning in my nose, when I'd been burned in so many other places. Stark white bones were left, and Otto watched in horror as his hands washed away from existence. She kept some of his finger bones, turning to me and offering them as a gift.

I wasn't sure why that broke me from the trance, but it did. I grabbed the bones, tucked them into my pocket, and spun the hilt of my sword in my hand. Otto's mouth was open on a soundless scream, and I straddled his chest, his breathing so rapid I knew he didn't have much time left.

Leaning in close to his ear, I whispered, "History will not remember your name. You will not be known as a conqueror. You will not be known as anything. For I will live on, even with these scars, *I will live.* Your bones will turn to dust in the earth, and only the worms will mourn you."

Without letting him respond, I planted my blade in his chest. His heart ceased, the last exhale left his lips, and his eyes stared up at the sky forever. I screamed, tears streaming down my face and onto his body as I put all of my weight on the sword's hilt. But my side stopped with the phantom burning. There hadn't been a moment since returning to Dusra where I *wasn't* aware of the scars. But now, I didn't even feel them. My clothing didn't brush against the ridges uncomfortably. The pure relief in that had me screaming again, my chest heaving with all the emotions mixing together. Daya turned to fight, unable to stand by and watch as more soldiers came closer.

Axel lifted me from Otto and he pulled me into his chest. He let me cry, Daya stopping anyone from getting close enough to hurt us. I peered back at Otto's lifeless body, and my crying ceased. My pain resolved. Daya pressed her boot into the stomach of a soldier for leverage and pulled her bloodied blade from him.

"You okay?" she asked, swiping a tear still running down my cheek with her free hand.

"I'm perfect."

With Otto gone, Abel dead, and Kaizer nowhere to be found, their army aimlessly fought. Many of these men and women weren't seasoned soldiers. It was evident in the hesitation they moved forward with. I'd been around enough warriors to spot them from afar, and it was sad the extent Kaizer went. All for the desire to conquer and for *my* woman. *Our* woman, I corrected. She was mine as much as she was Axel's. And if I was being honest, nobody owned her.

We had three teams of soldiers and had only used two to get this far. Sanjry was defeated, and wherever Kaizer was, he had to know. Paxx had the scepter staff. We didn't have the journal, but we didn't necessarily need it. We knew where Chuah was, and we knew what he wanted. The journal was a guise, but we certainly didn't want it to end somewhere it shouldn't be and create a new monster. A new fire burned in Daya after we took Otto down. Her face was covered in blood, her eyes shining like bright stars among the crusted crimson.

She hadn't tapped into her Acna power, and I wondered if she was saving it for Kaizer. The wings she was able to conjure without much issue, but tapping into the power of all her ancestors was something she had more difficulty with. But I felt the focus in her, and I was just waiting for the moment she unleashed all of that beautiful power. She and Axel cut to the left, but whimpering in the distance had me going in the opposite direction.

One of my lobos was on the ground with a sword in his chest and charred fur surrounding the wound. The sounds he made had my mind reverting back to my parents' death, but I knew he needed my help, so I stayed focused.

"Can you shift back?" I asked.

All he was able to do was a faint tip of his nose in confirmation.

"As soon as I pull this out, I need you to shift. I'll heal you once you're in your other form." I rubbed down his cheek.

His eyes blinked slowly, and I gripped the hilt of the sword as carefully as I could. Holding my gaze in his, I yanked the blade. He didn't shift immediately, and I panicked for just a moment until his body vibrated with the change. It was slow; most of us shifted in the blink of an eye, but I could see all the pain in his stare as he tried. As soon as he was back in his other form, I tore his shirt and pressed my hand against his umber skin.

"It's going to be okay," I said as his eyes rolled back.

The sword, by some sort of miracle, had missed his vital organs. I felt the tears through his muscles and a fracture in his ribs, but his heart still beat strong, and his lungs were pumping just fine. He grasped onto my forearm as the worst of it peaked. As much as I wished I could do this pain-free, it wasn't possible. I could help the pain after I was done mending the wound, but not before. My hands glowed yellow, finding another wound near his hip that needed attention. His fur was so thick in his lobo form that I didn't see it originally.

"Thank you," he rasped. "Had you not come when you did. . ."

I pulled my healing magic back in and smiled. "I was exactly where I needed to be. You're more than welcome. You should get back to camp."

Goddess, did it feel good to heal someone. He ran off, and I had been so focused on healing him that I didn't see the Sanjryan coming my way. The soldier's eyes went wide, slumping forward and exposing Ishani behind him.

"East side is almost wiped out. They're pushing everyone in this direction. That way we can finish this," she said as she tossed a braid over her shoulder.

As soon as the words left her mouth, a stampede of Sanjryan soldiers ran toward us. We were the only ones on this side and were outnumbered five to one. The fuckers seemed to notice it at the same time we did and smiled and joked with each other as they pressed closer.

"We need help," I spoke into Axel's mind.

Ishani, to my surprise, sheathed her weapon and stepped in front of me. My friend was typically overly positive, but I was a little worried she'd lost it. Until I remembered the blood-bending. I still wasn't used to the fact she was capable of such a thing. Part of me was hurt that she'd kept it from me, but I was the last one to judge for omissions.

The soldiers darted toward us, and Ishani simply lifted her hands. Something fell over her, her head falling back and a deep exhale pressing out between her lips. Every single one of the Sanjryan stopped mid-run, some of them balancing on one foot, others crouched down like they were ready to jump.

"Ish," I said, bewilderment in my tone.

She smiled as she snapped her fingers and the soldiers. . . disappeared. More specifically, the air was filled with their blood. A cloud of red haze surrounded us, the droplets suspended in the air. More Sanjryan soldiers appeared, Axel now joining us at our backs.

"Hey, what's going. . . " He trailed off as his gaze landed on his twin.

Ishani took another breath. With her shoulders square and her hands outstretched, the mist began to vibrate. The small droplets joined together, creating spears of sharp blood. It was the craziest thing I'd ever seen in my life—it didn't even seem possible. My mouth dropped open in amazement as I glanced over to find Axel with the same look on his face as mine. The Sanjryan soldiers didn't know what hit them. The blood spears flew through the air as if they were released from the world's strongest bow. They found their targets, ending them on impact.

Ishani's strong form shuddered slightly, and I was there immediately to hold her up.

"Thanks, Zuri," Ishani said as she wiped her brow.

"Um, no, thank you," I said. "That was. . ."

"Incredible," Axel finished for me.

"I didn't know if I'd be able to do it on that scale again," she laughed. *Laughed.*

I placed my hand on her and let it light with healing magic just in case, but she was perfectly fine.

"I'm fine this time," Ishani said. "Took a lot, but not in the same way as before."

Ishani was one of the few of us without blood smeared over every inch of our bodies, but not because she hadn't been in the fight. She always cleaned herself throughout fighting, something she'd done as long as I could remember. I'd heard Axel make an argument that using any extra magic could put her at a disadvantage, but she always continued doing it. She said she hated feeling all the lives on her, which I now knew meant more than it seemed.

Her emerald eyes narrowed on something behind me, and her lip pulled back. Daya's purple smoke exploded at my side, and her fingers tangled in mine immediately. She looked in the same direction as Ishani and sneered.

I turned, finally setting eyes on the king of Sanjry. His hair was pulled back in a messy bun, and it felt like centuries had passed since the last time I saw him. Where his skin was once blemish-free and smooth, patches of red were left behind. Well-rested eyes were now exhausted, small lines forming where there were none before.

"Remember the plan," I whispered to Daya.

Her fingers gripped mine tight, and I would have pulled away from the pain had it been anyone else. Kaizer stared at us unmoving, long enough for Paxx to find us too. The five of us stood like a wall. We didn't waiver as he made his way to where we stood. This side of the battle fought for each other and wouldn't stop any time soon.

Chapter Fifty-Seven

Kaizer

Otto and Abel were dead. More than half of my army was still without magic, and the other half were defeated. I'd been promised victory, power, and the woman I deserved. But now, all of it seemed out of my reach. All but Daya, who stared at me from across the battlefield with a hate she reserved specifically for me. Her new friends and family surrounded her, and the soldiers around us dissipated, removing themselves from the path between us.

Even with the gift from the Flame—or the god of Chaos—it wasn't enough. I didn't exactly care who I spoke with in the journal provided they followed through with their promises. When I'd seen the beasts Joseph brought into Sanjry—a gift from the Flame, I should have known then. I didn't *want* to know. He said that evil had to be fought with more evil. But those creatures, they were beyond evil. For the second time, I was convinced to use tactics that hurt my own soldiers. I had no idea where Joseph was now. He left early this morning with a witch and hadn't returned.

"I did all of this for you, you know," I spoke to Daya.

Zuri and Axel crowded her, and Paxx took a step in front of the both of them. I reminded myself to keep an eye out for him. He moved fast, too fast, the last time we'd been in proximity. Not even my advisers had registered his movement before he had a blade pressed to my neck.

"You did all of this for *you*," Daya snapped back.

That was partially true. But I did it for us. For what we could have been. I realized now there was no convincing her. She'd made her decision a long time ago, and I was a fool to think otherwise. My head felt overwhelmed by so many feelings and voices. It was hard to decipher what was me and what was the being in the journal. There was a simultaneous emptiness, like the things that made me *me* were taken and replaced with something else. Filled to the brim and unable to wade through the thick tar.

My hand twitched at my side, my left eye following suit. I hoped that none of them saw, but Daya's gaze fell to it immediately, her features going puzzled.

She thinks you're weak. What do we do to people who think us weak?

That voice. Not my voice. But my body reacted as if it was mine. My blood boiled, and my muscles went tight. My fangs exposed in a hiss, and I moved forward. Each step was hurried, and as if I didn't make the steps myself, I was before Daya. Only Daya, Zuri, and Axel remained. The rest of them ran off to continue fighting. There weren't too many left, but enough for this one-on-one battle to become something more.

A small sliver of my consciousness broke through, and my face relaxed momentarily as my lip quivered. "He promised me everything." It was quickly snuffed down, and I yelled, "You are MINE!"

Her furrowed brows rose high, and she abandoned whatever state of confusion she was in at my words. A phantom tugging pulled at my body, much like what happened in my mind. I knew being so close to the journal's influence had clouded my head, but it had yet to influence my body. Not until Joseph brought me some sort of black potion and said it would make me stronger. He'd cut into me, advising that it was needed for this type of potion. After that, everything inside me had changed.

Before I could assess it, Daya was already too close. I'd never seen a woman fight with such ferocity. Even when I'd seen her in battle, it was never like this. Gone was the leisure, cocky grin she typically wore as she swung her blade. When it was all a fun little game for her. The look of pure determination, of wrath, vengeance, and retribution replaced it. She'd rarely evoked fear in me, but the gut instinct that she was a predator and I was merely feeble prey rose in me with bile.

I'd barely blocked the last blow as I stumbled over a rock on the ground. She left me no space to be aware of my surroundings as she berated me with strike after strike. She twisted, swinging her blade low, and I stabbed mine into the ground at the last second to stop her from making contact. The metal impact echoed through the air, the force she used bending my blade and nearly shattering it.

I'd forgotten how fast she was, and as she spun again with my blade stuck in the earth, I had to protect myself solely with the armor on my body. Lifting my forearm, I stopped her from getting to my heart, but the definite snap of my bone within my armor sent pain coursing through me. I slid my blade up, forcing it between hers and my arm, but she pressed in harder. Her hair fell in front of her eyes, the only thing visible above her sword as she held it horizontally and continued pushing.

This was the closest I'd been to her since she left. I held strong, wanting to keep the proximity. I looked at the map of beauty marks across her face, how her violet eyes flashed with her power every couple of moments. Even covered in the blood of hundreds, her scent still wafted toward me with the wind. Her nose twitched with fury, her normally full lips tight.

She growled as she quickly pulled back, and it wasn't until she took a step back that I realized why. It was the warmth I realized first—hot and wet. My organs went into overdrive, every pump of my heart spilling more and more blood from the wound at my hip. I knew it should have crippled me with pain, but I tried my best to tuck it away.

"Daya," I said as I pressed one of my hands to the wound.

She held the dagger in her hand and let my blood drip to the floor. The drips suddenly suspended in the air, blobs of red floating like stars shooting across the sky. Daya winked before waving bye with her dagger in hand. I didn't understand what was happening. The blood continued floating, and the surrounding soldiers all burst. Blobs of their blood suspended with mine, like whatever force held us to the ground, didn't apply to them.

"What is—"

Axel walked through the mist of red. None of it touched him, but repelled from his body as he walked in my direction. I tried to move, but my feet were bolted to the ground. The sword in my hand turned into ash, and my magic was far from my reach. Axel's facial expression matched Daya's, so similar I wondered if they'd practiced. He stopped and stared me down. I tried to move from where I was, but I was still stuck. Axel said nothing, only bore his gaze into my soul for a long while until he finally spoke.

"I've wondered what I'd do when I finally came before you." Axel stepped around me, out of my sight, and passed my peripheral. "You've hurt many people. Your own, my own, those from Caldera."

Pain wrenched up my spine, every single vertebra feeling as if it was being pulled apart from the other. I couldn't do anything. My only option was to feel every ounce of the pain.

"Above all, you hurt people that *I* love."

My mouth opened on a scream. I could feel it bursting from me, but the sound never made it out. Axel stopped his pacing directly in front of me, and as if he had the gift of fire, my hand went up in flames. I gained back enough control to shake them in panic, but the flames only grew higher up my body.

"You think you can lay claim to Daya? Think you can torture Zuri without repercussions?"

Flames licked over my entire body, the smell of my exposed skin burning, the metal of my armor scorching hot enough it turned orange and then red.

"The only reason I'm not killing you now is because Daya has laid claim to *your* life. I'll be damned if I get in her way."

Everything went black. I floated in absolute nothingness. No people, no sky or clouds, or trees. No sounds, and for some reason, the lack of *everything* felt heavier than the presence of it. As if it would swallow me whole and never let me leave.

I gasped for breath. My vision was hazy, but my body was still locked up. I blinked, realizing that my body wasn't being held the same way as before, but I was tied up with heavy chains. Ones that I'd seen Lupe use. Made of some material that absorbed magic suppressant and continuously pushed it into the body it touched. I could still smell it in my nostrils, where they'd most likely made me inhale it.

The ground was covered in some sort of writing, swirling symbols I couldn't immediately decipher, but something told me I knew them. They glowed pink and green, pulsating with. . . the beat of my heart. I was surrounded by bodies; some I recognized, and others I didn't. All of them wearing the colors of Dusra and Caldera, none of my own. At the center of them was Daya. She didn't look the way I'd last seen her. Her body was free of all the blood, but that hate still burned in her gaze. I tried to pull from my bounds, but they were too tight. My lips moved to speak, but every effort to make a sound was thwarted by. . . something.

Daya stepped forward and pointed to one of the symbols. "Blood magic. It's a powerful thing. Something I haven't even tapped into, but a couple of my brujas have."

She watched as I struggled to speak—as I tried to plead with her. She mocked me, mouthing silent words until she kicked the dirt beneath the symbol, and my voice rushed back into my throat. I swallowed, trying to settle my rapid breathing.

"These other ones are far worse than merely holding your voice. So choose your words carefully," she said as she squatted down to my eye level.

"Why not kill me?" I asked.

There was hope in my voice, and I knew she detected it when she threw her head back and laughed. The laugh sent goosebumps all over my skin. It blared in the silence as no other soldier made a noise. Axel was glaring the same way he did before he broke whatever illusion he had me under. Zuri twisted the double daggers in her hand, her face blank but ready.

"I have questions, and you can't answer them dead."

I ran my tongue over my teeth, tasting blood. "What do you want to know?"

Daya pulled out my journal from somewhere behind her back. She flipped through the pages, and I fought the urge to yank it from her gasp. That thing that had wormed its way into my mind screamed that it was not in my possession.

"Do you know where the other pieces of the scepter are?"

"He did not assist with that. He doesn't know, or he would have had them centuries ago," I responded.

"So you just happened upon the staff?"

"Essentially."

It wasn't quite that simple. We'd had many dig sites. There wasn't much of Sanjry left with undisturbed soil. Caldera took much more time, but the moment that agreement was signed, I started searching. I'd kept Daya busy, and Lupe made sure she didn't go anywhere near the sites. Not that she knew the specifics of what we were looking for.

"You truly believe that you were born to rule it all?" she asked.

"Born, I'm not sure. But we're here now."

Daya sneered. "To be clear, your 'here' is without your magic, doused in suppressant, and within chains."

"I can still help you," I said.

"Help me what?"

Come on. Come on. Come on. How can we stay alive? I got it.

"Help you find the other pieces," I blurted.

"You just said you don't know where they are."

I had to think quickly. "I know where I've already looked and where I haven't. I can give you that information if you spare me."

"Half of it could be in Bonda. That's no use to me."

I racked my brain with how else I could get out of this. Had I used all that I had to offer? Was there anything left to give? There was no way this was what fate had in mind for me. To get this far and not be successful. That wall needed to come down, and I needed to be sitting upon the High Throne.

"There's someone in Bonda trying to bring the wall down, too. If we don't do it first, they will. Who do you think would be more prepared if they bring it down?"

"Are they doing it for Chuah, too?"

"I don't know what the person in that journal promised them. I know I am to be king."

"You don't think he promised the same to them?" she scoffed.

No, I didn't. My face said all I needed to, and Daya regarded me as if I was a poor, stupid boy.

"What kingdom are they from?" she asked.

I tilted my head and raised my brows. Indicating I wanted reassurance.

"You see these glyphs in front of you? There are four. I'm rather excited to use all of them, personally. We already used the first one. If I get to the last one, you die. Your blood will harden within your heart, and your life will cease instantly. Remember what I said. Choose your words carefully."

Before I could respond, she hovered her hand over the next glyph, and pressure built behind my eye. It intensified, and I was sure that it had to be pushing out of the socket.

"Air. In their Air kingdom!" I yelled, and she backed up.

"A human?" she said in disbelief.

"I have a feeling he prefers an underdog," I responded.

Daya didn't reply. She twisted her hand into a fist, and my eye burst from my skull.

Chapter Fifty-Eight

Dayanara

Fucking blood magic. Who knew. I'd heard some stories and was starting to understand why it had died out over the years. This shit was volatile as fuck, and I loved it. Kaizer doubled over as his eye burst, and I waited for him to get it together. The fact he thought he would come out of this with his life was comical, but hey, if it got him talking, that made things easier.

Kaizer was taking far too long to accept that he had lost one eye, so I turned to Axel and Zuri. "Air makes no sense. What can a human do?"

"We don't know what the state of Bonda is. Things could have changed vastly since our books were written," Axel reasoned.

"Just look at us." Zuri motioned to everything around us.

Kaizer let out one last exhale, and I sighed. "I'm ready to kill him. There's just something beautiful about revenge, ya know? Do I at least look hot out there?"

"Very," they both answered at the same time.

"Good." I turned quickly and flipped my hair, sashaying my hips a bit for the onlookers.

Blood dripped down Kaizer's face, a crater where his eye was. I sat across from him with my legs crossed and flipped my dagger in my hand. Tossing it from palm to palm, I pointed to the next glyph with my lips. "Curious what that one is?"

"I told you what I know," Kaizer said.

Ah, the defeat in his voice was decadent. There were some more. . . personal questions I wanted to ask. I snapped an airshield down around us so the soldiers couldn't hear. I kept Axel, Paxx, Ishani, and Zuri inside. That way they could stay in the know.

"At what point were you going to bring me into this plan?" I asked.

"After we were married."

"Oh, the classic 'I'm the man of the marriage. She'll do what I say,'" I responded.

Kaizer didn't reply.

"What was your plan for Dusra?" I asked.

"Well, I thought you'd lead our joined armies. Thought it would be easy."

I scoffed. "Where is Joseph? We haven't seen him."

"I—" He stuttered. "I really don't know."

Didn't seem like a lie, but also not what I wanted. I hovered my hand over the next rune and watched as he panicked over what would happen next. He jolted, falling over from where he was kneeling and down onto the ground. With his arms chained to his back, he couldn't do much to stop the splinters growing in his bones. Just the legs. Fissures would be running from his tibia up into his femur. The sound was muffled within his skin, but the faint sound of crackling filled the air. Reminded me of embers in a fire. How kismet.

"Just kill me," Kaizer groaned under his breath.

I dismantled the airshield. "What was that?"

"Just fucking kill me!" Kaizer yelled.

"I'm happy to oblige. One more thing, and I'll make it quick. Otherwise, we'll be here for a bit longer. You were never going to be able to take down the Piedra. Without the earthstone, and I'm not sure if you're aware, but you don't have the firestone." I waited for his response, and the flare of his nostrils and widening of his eyes told me he didn't. "Not to mention the likelihood of the rest of the scepter being in Bonda. So, how were you going to do it?"

Kaizer bristled, or as much bristling as he could do, while his legs were immobile. I nodded toward him for someone to assist and stop the squirming. One of the Dusran soldiers came over and sat him on his ass, and Kaizer screamed with the pain radiating from his body.

"The scepter could remake the world," he finally said. "Things would have to be destroyed before remaking it."

"Again. How?"

"Joseph said the Bondan was tasked with that. I was simply to gather the pieces of the scepter on this side and then pick up and rule."

The amount of trust this idiot put in Joseph should be studied. Hang a tiny carrot of power before a man, and they'll do anything to catch it.

"Well, you won't be doing that, now will you?"

"Where's my army?" he asked.

"Down at the bottom of this hill, listening to you beg for mercy." I smiled. "Don't worry about what will happen to them. They staked their own fates long ago."

"And my kingdom?"

"Hm, I'm not sure yet. You're leaving behind quite the mess. Half your population is delusional. So we'll see how well they're convinced that you've been lying to them."

That wasn't going to be easy. The Flame and the Embers were ingrained into Sanjryan culture. I had no desire to rule *what* they believed, but if they used it as a way to enact violence against the rest of Malva, that would be a problem. There'd be a lot of monitoring needed. Part of the reason I never wanted to be here in this position to start with. I wanted to rule my people—protect my people. Not everyone.

Kaizer was the last of the Curran lineage, he made sure of that. I wasn't even positive who the next in line was. There was a good chance they were just as crazy as him. Some sort of person would need to be put in place from our side. No idea who would want that job.

Kaizer hung his head. My inner circle stepped forward, bracketing me. They knew what was coming next, as did everyone watching. Kaizer had given up. He had nothing left to give us. It was quiet, the grass rustling in the wind the only sound. I'd hated a lot of things in this life. A lot of people. Hate was easier than anything else, certainly easier than love. I was born into a world of despair and pain. Kaizer had brought so much of it over the last decade, and then more than I even thought possible in recent months. His death wouldn't bring the resolution of it all. There was still a lot of work to be done. But it would certainly feel really fucking good.

"Any last words?" I asked.

The despairing look of defeat on his face morphed, the laxness in his muscles tightened. His lip pulled back to expose his teeth, and when he blinked, his navy eyes were replaced with black. The same pinpricks of light sparkled in them as his whole demeanor changed. He sat up straight and pulled his face into an iniquitous smile.

The voice he spoke of was not his. "If you want to know my plans, all you have to do is come ask me."

Kaizer didn't blink as he stared at me, his gaze ancient and *wrong*. I shifted on my feet, and he tracked the movement like a cat stalking a mouse. I snapped down an additional airshield around me and my inner circle.

"I'm sure I've already told you to go fuck yourself, Chuah," I quipped.

This crowd did not know his name. But the people surrounding me did. I felt the ripple of unease extend from person to person, settling in me as well, but I couldn't show it.

"Dayanara," Chuah said through Kaizer, and I wanted to rip the content right off his fucking face. "There's no need to fight it. What's coming is coming."

"I'll take my chances."

I'd told Lucia that making the impossible possible was something I took pride in, and I wouldn't be stopping now.

"I won't lie. You've put a kink in my plans. But rest assured, they will still be happening. They can't hold me back forever, and I feel them weakening by the day with all the chaos ensuing. Surely, there's something I can offer you."

It was my mouth that moved, but I swore my voice came at as more than just my own. "Your death."

My wings ripped out of my body, and I felt my skin go lit with power. I levitated, my wings flapping enough to keep me a few feet off the ground. I jutted my hands out as my Acna powers poured out of me. It burst from me like a geyser that had been dormant for a hundred years. The impact of it sent Kaizer/Chuah barreling through the air, and I used my other hand to stop him with an airshield.

I could see all the colors reflecting off the shield with the water of the river behind it. My body shot toward them, my wings stopping me as soon as I got to where he was pressed against the hardened air. I let him drop, and he hit the ground hard. His legs were broken, and the impact had dislocated his shoulder. His body burned, not like one from fire, but from one of pure essence.

"We defeated you once. We will do it again. This time, there will be no realm in which you live. No prison to keep you safe and away. When you are free, we will take great pleasure in ripping you piece by piece."

I didn't know where the words came from, and it still wasn't my voice. I realized then that at the forefront of my mind was Valentina. Her hate fueled me, the mixture of colors from my ancestors was still present, but the cerulean of her magic seemed to be the most prominent. The power assaulted him, his body vibrating with so much of it being forced into one small vessel. The black in his eyes faded back into blue, and the vile smile he'd worn morphed back into defeat. Kaizer's body evaporated into the air, no ashes or anything left behind.

The soldiers raged, cheering and throwing their helmets into the air at the official defeat of the Sanjryan king. I continued staring at the space where Kaizer once was. Thought about the many lights I'd seen his face in. I thought back to my mother—if she was also cheering me on from the spirit world. This, after all, was what she wanted. It was her goal. One of the few things we'd been aligned on when it all came to an end. I felt my Acna power retreat, my skin returning to normal, and the weight of my wings vanishing. Zuri wrapped her fingers in mine while my chest heaved, and Axel rubbed the place on my back where my wings just were.

"We need to find Joseph," I finally said.

"We should deal with the rest of the army first," Axel replied.

Scanning the crowd, I looked for Cat, who I found pushing her way through the crowd. She tucked her sword away and glanced back at the place where I'd destroyed Kaizer. "I was down there monitoring the Sanjryans, but damn."

"You hear anything about where Joseph might be?" I asked.

She shook her head, pushing some of her hair out of her face. "Nope, nothing yet."

"Can you take a team to Sanjry? We need to deal with them, but I don't want him to get too far. If you can find them, there are tunnels in the walls that can help you hide," I replied.

"Can do. Anybody you want to send with me?" Cat asked Ishani.

"Yeah, let me help you find them," Ishani responded.

The Sanjryan army was rallied into one area, not a ton left, but some had certainly fled while we took Kaizer down. There were a lot of missing witches, I knew that for sure. Kaizer keeping them at the camp while the others got doused in suppressant had saved them. Not for long.

Axel went to the front line, Akari and Ishani already barking out orders to the generals. I saw a blue cloud in the distance and watched Cat jump through a portal with a couple others. Row by row, the Sanjryans were forced to their knees. Another line of Sanjryan soldiers faced them, and I realized that they were the high-ranking.

"They been questioned?" I asked Ishani.

"Paxx is taking them now." She nodded toward where Paxx was bounding toward them.

"I'm going to go with him," I told Ishani.

"Have a feeling about something?" she asked.

"I just want to see if they know anything."

"We'll handle these," she said before going back to the others.

Zuri went to help the healers, and Axel was assisting Ishani, so I waved my hand to get their attention, pointing toward where Paxx was, and they nodded. There were about ten vampires following Paxx, no brujas. He led them toward their own camp, taking over a tent near the edge. The camp had been cleared when the last of their army was rounded up, and from the looks of it, they rampaged for anything we could have used. Some tents were torn down, others ripped and in piles, but the one we entered was completely empty.

Paxx saw me enter and gestured for me to come to the front. "You have something you want to question them about?"

"I want to hear what they say," I responded.

With Abel, Otto, and Kaizer dead, and Joseph missing, I wondered just how much this group knew. We'd seen some of them at that party on Flame Founding and heard them discussing plans. Lord Byrne was hesitant to join, and there might have been a reason for that. He had to tell them *something* to convince them either way.

Chapter Fifty-Nine

Dayanara

One of the Sanjryan generals was already dead. Unfortunately for him, Paxx didn't have a ton of patience left. We were all at our wit-ends. Personally, I was ready for a hot shower, laying down with two of the people who made our success possible, and going to sleep. One of the Sanjryan soldiers removed their helmet, and I recognized his silver hair. I waded to the back of the tent where he stood and watched Paxx yank another Sanjryan up to the front.

"Byrne," I said, and he turned his head toward me in confusion. "I was at your estate during Flame Founding."

"I was not aware," he responded.

"Yeah, I kept it that way for a reason."

Paxx punched the man in the jaw when he didn't answer his question. I waited to see if the guy would come back from it, but he was out cold. Paxx rolled his eyes and doused him in water to wake him up.

"So, I heard you had reservations about Kaizer's proposal." I inspected my dagger and used a rag nearby to clean off all the blood and dirt from today. "Why?"

Byrne looked up to where one of his fellow Sanjryans was gasping for air and back down at his hands. The man Paxx was torturing took one final loud gasp and then went quiet. Dead. Byrne peered back at me, and I just shrugged as I continued cleaning my weapon.

"What he was saying was too good to be true," Byrne whispered.

"Very much so. But what specifically?"

"That Sanjry would sit at the top of everything. That we'd get more land, more resources. That we'd never have to fight again."

"Yeah, that all sounds too good to be true. Why'd the rest of these idiots believe him?"

"He sold it well. Not to mention, half of them would do whatever Athena said. I almost bought into it with the hope that my people would stop dying. But my wife told me she could smell the crap on him."

"Ah, women always have to save the day."

He smiled weakly as he rubbed his chest. We watched everyone die one by one, barely getting anything out of them. They were all meatheads. Just like Byrne said, they only wanted what Kaizer promised. The same way Kaizer only wanted what *he* was promised. They all met the same end.

Byrne was the last one, and Paxx went to pull him up, but I lifted my hand to stop him. "Not this one. Will you tell us what you know?"

"My wife would hate that I died for that man. She didn't even want me to fight," Byrne sighed.

"We need someone we trust to help. That could be you and your wife. If you earn that trust."

"I also don't want to be viewed as a sellout," he sighed.

"Choice is yours. You can die for your pride if that's what you prefer," I responded.

Unfortunately both my patience and Paxx's were running quite low.

Byrne examined Paxx. "What is it you're looking for?"

"You heard what I asked the others. Information on the next steps and where Joseph is," Paxx answered.

"What do you know of the Embers?" Byrne said.

"Other than them being insane?" I asked.

Byrne chuckled. "They're a vast system. There are churches in every city, but there's always a main one. If he's not in the capital, I'd bet he's hiding out in one of those churches."

"Makes sense," I said to Paxx.

"He won't stay in one place for long. We need to know what he's doing next," Paxx answered.

"Don't think because they are churches they aren't dangerous," Byrne added, seriousness in his tone.

A shiver ran through me. "Oh, I've come face-to-face with a few violent ones."

That day at the Ritual, those were no docile acolytes. They were there for one reason, and that was to kill me. The realization that I had won my land back and that I had access to my home again hit me. My mother might have had something there. She wrote down *everything* and was always in her office. There could be something, even if it was a dead end. I knew I needed to go back there.

"What do you want to do with him, Daya?" Paxx asked.

"Have Axel arrange an agreement with him. He can bring his wife and any family to Dusra while we figure out what to do," I responded.

"Thank you." Byrne bowed his head.

"Your fate is in your hands. Don't fuck it up," I said as I walked out.

The moment I stepped out of the tent, I called to my wings and shot into the air. It was late now, the light of the sky long gone and replaced with the moon and stars. I had never taken to the sky solely for peace since I had this ability. I'd seen Axel do it several times, and I understood why now. That feeling I got by just looking at the moon was amplified soaring so close to it. It tingled over my body, expanding into my wings and every burning feather adorning them.

It was hard to slow down after a century and a half of fighting. The fight wasn't anywhere close to done. But in this small pocket of time, I allowed myself to fully sit in the peace. Even as I watched the pyres go up with our fallen soldiers. I reminded myself that I'd *earned* this moment. I'd given so much of myself. Like I'd told Zuri, some pieces we'd never get back. Sometimes, those jagged edges never fit back into our souls. They left scars. Ones that we'd never forget. A constant reminder of what we'd been through—but also of our accomplishments.

I'd earned this moment to be without the pressures of everything. Even if my mind screamed that I had to be doing something. That I should have already been moving to the next thing. My heart told me to relish in the moment of success.

I soared higher and higher until the atmosphere had my breath catching. The crisp air formed snowflakes on my fingers, and I watched each one crystallize as I floated. I flapped my wings as I turned my face to the stars.

My body lit, and I became one of them. I shone just as brightly, and I felt them all flare to match. When I could no longer stand the cold and the burning in my chest increased, I shot back down to the clouds. I remember thinking as a little girl that the clouds would be fun to play in. As I got older, I'd stare up at them during the day and think to myself that the sky seemed safer than where I was. I wondered if I could wrap myself in the fluff and hide. Remove myself from the things that sought my pain—or the people, more so.

I dreamed of hopping from one to the other in the company of the moon. She'd light the path to safety, and I'd join the stars as they watched over the land. That wasn't my reality, but it brought me comfort. Even when the sky was far beyond my reach, when I was stuck in some cavern or locked beneath the palace, I'd held onto the feeling. That same sentiment I'd found embodied in Zuri and Axel. Now, I only needed to find them to know peace.

As always, my gaze landed on the pair among the crowd. I circled in the sky, watching them walk together across the camp. They were both smiling, maybe even joking, and fuck did it make me happy. The same way I always found them, they always found me. Both turned to look back and up into the sky, spotting me. Shooting down to them, I flapped my wings to slow for a better landing than the one earlier.

"Hey, you two," I said as I wrapped my arms around them.

"Taking a victory lap?" Zuri asked.

"Something like that. Where are you going?"

"Took care of the last of the soldiers. We were going to find something to eat," Axel said.

My hunger hit me suddenly, and it looked like many of us had the same thought. The cooks weren't ready yet, and we watched as they scrambled around to finish the meal. Although we'd won, there was still a heaviness in the air. In war, there truly wasn't a winner. No matter who emerged victorious, there was always great loss on either side. Death wasn't viewed as a negative thing here in Caldera or in Dusra, I'd found out, but that didn't mean it didn't weigh on the living.

A beat picked up somewhere in the distance, and my senses went on overdrive for a moment. I quickly pulled my weapon but realized it wasn't a war drum beat. It was a song of joy. The musicians came closer, a mixture of Dusra and Caldera with instruments in hand. They sat at the edge of the opening, where we waited for food, and they played. Every note got someone else up from their seat. It wasn't a song I recognized immediately until I really listened. Two songs were playing, one by my people in Caldera and one by Dusra. They combined in perfect harmony, creating a tune that had never been heard before. One that represented us.

Zuri got up from beside me and started to move with the beat, holding out her hand for me to join her. The moment my fingers grazed hers, she squeezed it tight and spun me around. There was no need for us to hide our identities this time, and I smiled at that fact alone. Our feet moved in sync, and we were quickly pulled into the heart of the dancing. Soldiers, some I'd met, some I hadn't, danced with us, twirling and stomping and clapping in pure jubilation. Ishani pushed into my space, and I didn't miss the scan of the perimeter she did.

"Xavier wouldn't have danced with me if he was here, but not even having him here still feels odd," she said.

"Day by day," I responded and lifted her hands in the air with mine. "We'll be here every step of the way."

Ishani smiled wide and sighed. "Even with all the preparation we did, I just. . . "

"Hey, I know. Nobody is faulting you for how you feel. Trust me."

"Day by day," she repeated.

Zuri grabbed one of her hands, and Akari grabbed mine, and we formed a large circle of love for our sister. I could have imagined it, but I swore the moon shined down even brighter on our circle. I swore the silvery beams put a spotlight on us, the highlights in Ishani's hair growing brighter. She tossed her face to the sky, and a star in the atmosphere grew even brighter. Ishani reached her hand out to it with her other hand on her chest.

I knew a piece of what she was going through, and if it were me, I would have been angry at Xavier for not trying everything to stay here with me. My instinct would have been to drag him to the soul-tying ceremony and make him stay. But Ishani wasn't me. She knew that they were different, that they saw things in a completely different light. She knew that they had known love and tenderness. Even if it wasn't enough to make him stay, she knew it was real. Ishani knew that giving him this one thing was the right way to end their years of back and forth. Xavier knew what he could give and what he couldn't. I respected him for knowing what she needed. Not to say he wasn't good enough for her, but Ishani deserved someone who saw life how she did, or at least enough to encourage her.

Not everyone experienced life the same way. For some, things weighed heavier than others. We couldn't be blamed for how we coped through the atrocities of this world. I was just happy to have the ones I did now. Axel, always knowing when I was thinking about him, found us at the center.

He wasn't much of a dancer, but he had perfected a very simple side to side step move. Paxx was dancing with the girl I'd seen leave his tent in the Inbetween, Selina, I thought he said her name was. He held onto her as they spoke and moved, not seeming to notice anyone around them.

Axel upgraded to a newer dance with a little more pep in it, and Zuri returned to our sides. I grabbed them both and pulled them close. Their eyes sparkled, their hands holding me even tighter. As the music transitioned to another song, I leaned my forehead into the circle, Axel following suit, and then Zuri.

"I love you both so much," I whispered. "I hope you know that."

That string that tied us all together felt like it pulled tight, and we all exhaled at the same time. My finger burned, and the sensation traveled all the way up my forearm, across my bicep, and stopped at my chest. Voices whispered somewhere in the distance, four female voices. I knew that they sensed it, too. We stepped back and pulled up the sleeves covering our arms. A tattoo wrapped around our second fingers twisted around our wrists and up our arms. I pulled the top of my shirt to the side, finding a symbol shining on my chest. Three circles interlocked with each other. It pulsed, and I somehow just *knew* what it was. I could feel their lives, their essence in the tattoo. Every thud of their hearts, every breath they took, it was evident in the mark.

The steady beat of our matching hearts played its own tune, and for the rest of the evening, that was the sound we danced to.

Chapter Sixty

Dayanara

"Has anyone heard from Cat yet?" I asked.

Ishani shook her head as she chewed her breakfast. We were taking down the camp now. Most of the tents and supplies were already collapsed and packed. The Sanjryan tents were burned early this morning and the smoke on their land still billowed, dark and wide.

Zuri set her cup down and licked some of the orange juice from her lips. "Me either."

"We were going to have to go there either way, but I was hoping she'd be able to give us a heads-up about the state of Sanjry," I replied.

"The Team should be ready. Last I checked, they were replenishing their supplies. The rest of them are going to head back with Paxx," Ishani advised.

"You figure out how you're going to avoid bringing the entire palace down to the ground?" Zuri teased.

No, I really hadn't. I knew the moment I stepped into that stupid fucking place, the urge to bring it to rubble was unavoidable. The mission to find Joseph was more important, but maybe they could rebuild after I fucked the place up.

"I'm working on it," I said.

Ishani let out a loud whistle, and a group of soldiers ran over to where we sat.

"You all ready?" she asked them.

"Yes, Commander," they all replied in unison.

"Ready when you are." Ishani tilted her head toward me.

Axel had been out all night and only went to get some sleep a couple of hours ago. I hadn't asked him if he wanted to go to Sanjry or back to Dusra, I assumed he'd want to go with me, but there was more than just us right now. He was still a king with duties, and I couldn't blame him for that.

"Give me twenty minutes and meet me by the bridge," I told them all before turning to Zuri. "Want to come with me to check on Axel?"

Zuri quickly got up and followed as we went to where he was sleeping. He was so incredibly tired he didn't even find a tent. He'd found a flat piece of land and was passed out in the long grass. With his arm over his eyes and mouth hanging open, we listened to his soft snores for a moment before waking him. He opened his eyes slowly, and I flashed him my tits, which had him sitting up much faster. Axel pulled me down to the ground with him, and I yanked Zuri with me. We laughed as we playfully fought against him and finally settled.

"Coming to see where I'm going after this?" Axel asked.

"Reading my mind?" I asked.

"No, I just know that you're already thinking of what needs to be done."

"Well, what are you thinking of doing?" I asked.

"As much as I hate to say it, I need to return with the army." He sighed as he rubbed both me and Zuri's legs.

Part of me knew that was going to be the answer, but my heart still sank with the thought of being away from him. My old self would have laughed at me for such a thought.

I sighed. "I kind of figured."

"Ishani is better for this. She can help with a portal if needed. I need to get everything in order. There's a lot to handle," Axel responded.

Zuri nodded, and the disappointment at being separated was thick in the air.

"We won't make any decisions without you. We'll come back to Dusra before moving forward with anything," I reassured.

"Have you heard from Cat?" Axel asked.

"Nope. Not yet. We're going to one of the temples first to see if Joseph is there."

Axel scanned the sky like he was trying to determine what time it was. "Now?"

"In a couple of minutes," Zuri answered.

"All right." He kissed my lips. "Be safe."

Axel turned to Zuri, and they both awkwardly figured out the proper way to say goodbye. Apparently, they were more comfortable pushing their naked bodies up against each other than with these little casual moments. To be fair, we hadn't had many since then.

"Just kiss!" I yelled.

They did as I said, laughter bubbling up between their lips.

"We'll get the hang of this," Axel advised. "I know it doesn't need to be said, but protect each other."

We left him as he strapped his weapons back on, finding the team already together at the river's edge. Dusran vampires and witches, it looked like most of the Calderan brujas had gone back to check on the status of their homes. We weren't advised of any demolition outside of the initial sweeping. It didn't mean it was impossible, and I really hoped that there wouldn't need to be a ton of rebuilding. There was too much that needed to be handled within Sanjry's borders.

"Have you all been briefed?" I asked.

Ishani affirmed, and I quickly tapped each of my weapons to make sure that I didn't forget any. I'd lost all of my throwing knives, but thankfully, there were quite a few. . . retrieved before the pyre. Zuri mimicked my movements, and when I was sure we were good, we walked across the bridge. There were eight of us—a regular portal would work as long as they moved quickly. I decided to be on the safe side and have Ishani open it to the village. The night I met Axel, the Dusran inner council had stayed within the village, she knew it well enough to portal.

We stepped out between two Sanjryan homes, and I led the way. It seemed like the news might not have gotten back to the village, or maybe they just didn't care. But there was no screaming. Nobody appeared worried about what their tomorrow would bring.

"This is. . . weird," Zuri whispered.

"I expected a little bit of mayhem," Ishani added.

"We need to find Cat and see what is going on here. Let's get into the palace first," I said.

We lifted our cloaks and moved toward the palace wall. There were still a few guards posted, but not nearly as many as when I was here. We hid behind a line of shrubbery to determine how to get in. The guards looked to be covering a lot of the wall individually, and when they turned, I opened a portal to the passageways near my old bedchamber. There was a chance there was a detection spell, but Ishani didn't know the palace the way I did.

Zuri immediately ran over to one of the spy holes. "Nobody is in here."

That was a room that constantly had people in and out of it, although it was mostly soldiers. I wasn't exactly sure what I was looking for or where I'd find it, but we continued until we'd surveyed the whole length of the palace and made it to the river before the barracks.

"It's like nothing happened here," Ishani said, puzzled.

There was a part of the tunnel I hadn't explored, one that gave the impression it went beneath the river and toward the temple within the village. It couldn't hurt to go in this way. Hopefully, it kept us undetected. The muffled sound of rushing water ran over the stone ceiling, and moisture gathered on the walls. This tunnel wasn't nearly as clean as the others, with dirt and rubble covering most of the ground. We moved through as quickly as possible. I had no desire to be stuck beneath this thing if it crumbled.

The tunnel tilted up, a significantly steeper incline than the other side. The smell of wet earth faded and was replaced with the faint smell of burning coal. A grate at the end of the tunnel had us slowing and carefully approaching to see what was on the other side. Similar to the palace, the tunnels extended, but rather than a few spy holes every few feet, large wooden doors lined the corridor.

"Do you guys hear that?" I questioned.

It was faint and could have been something on the other side of the wall, but it blared against my senses. A whistling, but it sounded. . . wet. It went in and out at an even pace, but I couldn't pin down the direction.

"No," Ishani answered, and Zuri shook her head.

I closed my eyes and focused, tracking the sound and where it was traveling from. The grate was wide enough for us to pull our bodies through, not without an extra wiggle of my hips, but we made it through, and I quickly went toward the sound. It was drawing me in, and I let out a gasp as I realized what it was.

"Cat," I shrieked.

She leaned against a wall, her hand holding her stomach as blood soaked her clothing. So much blood. A pool of crimson formed around her, streaks of it running down the tunnel. Smudged handprints started at the center of the wall in the distance, descending until they stopped where she was.

Her normally almond skin was ashen, a faint green undertone as she breathed. Zuri slid through the blood on her knees and immediately started trying to heal her. When Cat lifted her shaky hand, we all realized it was too late. It wasn't just a wound she had, but an entire gaping hole through her stomach. The light of Zuri's magic still burned, and the edges of the wound slowly knit, but it wasn't fast enough. Healing magic could do a lot, but the wounded needed to have the energy.

"What happened?" I finally asked.

"He left a couple of beasts here," Cat exasperated. "We didn't see them coming. The others chased him into the room around the corner. I stayed back. There were too many."

"Fuck, fuck, fuck," I said as I joined in Zuri's healing.

"That room." Cat swallowed. "You can sense how wrong it is as soon as you open the door."

"What's in there?" Ishani asked.

"It feels like the opposite of essence. Anti-essence, something very, very bad," she replied.

Blood dripped from the cracked corners of her lips, and she closed her eyes. Each breath looked like it pained her and, in turn, pained me. Anybody but Cat. I hated that I even had the thought. But it was true. If I could have stopped this, had another soldier fall in her place I would have. Cat was too special. The only person from Caldera that truly knew me.

"Cat, I don't know what to do," I whispered.

Her smile was weak, but the crinkle in her eyes was there like always. She slid her hand through the blood on her stomach, and she grabbed mine. "I meant every word before the battle, Daya. I'm so proud of who you've become. This world needs you, I know you won't let them down."

"Stop fucking saying goodbye," I snapped and fished through my satchel for *something* to help. Anything. The contents of the bag spilled out, slipping through the blood, and I scrambled to pick them up.

"Daya," Zuri said as the glow in her hands went out. "Daya."

"No. Don't tell me to stop. There has to be something to help. What's the point of all this fucking power if I can't help!"

These crystals were useless. I flipped each one over, trying to see if they could at least stop the bleeding. The herbs I had would only help the pain but wouldn't knit her flesh back together. *The grimoire.*

"I need the grimoire." I lifted my hand to call to it, but Cat used more force than I thought she was capable of to pull me back toward her.

"You can't stop death. It comes for everyone in Iteria, even us," she said.

"I can't do this without you, Cat," I said as my throat constricted.

"You think I won't fuck with you from the spirit world?" she teased, but every word had too much space between it. She wasn't getting enough air in to speak.

I grabbed her body and pulled it toward me. She didn't have enough strength to embrace me back, but I felt her trying. Decades were lost when I failed to see what a good friend she was, how she was my only friend. Years we could have filled with laughter and joy. I didn't think anyone could have loved me the way she did—unconditionally. Not in a way where she wanted something back. My position never mattered to her. My power never mattered to her. Only me. She'd listened to me without question and filled in the gaps that I couldn't. Every time she'd tried to be kind ran through my mind. When I was filled with so much anger, I couldn't even see it. Now, when I could finally be a good friend to her, when I could pour into her what she'd poured into me, it was too late.

"This isn't fair," I said, my voice cracking. "I love you, you know? Even when it didn't seem like I did. I promise that's true."

"I've never expected you to be someone you aren't. Love looks different for every person. I never doubted it," she responded.

We all sat there as her heart slowed, and the whistling of her breaths turned into a full-on wheezing. The blood wasn't flowing out of the wound anymore, only a slow trickle.

"Do it," Cat said as she used every ounce of her strength to sit up.

She didn't need to spell out what she wanted. Zuri and Ishani helped her stand fully, and she lifted her chin, even if it wasn't as high as she wanted.

For the second time in my life, I pushed my dagger into the heart of someone I loved.

Chapter Sixty-One

Dayanara

I'd emptied a jar of cloves into my satchel and used my magic to sweep Cat's ashes inside. They'd be spread at Cape Coven, and her headstone would be beside her mother's. Tightening the lid, I took a deep breath and guided us toward the room she spoke of. As soon as we turned the corner, I saw the beasts Cat had taken down. There weren't just two or three, but ten of them lay dead on the ground. Their bodies were twisted unnaturally, some of their limbs separated from their bodies. I saw the one that killed her. One with a barbed tail that must have been the last one she killed. It lay at the very edge of the hall, right where the handprints on the wall started.

I took my sword, and I stabbed and chopped it until it was merely chunks of flesh. The others watched me, probably too afraid to say anything. I didn't have it in me to try to tell them I was okay. I wasn't. The door Cat spoke of sat at the end of the hall, a dead end and nowhere else to turn. It was the only one that looked like it had been replaced recently, but the handle was broken off.

A deep humming reverberated through the air, that sense of wrong Cat told us of evident. I knew what it was before I saw it. I'd felt it slither over my skin. I'd felt it inside my body. Ishani was the second to seem like she knew what we were going to open the door to. I slowly opened the door with my weapon raised, but there were no living beings within the room. There was blood, and there were a couple of dead vampires, but none living.

The thing that sent shivers up my spine, that had bile rising in my throat and my heart thudding against my chest was the wall of black. It moved and swirled, a circle of it shifting like someone had just gotten finished stirring a jar of ink. But it didn't stop. Splotches of the substance were splattered on the floor, some of the edges of it jagged. One of the soldiers stepped toward it and I held up my arm.

"What is it?" They asked.

I peered over at Ishani. "It's a portal."

"Where to?" Zuri asked.

"I'm assuming the Inbetween, but could be anywhere," I replied.

The thick liquid swirled on the wall, not flickering or fading. It was being fed constant power, and all of our gazes were stuck to it. I swore I could sense the residue on my skin from the last time I'd come in contact with this shit.

"Well, there's only one way to find out," I said.

Ishani moved to the front of the group and turned to face us, her back to the portal. "That is not a good idea."

"Joseph went through here," I responded.

"We don't know that," Zuri said.

"Cat said he went into this room. If he didn't come out, that means he went through here," I replied

None of them argued.

"I'll go and check if the coast is clear," a soldier said at my back.

I crossed my arms and stood tall. "No, none of you should take that risk,"

"All due respect, it's our job. If you don't come back, there's a much bigger problem than if we don't," the soldier said, and the rest of them grunted in agreement.

"He's right," Ishani added. "I told you, you're the future of Malva."

"Fine," I relented. "Go in, come right back, and tell us if it's safe."

His steps moved in slow motion toward the portal, and not a single one of us dared to make a sound. We all held our breath as he stuck his finger in it and rubbed the tar between his fingers. It wasn't like a witch portal, where the magic simply lapped over your skin as you passed through. This portal pushed back, resistance to his step so much that he had to put his shoulder in first. The inky black let him in, and he disappeared. He could have been gone for seconds, but it seemed like hours dragged on without a response.

Suddenly, he pressed his shoulder and head back toward our side and said, "We're good to g—"

His body was yanked back, and without another thought, we all ran toward the portal. My breathing hitched as the portal felt like it was trying to reject me. I slashed through with my nails, my power lit in my hand, but as soon as I got through, it vanished. So it was the Inbetween. I twirled as I tried to figure out specifically where in the Inbetween we were, and my gaze landed on our soldier.

He was being held with a knife to his neck by people in dark gray and black-speckled clothing. I put away my weapon and held my hands in the air, looking back over my shoulder for the others to follow suit.

"Where are we?" I asked. "We mean no harm. We just appeared here."

"Inbetween," one of the men responded quickly.

I glanced to my right, seeing the jagged rock of the Piedra towering over us. The men's coats were lined with fur, similar to what I'd seen on Bastian in the pub.

"Is Bastian your leader?" I asked. They all looked at each other, unsure if what I was saying was a threat, and I quickly continued. "I know him. Let him know Dayanara is here, and he'll advise that we aren't dangerous."

"We're taking the soldier," the one with the knife to our man said. "You all stay here."

"Very well." I nodded to our soldier, wishing I asked his name. I hope he knew we would do everything we could not to let him get hurt.

Ishani patted my back, and Zuri inspected the area where the portal spat us out. The other soldiers with us monitored the portal, and I realized then one of them was a lobo as they squatted down and sniffed the ground. His nose twitched as he stood and followed a path invisible to the rest of us.

"Someone else was here. I can smell fresh witch blood, too," the lobo said.

"We can't leave here yet. We can follow it once we're cleared. We need their leader on our side for what's coming," I advised.

Zuri and I had turned to drawing stupid shit in the dirt. Bastian was taking his sweet old time coming to where we were, so I was currently using a stick to remake a particularly vivid scene of the three of us having sex. Ishani had rolled her eyes once she realized what I was doing and turned to sharpening her knives. The other soldiers were sitting in the dirt with their eyes closed. Heavy footsteps bound toward us, and I quickly kicked the drawing, which I was almost done with. Didn't want them to think I was childish.

Bastian's hulking form came through a cave in the Piedra, and our soldier was no longer being held at knifepoint. We all relaxed at that site, and Bastian took a big bite out of some sort of dried meat. His jaw was working mighty hard to tear through it, but he gave no mind to how he chewed with his mouth open.

"Dayanara." He finally swallowed. "Not going to lie, I wasn't expecting you this soon."

"No kidding," I responded. "We actually didn't know where this portal led."

"You just jumped through this shit without knowing anything about it?" he laughed, and his belly shook.

"Well. . . yes. Has this always been here?"

Bastian shook his head. "Nope. Popped up a few hours ago. Had my men monitoring it because I was worried what would come through."

"Did they see a man come through?"

"Eike, what did you say you saw?"

"Freaky looking fellow. Had eyes that gave me shivers. Weird hair," he responded.

"Yeah, that is who we're here for," I said. "Where'd he go?"

"Went that way. I tried to track him, but he was running like hell. Couple women came through a little later. I went back to report to Bastian."

"I told them not to engage. With what we talked about in La Madama's pub, didn't want to take chances," Bastian replied.

"Understood." I trailed the path they said Joseph had taken with my eyes, but there were too many dead trees to see where he might have gone.

Bastian gestured to the Piedra. "Come on into the shelter. We can discuss more."

My magic beat beneath my skin, and I hoped we didn't have to be here too long. I didn't think about the fact that if we tried to make the trip through the Piedra, it could mean months without access to my magic. How they did it here, I had no idea. That was going to be torture.

The caves and tunnels within the Piedra were clearly man-made, smooth with lanterns hanging every few feet. There wasn't much outside light in the Inbetween itself. Without the lanterns, they'd be blind here. The sound of more heartbeats than I expected pressed against my senses. They came from every direction, above, below, from either side. Muffled by the stone, but they were there. Zuri's nose scrunched, and I assumed she was smelling what I was hearing.

Bastian opened a wide steel door, and even more tunnels appeared. It reminded me of a burrowing animal's den, some of them crossed over or traveled deep down, others were so steep they had steps embedded in the ground to climb.

"This is impressive," Ishani said.

"We've been here for a long time. Made it a home," Bastian responded.

It only got colder as we got deeper into the mountain, and I understood why they were covered in furs. The room Bastian brought us into thankfully had a fire burning in it, and I assumed we had to be semi-close to the edge of the mountain for a vent. A stone table sat in the middle, planks of wood across its surface. I stuck my finger between the slabs and they shifted, a textured map beneath the wood.

Bastian looked over his shoulder as he knocked on the wall, and I yanked my finger back. Wasn't sure how much he trusted me yet. Agreeing to take us through the Piedra was one thing, and I assumed there was going to be some form of payment. The ceiling had a large hole in it, and a rope dropped from the opening before two people cascaded down the rope and into the room.

My hand slid to my weapon at the fact their faces were covered and had large curved blades on their backs. They didn't turn to us, only to Bastian for directions. Bastian spoke to them in hushed tones, and we waited patiently for them to finish speaking.

"I sent them to find the man who came through the portal. They said he's deep within the mountain now, and that they don't expect him to survive," Bastian explained.

"He's trying to get to Chuah," I said as I shook my head.

"There must have been something given to him to create that portal. I don't know what, but he couldn't have done that himself," Zuri added.

"Even if Joseph makes it to him, he alone can't help him escape," Ishani replied.

"That we know of," I sighed.

"We have the opportunity to follow him before he gets too far," Zuri mumbled.

"We could be ready in a week," Bastian announced. "There's quite a bit of supplies needed for a trip like this. I sent a scout ahead to see if they could determine the safest path. They should be back by then as well."

Ishani watched Bastian. "Why are you helping us?"

"Ish," I snapped.

"I'm only asking because we've never joined forces before," she replied.

"I told Dayanara that we can feel the instability here. The mountain trembles, and I don't want to be unprepared. We aren't only helping you, you're helping us too. A mutual benefit."

"We have some things to take care of. A week would actually be great," I said, thinking of all the shit that would be happening in Sanjry. I also needed to spread Cat's ashes, and that was my top priority.

"Trust me, this mountain is not an easy thing to traverse. He won't get far in that much time. We know every inch of our side. The map is pretty detailed for the parts we haven't been to. I'm confident that if there is a way across, we'll find it."

"Why have you never tried?" Ishani pressed.

"Tried to risk our lives for no reward?" Bastian laughed. "You are as funny as you are pretty. We get across the mountain, and then what? We're hunted, can't go out in the day. We've been perfectly fine here. Only the threat to that peace is enough to make me want to try."

Ishani's eyes narrowed on him, but I surveyed the room. It was far simpler in decor and architecture than the rest of Malva, but they all seemed pretty comfortable and content here. I supposed anyone could get used to anything if it meant they would continue to survive.

"Do you really think the map will work?" I asked, not wanting to give voice to the possibility but also feeling like I needed to ask.

Bastian scratched the back of his head. "I don't know. The map has been in my family for centuries. We made everyone think it was simply a rumor. Mostly because we had no idea if it was real."

"I want to stop him, but going over there is going to be." Zuri shook her head. "My wolf remembers."

"We'll protect each other. This won't be our end," I reassured.

One of the soldiers behind me was fidgeting with something on the wall, and his scream startled us all as the floor shifted from beneath him, and a tunnel shot down. His holler faded, and one of Bastian's men dove down into the space.

"We'll retrieve your man," Bastian said before looking at the others. "Maybe you all don't touch anything else."

The soldiers huddled together with their hands at their side as Bastian walked us back outside. I rubbed my fingers together. They tingled like I'd fallen asleep atop them, and I squeezed my hands into fists before stretching my fingers out wide.

"It'll get better," Bastian said. "Takes some time, but it will."

I hadn't been here for a day yet, and I could barely take it. The soldier who took an involuntary trip through the mountain dragged his feet beside the man who rescued him. The other soldiers slapped him on the back of his head as he walked by.

"We'll be back in a week. Thank you for this," I said.

Bastian dipped his chin. We all stared at the portal, none of us wanting to be the first to jump in. My body repulsed, but I jumped through, the others on my heels. Ishani opened up another portal to the Dusran border, and the relief I felt as my feet hit the ground was substantial.

Chapter Sixty-Two

Dayanara

"I've got to go somewhere we've never been," I whispered as I lifted Cat's ashes into the air with my magic. "You've always been there when I needed you. I don't know how this magic works, but if you can find my ancestors, go to them. Let me know you're okay."

The voices I always heard here were clearer than ever, but they all spoke on top of each other. I sensed love and passion but also pain and regret. I wondered if this was how Paxx always felt. Cat's headstone was made by our best stonesmiths, the material so shiny I could see myself on the surface. The stone of her sanction sparkled even in the dim, foggy atmosphere. Bending down, I placed the remaining ashes on the soil and pushed the headstone down to the ground.

Zuri and Axel were at my back, though I couldn't see them through the fog. I knew they were there. I could feel their presence in the air as much as I could through my Verdaji mark. It was the only explanation, and even Akari said it looked exactly like the Verdaji she knew of. We all knew that we were meant for each other and didn't need confirmation of it, but damn, was it nice.

Especially regarding what we had to do next. Knowing that no matter what, I had people who loved me unconditionally to come home to… that kept me going. There was no doubt that even if this all went to shit, we'd protect each other and our little found family. All three of us didn't have much, if any, blood family left, but making our own was nice. Cat was part of that. She'd become integral in all of our lives, and we all grieved her.

I sat on the ground of all my dead kin. I hoped that all the brujas who had passed by the hand of Sanjryans sensed our victory. That they knew I avenged them. There was more to do, more to protect my coven from. I wasn't sure we'd ever be without threat, but I knew we were up for the fight. The warm breeze wrapped around me, but this one felt. . . familiar.

"Catalina Raiz, may you find eternal peace. I'll see you again."

The gust of wind rubbed against my cheek before flipping my hair over my face. I smiled, and swatted at her with a chuckle. She retreated from me and opened a path through the fog to Zuri and Axel. Both of their brows raised as they were startled by her, their faces relaxed like they understood what it was. Zuri lifted her hand and twisted, a tear falling down her cheek.

"She's saying goodbye." My lip wobbled.

"Goodbye, Catalina," Axel said with a tilt of his chin.

There weren't many deaths that impacted me in such a way, really just Cat and Ximena, but my heart told me that they'd find each other in the spirit world. Maybe Cat would catch Ximena up on anything she might have missed. I didn't know how it worked there, if they could all watch the living like the Acnas, but either way, I knew Ximena would comfort her.

With one more goodbye to my friend, I opened a portal back to the Calderan palace that had been plundered by the Sanjryans. There were quite a few brujas here cleaning and disposing of any traitors that were left behind. My boots thudded against the marble floor, and I ran my finger down the walls. I was acutely aware of every scar on my body—so much pain in the foundation of this structure. How many times had I wanted to be anywhere else but here? Now, I wanted to turn all that I suffered into something fucking beautiful. I didn't know where we'd end up at the end of this—if I'd be in Dusra or here. I did know that no matter what, these walls would be filled with love. If Zuri or I ever had children, they'd know this as a haven. A place they would find safety in no matter what. If we didn't have children, it would still be that for us and any of our loved ones who needed it.

Pushing the doors of the throne room open, I saw a younger version of myself running across the space. My two purple ponytails streamed behind me, holding my favorite doll. Before everything went to shit. She was who I did this for. If only she knew what she'd have to go through. I took the hand of my younger self, and she guided us over to the throne my mother used to sit upon. She folded her hands in front of her flowing skirt, and she smiled a fangless smile.

I laid my hands on the armrests, and I lowered myself slowly. As directed before I left, two brujas came into the throne room, and both Axel and Zuri spun to face them. I couldn't hold back the smirk on my face. They had two thrones matching mine lifted in the air with their magic, and they set them down directly in line with mine. I spread my arms in invitation for them, and the shock and appreciation had my gut tight.

The moment they sat down, the throne room filled with glowing eyes. All the Amapolas before me appeared, at least for me, because Zuri and Axel didn't seem to notice. They didn't bow, but the slight tilts of their heads, the admiration in their eyes, it was enough. I felt their pride in my chest. When I lifted my chin, they disappeared.

"We're going to fucking destroy Chuah."

Chapter Sixty-Three

Joseph

I ripped off the bottom of my robe before wrapping the strip of fabric around the blood gushing from my hand. The beasts that lived here hadn't shown their faces yet, but I knew my blood would only call them to me. Without any access to magic, I couldn't even stop the bleeding immediately.

The portal was a last resort, for if things took a turn. Which they did. How the witches found me in the secret tunnels, I wasn't sure. I'd been the sole person to leverage them for as long as I could remember. How I got around—how I obtained secrets to use against people in the palace. I'd never told Kaizer or his advisers of them, so it had to be the witch.

The portal was supposed to go directly to Chuah, but the little magic he had wasn't stable yet. Even many of the monsters he gave us died before we got to Sanjry. He was close to getting out, but not close enough. I had to help him.

He was going to remake the world, bring it back to the greatness it once was. When we were feared by all when we took what we wanted and didn't worry about the repercussions. This mountain that I was in—the Piedra—was never meant to exist. It was a constant reminder that we were too powerful for the other side. If that was the case, the other side should have been ours.

Kaizer was easy to convince, especially thanks to the years of Athena influencing him. My heart hurt. My daughter had long expressed her hate and disdain for me, but I did love her. It was easy to see how she would think otherwise. What I'd done to get us here was. . . unsavory. But she was supposed to be here to see what

I'd accomplish. Athena was supposed to sit at the top of all of it. With me as her adviser, of course, but that wasn't going to happen anymore.

Even if Kaizer had survived, he wasn't strong enough to handle what Chuah had to offer. I had hope, but I could see the decline. He let that witch destroy everything he could have had. Developing actual feelings for her wasn't supposed to happen. A simple agreement—one that I'd had more of a hand in than he really knew—that she was to wed him. Her mother thought she had to die, but I knew that she only needed to be subdued and controlled. Precisely like I'd done to the rest of the kingdom.

It was easy. They were all desperate for purpose. For a sense of unity. Especially the ones who were poor. They needed something to prove that their lives weren't worthless. That they could be rich in other ways. For if they were loved by the Flame in the same way as a king was, they had to be special. Giving them structure through rules, through things they *weren't* supposed to do, made it easy for them to see themselves as better than those that did. Gave them someone else to hate rather than themselves.

I didn't create the Flame, but I had been one of the people who turned it into what it was. The Embers were my followers. Believers who would do the unthinkable in my name. I wished I had time to bring some of them with me. They didn't know who our true leader was, that it was the god of Chaos I spoke to and not the Flame. They'd believe anything I said, and I knew there would be no problems once it was revealed.

I'd spent the same amount of time under Chuah's influence as Kaizer, and I knew he was part of me. Regret at not saving some of Chuah's blood I retrieved in the Inbetween coursed through me. But it was too late for that. I tried to listen to that part, the intuition extended by him as I weaved through the dark tunnels. There was no way to know how close I was or if I was even going in the right direction. But I believed that his hand was guiding me. I just hoped it guided me fast enough before the others caught up.

We had great things to do. The Bondan on the other side were seeing to it. They were so close to bringing Bonda to heel. We had to be patient. We were coming up on the trials they planned on leveraging. There was a chance we'd have to appease them and give the Bondans who assisted a small role in ruling. Regardless, it would all be ours.

Patience. That was all it took.

ACKNOWLEDGMENTS

As always, there are too many people to thank and not enough paper in the world! First, thank YOU the reader for sticking around for another book. I am eternally grateful, and it may be a biased opinion, but I think I have the best readers in the entire world. Thank you to my husband and daughters for supporting me through every book I write. Shout out to my alpha & beta team! Your feedback and assistance will never ever go unnoticed. To my besties, Nelle Nikole & Amber Nicole, thanks for being an incredible support system and just all around amazing people. Emma at EJL Editing, we did it again! Thank you for all of your patience, and reminding me that as much as I think I know what I'm doing, many times I do not lol Phil at Editing by Phi, your brain should be a national treasure. I don't know how you just *know* so many things. Incredible. I am oozing with joy and gratitude.

Thank you for taking this ride with me—to many more! (See a glimpse at my new series, Kuxtal Academy: The Beginning on the next page)

Glimpse at KATB

Read below for a look at *Kuxtal Academy: The Beginning*, Book one in the Kuxtal Academy series.

A new series blending urban fantasy, mayan mythology, and dark academia. With anxiety and dyslexia rep, elemental magic, shifters, and a unique magic system. AVAILABLE NOW in Kindle Unlimited.

First Chapter:

Celeste

If death was inevitable, the most noble thing you could do was die for a good cause.

We all had to meet our makers at some point. Everybody had an expiration date. You had one, your friends had one, even my nauseatingly cruel sister had one. I had one too.

My nose twitched, listening for the answers on the wind. Their scent carried in from the west. East it is then. Dying in the form of a *Manik* with the fear of being hunted coursing through my veins was not exactly ideal. If I stayed in this deer form though, then I couldn't talk. They would do anything to pry information from me if I was back in my fae form, and gods help me, that couldn't happen.

This knowledge would die here, right now. The world wasn't ready for this, not yet. I had to buy some time.

My girls, forgive me.

Cutting a sharp left, I braced against the pain of the branches smacking against my tapered muzzle. The cliffside was in view. Just a few more seconds, and it would all be over. I'd covered my bases the moment I caught word they were on to me. A secret was no longer a secret when more than yourself knew. I'd been betrayed, and though I would never find out by who, I hope they rotted in all nine hells. The work I had spent half a lifetime on would remain forever unfinished—my legacy, my memory, forever tarnished. None of that mattered anymore, as long as they were safe. I lacked the courage to destroy my research. Years of sleepless nights, thousands of pages, hundreds of books...all of that couldn't go to waste. I left a fail-safe, clues that only my Mira and Sienna could decipher. May the gods guide them. They were this world's last hope, the last puzzle piece, and they didn't even know yet. I could only hope I didn't make a mistake in doing what I did. Aurora and I had been close once, that sliver of our sisterly bond being the only reason I'd gone undiscovered for this long. That and our father forcing us to keep the secret, sealing us by blood oath. He was the one who came up with the plan to hide my *Manik* form. Due to my natural intelligence, everyone thought I was an *Eb*. But they were wrong.

I was the first deer-shifter since the old gods. I was the one who was supposed to bring in the new age, a new beginning. Our grandfather had spoken on the prophecy many times when we were children. "A Cynod secret," he had warned us. Once I emerged and the rift between Aurora and I had begun, she'd had to cut our twin connection and form relationships of her own. Some would say the wrong crowd, others would claim the right one. Either way, society latched their claws into her, and she'd never looked back.

They said the gods granted the damned three wishes as you walked the line between life and death. So three wishes ran through my mind as my hooves kicked dust off the edge of the mountain; One, Mira and Sienna would forgive me. Two, my sister would know I forgive her. Three, that in due time, the world would never discover the hidden truths of the Cynod, or they would destroy them all.

May my path be peaceful.

About the Author

Mikayla grew up on the east coast, and has always been a fan of anything fantasy related. As a Latina, she always wanted to see her and her family represented in these stories. She focuses on Mesoamerican/Caribbean mythologies, and hopes that her readers feel represented in every story. Mikayla is happily married and has two beautiful daughters who inspire her to be better daily.

For more about her books or to follow her on socials, visit mikayladhornedo .com/links